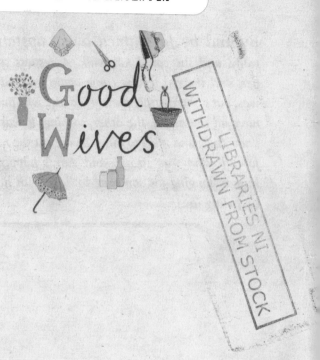

Good
Wives

By and by Jo roamed away upstairs, for it was rainy, and she could not walk. A restless spirit possessed her, and the old feeling came again, not bitter as it once was, but a sorrowfully patient wonder why one sister should have all she asked, the other nothing. It was not true; she knew that, and tried to put it away, but the natural craving for affection was strong, and Amy's happiness woke the hungry longing for someone to 'love with heart and soul, and cling to . . .'

LOUISA MAY ALCOTT

Good Wives

PUFFIN CLASSICS

PUFFIN BOOKS

UK | USA | Canada | Ireland | Australia
India | New Zealand | South Africa

Puffin Books is part of the Penguin Random House group of companies
whose addresses can be found at global.penguinrandomhouse.com.

puffinbooks.com

First published 1869
Published in Peacock Books 1965
Published in Puffin Books 1978
Reissued in this edition 2015

001

Set in 11.5/15pt Minion Pro
Typeset by Palimpsest Book Production Ltd, Falkirk, Stirlingshire
Printed in Great Britain by Clays Ltd, St Ives plc

A CIP catalogue record for this book is available from the British Library

ISBN: 978-0-141-36003-4

www.greenpenguin.co.uk

Penguin Random House is committed to a
sustainable future for our business, our readers
and our planet. This book is made from Forest
Stewardship Council® certified paper.

Contents

1

Gossip

In order that we may start afresh, and go to Meg's wedding with free minds, it will be well to begin with a little gossip about the Marches. And here let me premise, that if any of the elders think there is too much 'lovering' in the story, as I fear they may (I'm not afraid the young folks will make that objection), I can only say with Mrs March, 'What *can* you expect when I have four gay girls in the house, and a dashing young neighbour over the way?'

The three years that have passed have brought but few changes to the quiet family. The war is over, and Mr March safely at home, busy with his books and the small parish which found in him a minister by nature as by grace – a quiet, studious man, rich in the wisdom that is better than learning, the charity which calls all mankind 'brother', the piety that blossoms into character, making it august and lovely.

These attributes, in spite of poverty and the strict integrity which shut him out from the more worldly successes, attracted to him many admirable persons, as naturally as sweet herbs draw bees, and as naturally he gave them the honey into which fifty years of hard experience had distilled no bitter drop. Earnest young men found the grey-headed scholar as young at heart as they; thoughtful or troubled women instinctively brought their doubts and sorrows to him, sure of finding the gentlest sympathy, the wisest counsel; sinners told their sins to the pure-hearted old man, and were both rebuked and saved; gifted men found a companion in him; ambitious men caught glimpses of nobler ambitions than their own; and even worldlings confessed that his beliefs were beautiful and true, although 'they wouldn't pay'.

To outsiders, the five energetic women seemed to rule the house, and so they did in many things; but the quiet scholar, sitting among his books, was still the head of the family, the household conscience, anchor, and comforter for to him the busy, anxious women always turned in troublous times, finding him, in the truest sense of those sacred words, husband and father.

The girls gave their hearts into their mother's keeping, their souls into their father's; and to both parents, who lived and laboured so faithfully for them, they gave a love that grew with their growth, and bound them tenderly together by the sweetest tie which blesses life and outlives death.

Mrs March is as brisk and cheery, though rather greyer,

than when we saw her last, and just now so absorbed in Meg's affairs that the hospitals and homes, still full of wounded 'boys' and soldiers' widows, decidedly miss the motherly missionary's visits.

John Brooke did his duty manfully for a year, got wounded, was sent home, and not allowed to return. He received no stars or bars, but he deserved them, for he cheerfully risked all he had; and life and love are very precious when both are in full bloom. Perfectly resigned to his discharge, he devoted himself to getting well, preparing for business, and earning a home for Meg. With the good sense and sturdy independence that character-ized him, he refused Mr Laurence's more generous offers, and accepted the place of book-keeper, feeling better satis-fied to begin with an honestly earned salary than by running any risks with borrowed money.

Meg had spent the time in working as well as waiting, growing womanly in character, wise in housewifely arts, and prettier than ever; for love is a great beautifier. She had her girlish ambitions and hopes, and felt some disap-pointment at the humble way in which the new life must begin. Ned Moffat had just married Sallie Gardiner, and Meg couldn't help contrasting their fine house and carriage, many gifts, and splendid outfit, with her own, and secretly wishing she could have the same. But somehow envy and discontent soon vanished when she thought of all the patient love and labour John had put into the little home awaiting her; and when they sat together in the twilight, talking over their small plans, the future always grew so beautiful and bright that she forgot Sallie's splendour, and felt herself the richest, happiest girl in Christendom.

Jo never went back to Aunt March, for the old lady took such a fancy to Amy that she bribed her with the offer of drawing lessons from one of the best teachers going; and for the sake of this advantage Amy would have served a far harder mistress. So she gave her mornings to duty, her afternoons to pleasure, and prospered finely. Jo, meantime, devoted herself to literature and Beth, who remained delicate, long after the fever was a thing of the past. Not an invalid exactly, but never again the rosy, healthy creature she had been; yet always hopeful, happy, and serene, busy with the quiet duties she loved, everyone's friend, and an angel in the house, long before those who loved her most had learned to know it.

As long as the *Spread Eagle* paid her a dollar a column for her 'rubbish', as she called it, Jo felt herself a woman of means, and spun her little romances diligently. But great plans fermented in her busy brain and ambitious mind, and the old tin kitchen in the garret held a slowly increasing pile of blotted manuscript, which was one day to place the name of March upon the roll of fame.

Laurie, having dutifully gone to college to please his grandfather, was now getting through it in the easiest possible manner to please himself. A universal favourite, thanks to money, manners, much talent, and the kindest heart that ever got its owner into scrapes by trying to get other people out of them, he stood in great danger of being spoilt, and probably would have been, like many another promising boy, if he had not possessed a talisman against evil in the memory of the kind old man who was bound up in his success, the motherly friend who watched over him as if he were her son, and last, but not least by any means, the knowledge that four innocent girls loved, admired, and believed in him with all their hearts.

Being only 'a glorious human boy', of course he frolicked and flirted, grew dandified, aquatic, sentimental, or gymnastic, as college fashions ordained; hazed and was hazed, talked slang, and more than once came perilously near suspension and expulsion. But as high spirits and the love of fun were the causes of these pranks, he always managed to save himself by frank confession, honourable atonement, or the irresistible power of persuasion which he possessed in perfection. In fact, he rather prided himself on his narrow escapes, and liked to thrill the girls with graphic accounts of his triumphs over wrathful tutors, dignified professors, and vanquished enemies. The 'men of my class' were heroes in the eyes of the girls, who never wearied of the exploits of 'our fellows', and were frequently allowed to bask in the smiles of these great creatures, when Laurie brought them home with him.

Amy especially enjoyed this high honour, and became quite a belle among them; for her ladyship early felt and learned to use the gift of fascination with which she was endowed. Meg was too much absorbed in her private and particular John to care for any other lords of creation, and Beth too shy to do more than peep at them, and wonder how Amy dared to order them about so; but Jo felt quite in her element, and found it very difficult to refrain from imitating the gentlemanly attitudes, phrases, and feats, which seemed more natural to her than the decorums prescribed for young ladies. They all liked Jo immensely, but never fell in love with her, though very few escaped without paying the tribute of a sentimental sigh or two at Amy's shrine. And speaking of sentiment brings us very naturally to the 'Dovecote'.

That was the name of the little brown house which Mr Brooke had prepared for Meg's first home. Laurie had christened it, saying it was highly appropriate to the gentle lovers, who 'went on together like a pair of turtle doves, with first a bill and then a coo'. It was a tiny house, with a little garden behind and a lawn about as big as a pocket-handkerchief in front. Here Meg meant to have a fountain, shrubbery, and a profusion of lovely flowers; though just at present, the fountain was represented by a weather-beaten urn, very like a dilapidated slop-bowl; the shrub-bery consisted of several young larches, undecided whether to live or die; and the profusion of flowers was merely hinted by regiments of sticks, to show where seeds were planted. But inside, it was altogether charming, and the happy bride saw no fault from garret to cellar. To be sure, the hall was so narrow, it was fortunate that they had no piano, for one never could have been got in whole; the dining room was so small that six people were a tight fit; and the kitchen stairs seemed built for the express purpose of precipitating both servants and china pell-mell into the coal bin. But once got used to these slight blemishes, and nothing could be more complete, for good sense and good taste had presided over the furnishing, and the result was highly satisfactory. There were no marble-topped tables, long mirrors, or lace curtains in the little parlour, but simple furniture, plenty of books, a fine picture or two, a stand of flowers in the bay window, and, scattered all about, the pretty gifts which came from friendly hands, and were the fairer for the loving messages they brought.

I don't think the Parian Psyche Laurie gave lost any of its beauty because John put up the bracket it stood upon; that any upholsterer could have draped the plain muslin curtains more gracefully than Amy's artistic hand; or that any storeroom was ever better provided with good wishes, merry words, and happy hopes than that in which Jo and her mother put away Meg's few boxes, barrels, and bundles; and I am morally certain that the spandy-new kitchen never *could* have looked so cosy and neat if

Hannah had not arranged every pot and pan a dozen times over, and laid the fire all ready for lighting, the minute 'Mis. Brooke came home'. I also doubt if any young matron ever began life with so rich a supply of dusters, holders, and piece-bags; for Beth made enough to last till the silver wedding came round, and invented three different kinds of dishcloths for the express service of the bridal china.

People who hire all these things done for them never know what they lose; for the homeliest tasks get beautified if loving hands do them, and Meg found so many proofs of this, that everything in her small nest, from the kitchen roller to the silver vase on her parlour table was eloquent of home love and tender forethought.

What happy times they had planning together, what solemn shopping excursions; what funny mistakes they made, and what shouts of laughter arose over Laurie's ridiculous bargains. In his love of jokes, this young gentleman, though nearly through college, was as much of a boy as ever. His last whim had been to bring with him, on his weekly visits, some new, useful, and ingenious article for the young housekeeper. Now a bag of remark-able clothes pins; next, a wonderful nutmeg grater, which fell to pieces at the first trial; a knife-cleaner that spoilt all the knives; or a sweeper that picked the nap neatly off the carpet, and left the dirt; labour-saving soap that took the skin off one's hands; infallible cements which stuck firmly to nothing but the fingers of the deluded buyer; and every kind of tinware, from a toy savings-bank for odd pennies, to a wonderful boiler which would wash articles in its own steam, with every prospect of exploding in the process.

In vain Meg begged him to stop. John laughed at him, and Jo called him 'Mr Toodles'. He was possessed with a mania for patronizing Yankee ingenuity, and seeing his friends fitly furnished forth. So each week beheld some fresh absurdity.

Everything was done at last, even to Amy's arranging different coloured soaps to match the different coloured rooms, and Beth's setting the table for the first meal.

'Are you satisfied? Does it seem like home, and do you feel as if you should be happy here?' asked Mrs March, as she and her daughter went through the new kingdom, arm-in-arm for just then they seemed to cling together more tenderly than ever.

'Yes, Mother, perfectly satisfied, thanks to you all, and *so* happy that I can't talk about it,' answered Meg, with a look that was better than words.

'If she only had a servant or two it would be all right,' said Amy, coming out of the parlour, where she had been trying to decide whether the bronze Mercury looked best on the whatnot or the mantelpiece.

'Mother and I have talked that over, and I have made up my mind to try her way first. There will be so little to do, that, with Lotty to run my errands and help me here and there, I shall only have enough work to keep me from getting lazy or homesick,' answered Meg tranquilly.

'Sallie Moffat has four,' began Amy.

'If Meg had four the house wouldn't hold them, and master and missis would have to camp in the garden,' broke in Jo, who, enveloped in a big blue pinafore, was giving the last polish to the door handles.

'Sallie isn't a poor man's wife, and many maids are in keeping with her fine establishment. Meg and John begin humbly, but I have a feeling that there will be quite as much happiness in the little house as in the big one. It's a great mistake for young girls like Meg to leave themselves nothing to do but dress, give orders, and gossip. When I was first married I used to long for my new clothes to wear out or get torn, so that I might have the pleasure of mending them, for I got heartily sick of doing fancy work and tending my pocket-handkerchief.'

'Why didn't you go into the kitchen and make messes, as Sallie says she does, to amuse herself, though they never turn out well, and the servants laugh at her,' said Meg.

'I did, after a while; not to "mess", but to learn of Hannah how things should be done, that my servants need *not* laugh at me. It was play then but there came a time when I was truly grateful that I not only possessed the will but the power to cook wholesome food for my little girls, and help myself when I could no longer afford to hire help.

You begin at the other end, Meg, dear; but the lessons you learn now will be of use to you by and by, when John is a richer man, for the mistress of a house, however splendid, should know how work ought to be done, if she wishes to be well and honestly served.'

'Yes, Mother, I'm sure of that,' said Meg, listening respectfully to the little lecture; for the best of women will hold forth upon the all-absorbing subject of housekeeping. 'Do you know I like this room most of all in my baby-house,' added Meg, a minute after, as they went upstairs, and she looked into her well-stored linen closet.

Beth was there, laying the snowy piles smoothly on the shelves, and exulting over the goodly array. All three laughed as Meg spoke; for that linen closet was a joke. You see, having said that if Meg married 'that Brooke' she shouldn't have a cent of her money, Aunt March was rather in a quandary, when time had appeased her wrath and made her repent her vow. She never broke her word, and was much exercised in her mind how to get round it, and at last devised a plan whereby she could satisfy herself. Mrs Carrol, Florence's mamma, was ordered to buy, have made, and marked, a generous supply of house and table linen, and send it as *her* present, all of which was faithfully done; but the secret leaked out, and was greatly enjoyed by the family; for Aunt March tried to look utterly unconscious, and insisted that she could give nothing but the old-fashioned pearls, long promised to the first bride.

'That's a housewifely taste which I am glad to see. I had a young friend who set up housekeeping with six sheets, but she had finger-bowls for company, and that satisfied her,' said Mrs March, patting the damask tablecloths, with a truly feminine appreciation of their fineness.

'I haven't a single finger-bowl, but this is a "set out" that will last me all my days, Hannah says'; and Meg looked quite contented, as well she might.

'Toodles is coming,' cried Jo from below; and they all went down to meet Laurie, whose weekly visit was an Important event in their quiet lives.

A tall, broad-shouldered young fellow, with a cropped head, a felt-basin of a hat, and a fly-away coat, came tramping down the road at a great pace, walked over the low fence without stopping to open the gate, straight up to Mrs March, with both hands out, and a hearty:

'Here I am, Mother! Yes, it's all right.'

The last words were in answer to the look the elder lady gave him; a kindly, questioning look, which the handsome eyes met so frankly that the little ceremony closed, as usual, with a motherly kiss.

'For Mrs John Brooke, with the maker's congratulations and compliments. Bless you, Beth! What a refreshing spectacle you are, Jo. Amy, you are getting altogether too handsome for a single lady.'

As Laurie spoke, he delivered a brown paper parcel to Meg, pulled Beth's hair-ribbon, stared at Jo's big pinafore, and fell into an attitude of mock rapture before Amy, then shook hands all round, and everyone began to talk.

'Where is John?' asked Meg anxiously.

'Stopped to get the licence for tomorrow, ma'am.'

'Which side won the last match, Teddy?' enquired Jo, who persisted in feeling an interest in manly sports, despite her nineteen years.

'Ours, of course. Wish you'd been there to see.'

'How is the lovely Miss Randal?' asked Amy, with a significant smile.

'More cruel than ever; don't you see how I'm pining away?' and Laurie gave his broad chest a sounding slap and heaved a melodramatic sigh.

'What's the last joke? Undo the bundle and see, Meg,' said Beth, eyeing the knobby parcel with curiosity.

'It's a useful thing to have in the house in case of fire or thieves,' observed Laurie, as a watchman's rattle appeared, amid the laughter of the girls.

'Any time when John is away, and you get frightened, Mrs Meg, just swing that out of the front window, and it will rouse the neighbourhood in a jiffy. Nice thing, isn't it?' and Laurie gave them a sample of its powers that made them cover up their ears.

'There's gratitude for you! and speaking of gratitude reminds me to mention that you may thank Hannah for saving your wedding cake from destruction. I saw it going into your house as I came by, and if she hadn't defended it manfully I'd have had a pick at it, for it looked like a remarkably plummy one.'

'I wonder if you will ever grow up, Laurie,' said Meg, in a matronly tone.

'I'm doing my best, ma'am, but can't get much higher, I'm afraid, as six feet is about all men can do in these degenerate days,' responded the young gentleman, whose head was about level with the little chandelier. 'I suppose it would be profanation to eat anything in this spick and span new bower, so, as I'm tremendously hungry, I propose an adjournment,' he added presently.

'Mother and I are going to wait for John. There are some last things to settle,' said Meg, bustling away.

'Beth and I are going over to Kitty Bryant's to get more flowers for tomorrow,' added Amy, tying a picturesque hat over her picturesque curls, and enjoying the effect as much as anybody.

'Come, Jo, don't desert a fellow. I'm in such a state of exhaustion I can't get home without help. Don't take off your apron, whatever you do; it's peculiarly becoming,' said Laurie, as Jo bestowed his especial aversion in her capacious pocket and offered him her arm to support his feeble steps.

'Now, Teddy, I want to talk seriously to you about tomorrow,' began Jo, as they strolled away together. 'You *must* promise to behave well, and not cut up any pranks, and spoil our plans.'

'Not a prank.'

'And don't say funny things when we ought to be sober.'

'I never do; you are the one for that.'

'And I implore you not to look at me during the ceremony; I shall certainly laugh if you do.'

'You won't see me; you'll be crying so hard that the thick fog round you will obscure the prospect.'

'I never cry unless for some great affliction.'

'Such as fellows going to college, hey?' cut in Laurie, with a suggestive laugh.

'Don't be a peacock. I only moaned a trifle to keep the girls company.'

'Exactly. I say, Jo, how is Grandpa this week? Pretty amiable?'

'Very; why, have you got into a scrape, and want to know how he'll take it?' asked Jo rather sharply.

'Now, Jo, do you think I'd look your mother in the face, and say "All right," if it wasn't?' and Laurie stopped short with an injured air.

'No, I don't.'

'Then don't go and be suspicious; I only want some money,' said Laurie, walking on again, appeased by her hearty tone.

'You spend a great deal, Teddy.'

'Bless you, I don't spend it; it spends itself, somehow, and is gone before I know it.'

'You are so generous and kind-hearted that you let

people borrow, and can't say "No" to anyone. We heard about Henshaw, and all you did for him. If you always spent money in that way, no one would blame you,' said Jo warmly.

'Oh, he made a mountain out of a molehill. You wouldn't have me let that fine fellow work himself to death, just for the want of a little help, when he is worth a dozen of us lazy chaps, would you?'

'Of course not; but I don't see the use of your having seventeen waistcoats, endless neckties, and a new hat every time you come home. I thought you'd got over the dandy period; but every now and then it breaks out in a new spot. Just now it's the fashion to be hideous – to make your head look like a scrubbing-brush, wear a straitjacket, orange gloves, and clumping, square-toed boots. If it was cheap ugliness, I'd say nothing; but it costs as much as the other, and I don't get any satisfaction out of it.'

Laurie threw back his head, and laughed so heartily at this attack, that the felt-basin fell off, and Jo walked on it, which insult only afforded him an opportunity for expatiating on the advantages of a rough-and-ready costume, as he folded up the maltreated hat, and stuffed it into his pocket.

'Don't lecture any more, there's a good soul! I have enough all through the week, and like to enjoy myself when I come home. I'll get myself up regardless of expense, tomorrow, and be a satisfaction to my friends.'

'I'll leave you in peace if you'll *only* let your hair grow. I'm not aristocratic, but I do object to be seen with a person who looks like a young prize-fighter,' observed Jo severely.

'This unassuming style promotes study; that's why we adopt it,' returned Laurie, who certainly could not be accused of vanity, having voluntarily sacrificed a handsome curly crop to the demand for quarter of an inch long stubble.

'By the way, Jo, I think that little Parker is really getting desperate about Amy. He talks of her constantly, writes poetry, and moons about in a most suspicious manner. He'd better nip his little passion in the bud, hadn't he?' added Laurie in a confidential, elder-brotherly tone, after a minute's silence.

'Of course he had; we don't want any more marrying in this family for years to come. Mercy on us, what *are* the children thinking of?' and Jo looked as much scandalized as if Amy and little Parker were not yet in their teens.

'It's a fast age, and I don't know what we are coming to, ma'am. You are a mere infant, but you'll go next, Jo, and we'll be left lamenting,' said Laurie, shaking his head over the degeneracy of the times.

'Don't be alarmed; I'm not one of the agreeable sort. Nobody will want me, and it's a mercy, for there should always be one old maid in a family.'

'You won't give anyone a chance,' said Laurie, with a

sidelong glance, and a little more colour than before in his sunburnt face. 'You won't show the soft side of your character; and if a fellow gets a peep at it by accident, and can't help showing that he likes it, you treat him as Mrs Gummidge did her sweetheart – throw cold water over him – and get so thorny no one dares touch or look at you.'

'I don't like that sort of thing; I'm too busy to be worried with nonsense, and I think it's dreadful to break up families so. Now don't say any more about it; Meg's wedding has turned all our heads, and we talk of nothing but lovers and such absurdities. I don't wish to get cross, so let's change the subject'; and Jo looked quite ready to fling cold water on the slightest provocation.

Whatever his feelings might have been, Laurie found a vent for them in a long low whistle, and the fearful prediction, as they parted at the gate, 'Mark my words, Jo, you'll go next.'

2

The First Wedding

The June roses over the porch were awake bright and early on that morning, rejoicing with all their hearts in the cloudless sunshine, like friendly little neighbours, as they were. Quite flushed with excitement were their ruddy faces, as they swung in the wind, whispering to one another what they had seen; for some peeped in at the dining room windows, where the feast was spread, some climbed up to nod and smile at the sisters as they dressed the bride, others waved a welcome to those who came and went on various errands in garden, porch, and hall, and all, from the rosiest full-blown flower to the palest baby bud, offered their tribute of beauty and fragrance to the gentle mistress who had loved and tended them so long.

Meg looked very like a rose herself; for all that was best and sweetest in heart and soul seemed to bloom into her face that day, making it fair and tender, with a charm more beautiful than beauty. Neither silk, lace, nor orange-flowers would she have. 'I don't want to look strange or fixed up today,' she said. 'I don't want a fashionable wedding, but only those about me whom I love, and to them I wish to look and be my familiar self.'

So she made her wedding gown herself, sewing into it the tender hopes and innocent romances of a girlish heart. Her sisters braided up her pretty hair, and the only ornaments she wore were the lilies of the valley which 'her John' liked best of all the flowers that grew.

'You *do* look just like our own dear Meg, only so very sweet and lovely that I should hug you if it wouldn't crumple your dress,' cried Amy, surveying her with delight, when all was done.

'Then I am satisfied. But please hug and kiss me, everyone, and don't mind my dress; I want a great many crumples of this sort put into it today'; and Meg opened her arms to her sisters, who clung about her with April faces for a minute, feeling that the new love had not changed the old.

'Now I'm going to tie John's cravat for him, and then to stay a few minutes with Father quietly in the study'; and Meg ran down to perform these little ceremonies, and then to follow her mother wherever she went, conscious that, in spite of the smiles on the motherly face, there was a secret sorrow hid in the motherly heart at the flight of the first bird from the nest.

As the younger girls stand together, giving the last touches to their simple toilet, it may be a good time to tell of a few changes which three years have wrought in their appearance for all are looking their best just now.

Jo's angles are much softened; she has learned to carry herself with ease, if not grace. The curly crop has lengthened into a thick coil, more becoming to the small head atop of the tall figure. There is a fresh colour in her brown cheeks, a soft shine in her eyes, and only gentle words fall from her sharp tongue today.

Beth has grown slender, pale, and more quiet than ever; the beautiful, kind eyes are larger, and in them lies an expression that saddens one, although it is not sad itself. It is the shadow of pain which touches the young face with such pathetic patience; but Beth seldom complains, and always speaks hopefully of 'being better soon'.

Amy is with truth considered 'the flower of the family'; for at sixteen she has the air and bearing of a full-grown woman – not beautiful, but possessed of that indescribable charm called grace. One saw it in the lines of her figure, the make and motion of her hands, the flow of her dress, the droop of her hair – unconscious, yet harmonious, and as attractive to many as beauty itself. Amy's nose still afflicted her, for it never *would* grow Grecian; so did her mouth, being too wide, and having a decided chin. These offending features gave character to her whole face, but she never could see it, and consoled herself with her wonderfully fair complexion, keen blue eyes, and curls, more golden and abundant than ever.

All three wore suits of thin silver grey (their best gowns for the summer), with blush-roses in hair and bosom; and all three looked just what they were – fresh-faced, happy-hearted girls, pausing a moment in their busy lives to read with wistful eyes the sweetest chapter in the romance of womanhood.

There were to be no ceremonious performances, everything was to be as natural and homelike as possible; so when Aunt March arrived, she was scandalized to see the bride come running to welcome and lead her in, to find the bridegroom fastening up a garland that had fallen down, and to catch a glimpse of the paternal minister marching upstairs with a grave countenance, and a wine bottle under each arm.

'Upon my word, here's a state of things!' cried the old lady, taking the seat of honour prepared for her, and settling the folds of her lavender moire with a great rustle. 'You oughtn't to be seen till the last minute, child.'

'I'm not a show, Aunty, and no one is coming to stare at me, to criticize my dress, or count the cost of my luncheon. I'm too happy to care what anyone says or thinks, and I'm going to have my little wedding just as I like it. John, dear, here's your hammer'; and away went Meg to help 'that man' in his highly improper employment.

Mr Brooke didn't even say 'Thank you,' but as he stooped for the unromantic tool, he kissed his little bride behind the folding-door, with a look that made Aunt March whisk out her pocket-handkerchief, with a sudden dew in her sharp old eyes.

A crash, a cry, and a laugh from Laurie, accompanied by the indecorous exclamation, 'Jupiter Ammon! Jo's upset the cake again!' caused a momentary flurry, which was hardly over when a flock of cousins arrived, and 'the party came in', as Beth used to say when a child.

'Don't let that young giant come near me; he worries me worse than mosquitoes,' whispered the old lady to Amy, as the rooms filled, and Laurie's black head towered above the rest.

'He has promised to be very good today, and he *can* be perfectly elegant if he likes,' returned Amy, gliding away to warn Hercules to beware of the dragon, which warning caused him to haunt the old lady with a devotion that nearly distracted her.

There was no bridal procession, but a sudden silence fell upon the room as Mr March and the young pair took their places under the green arch. Mother and sisters gathered close, as if loath to give Meg up; the fatherly voice broke more than once, which only seemed to make the service more beautiful and solemn; the bridegroom's hand trembled visibly, and no one heard his replies; but Meg looked straight up in her husband's eyes, and said, 'I will!' with such tender trust in her own face and voice that her mother's heart rejoiced, and Aunt March sniffed audibly.

Jo did *not* cry, though she was very near it once, and was only saved from a demonstration by the consciousness that Laurie was staring fixedly at her, with a comical mixture of merriment and emotion in his wicked black eyes. Beth kept her face hidden on her mother's shoulder, but Amy stood like a graceful statue, with a most becoming ray of sunshine touching her white forehead and the flower in her hair.

It wasn't at all the thing, I'm afraid, but the minute she was fairly married, Meg cried, 'The first kiss for Marmee!' and, turning, gave it with her heart on her lips. During the next fifteen minutes she looked more like a rose than ever, for everyone availed themselves of their privileges to the fullest extent, from Mr Laurence to old Hannah, who, adorned with a headdress fearfully and wonderfully made, fell upon her in the hall, crying, with a sob and a chuckle, 'Bless you, deary, a hundred times! The cake ain't hurt a mite, and everything looks lovely.'

Everybody cleared up after that, and said something brilliant, or tried to, which did just as well, for laughter is ready when hearts are light. There was no display of gifts, for they were already in the little house, nor was there an elaborate breakfast, but a plentiful lunch of cake and fruit, dressed with flowers. Mr Laurence and Aunt March shrugged and smiled at one another when water, lemonade, and coffee were found to be the only sorts of nectar which the three Hebes carried round. No one said anything, however, till Laurie, who insisted on serving the bride, appeared before her, with a loaded salver in his hand and a puzzled expression in his face.

'Has Jo smashed all the bottles by accident,' he whispered, 'or am I merely labouring under a delusion that I saw some lying about loose this morning?'

'No; your grandfather kindly offered us his best, and Aunt March actually sent some, but Father put away a little for Beth, and dispatched the rest to the Soldiers' Home. You know he thinks that wine should be used only in illness, and Mother says that neither she nor her daughters will ever offer it to any young man under her roof.'

Meg spoke seriously, and expected to see Laurie frown or laugh; but he did neither, for after a quick look at her, he said, in his impetuous way, 'I like that! for I've seen enough harm done to wish other women would think as you do.'

'You are not made wise by experience, I hope?' and there was an anxious accent in Meg's voice.

'No; I give you my word for it. Don't think too well of me, either; this is not one of my temptations. Being brought up where wine is as common as water, and almost as harmless, I don't care for it; but when a pretty girl offers it, one doesn't like to refuse, you see.'

'But you will, for the sake of others, if not for your own. Come, Laurie, promise, and give me one more reason to call this the happiest day of my life.'

A demand so sudden and so serious made the young man hesitate a moment, for ridicule is often harder to bear than self-denial. Meg knew that if he gave the promise he would keep it at all costs; and, feeling her power, used it as a woman may for her friend's good. She did not speak, but she looked up at him with a face made very eloquent by happiness, and a smile which said, 'No one can refuse me anything today.' Laurie certainly could not; and, with an answering smile, he gave her his hand, saying heartily, 'I promise, Mrs Brooke!'

'I thank you, very, very much.'

'And I drink "long life to your resolution," Teddy,' cried Jo, baptizing him with a splash of lemonade, as she waved her glass, and beamed approvingly upon him.

So the toast was drunk, the pledge made, and loyally kept, in spite of many temptations; for, with instinctive wisdom, the girls had seized a happy moment to do their friend a service, for which he thanked them all his life.

After lunch, people strolled about, by twos and threes, through house and garden, enjoying the sunshine without and within. Meg and John happened to be standing together in the middle of the grass plot, when Laurie was seized with an inspiration which put the finishing touch to this unfashionable wedding.

'All the married people take hands and dance round the new-made husband and wife, as the Germans do, while we bachelors and spinsters prance in couples outside!' cried Laurie, promenading down the path with Amy, with such infectious spirit and skill that everyone else followed their example without a murmur. Mr and Mrs March, Aunt and Uncle Carrol, began it; others rapidly joined in; even Sallie Moffat, after a moment's hesitation, threw her train over her arm, and whisked Ned into the ring. But the crowning joke was Mr Laurence and Aunt March; for when the stately old gentleman chasséd solemnly up to the old lady, she just tucked her cane under her arm, and hopped briskly away to join hands with the rest, and dance about the bridal pair, while the young folks pervaded the garden, like butterflies on a midsummer day.

Want of breath brought the impromptu ball to a close, and then people began to go.

'I wish you well, my dear, I heartily wish you well; but I think you'll be sorry for it,' said Aunt March to Meg, adding to the bridegroom, as he led her to the carriage, 'You've got a treasure, young man, see that you deserve it.'

'That is the prettiest wedding I've been to for an age, Ned, and I don't see why, for there wasn't a bit of style about it,' observed Mrs Moffat to her husband, as they drove away.

'Laurie, my lad, if you ever want to indulge in this sort of thing, get one of those little girls to help you, and I shall be perfectly satisfied,' said Mr Laurence, settling himself in his easy chair to rest, after the excitement of the morning.

'I'll do my best to gratify you, sir,' was Laurie's unusually dutiful reply, as he carefully unpinned the posy Jo had put in his buttonhole.

The little house was not far away, and the only bridal journey Meg had was the quiet walk with John, from the old home to the new. When she came down, looking like a pretty Quakeress in her dove-coloured suit and straw bonnet tied with white, they all gathered about her to say 'goodbye,' as tenderly as if she had been going to make the grand tour.

'Don't feel that I am separated from you, Marmee, dear, or that I love you any the less for loving John so much,' she said, clinging to her mother, with full eyes, for a moment. 'I shall come every day, Father, and expect to keep my old place in all your hearts, though I *am* married. Beth is going to be with me a great deal, and the other girls will drop in now and then to laugh at my housekeeping struggles. Thank you all for my happy wedding day. Goodbye, goodbye!'

They stood watching her, with faces full of love and hope and tender pride, as she walked away, leaning on her husband's arm, with her hands full of flowers, and the June sunshine brightening her happy face – and so Meg's married life began.

3

Artistic Attempts

It takes people a long time to learn the difference between talent and genius, especially ambitious young men and women. Amy was learning this distinction through much tribulation; for, mistaking enthusiasm for inspiration, she attempted every branch of art with youthful audacity. For a long time there was a lull in the 'mud-pie' business, and she devoted herself to the finest pen-and-ink drawing, in which she showed such taste and skill that her graceful handiwork proved both pleasant and profitable. But overstrained eyes soon caused pen and ink to be laid aside for a bold attempt at poker sketching. While this attack lasted, the family lived in constant fear of a conflagration; for the odour of burning wood pervaded the house at all hours; smoke issued from attic and shed with alarming frequency, red-hot pokers lay about promiscuously, and Hannah never went to bed without a pail of water and the dinner-bell at her door, in case of fire. Raphael's face was found boldly executed on the under side of the moulding-board, and Bacchus on the head of a beer barrel; a chanting cherub adorned the cover of the sugar bucket, and attempts to portray Romeo and Juliet supplied kindlings for some time.

From fire to oil was a natural transition for burnt fingers, and Amy fell to painting with undiminished ardour. An artist friend fitted her out with his cast-off palettes, brushes, and colours; and she daubed away, producing pastoral and marine views such as were never seen on land or sea. Her monstrosities in the way of cattle would have taken prizes at an agricultural fair; and the perilous pitching of her vessels would have produced sea-sickness in the most nautical observer, if the utter disregard to all known rules of shipbuilding and rigging had not convulsed him with laughter at the first glance. Swarthy boys and dark-eyed Madonnas, staring at you from one corner of the studio, suggested Murillo; oily-brown shadows of faces, with a lurid streak in the wrong place, meant Rembrandt; buxom ladies and dropsical infants, Rubens; and Turner appeared in tempests of blue thunder, orange lightning, brown rain, and purple clouds, with a tomato-coloured splash in the middle, which might be the sun or a buoy, a sailor's shirt or a king's robe, as the spectator pleased.

Charcoal portraits came next; and the entire family hung in a row, looking as wild and crocky as if just evoked from a coal bin. Softened into crayon sketches, they did better; for the likenesses were good, and Amy's hair, Jo's nose, Meg's mouth, and Laurie's eyes were pronounced 'wonderfully fine'. A return to clay and plaster followed, and ghostly casts of her acquaintances haunted corners of the house, or tumbled off closet shelves on to people's heads. Children were enticed in as models, till their incoherent accounts of her mysterious doings caused Miss Amy to be regarded in the light of a young ogress. Her efforts in this line, however, were brought to an abrupt close by an untoward accident, which quenched her ardour. Other models failing her for a time, she undertook to cast her own pretty foot, and the family were one day alarmed by an unearthly bumping and screaming, and running to the rescue, found the young enthusiast hopping wildly about the shed, with her foot held in a panful of plaster, which had hardened with unexpected rapidity. With much difficulty and some danger she was dug out; for Jo was so overcome with laughter while she excavated, that her knife went too far, cut the poor foot, and left a lasting memorial of one artistic attempt, at least.

After this Amy subsided, till a mania for sketching from nature set her to haunting river, field, and wood for picturesque studies, and sighing for ruins to copy. She caught endless colds sitting on damp grass to book 'a delicious bit', composed of a stone, a stump, one mushroom, and a broken mullein stalk, or a 'heavenly mass of clouds', that looked like a choice display of feather beds when done. She sacrificed her complexion floating on the river in the midsummer sun, to study light and shade, and got a wrinkle over her nose, trying after 'points of sight', or whatever the squint-and-string performance is called.

If 'genius is eternal patience', as Michael Angelo affirms, Amy certainly had some claim to the divine attribute, for she persevered in spite of all obstacles, failures, and discouragements, firmly believing that in time she should do something worthy to be called 'high art'.

She was learning, doing, and enjoying other things, meanwhile, for she had resolved to be an attractive and accomplished woman, even if she never became a great artist. Here she succeeded better; for she was one of those happily created beings who please without effort, make friends everywhere, and take life so gracefully and easily – that less fortunate souls are tempted to believe that such are born under a lucky star. Everybody liked her, for among her good gifts was tact. She had an instinctive sense of what was pleasing and proper, always said the right thing to the right person, did just what suited the time and place, and was so self-possessed that her sisters used to say, 'If Amy went to court without any rehearsal beforehand, she'd know exactly what to do.'

One of her weaknesses was a desire to move in 'our best society', without being quite sure what the *best* really was. Money, position, fashionable accomplishments, and elegant manners were most desirable things in her eyes, and she liked to associate with those who possessed them, often mistaking the false for the true, and admiring what was not admirable. Never forgetting that by birth she was a gentlewoman, she cultivated her aristocratic tastes and feelings, so that when the opportunity came she might be ready to take the place from which poverty now excluded her.

'My lady', as her friends called her, sincerely desired to be a genuine lady, and was so at heart, but had yet to learn that money cannot buy refinement of nature, that rank does not always confer nobility, and that true breeding makes itself felt in spite of external drawbacks.

'I want to ask a favour of you, Mamma,' Amy said, coming in, with an important air, one day.

'Well, little girl, what is it?' replied her mother, in whose eyes the stately young lady still remained 'the baby'.

'Our drawing class breaks up next week, and before the girls separate for the summer, I want to ask them out here for a day. They are wild to see the river, sketch the broken bridge, and copy some of the things they admire in my book. They have been very kind to me in many ways, and I am grateful, for they are all rich, and know I am poor, yet they never made any difference.'

'Why should they?' and Mrs March put the question with what the girls called her 'Maria Theresa air'.

'You know as well as I that it *does* make a difference with nearly everyone, so don't ruffle up, like a dear, motherly hen, when your chickens get pecked by smarter birds;

the ugly duckling turned out a swan, you know'; and Amy smiled without bitterness, for she possessed a happy temper and hopeful spirit.

Mrs March laughed, and smoothed down her maternal pride as she asked:

'Well, my swan, what is your plan?'

'I should like to ask the girls out to lunch next week, to take them a drive to the places they want to see, a row on the river, perhaps, and make a little artistic fête for them.'

'That looks feasible. What do you want for lunch? Cake, sandwiches, fruit, and coffee will be all that is necessary, I suppose?'

'Oh dear, no! we must have cold tongue and chicken, French chocolate and ice cream, besides. The girls are used to such things, and I want my lunch to be proper and elegant, though I *do* work for my living.'

'How many young ladies are there?' asked her mother, beginning to look sober.

'Twelve or fourteen in the class, but I dare say they won't all come.'

'Bless me, child, you will have to charter an omnibus to carry them about.'

'Why, Mother, how *can* you think of such a thing? Not more than six or eight will probably come, so I shall hire a beach wagon, and borrow Mr Laurence's cherry-bounce.' (Hannah's pronunciation of charabanc.)

'All this will be expensive, Amy.'

'Not very; I've calculated the cost, and I'll pay for it myself.'

'Don't you think, dear, that as these girls are used to such things, and the best we can do will be nothing new, that some simpler plan would be pleasanter to them, as a change, if nothing more, and much better for us than buying or borrowing what we don't need, and attempting a style not in keeping with our circumstances?'

'If I can't have it as I like, I don't care to have it at all. I know that I can carry it out perfectly well, if you and the girls will help a little; and I don't see why I can't if I'm willing to pay for it,' said Amy, with the decision which opposition was apt to change into obstinacy.

Mrs March knew that experience was an excellent teacher, and when it was possible she left her children to learn alone the lessons which she would gladly have made easier, if they had not objected to taking advice as much as they did salts and senna.

'Very well, Amy; if your heart is set upon it, and you see your way through without too great an outlay of money, time, and temper, I'll say no more. Talk it over with the girls, and whichever way you decide, I'll do my best to help you.'

'Thanks, Mother; you are always *so* kind'; and away went Amy to lay her plan before her sisters.

Meg agreed at once, and promised her aid, gladly

offering anything she possessed, from her little house itself to her very best salt spoons. But Jo frowned upon the whole project, and would have nothing to do with it at first.

'Why in the world should you spend your money, worry your family, and turn the house upside-down for a parcel of girls who don't care a sixpence for you? I thought you had too much pride and sense to truckle to any mortal woman just because she wears French boots and rides in a coupé,' said Jo, who, being called from the tragical climax of her novel, was not in the best mood for social enterprises.

'I *don't* truckle, and I hate being patronized as much as you do!' returned Amy indignantly, for the two still jangled when such questions arose. 'The girls do care for me, and I for them, and there's a great deal of kindness and sense and talent among them, in spite of what you call fashionable nonsense. You don't care to make people like you, to go into good society, and cultivate your manners and tastes. I do, and I mean to make the most of every chance that comes. *You* can go through the world with your elbows out and your nose in the air, and call it independence, if you like. That's not my way.'

When Amy whetted her tongue and freed her mind she usually got the best of it, for she seldom failed to have common sense on her side, while Jo carried her love of liberty and hate of conventionalities to such an unlimited extent that she naturally found herself worsted in an argument. Amy's definition of Jo's idea of independence was such a good hit that both burst out laughing, and the discussion took a more amiable turn. Much against her will, Jo at length consented to sacrifice a day to Mrs Grundy, and help her sister through what she regarded as 'a nonsensical business'.

The invitations were sent, nearly all accepted, and the following Monday was set apart for the grand event. Hannah was out of humour because her week's work was deranged, and prophesied that 'ef the washin' and ironin' warn't done reg'lar nothin' would go well anywheres'. This hitch in the mainspring of the domestic machinery had a bad effect upon the whole concern; but Amy's motto was *Nil desperandum*, and having made up her mind what to do, she proceeded to do it in spite of all obstacles. To begin with, Hannah's cooking didn't turn out well: the chicken was tough, the tongue too salt, and the chocolate wouldn't froth properly. Then the cake and ice cost more than Amy expected, so did the wagon; and various other expenses, which seemed trifling at the outset, counted up rather alarmingly afterwards. Beth got cold and took to her bed, Meg had an unusual number of callers to keep her at home, and Jo was in such a divided state of mind that her breakages, accidents, and mistakes were uncommonly numerous, serious, and trying.

'If it hadn't been for Mother I never should have got

through,' as Amy declared afterwards, and gratefully remembered when 'the best joke of the season' was entirely forgotten by everybody else.

If it was not fair on Monday, the young ladies were to come on Tuesday – an arrangement which aggravated Jo and Hannah to the last degree. On Monday morning the weather was in that undecided state which is more exasperating than a steady pour. It drizzled a little, shone a little, blew a little, and didn't make up its mind till it was too late for anyone else to make up theirs. Amy was up at dawn, hustling people out of their beds and through their breakfasts, that the house might be got in order. The parlour struck her as looking uncommonly shabby; but without stopping to sigh for what she had not, she skilfully made the best of what she had, arranging chairs over the worn places in the carpet, covering stains on the walls with pictures framed in ivy, and filling up empty corners with home-made statuary, which gave an artistic air to the room, as did the lovely vases of flowers Jo scattered about.

The lunch looked charmingly; and as she surveyed it, she sincerely hoped it would taste well, and that the borrowed glass, china, and silver would get safely home again. The carriages were promised, Meg and Mother were all ready to do the honours, Beth was able to help Hannah behind the scenes, Jo had engaged to be as lively and amiable as an absent mind, an aching head, and a very decided disapproval of everybody and everything would allow, and, as she wearily dressed, Amy cheered herself with anticipations of the happy moment when, lunch safely over, she should drive away with her friends for an afternoon of artistic delights; for the 'cherry-bounce' and the broken bridge were her strong points.

Then came two hours of suspense, during which she vibrated from parlour to porch, while public opinion varied like the weathercock. A smart shower at eleven had evidently quenched the enthusiasm of the young ladies who were to arrive at twelve, for nobody came; and at two the exhausted family sat down in a blaze of sunshine to consume the perishable portions of the feast, that nothing might be lost.

'No doubt about the weather today; they will certainly come, so we must fly round and be ready for them,' said Amy, as the sun woke her next morning. She spoke briskly, but in her secret soul she wished she had said nothing about Tuesday, for her interest, like her cake, was getting a little stale.

'I can't get any lobsters, so you will have to do without salad today,' said Mr March, coming in half an hour later, with an expression of placid despair.

'Use the chicken, then; the toughness won't matter in a salad,' advised his wife.

'Hannah left it on the kitchen table a minute, and the

kittens got at it. I'm very sorry, Amy,' added Beth, who was still a patroness of cats.

'Then I *must* have a lobster, for tongue alone won't do,' said Amy decidedly.

'Shall I rush into town and demand one?' asked Jo, with the magnanimity of a martyr.

'You'd come bringing it home under your arm, without any paper, just to try me. I'll go myself,' answered Amy, whose temper was beginning to fail.

Shrouded in a thick veil and armed with a genteel travelling basket, she departed, feeling that a cool drive would soothe her ruffled spirit, and fit her for the labours of the day. After some delay, the object of her desire was procured, likewise a bottle of dressing, to prevent further loss of time at home, and off she drove again, well pleased with her own forethought.

As the omnibus contained only one other passenger, a sleepy old lady, Amy pocketed her veil, and beguiled the tedium of the way by trying to find out where all her money had gone to. So busy was she with her card full of refractory figures that she did not observe a newcomer, who entered without stopping the vehicle, till a masculine voice said, 'Good morning, Miss March,' and, looking up, she beheld one of Laurie's most elegant college friends. Fervently hoping that he would get out before she did, Amy utterly ignored the basket at her feet, and, congratulating herself that she had on her new travelling dress, returned the young man's greeting with her usual suavity and spirit.

They got on excellently; for Amy's chief care was soon set at rest by learning that the gentleman would leave first, and she was chatting away in a peculiarly lofty strain, when the old lady got out. In stumbling to the door, she upset the basket, and – oh, horror! – the lobster, in all its vulgar size and brilliancy, was revealed to the high-born eyes of a Tudor.

'By Jove, she's forgotten her dinner!' cried the unconscious youth, poking the scarlet monster into its place with his cane, and preparing to hand out the basket after the old lady.

'Please don't – it's – it's mine,' murmured Amy, with a face nearly as red as her fish.

'Oh, really, I beg pardon; it's an uncommonly fine one, isn't it?' said Tudor, with great presence of mind, and an air of sober interest that did credit to his breeding.

Amy recovered herself in a breath, set her basket boldly on the seat, and said, laughing:

'Don't you wish you were to have some of the salad he's to make, and to see the charming young ladies who are to eat it?'

Now that was tact, for two of the ruling foibles of the masculine mind were touched: the lobster was instantly surrounded by a halo of pleasing reminiscences, and curiosity about 'the charming young ladies' diverted his mind from the comical mishap.

'I suppose he'll laugh and joke over it with Laurie, but I shan't see them; that's a comfort,' thought Amy, as Tudor bowed and departed.

She did not mention this meeting at home (though she discovered that, thanks to the upset, her new dress was much damaged by the rivulets of dressing that meandered down the skirt), but went through with the preparations which now seemed more irksome than before; and at twelve o'clock all was ready again. Feeling that the neighbours were interested in her movements, she wished to efface the memory of yesterday's failure by a grand success today; so she ordered the 'cherry-bounce', and drove away in state to meet and escort her guests to the banquet.

'There's the rumble, they're coming! I'll go into the porch to meet them; it looks hospitable, and I want the poor child to have a good time after all her trouble,' said Mrs March, suiting the action to the word. But after one glance, she retired, with an indescribable expression, for, looking quite lost in the big carriage, sat Amy and one young lady.

'Run, Beth, and help Hannah clear half the things off the table; it will be too absurd to put a luncheon for twelve before a single girl,' cried Jo, hurrying away to the lower regions, too excited to stop even for a laugh.

In came Amy, quite calm, and delightfully cordial to the one guest who had kept her promise; the rest of the family, being of a dramatic turn, played their parts equally well, and Miss Eliott found them a most hilarious set; for it was impossible to entirely control the merriment which possessed them. The remodelled lunch being gaily partaken of, the studio and garden visited, and art discussed with enthusiasm, Amy ordered a buggy (alas for the elegant cherry-bounce!) and drove her friend quietly about the neighbourhood till sunset when 'the party went out'.

As she came walking in, looking very tired, but as composed as ever, she observed that every vestige of the unfortunate fête had disappeared, except a suspicious pucker about the corners of Jo's mouth.

'You've had a lovely afternoon for your drive, dear,' said her mother, as respectfully as if the whole twelve had come.

'Miss Eliott is a very sweet girl, and seemed to enjoy herself, I thought,' observed Beth, with unusual warmth.

'Could you spare me some of your cake? I really need some, I have so much company, and I can't make such delicious stuff as yours,' asked Meg soberly.

'Take it all; I'm the only one here who likes sweet things, and it will mould before I can dispose of it,' answered Amy, thinking with a sigh of the generous store she had laid in for such an end as this.

'It's a pity Laurie isn't here to help us,' began Jo, as they sat down to ice cream and salad for the second time in two days.

A warning look from her mother checked any further remarks, and the whole family ate in heroic silence, till Mr March mildly observed, 'Salad was one of the favourite dishes of the ancients, and Evelyn –' Here a general explosion of laughter cut short the 'history of sallets', to the great surprise of the learned gentleman.

'Bundle everything into a basket and send it to the Hummels: Germans like messes. I'm sick of the sight of this; and there's no reason you should all die of a surfeit because I've been a fool,' cried Amy, wiping her eyes.

'I thought I *should* have died when I saw you two girls rattling about in the what-you-call-it, like two little kernels in a very big nutshell, and Mother waiting in state to receive the throng,' sighed Jo, quite spent with laughter.

'I'm very sorry you were disappointed, dear, but we all did our best to satisfy you,' said Mrs March, in a tone full of motherly regret.

'I *am* satisfied; I've done what I undertook, and it's not my fault that it failed; I comfort myself with that,' said Amy, with a little quiver in her voice. 'I thank you all very much for helping me, and I'll thank you still more if you won't allude to it for a month, at least.'

No one did for several months; but the word 'fête' always produced a general smile, and Laurie's birthday gift to Amy was a tiny coral lobster in the shape of a charm for her watchguard.

4

Literary Lessons

Fortune suddenly smiled upon Jo, and dropped a good-luck penny in her path. Not a golden penny, exactly, but I doubt if half a million would have given more real happiness than did the little sum that came to her in this wise.

Every few weeks she would shut herself up in her room, put on her scribbling suit, and 'fall into a vortex', as she expressed it, writing away at her novel with all her heart and soul, for till that was finished she could find no peace. Her 'scribbling suit' consisted of a black woollen pinafore on which she could wipe her pen at will, and a cap of the same material, adorned with a cheerful red bow, into which she bundled her hair when the decks were cleared for action. This cap was a beacon to the enquiring eyes of her family, who during these periods kept their distance, merely popping in their heads semi-occasionally, to ask, with interest, 'Does genius burn, Jo?' They did not always venture even to ask this question, but took an observation of the cap, and judged accordingly. If this expressive article of dress was drawn low upon the forehead, it was a sign that hard work was going on; in exciting moments it was pushed rakishly askew; and when despair seized the author it was plucked wholly off, and cast upon the floor. At such times the intruder silently withdrew; and not until the red bow was seen gaily erect upon the gifted brow, did anyone dare address Jo.

She did not think herself a genius by any means; but when the writing fit came on, she gave herself up to it with entire abandon, and led a blissful life, unconscious of want, care, or bad weather, while she sat safe and happy in an imaginary world, full of friends almost as real and dear to her as any in the flesh. Sleep forsook her eyes, meals stood untasted, day and night were all too short to enjoy the happiness which blessed her only at such times, and made these hours worth living, even if they bore no other fruit. The divine afflatus usually lasted a week or two, and then she emerged from her 'vortex', hungry, sleepy, cross, or despondent.

She was just recovering from one of these attacks when she was prevailed upon to escort Miss Crocker to a lecture, and in return for her virtue was rewarded with a new idea. It was a People's Course, the lecture on the Pyramids, and Jo rather wondered at the choice of such a subject for such an audience, but took it for granted that some great social evil would be remedied or some great want supplied by unfolding the glories of the Pharaohs to an audience whose thoughts were busy with the price of coal and flour, and whose lives were spent in trying to solve harder riddles than that of the Sphinx.

They were early; and while Miss Crocker set the heel of her stocking, Jo amused herself by examining the faces of the people who occupied the seat with them. On her left were two matrons, with massive foreheads, and bonnets to match, discussing Woman's Rights and making tatting. Beyond sat a pair of humble lovers, artlessly holding each other by the hand, a sombre spinster eating peppermints out of a paper bag, and an old gentleman taking his preparatory nap behind a yellow bandanna. On her right, her only neighbour was a studious-looking lad absorbed in a newspaper.

It was a pictorial sheet, and Jo examined the work of art nearest her, idly wondering what unfortuitous concatenation of circumstances needed the melodramatic illustration of an Indian in full war costume, tumbling over a precipice with a wolf at his throat, while two infuriated young gentlemen, with unnaturally small feet and big eyes, were stabbing each other close by, and a dishevelled female was flying away in the background with her mouth wide open. Pausing to turn a page, the lad saw her looking, and, with boyish good nature, offered half his paper, saying bluntly, 'Want to read it? That's a first-rate story.'

Jo accepted it with a smile, for she had never outgrown her liking for lads, and soon found herself involved in the usual labyrinth of love, mystery, and murder, for the story belonged to that class of light literature in which the passions have a holiday, and when the author's invention fails, a grand catastrophe clears the stage of one half the dramatis personae, leaving the other half to exult over their downfall.

'Prime, isn't it?' asked the boy, as her eye went down the last paragraph of her portion.

'I think you and I could do as well as that if we tried,' returned Jo, amused at his admiration of the trash.

'I should think I was a pretty lucky chap if I could. She makes a good living out of such stories, they say'; and he pointed to the name of Mrs S. L. A. N. G. Northbury, under the title of the tale.

'Do you know her?' asked Jo, with sudden interest.

'No; but I read all her pieces, and I know a fellow who works in the office where this paper is printed.'

'Do you say she makes a good living out of stories like this?' and Jo looked more respectfully at the agitated group and thickly sprinkled exclamation points that adorned the page.

'Guess she does! She knows just what folks like, and gets paid well for writing it.'

Here the lecture began, but Jo heard very little of it, for while Prof. Sands was prosing away about Belzoni, Cheops, scarabei, and hieroglyphics, she was covertly taking down the address of the paper, and boldly resolving to try for

the hundred-dollar prize offered in its columns for a sensational story. By the time the lecture ended and the audience awoke, she had built up a splendid fortune for herself
(not the first founded upon paper), and was already deep
in the concoction of her story, being unable to decide
whether the duel should come before the elopement or
after the murder.

She said nothing of her plan at home, but fell to work
next day, much to the disquiet of her mother, who always
looked a little anxious when 'genius took to burning'. Jo
had never tried this style before, contenting herself with
very mild romances for the *Spread Eagle*. Her theatrical
experience and miscellaneous reading were of service now,
for they gave her some idea of dramatic effect, and
supplied plot, language, and costumes. Her story was as
full of desperation and despair as her limited acquaintance
with those uncomfortable emotions enabled her to make
it, and, having located it in Lisbon, she wound up with
an earthquake, as a striking and appropriate denouement.
The manuscript was privately dispatched, accompanied
by a note, modestly saying that if the tale didn't get the
prize, which the writer hardly dared expect, she would be
very glad to receive any sum it might be considered worth.

Six weeks is a long time to wait, and a still longer time
for a girl to keep a secret; but Jo did both, and was just
beginning to give up all hope of ever seeing her manuscript
again, when a letter arrived which almost took her breath

away; for on opening it, a cheque for a hundred dollars fell into her lap. For a minute she stared at it as if it had been a snake, then she read her letter and began to cry. If the amiable gentleman who wrote that kindly note could have known what intense happiness he was giving a fellow creature, I think he would devote his leisure hours, if he has any, to that amusement; for Jo valued the letter more than the money, because it was encouraging; and after years of effort it was *so* pleasant to find that she had learned to do something, though it was only to write a sensation story.

A prouder young woman was seldom seen than she, when, having composed herself, she electrified the family by appearing before them with the letter in one hand, the cheque in the other, announcing that she had won the prize. Of course there was a great jubilee, and when the story came everyone read and praised it; though after her father had told her that the language was good, the romance fresh and hearty, and the tragedy quite thrilling, he shook his head, and said in his unworldly way:

'You can do better than this, Jo. Aim at the highest, and never mind the money.'

'*I* think the money is the best part of it. What *will* you do with such a fortune?' asked Amy, regarding the magic slip of paper with a reverential eye.

'Send Beth and Mother to the seaside for a month or two,' answered Jo promptly.

'Oh, how splendid! No, I can't do it, dear, it would be so selfish,' cried Beth, who had clapped her thin hands, and taken a long breath, as if pining for fresh ocean breezes; then stopped herself, and motioned away the cheque which her sister waved before her.

'Ah, but you shall go, I've set my heart on it; that's what I tried for, and that's why I succeeded. I never get on when I think of myself alone, so it will help me to work for you, don't you see? Besides, Marmee needs the change, and she won't leave you, so you *must* go. Won't it be fun to see you come home plump and rosy again? Hurrah for Dr Jo, who always cures her patients!'

To the seaside they went, after much discussion; and though Beth didn't come home as plump and rosy as could be desired, she was much better, while Mrs March declared she felt ten years younger; so Jo was satisfied with the investment of her prize money, and fell to work with a cheery spirit, bent on earning more of those delightful cheques. She did earn several that year, and began to feel herself a power in the house; for by the magic of a pen her 'rubbish' turned into comforts for them all. 'The Duke's Daughter' paid the butcher's bill, 'The Phantom Hand' put down a new carpet, and the 'Curse of the Coventrys' proved the blessing of the Marches in the way of groceries and gowns.

Wealth is certainly a most desirable thing, but poverty has its sunny side, and one of the sweet uses of adversity is the genuine satisfaction which comes from hearty work of head or hand; and to the inspiration of necessity, we owe half the wise, beautiful, and useful blessings of the world. Jo enjoyed a taste of this satisfaction, and ceased to envy richer girls, taking great comfort in the knowledge that she could supply her own wants, and need ask no one for a penny.

Little notice was taken of her stories, but they found a market; and, encouraged by this fact, she resolved to make a bold stroke for fame and fortune. Having copied her novel for the fourth time, read it to all her confidential friends, and submitted it with fear and trembling to three publishers, she at last disposed of it, on condition that she would cut it down one-third, and omit all the parts which she particularly admired.

'Now I must either bundle it back into my tin kitchen to mould, pay for printing it myself, or chop it up to suit purchasers, and get what I can for it. Fame is a very good thing to have in the house, but cash is more convenient; so I wish to take the sense of the meeting on this important subject,' said Jo, calling a family council.

'Don't spoil your book, my girl, for there is more in it than you know, and the idea is well worked out. Let it wait and ripen,' was her father's advice; and he practised as he preached, having waited patiently thirty years for fruit of his own to ripen, and being in no haste to gather it, even now, when it was sweet and mellow.

'It seems to me that Jo will profit more by making the trial than by waiting,' said Mrs March. 'Criticism is the best test of such work, for it will show her both unsuspected merits and faults, and help her to do better next time. We are too partial; but the praise and blame of outsiders will prove useful, even if she gets but little money.'

'Yes,' said Jo, knitting her brows, 'that's just it; I've been fussing over the thing so long, I really don't know whether it's good, bad, or indifferent. It will be a great help to have cool, impartial persons take a look at it, and tell me what they think of it.'

'I wouldn't leave out a word of it; you'll spoil it if you do, for the interest of the story is more in the minds than in the actions of the people, and it will be all a muddle if you don't explain as you go on,' said Meg, who firmly believed that this book was the most remarkable novel ever written.

'But Mr Allen says, "Leave out the explanations, make it brief and dramatic, and let the characters tell the story,"' interrupted Jo, turning to the publisher's note.

'Do as he tells you; he knows what will sell, and we don't. Make a good, popular book, and get as much money as you can. By and by, when you've got a name, you can afford to digress, and have philosophical and metaphysical people in your novels,' said Amy, who took a strictly practical view of the subject.

'Well,' said Jo, laughing, 'if my people *are* "philosophical and metaphysical," it isn't my fault, for I know nothing about such things, except what I hear Father say, sometimes. If I've got some of his wise ideas jumbled up with my romance, so much the better for me. Now, Beth, what do you say?'

'I should so like to see it printed *soon,*' was all Beth said, and smiled in saying it; but there was an unconscious emphasis on the last word, and a wistful look in the eyes that never lost their childlike candour, which chilled Jo's heart, for a minute, with a foreboding fear, and decided her to make her little venture 'soon'.

So, with Spartan firmness, the young authoress laid her first-born on her table, and chopped it up as ruthlessly as any ogre. In the hope of pleasing everyone, she took everyone's advice; and, like the old man and his donkey in the fable, suited nobody.

Her father liked the metaphysical streak which had unconsciously got into it; so that was allowed to remain, though she had her doubts about it. Her mother thought that there *was* a trifle too much description; out, therefore, it nearly all came, and with it many necessary links in the story. Meg admired the tragedy; so Jo piled up the agony to suit her, while Amy objected to the fun, and, with the best intentions in life, Jo quenched the sprightly scenes which relieved the sombre character of the story. Then, to complete the ruin, she cut it down one-third, and confidingly sent the poor little romance, like a picked robin, out into the big, busy world, to try its fate.

Well, it was printed, and she got three hundred dollars for it; likewise plenty of praise and blame, both so much greater than she expected that she was thrown into a state of bewilderment, from which it took her some time to recover.

'You said, Mother, that criticism would help me; but how can it, when it's so contradictory that I don't know whether I've written a promising book or broken all the ten commandments?' cried poor Jo, turning over a heap of notices, the perusal of which filled her with pride and joy one minute, wrath and dire dismay the next. 'This man says, "An exquisite book, full of truth, beauty, and earnestness; all is sweet, pure, and healthy,"' continued the perplexed authoress. 'The next, "The theory of the book is bad, full of morbid fancies, spiritualistic ideas, and unnatural characters." Now, as I had no theory of any kind, don't believe in Spiritualism, and copied my characters from life, I don't see how this critic *can* be right. Another says, "It's one of the best American novels which has appeared for years" (I know better than that); and the next asserts that "though it is original, and written with great force and feeling, it is a dangerous book." 'Tisn't! Some make fun of it, some over-praise, and nearly all insist that I had a deep theory to expound, when I only wrote it for the pleasure and the money. I wish I'd printed it whole or not at all, for I do hate to be so misjudged.'

Her family and friends administered comfort and commendation liberally; yet it was a hard time for sensitive, high-spirited Jo, who meant so well, and had apparently done so ill. But it did her good, for those whose opinion had real value gave her the criticism which is an author's best education; and when the first soreness was over, she could laugh at her poor little book, yet believe in it still, and feel herself the wiser and stronger for the buffeting she had received.

'Not being a genius, like Keats, it won't kill me,' she said stoutly; 'and I've got the joke on my side, after all; for the parts that were taken straight out of real life are denounced as impossible and absurd, and the scenes that I made up out of my own silly head are pronounced "charmingly natural, tender, and true." So I'll comfort myself with that, and when I'm ready, I'll up again and take another.'

5

Domestic Experiences

Like most other young matrons, Meg began her married life with the determination to be a model housekeeper. John should find home a paradise; he should always see a smiling face, should fare sumptuously every day, and never know the loss of a button. She brought so much love, energy, and cheerfulness to the work that she could not but succeed, in spite of some obstacles. Her paradise was not a tranquil one; for the little woman fussed, was over-anxious to please, and bustled about like a true Martha, cumbered with many cares. She was too tired, sometimes, even to smile; John grew dyspeptic after a course of dainty dishes, and ungratefully demanded plain fare. As for buttons, she soon learned to wonder where they went, to shake her head over the carelessness of men, and to threaten to make him sew them on himself, and then see if *his* work would stand impatient tugs and clumsy fingers any better than hers.

They were very happy, even after they discovered that they couldn't live on love alone. John did not find Meg's beauty diminished, though she beamed at him from behind the familiar coffee-pot; nor did Meg miss any of the romance from the daily parting, when her husband followed up his kiss with the tender enquiry, 'Shall I send home veal or mutton for dinner, darling?' The little house ceased to be a glorified bower, but it became a home, and the young couple soon felt that it was a change for the better. At first they played keep-house, and frolicked over it like children; then John took steadily to business, feeling the cares of the head of a family upon his shoulders; and Meg laid by her cambric wrappers, put on a big apron, and fell to work, as before said, with more energy than discretion.

While the cooking mania lasted she went through *Mrs Cornelius's Recipe Book* as if it were a mathematical exercise, working out the problems with patience and care. Sometimes her family were invited in to help eat up a too bounteous feast of successes, or Lotty would be privately dispatched with a batch of failures, which were to be concealed from all eyes in the convenient stomachs of the little Hummels. An evening with John over the account books usually produced a temporary lull in the culinary enthusiasm, and a frugal fit would ensue, during which the poor man was put through a course of bread pudding, hash, and warmed-over coffee, which tried his soul, although he bore it with praiseworthy fortitude. Before the golden mean was found, however, Meg added to her domestic possessions what young couples seldom get on long without – a family jar.

Fired with a housewifely wish to see her storeroom stocked with home-made preserves, she undertook to put up her own currant jelly. John was requested to order home a dozen or so of little pots, and an extra quantity of sugar, for their own currants were ripe, and were to be attended to at once. As John firmly believed that 'my wife' was equal to anything, and took a natural pride in her skill, he resolved that she should be gratified, and their only crop of fruit laid by in a most pleasing form for winter use. Home came four dozen delightful little pots, half a barrel of sugar, and a small boy to pick the currants for her. With her pretty hair tucked into a little cap, arms bared to the elbow, and a checked apron which had a coquettish look in spite of the bib, the young housewife fell to work, feeling no doubts about her success; for hadn't she seen Hannah do it hundreds of times? The array of pots rather amazed her at first, but John was so fond of jelly, and the nice little jars would look so well on the top shelf, that Meg resolved to fill them all, and spent a long day picking, boiling, straining, and fussing over her jelly. She did her best; she asked advice of Mrs Cornelius; she racked her brain to remember what Hannah did that she had left undone; she reboiled, resugared, and restrained, but that dreadful stuff wouldn't 'jell'.

She longed to run home, bib and all, and ask Mother

to lend a hand, but John and she had agreed that they would never annoy anyone with their private worries, experiments, or quarrels. They had laughed over that last word as if the idea it suggested was a most preposterous one; but they had held to their resolve, and whenever they could get on without help they did so, and no one interfered, for Mrs March had advised the plan. So Meg wrestled alone with the refractory sweetmeats all that hot summer day, and at five o'clock sat down in her topsy-turvy kitchen, wrung her bedaubed hands, lifted up her voice and wept.

Now, in the first flush of the new life, she had often said:

'My husband shall always feel free to bring a friend home whenever he likes. I shall always be prepared; there shall be no flurry, no scolding, no discomfort, but a neat house, a cheerful wife, and a good dinner. John, dear, never stop to ask my leave, invite whom you please, and be sure of a welcome from me.'

How charming that was, to be sure! John quite glowed with pride to hear her say it, and felt what a blessed thing it was to have a superior wife. But, although they had had company from time to time, it never happened to be unexpected, and Meg had never had an opportunity to distinguish herself till now. It always happens so in this vale of tears; there is an inevitability about such things which we can only wonder at, deplore, and bear as we best can.

If John had not forgotten all about the jelly, it really would have been unpardonable in him to choose that day, of all the days in the year, to bring a friend home to dinner unexpectedly. Congratulating himself that a handsome repast had been ordered that morning, feeling sure that it would be ready to the minute, and indulging in pleasant anticipations of the charming effect it would produce, when his pretty wife came running out to meet him, he escorted his friend to his mansion, with the irrepressible satisfaction of a young host and husband.

It is a world of disappointments, as John discovered when he reached the Dovecote. The front door usually stood hospitably open; now it was not only shut, but locked, and yesterday's mud still adorned the steps. The parlour windows were closed and curtained, no picture of the pretty wife sewing on the piazza, in white, with a distracting little bow in her hair, or a bright-eyed hostess, smiling a shy welcome as she greeted her guest. Nothing of the sort, for not a soul appeared, but a sanguinary-looking boy asleep under the currant bushes.

'I'm afraid something has happened. Step into the garden, Scott, while I look up Mrs Brooke,' said John, alarmed at the silence and solitude.

Round the house he hurried, led by a pungent smell of burnt sugar, and Mr Scott strolled after him, with a queer look on his face. He paused discreetly at a distance when Brooke disappeared; but he could both see and hear, and, being a bachelor, enjoyed the prospect mightily.

In the kitchen reigned confusion and despair; one edition of jelly was trickled from pot to pot, another lay upon the floor, and a third was burning gaily on the stove. Lotty, with Teutonic phlegm, was calmly eating bread and currant wine, for the jelly was still in a hopelessly liquid state, while Mrs Brooke, with her apron over her head, sat sobbing dismally.

'My dearest girl, what is the matter?' cried John, rushing in, with awful visions of scalded hands, sudden news of affliction, and secret consternation at the thought of the guest in the garden.

'O John, I *am* so tired and hot and cross and worried! I've been at it till I'm worn out. Do come and help me or I *shall* die!' and the exhausted housewife cast herself upon his breast, giving him a sweet welcome in every sense of the word, for her pinafore had been baptized at the same time as the floor.

'What worries you, dear? Has anything dreadful happened?' asked the anxious John, tenderly kissing the crown of the little cap, which was all askew.

'Yes,' sobbed Meg despairingly.

'Tell me quick, then. Don't cry, I can bear anything better than that. Out with it, love.'

'The – the jelly won't jell and I don't know what to do!'

John Brooke laughed then as he never dared to laugh

afterwards; and the derisive Scott smiled involuntarily as he heard the hearty peal, which put the finishing stroke to poor Meg's woe.

'Is that all? Fling it out of the window, and don't bother any more about it. I'll buy you quarts if you want it; but for heaven's sake don't have hysterics, for I've brought Jack Scott home to dinner, and –'

John got no further, for Meg cast him off, and clasped her hands with a tragic gesture as she fell into a chair, exclaiming in a tone of mingled indignation, reproach, and dismay:

'A man to dinner, and everything in a mess! John Brooke, how *could* you do such a thing?'

'Hush, he's in the garden! I forgot the confounded jelly, but it can't be helped now,' said John, surveying the prospect with an anxious eye.

'You ought to have sent word, or told me this morning, and you ought to have remembered how busy I was,' continued Meg petulantly; for even turtle doves will peck when ruffled.

'I didn't know it this morning, and there was no time to send word, for I met him on the way out. I never thought of asking leave, when you have always told me to do as I liked. I never tried it before, and hang me if I ever do again!' added John, with an aggrieved air.

'I should hope not! Take him away at once; I can't see him, and there isn't any dinner.'

'Well, I like that! Where's the beef and vegetables I sent home, and the pudding you promised?' cried John, rushing to the larder.

'I hadn't time to cook anything; I meant to dine at Mother's. I'm sorry, but I was *so* busy'; and Meg's tears began again.

John was a mild man, but he was human; and after a long day's work, to come home tired, hungry, and hopeful, to find a chaotic house, an empty table, and a cross wife was not exactly conducive to repose of mind or manner. He restrained himself, however, and the little squall would have blown over, but for one unlucky word.

'It's a scrape, I acknowledge; but if you will lend a hand, we'll pull through, and have a good time yet. Don't cry, dear, but just exert yourself a bit, and knock us up something to eat. We're both as hungry as hunters, so we shan't mind what it is. Give us the cold meat, and bread and cheese; we won't ask for jelly.'

He meant it for a good-natured joke; but that one word sealed his fate. Meg thought it was *too* cruel to hint about her sad failure, and the last atom of patience vanished as he spoke.

'You must get yourself out of the scrape as you can; I'm too used up to "exert" myself for anyone. It's like a man to propose a bone and vulgar bread and cheese for company. I won't have anything of the sort in my house. Take that Scott up to Mother's, and tell him I'm away, sick, dead – anything. I won't see him, and you two can laugh at me and my jelly as much as you like: you won't have anything else here'; and having delivered her defiance all in one breath, Meg cast away her pinafore, and precipitately left the field to bemoan herself in her own room.

What those two creatures did in her absence she never knew; but Mr Scott was not taken 'up to Mother's', and when Meg descended, after they had strolled away together, she found traces of a promiscuous lunch which filled her with horror. Lotty reported that they had eaten 'a much, and greatly laughed, and the master bid her throw away all the sweet stuff, and hide the pots'.

Meg longed to go and tell Mother; but a sense of shame at her own shortcomings, of loyalty to John, 'who might be cruel, but nobody should know it,' restrained her; and after a summary clearing up, she dressed herself prettily, and sat down to wait for John to come and be forgiven.

Unfortunately, John didn't come, not seeing the matter in that light. He had carried it off as a good joke with Scott, excused his little wife as well as he could, and played the host so hospitably that his friend enjoyed the impromptu dinner, and promised to come again. But John was angry, though he did not show it; he felt that Meg had got him into a scrape, and then deserted him in his hour of need. 'It wasn't fair to tell a man to bring folks home any time, with perfect freedom, and when he took you at your word, to flame up and blame him, and leave him in the lurch, to be laughed at or pitied. No, by George, it wasn't! and Meg must know it.' He had fumed inwardly during the feast, but when the flurry was over, and he strolled home, after seeing Scott off, a milder mood came over him. 'Poor little thing! it was hard upon her when she tried so heartily to please me. She was wrong, of course, but then she is young. I must be patient and teach her.' He hoped she had not gone home – he hated gossip and interference. For a minute he was ruffled again at the mere thought of it; and then the fear that Meg would cry herself sick softened his heart, and sent him on at a quicker pace, resolving to be calm and kind, but firm, quite firm, and show her where she had failed in her duty to her spouse.

Meg likewise resolved to be 'calm and kind, but firm', and show *him* his duty. She longed to run to meet him, and beg pardon, and be kissed and comforted, as she was sure of being; but, of course, she did nothing of the sort, and when she saw John coming, began to hum quite naturally, as she rocked and sewed, like a lady of leisure in her best parlour.

John was a little disappointed not to find a tender Niobe; but, feeling that his dignity demanded the first apology, he made none, only came leisurely in, and laid himself upon the sofa, with the singularly relevant remark:

'We are going to have a new moon, my dear.'

'I've no objection,' was Meg's equally soothing remark.

A few other topics of general interest were introduced by Mr Brooke, and wet-blanketed by Mrs Brooke, and conversation languished. John went to one window, unfolded his paper, and wrapped himself in it, figuratively speaking. Meg went to the other window, and sewed as if new rosettes for her slippers were among the necessaries of life. Neither spoke; both looked quite 'calm and firm', and both felt desperately uncomfortable.

'Oh dear,' thought Meg, 'married life is very trying, and does need infinite patience, as well as love, as Mother says.' The word 'Mother' suggested other maternal counsels, given long ago, and received with unbelieving protests.

'John is a good man, but he has his faults, and you must learn to see and bear with them, remembering your own. He is very decided, but never will be obstinate, if you reason kindly, not oppose impatiently. He is very accurate, and particular about the truth – a good trait, though you call him "fussy". Never deceive him by look or word, Meg, and he will give you the confidence you deserve, the support you need. He has a temper, not like ours – one flash, and then all over – but the white, still anger, that is seldom stirred, but once kindled, is hard to quench. Be careful, very careful, not to wake this anger against yourself, for peace and happiness depend on keeping his respect. Watch yourself, be the first to ask pardon if you both err, and guard against the little piques, misunderstandings, and hasty words that often pave the way for bitter sorrow and regret.'

These words came back to Meg, as she sat sewing in the sunset, especially the last. This was the first serious disagreement; her own hasty speeches sounded both silly and unkind, as she recalled them, her own anger looked childish now, and thoughts of poor John coming home to such a scene quite melted her heart. She glanced at him with tears in her eyes, but he did not see them; she put down her work and got up, thinking, 'I *will* be the first to say, "Forgive me", but he did not seem to hear her; she went very slowly across the room, for pride was hard to swallow, and stood by him, but he did not turn his head. For a minute she felt as if she really couldn't do it; then came the thought, 'This is the beginning, I'll do my part, and have nothing to reproach myself with,' and stooping down, she softly kissed her husband on the forehead. Of course that settled it; the penitent kiss was better than a world of words, and John had her on his knee in a minute, saying tenderly:

'It was too bad to laugh at the poor little jelly-pots. Forgive me, dear, I never will again!'

But he did, oh bless you, yes, hundreds of times, and so did Meg, both declaring that it was the sweetest jelly they ever made; for family peace was preserved in that little family jar.

After this, Meg had Mr Scott to dinner by special invitation, and served him up a pleasant feast without a cooked wife for the first course; on which occasion she was so gay and gracious, and made everything go off so charmingly, that Mr Scott told John he was a happy fellow, and shook his head over the hardships of bachelorhood all the way home.

In the autumn, new trials and experiences came to Meg. Sallie Moffat renewed her friendship, was always running out for a dish of gossip at the little house, or inviting 'that poor dear' to come in and spend the day at the big house. It was pleasant, for in dull weather Meg often felt lonely; all were busy at home, John absent till night, and nothing to do but sew, or read, or potter about. So it naturally fell out that Meg got into the way of gadding and gossiping with her friend. Seeing Sallie's pretty things made her long for such, and pity herself because she had not got them. Sallie was very kind, and often offered her the coveted trifles; but Meg declined them, knowing that John wouldn't like it; and then this foolish little woman went and did what John disliked infinitely worse.

She knew her husband's income, and she loved to feel that he trusted her, not only with his happiness, but what some men seem to value more – his money. She knew where it was, was free to take what she liked, and all he asked was that she should keep account of every penny, pay bills once a month, and remember that she was a poor man's wife. Till now, she had done well, been prudent and exact, kept her little account books neatly, and showed them to him monthly without fear. But that autumn the serpent got into Meg's paradise, and tempted her, like many a modern Eve, not with apples, but with dress. Meg didn't like to be pitied and made to feel poor; it irritated her, but she was ashamed to confess it, and now and then she tried to console herself by buying something pretty, so that Sallie needn't think she had to economize. She always felt wicked after it, for the pretty things were seldom necessaries; but then they cost so little, it wasn't worth worrying about; so the trifles increased unconsciously, and in the shopping excursions she was no longer a passive looker-on.

But the trifles cost more than one would imagine; and when she cast up her accounts at the end of the month, the sum total rather scared her. John was busy that month, and left the bills to her; the next month he was absent; but the third he had a grand quarterly settling up, and Meg never forgot it. A few days before she had done a dreadful thing, and it weighed upon her conscience. Sallie had been buying silks, and Meg longed for a new one – just a handsome light one for parties, her black silk was so common, and thin things for evening wear were only proper for girls. Aunt March usually gave the sisters a present of twenty-five dollars apiece at New Year, that was only a month to wait, and here was a lovely violet silk going at a bargain, and she had the money, if she only dared to take it. John always said what was his was hers;

but would he think it right to spend not only the prospective five-and-twenty, but another five-and-twenty out of the household fund? That was the question. Sallie had urged her to do it, had offered to loan the money, and with the best intentions in life, had tempted Meg beyond her strength. In an evil moment the shopman held up the lovely, shimmering folds, and said, 'A bargain, I assure you, ma'am.' She answered, 'I'll take it' and it was cut off and paid for, and Sallie had exulted, and she had laughed as if it were a thing of no consequence, and driven away, feeling as if she had stolen something, and the police were after her.

When she got home, she tried to assuage the pangs of remorse by spreading forth the lovely silk; but it looked less silvery now, didn't become her, after all, and the words 'fifty dollars' seemed stamped like a pattern down each breadth. She put it away; but it haunted her, not delightfully, as a new dress should, but dreadfully, like the ghost of a folly that was not easily laid. When John got out his books that night, Meg's heart sank, and for the first time in her married life, she was afraid of her husband. The kind, brown eyes looked as if they could be stern; and though he was unusually merry, she fancied he had found her out, but didn't mean to let her know it. The house bills were all paid, the books all in order. John had praised her, and was undoing the old pocket-book which they called the 'bank', when Meg, knowing that it was quite empty, stopped his hand, saying nervously:

'You haven't seen my private expense book yet.'

John never asked to see it; but she always insisted on his doing so, and used to enjoy his masculine amazement at the queer things women wanted, and made him guess what 'piping' was, demand fiercely the meaning of a 'hug-me-tight', or wonder how a little thing composed of three rosebuds, a bit of velvet, and a pair of strings, could possibly be a bonnet, and cost five or six dollars. That night he looked as if he would like the fun of quizzing her figures and pretending to be horrified at her extravagance, as he often did, being particularly proud of his prudent wife.

The little book was brought slowly out, and laid down before him. Meg got behind his chair under pretence of smoothing the wrinkles out of his tired forehead, and standing there, she said, with her panic increasing with every word:

'John, dear, I'm ashamed to show you my book, for I've really been dreadfully extravagant lately. I go about so much I must have things, you know, and Sallie advised my getting it, so I did; and my New Year's money will partly pay for it: but I was sorry after I'd done it, for I knew you'd think it wrong in me.'

John laughed, and drew her round beside him, saying good-humouredly, 'Don't go and hide. I won't beat you if you *have* got a pair of killing boots; I'm rather proud of my wife's feet, and don't mind if she does pay eight or nine dollars for her boots, if they are good ones.'

That had been one of her last 'trifles', and John's eye had fallen on it as he spoke. 'Oh, what *will* he say when he comes to that awful fifty dollars!' thought Meg, with a shiver.

'It's worse than boots, it's a silk dress,' she said, with the calmness of desperation, for she wanted the worst over.

'Well, dear, what is the "dem'd total", as Mr Mantalini says?'

That didn't sound like John, and she knew he was looking up at her with the straightforward look that she had always been ready to meet and answer with one as frank till now. She turned the page and her head at the same time, pointing to the sum which would have been bad enough without the fifty, but which was appalling to her with that added. For a minute the room was very still; then John said slowly – but she could feel it cost him an effort to express no displeasure:

'Well, I don't know that fifty is much for a dress, with all the furbelows and notions you have to have to finish it off these days.'

'It isn't made or trimmed,' sighed Meg faintly, for a sudden recollection of the cost still to be incurred quite overwhelmed her.

'Twenty-five yards of silk seems a good deal to cover

one small woman, but I've no doubt my wife will look as fine as Ned Moffat's when she gets it on,' said John dryly.

'I know you are angry, John, but I can't help it. I don't mean to waste your money, and I didn't think those little things would count up so. I can't resist them when I see Sallie buying all she wants, and pitying me because I don't. I try to be contented, but it is hard, and I'm tired of being poor.'

The last words were spoken so low she thought he did not hear them, but he did, and they wounded him deeply, for he had denied himself many pleasures for Meg's sake. She could have bitten her tongue out the minute she had said it, for John pushed the books away, and got up, saying, with a little quiver in his voice, 'I was afraid of this; I do my best, Meg.' If he had scolded her, or even shaken her, it would not have broken her heart like those few words. She ran to him and held him close, crying, with repentant tears, 'O John, my dear, kind, hard-working boy, I didn't mean it! It was so wicked, so untrue and ungrateful, how could I say it! Oh, how could I say it!'

He was very kind, forgave her readily, and did not utter one reproach; but Meg knew that she had done and said a thing which would not be forgotten soon, although he might never allude to it again. She had promised to love him for better or worse; and then she, his wife, had reproached him with his poverty, after spending his earnings recklessly. It was dreadful; and the worst of it was

John went on so quietly afterwards, just as if nothing had happened, except that he stayed in town later, and worked at night when she had gone to cry herself to sleep. A week of remorse nearly made Meg sick; and the discovery that John had countermanded the order for his new greatcoat reduced her to a state of despair which was pathetic to behold. He had simply said, in answer to her surprised enquiries as to the change, 'I can't afford it, my dear'.

Meg said no more, but a few minutes after he found her in the hall, with her face buried in the old greatcoat, crying as if her heart would break.

They had a long talk that night, and Meg learned to love her husband better for his poverty, because it seemed to have made a man of him, given him the strength and courage to fight his own way, and taught him a tender patience with which to bear and comfort the natural longings and failures of those he loved.

Next day she put her pride in her pocket, went to Sallie, told the truth, and asked her to buy the silk as a favour. The good-natured Mrs Moffat willingly did so, and had the delicacy not to make her a present of it immediately afterwards. Then Meg ordered home the greatcoat, and, when John arrived, she put it on, and asked him how he liked her new silk gown. One can imagine what answer he made, how he received his present, and what a blissful state of things ensued. John came home early, Meg gadded no more; and that greatcoat was put on in the morning by a very happy husband, and taken off at night by a most devoted little wife. So the year rolled round, and at midsummer there came to Meg a new experience – the deepest and tenderest of a woman's life.

Laurie came sneaking into the kitchen of the Dovecote, one Saturday, with an excited face, and was received with the clash of cymbals, for Hannah clapped her hands with a saucepan in one and the cover in the other.

'How's the little mamma? Where is everybody? Why didn't you tell me before I came home?' began Laurie, in a loud whisper.

'Happy as a queen, the dear! Every soul of 'em is upstairs a worshipin'; we didn't want no hurrycanes round. Now you go into the parlour, and I'll send 'em down to you,' with which somewhat involved reply Hannah vanished, chuckling ecstatically.

Presently Jo appeared, proudly bearing a flannel bundle laid forth upon a large pillow. Jo's face was very sober, but her eyes twinkled, and there was an odd sound in her voice of repressed emotion of some sort.

'Shut your eyes and hold out your arms,' she said invitingly.

Laurie backed precipitately into a corner, and put his hands behind him with an imploring gesture: 'No, thank you, I'd rather not. I shall drop it or smash it, as sure as fate.'

'Then you shan't see your nevvy,' said Jo decidedly, turning as if to go.

'I will, I will! only you must be responsible for damages'; and, obeying orders, Laurie heroically shut his eyes while something was put into his arms. A peal of laughter from Jo, Amy, Mrs March, Hannah, and John caused him to open them the next minute, to find himself invested with two babies instead of one.

No wonder they laughed, for the expression of his face was droll enough to convulse a Quaker, as he stood and stared wildly from the unconscious innocents to the hilarious spectators, with such dismay that Jo sat down on the floor and screamed.

'Twins, by Jupiter!' was all he said for a minute; then, turning to the women with an appealing look that was comically piteous, he added, 'Take 'em quick, somebody! I'm going to laugh, and I shall drop 'em.'

John rescued his babies, and marched up and down, with one on each arm, as if already initiated into the mysteries of baby tending, while Laurie laughed till the tears ran down his cheeks.

'It's the best joke of the season, isn't it? I wouldn't have you told, for I set my heart on surprising you, and flatter myself I've done it,' said Jo, when she got her breath.

'I never was more staggered in my life. Isn't it fun? Are they boys? What are you going to name them? Let's have another look. Hold me up, Jo; for upon my life it's one too many for me,' returned Laurie, regarding the infants with the air of a big, benevolent Newfoundland looking at a pair of infantile kittens.

'Boy and girl. Aren't they beauties?' said the proud papa, beaming upon the little, red squirmers as if they were unfledged angels.

'Most remarkable children I ever saw. Which is which?' and Laurie bent like a well-sweep to examine the prodigies.

'Amy put a blue ribbon on the boy and a pink on the girl, French fashion, so you can always tell. Besides, one has blue eyes and one brown. Kiss them, Uncle Teddy,' said wicked Jo.

'I'm afraid they mightn't like it,' began Laurie, with unusual timidity in such matters.

'Of course they will; they are used to it now. Do it this minute, sir!' commanded Jo, fearing he might propose a proxy.

Laurie screwed up his face, and obeyed with a gingerly peck at each little cheek that produced another laugh, and made the babies squeal.

'There, I knew they didn't like it! That's the boy, see him kick; he hits out with his fists like a good one. Now then, young Brooke, pitch into a man of your own size, will you?' cried Laurie, delighted with a poke in the face from a tiny fist, flapping aimlessly about.

'He's to be named John Laurence, and the girl Margaret, after Mother and Grandmother. We shall call her Daisy, so as not to have two Megs, and I suppose the mannie will be Jack, unless we find a better name,' said Amy, with aunt-like interest.

'Name him Demijohn, and call him "Demi" for short,' said Laurie.

'Daisy and Demi – just the thing! I *knew* Teddy would do it,' cried Jo, clapping her hands.

Teddy certainly had done it that time, for the babies were 'Daisy' and 'Demi' to the end of the chapter.

6

Calls

'Come, Jo, it's time.'

'For what?'

'You don't mean to say you have forgotten that you promised to make half a dozen calls with me today?'

'I've done a good many rash and foolish things in my life, but I don't think I ever was mad enough to say I'd make six calls in one day, when a single one upsets me for a week.'

'Yes, you did; it was a bargain between us. I was to finish the crayon of Beth for you, and you were to go properly with me, and return our neighbours' visits.'

'If it was fair – that was in the bond; and I stand to the letter of my bond, Shylock. There is a pile of clouds in the east; it's *not* fair, and I don't go.'

'Now, that's shirking. It's a lovely day, no prospect of rain, and you pride yourself on keeping promises; so be honourable; come and do your duty, and then be at peace for another six months.'

At that minute Jo was particularly absorbed in dress-making for she was mantua-maker to the family, and took especial credit to herself because she could use a needle as well as a pen. It was very provoking to be arrested in the act of a first trying-on, and ordered out to make calls in her best array, on a warm July day. She hated calls of the formal sort, and never made any till Amy compelled her with a bargain, bribe, or promise. In the present instance, there was no escape; and having clashed her scissors rebelliously, while protesting that she smelt thunder, she gave in, put away her work, and taking up her hat and gloves with an air of resignation, told Amy the victim was ready.

'Jo March, you are perverse enough to provoke a saint! You don't intend to make calls in that state, I hope,' cried Amy, surveying her with amazement.

'Why not? I'm neat and cool and comfortable, quite proper for a dusty walk on a warm day. If people care more for my clothes than they do for me, I don't wish to see them. You can dress for both, and be as elegant as you please: it pays for you to be fine; it doesn't for me, and furbelows only worry me.'

'Oh dear!' sighed Amy; 'now she's in a contrary fit, and will drive me distracted before I can get her properly ready. I'm sure it's no pleasure to me to go today, but it's a debt we owe society, and there's no one to pay it but you and me. I'll do anything for you, Jo, if you'll only dress yourself nicely, and come and help me do the civil. You can talk so well, look so aristocratic in your best things, and behave so beautifully, if you try, that I'm proud of you. I'm afraid to go alone; do come and take care of me.'

'You're an artful little puss to flatter and wheedle your cross old sister in that way. The idea of my being aristocratic and well bred, and your being afraid to go anywhere alone! I don't know which is the most absurd. Well, I'll go if I must, and do my best. You shall be commander of the expedition, and I'll obey blindly; will that satisfy you?' said Jo, with a sudden change from perversity to lamb-like submission.

'You're a perfect cherub! Now put on all your best things, and I'll tell you how to behave at each place, so that you will make a good impression. I want people to like you, and they would if you'd only try to be a little more agreeable. Do your hair the pretty way, and put the pink rose in your bonnet; it's becoming, and you look too sober in your plain suit. Take your light gloves and the embroidered handkerchief. We'll stop at Meg's, and borrow her white sunshade, and then you can have my dove-coloured one.'

While Amy dressed, she issued her orders, and Jo obeyed them; not without entering her protest, however, for she sighed as she rustled into her new organdie, frowned darkly at herself as she tied her bonnet strings in an irreproachable bow, wrestled viciously with pins as she put on her collar, wrinkled up her features generally as she shook out the handkerchief, whose embroidery was as irritating to her nose as the present mission was to her feelings; and when she had squeezed her hands into tight gloves with three buttons and a tassel, as the last touch of elegance, she turned to Amy with an imbecile expression of countenance, saying meekly:

'I'm perfectly miserable; but if you consider me presentable, I die happy.'

'You are highly satisfactory; turn slowly round, and let me get a careful view.' Jo revolved, and Amy gave a touch here and there, then fell back, with her head on one side, observing graciously, 'Yes, you'll do; your head is all I could ask, for that white bonnet *with* the rose is quite ravishing. Hold back your shoulders, and carry your hands easily, no matter if your gloves do pinch. There's one thing you can do well, Jo, that is, wear a shawl – I can't; but it's very nice to see you, and I'm so glad Aunt March gave you that lovely one; it's simple, but handsome, and those folds over the arm are really artistic. Is the point of my mantle in the middle, and have I looped my dress evenly? I like to show my boots, for my feet *are* pretty, though my nose isn't.'

'You are a thing of beauty and a joy for ever,' said Jo, looking through her hand with the air of a connoisseur at the blue feather against the gold hair. 'Am I to drag my best dress through the dust, or loop it up, please, ma'am?'

'Hold it up when you walk, but drop it in the house;

the sweeping style suits you best, and you must learn to trail your skirts gracefully. You haven't half buttoned one cuff; do it at once. You'll never look finished if you are not careful about the little details, for they make up the pleasing whole.'

Jo sighed, and proceeded to burst the buttons off her glove, in doing up her cuff; but at last both were ready, and sailed away, looking as 'pretty as picters', Hannah said, as she hung out of the upper window to watch them.

'Now, Jo dear, the Chesters consider themselves very elegant people, so I want you to put on your best deportment. Don't make any of your abrupt remarks, or do anything odd, will you? Just be calm, cool, and quiet – that's safe and ladylike; and you can easily do it for fifteen minutes,' said Amy, as they approached the first place, having borrowed the white parasol and been inspected by Meg, with a baby on each arm.

'Let me see. "Calm, cool, and quiet" – yes, I think I can promise that. I've played the part of a prim young lady on the stage, and I'll try it off. My powers are great, as you shall see; so be easy in your mind, my child.'

Amy looked relieved, but naughty Jo took her at her word for, during the first call, she sat with every limb gracefully composed, every fold correctly draped, calm as a summer sea, cool as a snowbank, and as silent as a sphinx. In vain Mrs Chester alluded to her 'charming novel', and the Misses Chester introduced parties, picnics, the opera, and the fashions; each and all were answered by a smile, a bow, and a demure 'Yes' or 'No', with the chill on. In vain Amy telegraphed the word 'Talk', tried to draw her out, and administered covert pokes with her foot. Jo sat as if blandly unconscious of it all, with deportment like Maud's face, 'icily regular, splendidly null'.

'What a haughty, uninteresting creature that oldest Miss March is!' was the unfortunately audible remark of one of the ladies, as the door closed upon their guests. Jo laughed noiselessly all through the hall, but Amy looked disgusted at the failure of her instructions, and very naturally laid the blame upon Jo.

'How could you mistake me so? I merely meant you to be properly dignified and composed, and you made yourself a perfect stock and stone. Try to be sociable at the Lambs', gossip as other girls do, and be interested in dress and flirtations and whatever nonsense comes up. They move in the best society, are valuable persons for us to know, and I wouldn't fail to make a good impression there for anything.'

'I'll be agreeable; I'll gossip and giggle, and have horrors and raptures over any trifle you like. I rather enjoy this, and now I'll imitate what is called "a charming girl"; I can do it, for I have May Chester as a model, and I'll improve upon her. See if the Lambs don't say, "What a lively, nice creature that Jo March is!"'

Amy felt anxious, as well she might, for when Jo turned

freakish there was no knowing where she would stop. Amy's face was a study when she saw her sister skim into the next drawing room, kiss all the young ladies with effusion, beam graciously upon the young gentlemen, and join in the chat with a spirit which amazed the beholder. Amy was taken possession of by Mrs Lamb, with whom she was a favourite, and forced to hear a long account of Lucretia's last attack, while three delightful young gentlemen hovered near, waiting for a pause when they might rush in and rescue her. So situated, she was powerless to check Jo, who seemed possessed by a spirit of mischief, and talked away as volubly as the old lady. A knot of heads gathered about her, and Amy strained her ears to hear what was going on; for broken sentences filled her with alarm, round eyes and uplifted hands tormented her with curiosity, and frequent peals of laughter made her wild to share the fun. One may imagine her suffering on overhearing fragments of this sort of conversation:

'She rides splendidly – who taught her?'

'No one; she used to practise mounting, holding the reins, and sitting straight on an old saddle in a tree. Now she rides anything, for she doesn't know what fear is, and the stableman lets her have horses cheap, because she trains them to carry ladies so well. She has such a passion for it, I often tell her if everything else fails she can be a horse-breaker, and get her living so.'

At this awful speech Amy contained herself with difficulty, for the impression was being given that she was
rather a fast young lady, which was her especial aversion.
But what could she do? for the old lady was in the middle
of her story, and long before it was done Jo was off again,
making more droll revelations, and committing still more
fearful blunders.

'Yes, Amy was in despair that day, for all the good beasts
were gone, and of three left, one was lame, one blind, and
the other so balky that you had to put dirt in his mouth
before he would start. Nice animal for a pleasure party,
wasn't it?'

'Which did she choose?' asked one of the laughing
gentlemen, who enjoyed the subject.

'None of them; she heard of a young horse at the farm-
house over the river, and, though a lady had never ridden
him, she resolved to try, because he was handsome and
spirited. Her struggles were really pathetic; there was no
one to bring the horse to the saddle, so she took the saddle
to the horse. My dear creature, she actually rowed it over
the river, put it on her head, and marched up to the barn
to the utter amazement of the old man!'

'Did she ride the horse?'

'Of course she did, and had a capital time. I expected
to see her brought home in fragments, but she managed
him perfectly, and was the life of the party.'

'Well, I call that plucky!' and young Mr Lamb turned

an approving glance upon Amy, wondering what his mother could be saying to make the girl look so red and uncomfortable.

She was still redder and more uncomfortable a moment after, when a sudden turn in the conversation introduced the subject of dress. One of the young ladies asked Jo where she got the pretty drab hat she wore to the picnic; and stupid Jo, instead of mentioning the place where it was bought two years ago, must needs answer, with unnecessary frankness, 'Oh, Amy painted it; you can't buy those soft shades, so we paint ours any colour we like. It's a great comfort to have an artistic sister.'

'Isn't that an original idea?' cried Miss Lamb, who found Jo great fun.

'That's nothing compared to some of her brilliant performances. There's nothing the child can't do. Why, she wanted a pair of blue boots for Sallie's party, so she just painted her soiled white ones the loveliest shade of sky-blue you ever saw, and they looked exactly like satin,' added Jo, with an air of pride in her sister's accomplishments that exasperated Amy till she felt that it would be a relief to throw her card-case at her.

'We read a story of yours the other day, and enjoyed it very much,' observed the elder Miss Lamb, wishing to compliment the literary lady, who did not look the character just then, it must be confessed.

Any mention of her 'works' always had a bad effect

upon Jo, who either grew rigid and looked offended, or changed the subject with a brusque remark, as now. 'Sorry you could find nothing better to read. I write that rubbish because it sells, and ordinary people like it. Are you going to New York this winter?'

As Miss Lamb had 'enjoyed' the story, this speech was not exactly grateful or complimentary. The minute it was made Jo saw her mistake; but, fearing to make the matter worse, suddenly remembered that it was for her to make the first move towards departure, and did so with an abruptness that left three people with half-finished sentences in their mouths.

'Amy, we *must* go. *Good*bye, dear; *do* come and see us; we are *pining* for a visit. I don't dare to ask *you*, Mr Lamb, but if you *should* come, I don't think I shall have the heart to send you away.'

Jo said this with such a droll imitation of May Chester's gushing style that Amy got out of the room as rapidly as possible, feeling a strong desire to laugh and cry at the same time.

'Didn't I do that well?' asked Jo, with a satisfied air, as they walked away.

'Nothing could have been worse,' was Amy's crushing reply. 'What possessed you to tell those stories about my saddle, and the hats and boots, and all the rest of it?'

'Why, it's funny, and amuses people. They know we are poor, so it's no use pretending that we have grooms, buy three or four hats a season, and have things as easy and fine as they do.'

'You needn't go and tell them all our little shifts, and expose our poverty in that perfectly unnecessary way. You haven't a bit of proper pride, and never will learn when to hold your tongue and when to speak,' said Amy despairingly.

Poor Jo looked abashed, and silently chafed the end of her nose with the stiff handkerchief, as if performing a penance for her misdemeanours.

'How shall I behave here?' she asked, as they approached the third mansion.

'Just as you please; I wash my hands of you,' was Amy's short answer.

'Then I'll enjoy myself. The boys are at home, and we'll have a comfortable time. Goodness knows I need a little change, for elegance has a bad effect upon my constitution,' returned Jo gruffly, being disturbed by her failures to suit.

An enthusiastic welcome from three big boys and several pretty children speedily soothed her ruffled feelings; and, leaving Amy to entertain the hostess and Mr Tudor, who happened to be calling likewise, Jo devoted herself to the young folks, and found the change refreshing. She listened to college stories with deep interest, caressed pointers and poodles without a murmur, agreed heartily that 'Tom Brown was a brick', regardless of the improper form of praise; and when one lad proposed a visit to his turtle tank, she went with an alacrity which caused Mamma to smile upon her, as that motherly lady settled the cap which was left in a ruinous condition by filial hugs, bear-like but affectionate, and dearer to her than the most faultless coiffure from the hands of an inspired Frenchwoman.

Leaving her sister to her own devices, Amy proceeded to enjoy herself to her heart's content. Mr Tudor's uncle had married an English lady who was third cousin to a living lord, and Amy regarded the whole family with great respect; for, in spite of her American birth and breeding, she possessed that reverence for titles which haunts the best of us – that unacknowledged loyalty to the early faith in kings which set the most democratic nation under the sun in a ferment at the coming of a royal yellow-haired laddie, some years ago, and which still has something to do with the love the young country bears the old, like that of a big son for an imperious little mother, who held him while she could, and let him go with a farewell scolding when he rebelled. But even the satisfaction of talking with a distant connection of the British nobility did not render Amy forgetful of time; and when the proper number of minutes had passed, she reluctantly tore herself from this aristocratic society, and looked about for Jo, fervently hoping that her incorrigible sister would not be found in any position which should bring disgrace upon the name of March.

It might have been worse, but Amy considered it bad; for Jo sat on the grass, with an encampment of boys about her, and a dirty-footed dog reposing on the skirt of her state and festival dress, as she related one of Laurie's pranks to her admiring audience. One small child was poking turtles with Amy's cherished parasol, a second was eating gingerbread over Jo's best bonnet, and a third playing ball with her gloves. But all were enjoying themselves; and when Jo collected her damaged property to go, her escort accompanied her, begging her to come again, 'it was such fun to hear about Laurie's larks'.

'Capital boys, aren't they? I feel quite young and brisk again after that,' said Jo, strolling along with her hands behind her, partly from habit, partly to conceal the bespattered parasol.

'Why do you always avoid Mr Tudor?' asked Amy, wisely refraining from any comment upon Jo's dilapidated appearance.

'Don't like him; he puts on airs, snubs his sisters, worries his father, and doesn't speak respectfully of his mother. Laurie says he is fast, and *I* don't consider him a desirable acquaintance; so I let him alone.'

'You might treat him civilly, at least. You gave him a cool nod; and just now you bowed and smiled in the politest way to Tommy Chamberlain, whose father keeps a grocery store. If you had just reversed the nod and the bow, it would have been right,' said Amy reprovingly.

'No, it wouldn't,' returned perverse Jo; 'I neither like, respect, nor admire Tudor, though his grandfather's uncle's nephew's niece *was* third cousin to a lord. Tommy is poor and bashful and good and very clever; I think well of him, and like to show that I do, for he *is* a gentleman in spite of the brown-paper parcels.'

'It's no use trying to argue with you,' began Amy.

'Not the least, my dear,' interrupted Jo; 'so let us look amiable, and drop a card here, as the Kings are evidently out, for which I'm deeply grateful.'

The family card-case having done its duty, the girls walked on, and Jo uttered another thanksgiving on reaching the fifth house, and being told that the young ladies were engaged.

'Now let us go home, and never mind Aunt March today. We can run down there any time, and it's really a pity to trail through the dust in our best bibs and tuckers, when we are tired and cross.'

'Speak for yourself, if you please. Aunt likes to have us pay her the compliment of coming in style, and making a formal call; it's a little thing to do, but it gives her pleasure, and I don't believe it will hurt your things half so much as letting dirty dogs and clumping boys spoil them. Stoop down, and let me take the crumbs off of your bonnet.'

'What a good girl you are, Amy!' said Jo, with a repentant glance from her own damaged costume to that of her sister, which was fresh and spotless still. 'I wish it was as easy for me to do little things to please people as it is for you. I think of them, but it takes too much time to do them; so I wait for a chance to confer a great favour, and let the small ones slip; but they tell best in the end, I fancy.'

Amy smiled, and was mollified at once, saying with a maternal air:

'Women should learn to be agreeable, particularly poor ones; for they have no other way of repaying the kindnesses they receive. If you'd remember that, and practise it, you'd be better liked than I am, because there is more of you.'

'I'm a crotchety old thing, and always shall be, but I'm willing to own that you are right; only it's easier for me to risk my life for a person than to be pleasant to him when I don't feel like it. It's a great misfortune to have such strong likes and dislikes, isn't it?'

'It's a greater not to be able to hide them. I don't mind saying that I don't approve of Tudor any more than you do; but I'm not called upon to tell him so neither are you, and there is no use in making yourself disagreeable because he is.'

'But I think girls ought to show when they disapprove of young men; and how can they do it except by their manners? Preaching does not do any good, as I know to my sorrow, since I've had Teddy to manage; but there are many little ways in which I can influence him without a word, and I say we *ought* to do it to others if we can.'

'Teddy is a remarkable boy, and can't be taken as a sample of other boys,' said Amy, in a tone of solemn conviction, which would have convulsed the 'remarkable boy', if he had heard it. 'If we were belles, or women of wealth and position, we might do something, perhaps; but for us to frown at one set of young gentlemen because we don't approve of them, and smile upon another set because we do, wouldn't have a particle of effect, and we should only be considered odd and puritanical.'

'So we are to countenance things and people which we detest, merely because we are not belles and millionaires, are we? That's a nice sort of morality.'

'I can't argue about it, I only know that it's the way of the world; and people who set themselves against it only get laughed at for their pains. I don't like reformers, and I hope you will never try to be one.'

'I do like them, and I shall be one if I can; for in spite of the laughing, the world would never get on without them. We can't agree about that, for you belong to the old set, and I to the new: you will get on the best, but I shall have the liveliest time of it. I should rather enjoy the brickbats and hooting, I think.'

'Well, compose yourself now, and don't worry Aunt with your new ideas.'

'I'll try not to, but I'm always possessed to burst out

with some particularly blunt speech or revolutionary sentiment before her; it's my doom, and I can't help it.'

They found Aunt Carrol with the old lady, both absorbed in some very interesting subject; but they dropped it as the girls came in, with a conscious look which betrayed that they had been talking about their nieces. Jo was not in a good humour, and the perverse fit returned; but Amy, who had virtuously done her duty, kept her temper, and pleased everybody, was in a most angelic frame of mind. This amiable spirit was felt at once, and both the aunts 'my deared' her affectionately, looking what they afterwards said emphatically – 'That child improves every day.'

'Are you going to help about the fair, dear?' asked Mrs Carrol, as Amy sat down beside her with the confiding air elderly people like so well in the young.

'Yes, Aunt. Mrs Chester asked me if I would, and I offered to tend a table, as I have nothing but my time to give.'

'I'm not,' put in Jo decidedly. 'I hate to be patronized, and the Chesters think it's a great favour to allow us to help with their highly connected fair. I wonder you consented, Amy; they only want you to work.'

'I am willing to work; it's for the freedmen as well as the Chesters, and I think it very kind of them to let me share the labour and the fun. Patronage does not trouble me when it is well meant.'

'Quite right and proper. I like your grateful spirit, my dear; it's a pleasure to help people who appreciate our efforts: some do not, and that is trying,' observed Aunt March, looking over her spectacles at Jo, who sat apart, rocking herself, with a somewhat morose expression.

If Jo had only known what a great happiness was wavering in the balance for one of them, she would have turned dove-like in a minute; but, unfortunately, we don't have windows in our breasts, and cannot see what goes on in the minds of our friends; better for us that we cannot as a general thing, but now and then it would be such a comfort, such a saving of time and temper. By her next speech, Jo deprived herself of several years of pleasure, and received a timely lesson in the art of holding her tongue.

'I don't like favours; they oppress and make me feel like a slave. I'd rather do everything for myself, and be perfectly independent.'

'Ahem!' coughed Aunt Carrol softly, with a look at Aunt March.

'I told you so,' said Aunt March, with a decided nod to Aunt Carrol.

Mercifully unconscious of what she had done, Jo sat with her nose in the air, and a revolutionary aspect which was anything but inviting.

'Do you speak French, dear?' asked Mrs Carrol, laying her hand on Amy's.

'Pretty well, thanks to Aunt March, who lets Esther talk to me as often as I like,' replied Amy, with a grateful look, which caused the old lady to smile affably.

'How are you about languages?' asked Mrs Carrol of Jo.

'Don't know a word; I'm very stupid about studying anything; can't bear French, it's such a slippery, silly sort of language,' was the brusque reply.

Another look passed between the ladies, and Aunt March said to Amy, 'You are quite strong and well, now, dear, I believe? Eyes don't trouble you any more, do they?'

'Not at all, thank you, ma'am. I'm very well, and mean to do great things next winter, so that I may be ready for Rome, whenever that joyful time arrives.'

'Good girl! You deserve to go, and I'm sure you will some day,' said Aunt March, with an approving pat on the head, as Amy picked up her ball for her.

> '*Cross-patch, draw the latch,*
> *Sit by the fire and spin,*'

squalled Polly, bending down from his perch on the back of her chair to peep into Jo's face, with such a comical air of impertinent enquiry that it was impossible to help laughing.

'Most observing bird,' said the old lady.

'Come and take a walk, my dear?' cried Polly, hopping

towards the china-closet, with a look suggestive of lump-sugar.

'Thank you, I will. Come, Amy'; and Jo brought the visit to an end, feeling more strongly than ever that calls did have a bad effect upon her constitution. She shook hands in a gentlemanly manner, but Amy kissed both the aunts, and the girls departed, leaving behind them the impression of shadow and sunshine; which impression caused Aunt March to say, as they vanished:

'You'd better do it, Mary; I'll supply the money,' and Aunt Carrol to reply decidedly, 'I certainly will, if her father and mother consent.'

7

Consequences

M rs Chester's fair was so very elegant and select that it was considered a great honour by the young ladies of the neighbourhood to be invited to take a table, and everyone was much interested in the matter. Amy was asked, but Jo was not, which was fortunate for all parties, as her elbows were decidedly akimbo at this period of her life, and it took a good many hard knocks to teach her how to get on easily. The 'haughty, uninteresting creature' was let severely alone; but Amy's talent and taste were duly complimented by the offer of the art table, and she exerted herself to prepare and secure appropriate and valuable contributions to it.

Everything went on smoothly till the day before the fair opened; then there occurred one of the little skirmishes which it is almost impossible to avoid, when some five-and-twenty women, old and young, with all their private piques and prejudices, try to work together.

May Chester was rather jealous of Amy because the latter was a greater favourite than herself; and, just at this time, several trifling circumstances occurred to increase the feeling. Amy's dainty pen-and-ink work entirely eclipsed May's painted vases – that was one thorn; then the all-conquering Tudor had danced four times with Amy, at a late party, and only once with May – that was thorn number two; but the chief grievance that rankled in her soul, and gave her an excuse for her unfriendly conduct, was a rumour which some obliging gossip had whispered to her, that the March girls had made fun of her at the Lambs'. All the blame of this should have fallen upon Jo, for her naughty imitation had been too lifelike to escape detection, and the frolicsome Lambs had permitted the joke to escape. No hint of this had reached the culprits, however, and Amy's dismay can be imagined, when, the very evening before the fair, as she was putting the last touches to her pretty table, Mrs Chester, who, of course, resented the supposed ridicule of her daughter, said, in a bland tone, but with a cold look:

'I find, dear, that there is some feeling among the young ladies about my giving this table to anyone but my girls. As this is the most prominent, and some say the most attractive table of all, and they are the chief getters-up of the fair, it is thought best for them to take this place. I'm sorry, but I know you are too sincerely interested in the cause to mind a little personal disappointment, and you shall have another table if you like.'

Mrs Chester had fancied beforehand that it would be

easy to deliver this little speech; but when the time came, she found it rather difficult to utter it naturally, with Amy's unsuspicious eyes looking straight at her, full of surprise and trouble.

Amy felt that there was something behind this, but could not guess what, and said quietly, feeling hurt, and showing that she did:

'Perhaps you had rather I took no table at all?'

'Now, my dear, don't have any ill feeling, I beg; it's merely a matter of expediency, you see; my girls will naturally take the lead, and this table is considered their proper place. *I* think it very appropriate to you, and feel very grateful for your efforts to make it so pretty; but we must give up our private wishes, of course, and I will see that you have a good place elsewhere. Wouldn't you like the flower table? The little girls undertook it, but they are discouraged. You could make a charming thing of it, and the flower table is always attractive, you know.'

'Especially to gentlemen,' added May, with a look which enlightened Amy as to one cause of her sudden fall from favour. She coloured angrily, but took no other notice of that girlish sarcasm, and answered, with unexpected amiability:

'It shall be as you please, Mrs Chester. I'll give up my place here at once, and attend to the flowers, if you like.'

'You can put your own things on your own table, if you prefer,' began May, feeling a little conscience-stricken, as she looked at the pretty racks, the painted shells, and quaint illuminations Amy had so carefully made and so gracefully arranged. She meant it kindly, but Amy mistook her meaning, and said quickly:

'Oh, certainly, if they are in your way'; and sweeping her contributions into her apron, pell-mell, she walked off, feeling that herself and her works of art had been insulted past forgiveness.

'Now she's mad. Oh dear, I wish I hadn't asked you to speak, Mamma,' said May, looking disconsolately at the empty spaces on her table.

'Girls' quarrels are soon over,' returned her mother, feeling a trifle ashamed of her own part in this one, as well she might.

The little girls hailed Amy and her treasures with delight, which cordial reception somewhat soothed her perturbed spirit, and she fell to work, determined to succeed florally, if she could not artistically. But everything seemed against her: it was late, and she was tired; everyone was too busy with their own affairs to help her; and the little girls were only hindrances, for the dears fussed and chattered like so many magpies, making a great deal of confusion in their artless efforts to preserve the most perfect order. The evergreen arch wouldn't stay firm after she got it up, but wiggled and threatened to tumble down on her head when the hanging baskets were filled; her best tile got a splash of water, which left a sepia tear on the Cupid's cheek; she bruised her hands with hammering, and got cold working in a draught, which last affliction filled her with apprehensions for the morrow. Any girl-reader who has suffered like afflictions will sympathize with poor Amy, and wish her well through with her task.

There was great indignation at home when she told her story that evening. Her mother said it was a shame, but told her she had done right; Beth declared she wouldn't go to the fair at all; and Jo demanded why she didn't take all her pretty things and leave those mean people to get on without her.

'Because they are mean is no reason why I should be. I hate such things, and though I think I've a right to be hurt, I don't intend to show it. They will feel that more than angry speeches or huffy actions, won't they, Marmee?'

'That's the right spirit, my dear; a kiss for a blow is always best, though it's not very easy to give it sometimes,' said her mother, with the air of one who had learned the difference between preaching and practising.

In spite of various very natural temptations to resent and retaliate, Amy adhered to her resolution all the next day, bent on conquering her enemy by kindness. She began well, thanks to a silent reminder that came to her unexpectedly, but most opportunely. As she arranged her table that morning, while the little girls were in an ante-room filling the baskets, she took up her pet production – a little book, the antique cover of which her father had found among his treasures, and in which, on leaves of vellum, she had beautifully illuminated different texts. As she turned the pages, rich in dainty devices, with very pardonable pride, her eye fell upon one verse that made her stop and think. Framed in a brilliant scroll-work of scarlet, blue, and gold, with little spirits of goodwill helping one another up and down among the thorns and flowers, were the words, 'Thou shalt love thy neighbour as thyself'.

'I ought, but I don't,' thought Amy, as her eye went from the bright page to May's discontented face behind the big vases, that could not hide the vacancies her pretty work had once filled. Amy stood a minute, turning the leaves in her hand, reading on each some sweet rebuke for all heart-burnings and uncharitableness of spirit. Many wise and true sermons are preached us every day by unconscious ministers in street, school, office, or home; even a fair table may become a pulpit, if it can offer the good and helpful words which are never out of season. Amy's conscience preached her a little sermon from that text, then and there; and she did what many of us do not always do – took the sermon to heart, and straightway put it in practice.

A group of girls were standing about May's table, admiring the pretty things, and talking over the change of saleswomen. They dropped their voices, but Amy knew they were speaking of her, hearing one side of the story, and judging accordingly. It was not pleasant, but a better spirit had come over her, and presently a chance offered for proving it. She heard May say sorrowfully:

'It's too bad, for there is no time to make other things, and I don't want to fill up with odds and ends. The table was just complete then: now it's spoilt.'

'I dare say she'd put them back if you asked her,' suggested someone.

'How could I after all the fuss?' began May, but she did not finish, for Amy's voice came across the hall, saying pleasantly:

'You may have them, and welcome, without asking, if you want them. I was just thinking I'd offer to put them back, for they belong to your table rather than mine. Here they are; please take them, and forgive me if I was hasty in carrying them away last night.'

As she spoke, Amy returned her contribution, with a nod and a smile, and hurried away again, feeling that it was easier to do a friendly thing than it was to stay and be thanked for it.

'Now, I call that lovely of her, don't you?' cried one girl.

May's answer was inaudible; but another young lady, whose temper was evidently a little soured by making lemonade, added, with a disagreeable laugh, 'Very lovely; for she knew she wouldn't sell them at her own table.'

Now, that was hard; when we make little sacrifices we like to have them appreciated, at least; and for a minute Amy was sorry she had done it, feeling that virtue was not always its own reward. But it is – as she presently discovered; for her spirits began to rise, and her table to blossom under her skilful hands; the girls were very kind, and that one little act seemed to have cleared the atmosphere amazingly.

It was a very long day, and a hard one to Amy, as she sat behind her table, often quite alone, for the little girls deserted very soon: few cared to buy flowers in summer, and her bouquets began to droop long before night.

The art table *was* the most attractive in the room; there was a crowd about it all day long, and the tenders were constantly flying to and fro with important faces and rattling money boxes. Amy often looked wistfully across, longing to be there, where she felt at home and happy, instead of in a corner with nothing to do. It might seem no hardship to some of us; but to a pretty, blithe young girl, it was not only tedious, but very trying; and the thought of being found there in the evening by her family, and Laurie and his friends, made it a real martyrdom.

She did not go home till night, and then she looked so pale and quiet that they knew the day had been a hard one, though she made no complaint, and did not even tell what she had done. Her mother gave her an extra cordial cup of tea, Beth helped her dress, and made a charming little wreath for her hair, while Jo astonished her family by getting herself up with unusual care, and hinting darkly that the tables were about to be turned.

'Don't do anything rude, pray, Jo. I won't have any fuss made, so let it all pass, and behave yourself,' begged Amy, as she departed early, hoping to find a reinforcement of flowers to refresh her poor little table.

'I merely intend to make myself entrancingly agreeable to everyone I know, and to keep them in your corner as long as possible. Teddy and his boys will lend a hand, and we'll have a good time yet,' returned Jo, leaning over the gate to watch for Laurie. Presently the familiar tramp was heard in the dusk, and she ran out to meet him.

'Is that my boy?'

'As sure as this is my girl!' and Laurie tucked her hand under his arm, with the air of a man whose every wish was gratified.

'O Teddy, such doings!' and Jo told Amy's wrongs with sisterly zeal.

'A flock of our fellows are going to drive over by and by, and I'll be hanged if I don't make them buy every flower she's got, and camp down before her table after-wards,' said Laurie, espousing her cause with warmth.

'The flowers are not at all nice, Amy says, and the fresh ones may not arrive in time. I don't wish to be unjust or suspicious, but I shouldn't wonder if they never came at all. When people do one mean thing they are very likely to do another,' observed Jo, in a disgusted tone.

'Didn't Hayes give you the best out of our gardens? I told him to.'

'I didn't know that; he forgot, I suppose; and, as your grandpa was poorly, I didn't like to worry him by asking, though I did want some.'

'Now, Jo, how could you think there was any need of asking! They are just as much yours as mine. Don't we always go halves in everything!' began Laurie, in the tone that always made Jo turn thorny.

'Gracious, I hope not! Half of some of your things wouldn't suit me at all. But we mustn't stand philandering here; I've got to help Amy, so you go and make yourself splendid; and if you'll be so very kind as to let Hayes take a few nice flowers up to the hall, I'll bless you for ever.'

'Couldn't you do it now?' asked Laurie, so suggestively that Jo shut the gate in his face with inhospitable haste, and called through the bars, 'Go away, Teddy, I'm busy.'

Thanks to the conspirators, the tables *were* turned that night; for Hayes sent up a wilderness of flowers, with a lovely basket, arranged in his best manner, for a centre-piece; then the March family turned out *en masse*, and Jo exerted herself to some purpose, for people not only came, but stayed, laughing at her nonsense, admiring Amy's taste, and apparently enjoying themselves very much. Laurie and his friends gallantly threw themselves into the breach, bought up the bouquets, encamped before the table, and made that corner the liveliest spot in the room. Amy was in her element now, and, out of gratitude, if nothing more, was as sprightly and gracious as possible – coming to the conclusion, about that time, that virtue *was* its own reward after all.

Jo behaved herself with exemplary propriety; and when Amy was happily surrounded by her guard of honour, Jo circulated about the hall, picking up various bits of gossip, which enlightened her upon the subject of the Chester change of base. She reproached herself for her share of the ill feeling, and resolved to exonerate Amy as soon as possible; she also discovered what Amy had done about the things in the morning, and considered her a model of magnanimity. As she passed the art table, she glanced over it for her sister's things, but saw no signs of them. 'Tucked away out of sight, I dare say,' thought Jo, who could forgive her own wrongs, but hotly resented any insult offered to her family.

'Good evening, Miss Jo. How does Amy get on?' asked May, with a conciliatory air, for she wanted to show that she also could be generous.

'She has sold everything she had that was worth selling, and now she is enjoying herself. The flower table is always attractive, you know, "especially to gentlemen".'

Jo *couldn't* resist giving that little slap, but May took it so meekly she regretted it a minute after, and fell to praising the great vases, which still remained unsold.

'Is Amy's illumination anywhere about? I took a fancy to buy that for Father,' said Jo, very anxious to learn the fate of her sister's work.

'Everything of Amy's sold long ago; I took care that the right people saw them, and they made a nice little sum of money for us,' returned May, who had overcome sundry small temptations, as well as Amy, that day.

Much gratified, Jo rushed back to tell the good news; and Amy looked both touched and surprised by the report of May's words and manner.

'Now, gentlemen, I want you to go and do your duty by the other tables as generously as you have by mine – especially the art table,' she said, ordering out 'Teddy's Own', as the girls called the college friends.

'"Charge, Chester, charge!" is the motto for that table; but do your duty like men, and you'll get your money's worth of *art* in every sense of the word,' said the irrepressible Jo, as the devoted phalanx prepared to take the field.

'To hear is to obey, but March is fairer far than May,' said little Parker, making a frantic effort to be both witty and tender, and getting promptly quenched by Laurie, who said, 'Very well, my son, for a small boy!' and walked him off, with a paternal pat on the head.

'Buy the vases,' whispered Amy to Laurie, as a final heaping of coals of fire on her enemy's head.

To May's great delight, Mr Laurence not only bought the vases, but pervaded the hall with one under each arm. The other gentlemen speculated with equal rashness in all sorts of frail trifles, and wandered helplessly about afterwards, burdened with wax flowers, painted fans, filigree portfolios, and other useful and appropriate purchases.

Aunt Carrol was there, heard the story, looked pleased, and said something to Mrs March in a corner, which made the latter lady beam with satisfaction, and watch Amy with a face full of mingled pride and anxiety, though she did not betray the cause of her pleasure till several days later.

The fair was pronounced a success; and when May bade Amy goodnight, she did not 'gush' as usual, but gave her an affectionate kiss, and a look which said, 'Forgive and forget'. That satisfied Amy; and when she got home she found the vases paraded on the parlour chimney piece, with a great bouquet in each. 'The reward of merit for a magnanimous March,' as Laurie announced with a flourish.

'You've a deal more principle and generosity and nobleness of character than I ever gave you credit for, Amy. You've behaved sweetly, and I respect you with all my heart,' said Jo warmly, as they brushed their hair together late that night.

'Yes, we all do, and love her for being so ready to forgive. It must have been dreadfully hard, after working so long, and setting your heart on selling your own pretty things. I don't believe I could have done it as kindly as you did,' added Beth from her pillow.

'Why, girls, you needn't praise me so; I only did as I'd be done by. You laugh at me when I say I want to be a lady, but I mean a true gentlewoman in mind and manners, and I try to do it as far as I know how. I can't explain exactly, but I want to be above the little meannesses and follies and faults that spoil so many women. I'm far from it now, but I do my best, and hope in time to be what Mother is.'

Amy spoke earnestly, and Jo said, with a cordial hug:

'I understand now what you mean, and I'll never laugh at you again. You are getting on faster than you think, and I'll take lessons of you in true politeness, for you've learned the secret, I believe. Try away, deary; you'll get your reward some day, and no one will be more delighted than I shall.'

A week later Amy did get her reward, and poor Jo found it hard to be delighted. A letter came from Aunt Carrol, and Mrs March's face was illuminated to such a degree, when she read it, that Jo and Beth, who were with her, demanded what the glad tidings were.

'Aunt Carrol is going abroad next month, and wants –'

'Me to go with her!' burst in Jo, flying out of her chair in an uncontrollable rapture.

'No, dear, not you; it's Amy.'

'O Mother! she's too young; it's my turn first. I've wanted it so long – it would do me so much good, and be so altogether splendid – I *must* go.'

'I'm afraid it's impossible, Jo. Aunt says Amy, decidedly, and it is not for us to dictate when she offers such a favour.'

'It's always so. Amy has all the fun and I have all the work. It isn't fair, oh, it isn't fair!' cried Jo passionately.

'I'm afraid it is partly your own fault, dear. When Aunt spoke to me the other day, she regretted your blunt manners and too independent spirit; and here she writes, as if quoting something you had said – "I planned at first to ask Jo; but as 'favours burden her', and she 'hates French', I think I won't venture to invite her. Amy is more docile, and will make a good companion for Flo, and receive gratefully any help the trip may give her.'"

'Oh, my tongue, my abominable tongue! why can't I learn to keep it quiet?' groaned Jo, remembering words which had been her undoing. When she had heard the explanation of the quoted phrases, Mrs March said sorrowfully:

'I wish you could have gone, but there is no hope of it this time; so try to bear it cheerfully, and don't sadden Amy's pleasure by reproaches or regrets.'

'I'll try,' said Jo, winking hard, as she knelt down to pick up the basket she had joyfully upset. 'I'll take a leaf out of her book, and try not only to seem glad, but to be so, and not grudge her one minute of happiness; but it won't be easy, for it is a dreadful disappointment'; and poor Jo bedewed the little fat pincushion she held with several very bitter tears.

'Jo, dear, I'm very selfish, but I couldn't spare you, and I'm glad you are not going quite yet,' whispered Beth, embracing her, basket and all, with such a clinging touch and loving face, that Jo felt comforted in spite of the sharp regret that made her want to box her own ears, and humbly beg Aunt Carrol to burden her with this favour, and see how gratefully she would bear it.

By the time Amy came in, Jo was able to take her part in the family jubilation; not quite as heartily as usual, perhaps, but without repinings at Amy's good fortune. The young lady herself received the news as tidings of great joy, went about in a solemn sort of rapture, and began to sort her colours and pack her pencils that evening, leaving such trifles as clothes, money, and passports to those less absorbed in visions of art than herself.

'It isn't a mere pleasure trip to me, girls,' she said impressively, as she scraped her best palette. 'It will decide my career; for if I have any genius, I shall find it out in Rome, and will do something to prove it.'

'Suppose you haven't?' said Jo, sewing away, with red eyes, at the new collars which were to be handed over to Amy.

'Then I shall come home and teach drawing for my living,' replied the aspirant for fame, with philosophic composure; but she made a wry face at the prospect, and scratched away at her palette as if bent on vigorous measures before she gave up her hopes.

'No, you won't; you hate hard work, and you'll marry some rich man, and come home to sit in the lap of luxury all your days,' said Jo.

'Your predictions sometimes come to pass, but I don't believe that one will. I'm sure I wish it would, for if I can't be an artist myself, I should like to be able to help those who are,' said Amy, smiling, as if the part of Lady Bountiful would suit her better than that of a poor drawing teacher.

'Hum!' said Jo, with a sigh; 'if you wish it you'll have it, for your wishes are always granted – mine never.'

'Would you like to go?' asked Amy, thoughtfully patting her nose with her knife.

'Rather!'

'Well, in a year or two I'll send for you, and we'll dig in the Forum for relics, and carry out all the plans we've made so many times.'

'Thank you; I'll remind you of your promise when that joyful day comes, if it ever does,' returned Jo, accepting the vague but magnificent offer as gratefully as she could.

There was not much time for preparation, and the house was in a ferment till Amy was off. Jo bore up very well till the last flutter of blue ribbon vanished, when she retired to her refuge, the garret, and cried till she couldn't cry any more. Amy likewise bore up stoutly till the steamer sailed; then, just as the gangway was about to be withdrawn, it suddenly came over her that a whole ocean was soon to roll between her and those who loved her best, and she clung to Laurie, the last lingerer, saying with a sob:

'Oh, take care of them for me; and if anything should happen –'

'I will, dear, I will; and if anything happens, I'll come and comfort you,' whispered Laurie, little dreaming that he would be called upon to keep his word.

So Amy sailed away to find the old world, which is always new and beautiful to young eyes, while her father and friend watched her from the shore, fervently hoping that none but gentle fortunes would befall the happy-hearted girl, who waved her hand to them till they could see nothing but the summer sunshine dazzling on the sea.

8

Our Foreign Correspondent

London

Dearest People, – Here I really sit at a front window of the Bath Hotel, Piccadilly. It's not a fashionable place, but Uncle stopped here years ago, and won't go anywhere else; however, we don't mean to stay long, so it's no great matter. Oh, I can't begin to tell you how I enjoy it all! I never can, so I'll only give you bits out of my notebook, for I've done nothing but sketch and scribble since I started.

I sent a line from Halifax, when I felt pretty miserable, but after that I got on delightfully, seldom ill, on deck all day, with plenty of pleasant people to amuse me. Everyone was very kind to me, especially the officers. Don't laugh, Jo; gentlemen really are very necessary aboard ship, to hold on to, or to wait upon one; and as they have nothing to do, it's a mercy to make them useful, otherwise they would smoke themselves to death, I'm afraid.

Aunt and Flo were poorly all the way, and liked to be let alone, so when I had done what I could for them, I went and enjoyed myself. Such walks on deck, such sunsets, such splendid air and waves! It was almost as exciting as riding a fast horse, when we went rushing on so grandly. I wish Beth could have come, it would have done her so much good; as for Jo, she would have gone up and sat on the main-top jib, or whatever the high thing is called, made friends with the engineers, and tooted on the captain's speaking-trumpet, she'd have been in such a state of rapture.

It was all heavenly, but I was glad to see the Irish coast, and found it very lovely, so green and sunny, with brown cabins here and there, ruins on some of the hills, and gentlemen's country seats in the valleys, with deer feeding in the parks. It was early in the morning, but I didn't regret getting up to see it, for the bay was full of little boats, the shore *so* picturesque, and a rosy sky overhead. I never shall forget it.

At Queenstown one of my new acquaintances left us – Mr Lennox – and when I said something about the Lakes of Killarney, he sighed and sung, with a look at me:

> '*Oh, have you e'er heard of Kate Kearney?*
> *She lives on the banks of Killarney;*
> *From the glance of yer eye,*

> Shun danger and fly,
> For fatal's the glance of Kate Kearney.'

Wasn't that nonsensical?

We only stopped at Liverpool a few hours. It's a dirty, noisy place, and I was glad to leave it. Uncle rushed out and bought a pair of dog-skin gloves, some ugly, thick shoes, and an umbrella, and got shaved *à la* mutton-chop, the first thing. Then he flattered himself that he looked like a true Briton; but the first time he had the mud cleaned off his shoes, the little bootblack knew that an American stood in them, and said, with a grin, 'There yer har, sir. I've give 'em the latest Yankee shine.' It amused Uncle immensely. Oh, I *must* tell you what that absurd Lennox did! He got his friend Ward, who came on with us, to order a bouquet for me, and the first thing I saw in my room was a lovely one, with 'Robert Lennox's compliments', on the card. Wasn't that fun, girls? I like travelling.

I never *shall* get to London if I don't hurry. The trip was like riding through a long picture-gallery, full of lovely landscapes. The farmhouses were my delight; with thatched roofs, ivy up to the eaves, latticed windows, and stout women with rosy children at the doors. The very cattle looked more tranquil than ours, as they stood knee-deep in clover, and the hens had a contented cluck, as if they never got nervous, like Yankee biddies. Such perfect colour I never saw – the grass so green, sky so blue, grain so yellow, woods so dark – I was in a rapture all the way. So was Flo; and we kept bounding from one side to the other, trying to see everything while we were whisking along at the rate of sixty miles an hour. Aunt was tired and went to sleep, but Uncle read his guide-book, and wouldn't be astonished at anything. This is the way he went on: Amy, flying up – 'Oh, that must be Kenilworth, that grey place among the trees!' Flo, darting to my window – 'How sweet! We must go there some time, won't we, Papa?' Uncle, calmly admiring his boots – 'No, my dear, not unless you want beer – that's a brewery.'

A pause – then Flo cried out, 'Bless me, there's a gallows and a man going up.' 'Where, where?' shrieks Amy, staring out at two tall posts with a cross-beam and some dangling chains. 'A colliery,' remarks Uncle, with a twinkle of the eye. 'Here's a lovely flock of lambs all lying down,' says Amy. 'See, Papa, aren't they pretty!' added Flo sentimentally. 'Geese, young ladies,' returns Uncle, in a tone that keeps us quiet till Flo settles down to enjoy *The Flirtations of Capt. Cavendish*, and I have the scenery all to myself.

Of course it rained when we got to London, and there was nothing to be seen but fog and umbrellas. We rested, unpacked, and shopped a little between the showers. Aunt Mary got me some new things, for I came off in such a hurry I wasn't half ready. A white hat and blue feather, a muslin dress to match, and the loveliest mantle you ever saw. Shopping in Regent Street is perfectly splendid; things seem so cheap – nice ribbons only sixpence a yard. I laid in a stock, but shall get my gloves in Paris. Doesn't that sound sort of elegant and rich?

Flo and I, for the fun of it, ordered a hansom cab, while Aunt and Uncle were out, and went for a drive, though we learned afterwards that it wasn't the thing for young ladies to ride in them alone. It was so droll! for when we were shut in by the wooden apron, the man drove so fast that Flo was frightened, and told me to stop him. But he was up outside behind somewhere, and I couldn't get at him. He didn't hear me call, nor see me flap my parasol in front, and there we were, quite helpless, rattling away, and whirling around corners at a breakneck pace. At last, in my despair, I saw a little door in the roof, and on poking it open, a red eye appeared, and a beery voice said:

'Now then, mum?'

I gave my order as soberly as I could, and slamming down the door, with an 'Aye, aye, mum,' the man made his horse walk, as if going to a funeral. I poked again, and said, 'A little faster'; then off he went, helter-skelter, as before, and we resigned ourselves to our fate.

Today was fair, and we went to Hyde Park, close by, for we are more aristocratic than we look. The Duke of Devonshire lives near. I often see his footmen lounging at the back gate; and the Duke of Wellington's house is not far off. Such sights as I saw, my dear! It was as good as Punch, for there were fat dowagers rolling about in their red and yellow coaches, with gorgeous Jeameses in silk stockings and velvet coats, up behind, and powdered coachmen in front. Smart maids, with the rosiest children I ever saw; handsome girls, looking half asleep; dandies, in queer English hats and lavender kids, lounging about, and tall soldiers, in short red jackets and muffin caps stuck on one side, looking so funny I longed to sketch them.

Rotten Row means 'Route de Roi', or the king's way; but now it's more like a riding-school than anything else. The horses are splendid, and the men, especially the grooms, ride well; but the women are stiff, and bounce, which isn't according to our rules. I longed to show them a tearing American gallop, for they trotted solemnly up and down, in their scant habits and high hats, looking like the women in a toy Noah's Ark. Everyone rides – old men, stout ladies, little children – and the young folks do a deal of flirting here; I saw a pair exchange rosebuds, for it's the thing to wear one in the buttonhole, and I thought it rather a nice little idea.

In the P.M. to Westminster Abbey; but don't expect me to describe it, that's impossible – so I'll only say it was sublime! This evening we are going to see Fechter, which will be an appropriate end to the happiest day of my life.

Midnight

It's very late, but I can't let my letter go in the morning without telling you what happened last evening. Who do you think came in, as we were at tea? Laurie's English friends, Fred and Frank Vaughn! I was *so* surprised, for I shouldn't have known them but for the cards. Both are tall fellows, with whiskers; Fred handsome in the English style, and Frank much better, for he only limps slightly, and uses no crutches. They had heard from Laurie where we were to be, and came to ask us to their house; but Uncle won't go, so we shall return the call, and see them as we can. They went to the theatre with us, and we did have *such* a good time, for Frank devoted himself to Flo, and Fred and I talked over past, present, and future fun as if we had known each other all our days. Tell Beth Frank asked for her, and was sorry to hear of her ill health. Fred laughed when I spoke of Jo, and sent his 'respectful compliments to the big hat'. Neither of them had forgotten Camp Laurence, or the fun we had there. What ages ago it seems, doesn't it?

Aunt is tapping on the wall for the third time, so I *must* stop. I really feel like a dissipated London fine lady, writing here so late, with my room full of pretty things, and my head a jumble of parks, theatres, new gowns, and gallant creatures who say 'Ah!' and twirl their blond moustaches with the true English lordliness. I long to see you all, and in spite of my nonsense am, as ever, your loving

Amy

Paris

Dear Girls, – In my last I told you about our London visit – how kind the Vaughns were, and what pleasant parties they made for us. I enjoyed the trips to Hampton Court and the Kensington Museums more than anything else – for at Hampton I saw Raphael's cartoons, and, at the Museum, rooms full of pictures by Turner, Lawrence, Reynolds, Hogarth, and the other great creatures. The day in Richmond Park was charming, for we had a regular English picnic, and I had more splendid oaks and groups of deer than I could copy; also heard a nightingale, and saw larks go up. We 'did' London to our hearts' content, thanks to

Fred and Frank, and were sorry to go away; for, though English people are slow to take you in, when they once make up their minds to do it they cannot be outdone in hospitality, *I* think. The Vaughns hope to meet us in Rome next winter, and I shall be dreadfully disappointed if they don't, for Grace and I are great friends, and the boys very nice fellows – especially Fred.

Well, we were hardly settled here, when he turned up again, saying he had come for a holiday, and was going to Switzerland. Aunt looked sober at first, but he was so cool about it she couldn't say a word; and now we get on nicely, and are very glad he came, for he speaks French like a native, and I don't know what we should do without him. Uncle doesn't know ten words, and insists on talking English very loud, as if that would make people understand him. Aunt's pronunciation is old-fashioned, and Flo and I, though we flattered ourselves that we knew a good deal, find we don't, and are very grateful to have Fred do the 'parley vooing', as Uncle calls it.

Such delightful times as we are having! sightseeing from morning till night, stopping for nice lunches in the gay cafés, and meeting with all sorts of droll adventures. Rainy days I spend in the Louvre, revelling in pictures. Jo would turn up her haughty nose at some of the finest, because she has no soul for art; but *I* have, and I'm cultivating eye and taste as fast as I can. She would like the relics of great people better, for I've seen her Napoleon's cocked hat and grey coat, his baby's cradle and his old toothbrush; also Marie Antoinette's little shoe, the ring of Saint Denis, Charlemagne's sword, and many other interesting things. I'll talk for hours about them when I come, but haven't time to write.

The Palais Royale is a heavenly place – so full of *bijouterie* and lovely things that I'm nearly distracted because I can't buy them. Fred wanted to get me some, but of course I didn't allow it. Then the Bois and the Champs Elysees are *très magnifique*. I've seen the imperial family several times – the emperor an ugly, hard-looking man, the empress pale and pretty, but dressed in bad taste, *I* thought – purple dress, green hat, and yellow gloves. Little Nap. is a handsome boy, who sits chatting to his tutor, and kisses his hand to the people as he passes in his four-horse barouche, with postilions in red satin jackets, and a mounted guard before and behind.

We often walk in the Tuileries Gardens, for they are lovely, though the antique Luxembourg Gardens suit me better. Père la Chaise is very curious, for many of the tombs are like small rooms, and, looking in, one sees a table, with images or pictures of the dead, and chairs for the mourners to sit in when they come to lament. That is so Frenchy.

Our rooms are on the Rue de Rivoli, and, sitting in the balcony, we look up and down the long brilliant street. It is so pleasant that we spend our evenings talking there, when too tired with our day's work to go out. Fred is very entertaining, and is altogether the most agreeable young man I ever knew – except Laurie, whose manners are more charming. I wish Fred was dark, for I don't fancy light men; however, the Vaughns are very rich, and come of an excellent family, so I won't find fault with their yellow hair, as my own is yellower.

Next week we are off to Germany and Switzerland; and, as we shall travel fast, I shall only be able to give you hasty letters. I keep my diary, and try to 'remember correctly and describe clearly all that I see and admire', as Father advised. It is good practice for me, and, with my sketch-book, will give you a better idea of my tour than these scribbles.

Adieu; I embrace you tenderly.

Votre Amie

Heidelberg

My Dear Mamma, – Having a quiet hour before we leave for Berne, I'll try to tell you what has happened, for some of it is very important, as you will see.

The sail up the Rhine was perfect, and I just sat and enjoyed it with all my might. Get Father's old guide-books, and read about it; I haven't words beautiful enough to describe it. At Coblenz we had a lovely time, for some students from Bonn, with whom Fred got acquainted on the boat, gave us a serenade. It was a moonlight night, and, about one o'clock, Flo and I were waked by the most delicious music under our windows. We flew up, and hid behind the curtains; but sly peeps showed us Fred and the students singing away down below. It was the most romantic thing I ever saw – the river, the bridge of boats, the great fortress opposite, moonlight everywhere, and music fit to melt a heart of stone.

When they were done we threw down some flowers, and saw them scramble for them, kiss their hands to the invisible ladies, and go laughing away – to smoke and drink beer, I suppose. Next morning Fred showed me one of the crumpled flowers in his vest-pocket, and looked very sentimental. I laughed at him, and said I didn't throw it, but Flo, which seemed to disgust him, for he tossed it out of the window, and turned sensible again. I'm afraid I'm going to have trouble with that boy, it begins to look like it.

The baths at Nassau were very gay, so was Baden-Baden, where Fred lost some money, and I scolded him. He needs someone to look after him when Frank is not with him. Kate said once she hoped he'd marry soon, and I quite agree with her that would be well for him. Frankfurt was delightful; I saw Goethe's house, Schiller's statue, and Dannecker's famous 'Ariadne'. It was very lovely, but I should have enjoyed it more if I had known the story better. I didn't like to ask, as everyone knew it, or pretended they did. I wish Jo would tell me all about it; I ought to have read more, for I find I don't know anything, and it mortifies me.

Now comes the serious part – for it happened here, and Fred is just gone. He has been so kind and jolly that we all got quite fond of him; I never thought of anything but a travelling friendship, till the serenade night. Since then I've begun to feel that the moonlight walks, balcony talks, and daily adventures were something more to him than fun. I haven't flirted, Mother, truly, but remembered what you said to me, and have done my very best. I can't help it if people like me; I don't try to make them, and it worries me if I don't care for them, though Jo says I haven't got any heart. Now I know Mother will shake her head, and the girls say, 'Oh, the mercenary little wretch!' but I've made up my mind, and, if Fred asks me, I shall accept him, though I'm not madly in love. I like him, and we get on comfortably together. He is handsome, young, clever enough, and very rich – ever so much richer than the Laurences.

I don't think his family would object, and I should be very happy, for they are all kind, well bred, generous people, and they like me. Fred, as the eldest twin, will have the estate, I suppose, and such a splendid one as it is! A city house in a fashionable street, not so showy as our big houses, but twice as comfortable, and full of solid luxury, such as English people believe in. I like it, for it's genuine. I've seen the plate, the family jewels, the old servants, and pictures of the country place, with its park, great house, lovely grounds, and fine horses. Oh, it would be all I should ask! and I'd rather have it than any title such as girls snap up so readily, and find nothing behind. I may be mercenary, but I hate poverty, and don't mean to bear it a minute longer than I can help. One of us *must* marry well; Meg didn't, Jo won't, Beth can't yet, so I shall, and make everything cosy all round. I wouldn't marry a man I hated or despised. You may be sure of that; and, though Fred is not my model hero, he does very well, and, in time, I should get fond enough of him if he was very fond of me, and let me do just as I liked. So I've been turning the matter over in my mind the last week, for it was impossible to help seeing that Fred liked me. He said nothing, but little things showed it; he never goes with Flo, always gets on my side of the carriage, table, or promenade, looks sentimental when we are alone, and frowns at anyone else who ventures to speak to me. Yesterday, at dinner, when an Austrian officer stared at us, and then said something to his friend – a rakish-looking baron – about 'ein wonderschönes Blöndchen', Fred looked as fierce as a lion, and cut his meat so savagely, it nearly flew off his plate. He isn't one of the cool, stiff Englishmen, but is rather peppery, for he has Scotch blood in him, as one might guess from his bonnie blue eyes.

Well, last evening we went up to the castle about sunset – at least all of us but Fred, who was to meet us there, after going to the poste restante for letters. We had a charming time poking about the ruins, the vaults where the monster tun is, and the beautiful gardens made by the elector, long ago, for his English wife. I liked the great terrace best, for the view was divine; so, while the rest went to see the rooms inside, I sat there trying to sketch the grey stone lion's head on the wall, with scarlet woodbine sprays hanging round it. I felt as if I'd got into a romance, sitting there, watching the Neckar rolling through the valley, listening to the music of the Austrian band below, and waiting for my lover, like a real storybook girl. I had a feeling that something was going to happen, and I was ready for it. I didn't feel blushy or quakey, but quite cool, and only a little excited.

By and by I heard Fred's voice, and then he came

hurrying through the great arch to find me. He looked so troubled that I forgot all about myself, and asked what the matter was. He said he'd just got a letter begging him to come home, for Frank was very ill; so he was going at once, in the night train, and only had time to say goodbye. I was very sorry for him, and disappointed for myself, but only for a minute, because he said, as he shook hands – and said it in a way that I could not mistake – 'I shall soon come back; you won't forget me, Amy?'

I didn't promise, but I looked at him, and he seemed satisfied, and there was no time for anything but messages and goodbyes, for he was off in an hour, and we all miss him very much. I know he wanted to speak, but I think, from something he once hinted, that he had promised his father not to do anything of the sort yet awhile, for he is a rash boy, and the old gentleman dreads a foreign daughter-in-law. We shall soon meet in Rome; and then, if I don't change my mind, I'll say 'Yes, thank you,' when he says 'Will you, please?'

Of course this is all *very private*, but I wished you to know what was going on. Don't be anxious about me; remember I am your 'prudent Amy', and be sure I will do nothing rashly. Send me as much advice as you like; I'll use it if I can. I wish I could see you for a good talk, Marmee. Love and trust me. – Ever your

Amy

9

Tender Troubles

'Jo, I'm anxious about Beth.'

'Why, Mother, she has seemed unusually well since the babies came.'

'It's not her health that troubles me now; it's her spirits. I'm sure there is something on her mind, and I want you to discover what it is.'

'What makes you think so, Mother?'

'She sits alone a good deal, and doesn't talk to her father as much as she used. I found her crying over the babies the other day. When she sings, the songs are always sad ones, and now and then I see a look in her face that I don't understand. This isn't like Beth, and it worries me.'

'Have you asked her about it?'

'I have tried once or twice; but she either evaded my questions, or looked so distressed that I stopped. I never force my children's confidence, and I seldom have to wait for it long.'

Mrs March glanced at Jo as she spoke, but the face

opposite seemed quite unconscious of any secret disquietude but Beth's; and, after sewing thoughtfully for a minute, Jo said:

'I think she is growing up, and so begins to dream dreams, and have hopes and fears and fidgets, without knowing why, or being able to explain them. Why, Mother, Beth's eighteen, but we don't realize it, and treat her like a child, forgetting she's a woman.'

'So she is. Dear heart, how fast you do grow up,' returned her mother, with a sigh and a smile.

'Can't be helped, Marmee, so you must resign yourself to all sorts of worries, and let your birds hop out of the nest, one by one. I promise never to hop very far, if that is any comfort to you.'

'It is a great comfort, Jo; I always feel strong when you are at home, now Meg is gone. Beth is too feeble and Amy too young to depend upon; but when the tug comes, you are always ready.'

'Why, you know I don't mind hard jobs much, and there must always be one scrub in a family. Amy is splendid in fine works, and I'm not; but I feel in my element when all the carpets are to be taken up, or half the family fall sick at once. Amy is distinguishing herself abroad; but if anything is amiss at home, I'm your man.'

'I leave Beth to your hands, then, for she will open her tender little heart to her Jo sooner than to anyone else. Be very kind, and don't let her think anyone watches or talks about her. If she only would get quite strong and cheerful again, I shouldn't have a wish in the world.'

'Happy woman! I've got heaps.'

'My dear, what are they?'

'I'll settle Bethy's troubles, and then I'll tell you mine. They are not very wearing, so they'll keep'; and Jo stitched away, with a wise nod which set her mother's heart at rest about her, for the present at least.

While apparently absorbed in her own affairs, Jo watched Beth; and, after many conflicting conjectures, finally settled upon one which seemed to explain the change in her. A slight incident gave Jo the clue to the mystery, she thought, and lively fancy, loving heart did the rest. She was affecting to write busily one Saturday afternoon, when she and Beth were alone together; yet as she scribbled, she kept her eye on her sister, who seemed unusually quiet. Sitting at the window, Beth's work often dropped into her lap, and she leaned her head upon her hand, in a dejected attitude, while her eyes rested on the dull, autumnal landscape. Suddenly someone passed below, whistling like an operatic blackbird, and a voice called out:

'All serene! Coming in tonight.'

Beth started, leaned forward, smiled and nodded, watched the passer-by till his quick tramp died away, then said softly, as if to herself:

'How strong and well and happy that dear boy looks.'

'Hum!' said Jo, still intent upon her sister's face; for the bright colour faded as quickly as it came, the smile vanished, and presently a tear lay shining on the window ledge. Beth whisked it off, and glanced apprehensively at Jo; but she was scratching away at a tremendous rate, apparently engrossed in 'Olympia's Oath'. The instant Beth turned, Jo began her watch again, saw Beth's hand go quietly to her eyes more than once, and, in her half-averted face, read a tender sorrow that made her own eyes fill. Fearing to betray herself, she slipped away, murmuring something about needing more paper.

'Mercy on me, Beth loves Laurie!' she said, sitting down in her own room, pale with the shock of the discovery which she believed she had just made. 'I never dreamt of such a thing. What *will* Mother say? I wonder if he –' There Jo stopped, and turned scarlet with a sudden thought. 'If he shouldn't love back again, how dreadful it would be. He must; I'll make him!' and she shook her head threateningly at the picture of the mischievous-looking boy laughing at her from the wall. 'Oh dear, we *are* growing up with a vengeance. Here's Meg married and a mamma, Amy flourishing away at Paris, and Beth in love. I'm the only one that has sense enough to keep out of mischief.' Jo thought intently for a minute, with her eyes fixed on the picture; then she smoothed out her wrinkled forehead, and said, with a decided nod at the face opposite, 'No, thank you, sir; you're very charming, but you've no more stability than a weathercock; so you needn't write touching notes, and smile in that insinuating way, for it won't do a bit of good, and I won't have it.'

Then she sighed, and fell into a reverie, from which she did not wake till the early twilight sent her down to take new observations, which only confirmed her suspicion. Though Laurie flirted with Amy and joked with Jo, his manner to Beth had always been peculiarly kind and gentle, but so was everybody's; therefore, no one thought of imagining that he cared more for her than for the others. Indeed, a general impression had prevailed in the family, of late, that 'our boy' was getting fonder than ever of Jo, who, however, wouldn't hear a word upon the subject, and scolded violently if anyone dared to suggest it. If they had known the various tender passages of the past year, or rather attempts at tender passages which had been nipped in the bud, they would have had the immense satisfaction of saying, 'I told you so'. But Jo hated 'philandering', and wouldn't allow it, always having a joke or a smile ready at the least sign of impending danger.

When Laurie first went to college, he fell in love about once a month; but these small flames were as brief as ardent, did no damage, and much amused Jo, who took great interest in the alternations of hope, despair, and resignation which were confided to her in their weekly conferences. But there came a time when Laurie ceased to worship at many shrines, hinted darkly at one all-absorbing passion, and indulged occasionally in Byronic fits of gloom. Then he avoided the tender subject altogether, wrote philosophical notes to Jo, turned studious, and gave out that he was going to 'dig', intending to graduate in a blaze of glory. This suited the young lady better than twilight confidences, tender pressures of the hand, and eloquent glances of the eye; for with Jo, brain developed earlier than heart, and she preferred imaginary heroes to real ones, because, when tired of them, the former could be shut up in the tin-kitchen till called for, and the latter were less manageable.

Things were in this state when the grand discovery was made, and Jo watched Laurie that night as she had never done before. If she had not got the new idea into her head, she would have seen nothing unusual in the fact that Beth was very quiet, and Laurie very kind to her. But having given the rein to her lively fancy, it galloped away with her at a great pace; and common sense, being rather weakened by a long course of romance writing, did not come to the rescue. As usual, Beth lay on the sofa, and Laurie sat in a low chair close by, amusing her with all sorts of gossip; for she depended on her weekly 'spin', and he never disappointed her. But that evening, Jo fancied that Beth's eyes rested on the lively, dark face beside her with peculiar pleasure, and that she listened with intense interest to an account of some exciting cricket match, though the phrases, 'caught off a tice', 'stumped off his ground', and 'the leg hit for three', were as intelligible to her as Sanscrit. She also fancied, having set her heart upon seeing it, that she saw a certain increase of gentleness in Laurie's manner, that he dropped his voice now and then, laughed less than usual, was a little absent-minded, and settled the afghan over Beth's feet with an assiduity that was really almost tender.

'Who knows? Stranger things have happened,' thought Jo, as she fussed about the room. 'She will make quite an angel of him, and he will make life delightfully easy and pleasant for the dear, if they only love each other. I don't see how he can help it; and I do believe he would if the rest of us were out of the way.'

As everyone *was* out of the way but herself, Jo began to feel that she ought to dispose of herself with all speed. But where should she go? and burning to lay herself upon the shrine of sisterly devotion, she sat down to settle that point.

Now, the old sofa was a regular patriarch of a sofa – long, broad, well cushioned, and low; a trifle shabby, as well it might be, for the girls had slept and sprawled on it as babies, fished over the back, rode on the arms, and had menageries under it as children, and rested tired heads, dreamed dreams, and listened to tender talk on it as young women. They all loved it, for it was a family refuge, and one corner had always been Jo's favourite lounging place. Among the many pillows that adorned the venerable couch was one, hard, round, covered with prickly horse-hair, and furnished with a knobby button at each end; this repulsive pillow was her especial property, being used as a weapon of defence, a barricade, or a stern preventive of too much slumber.

Laurie knew this pillow well, and had cause to regard it with deep aversion, having been unmercifully pummelled with it in former days, when romping was allowed, and now frequently debarred by it from taking the seat he most coveted, next to Jo in the sofa corner. If 'the sausage', as they called it, stood on end, it was a sign that he might approach and repose; but if it lay flat across the sofa, woe to the man, woman, or child who dared disturb it! That evening Jo forgot to barricade her corner, and had not been in her seat five minutes, before a massive form appeared beside her, and with both arms spread over the sofa-back, both long legs stretched out before him, Laurie exclaimed, with a sigh of satisfaction:

'Now, *this* is filling at the price.'

'No slang,' snapped Jo, slamming down the pillow. But it was too late, there was no room for it; and, coasting on to the floor, it disappeared in a most mysterious manner.

'Come, Jo, don't be thorny. After studying himself to a skeleton all the week, a fellow deserves petting, and ought to get it.'

'Beth will pet you; I'm busy.'

'No, she's not to be bothered with me; but you like that

sort of thing, unless you've suddenly lost your taste for it. Have you? Do you hate your boy, and want to fire pillows at him?'

Anything more wheedlesome than that touching appeal was seldom heard, but Jo quenched 'her boy' by turning on him with the stern query:

'How many bouquets have you sent Miss Randal this week?'

'Not one, upon my word. She's engaged. Now then.'

'I'm glad of it; that's one of your foolish extravagances – sending flowers and things to girls for whom you don't care two pins,' continued Jo reprovingly.

'Sensible girls, for whom I do care whole papers of pins, won't let me send them "flowers and things", so what can I do? My feelings must have a *went*.'

'Mother doesn't approve of flirting, even in fun; and you do flirt desperately, Teddy.'

'I'd give anything if I could answer, "So do you." As I can't, I'll merely say that I don't see any harm in that pleasant little game, if all parties understand that it's only play.'

'Well, it does look pleasant, but I can't learn how it's done. I've tried, because one feels awkward in company, not to do as everybody else is doing; but I don't seem to get on,' said Jo, forgetting to play Mentor.

'Take lessons of Amy; she has a regular talent for it.'

'Yes, she does it very prettily, and never seems to go

too far. I suppose it's natural to some people to please without trying, and others to always say and do the wrong thing in the wrong place.'

'I'm glad you can't flirt; it's really refreshing to see a sensible, straightforward girl, who can be jolly and kind without making a fool of herself. Between ourselves, Jo, some of the girls I know really do go on at such a rate I'm ashamed of them. They don't mean any harm, I'm sure; but if they knew how we fellows talked about them afterwards, they'd mend their ways, I fancy.'

'They do the same; and, as their tongues are the sharpest, you fellows get the worst of it, for you are as silly as they, every bit. If you behaved properly, they would; but knowing you like their nonsense, they keep it up, and then you blame them.'

'Much you know about it, ma'am,' said Laurie, in a superior tone. 'We don't like romps and flirts, though we may act as if we did sometimes. The pretty, modest girls are never talked about, except respectfully, among gentlemen. Bless your innocent soul! If you could be in my place for a month you'd see things that would astonish you a trifle. Upon my word, when I see one of those harum-scarum girls, I always want to say with our friend Cock Robin:

> 'Out upon you, fie upon you,
> Bold-faced jig!'

It was impossible to help laughing at the funny conflict between Laurie's chivalrous reluctance to speak ill of womankind, and his very natural dislike of the unfeminine folly of which fashionable society showed him many samples. Jo knew that 'young Laurence' was regarded as a most eligible *parti* by worldly mammas, was much smiled upon by their daughters, and flattered enough by ladies of all ages to make a coxcomb of him; so she watched him rather jealously, fearing he would be spoilt, and rejoiced more than she confessed to find that he still believed in modest girls. Returning suddenly to her admonitory tone, she said, dropping her voice, 'If you *must* have a *went*, Teddy, go and devote yourself to one of the "pretty, modest girls" whom you do respect, and not waste your time with the silly ones.'

'You really advise it?' and Laurie looked at her with an odd mixture of anxiety and merriment in his face.

'Yes, I do; but you'd better wait till you are through college, on the whole, and be fitting yourself for the place meantime. You're not half good enough for – well, whoever the modest girl may be,' and Jo looked a little queer likewise, for a name had almost escaped her.

'That I'm not!' acquiesced Laurie, with an expression of humility quite new to him, as he dropped his eyes, and absently wound Jo's apron tassel round his finger.

'Mercy on us, this will never do,' thought Jo; adding aloud, 'Go and sing to me. I'm dying for some music, and always like yours.'

'I'd rather stay here, thank you.'

'Well, you can't; there isn't room. Go and make yourself useful, since you are too big to be ornamental. I thought you hated to be tied to a woman's apron string?' retorted Jo, quoting certain rebellious words of his own.

'Ah, that depends on who wears the apron!' and Laurie gave an audacious tweak at the tassel.

'Are you going?' demanded Jo, diving for the pillow.

He fled at once, and the minute it was well 'Up with the bonnets of bonnie Dundee,' she slipped away, to return no more till the young gentleman had departed in high dudgeon.

Jo lay long awake that night, and was just dropping off when the sound of a stifled sob made her fly to Beth's bedside, with the anxious enquiry, 'What is it, dear?'

'I thought you were asleep,' sobbed Beth.

'Is it the old pain, my precious?'

'No; it's a new one; but I can bear it,' and Beth tried to check the tears.

'Tell me all about it, and let me cure it as I often did the other.'

'You can't; there is no cure.' There Beth's voice gave way, and, clinging to her sister, she cried so despairingly that Jo was frightened.

'Where is it? Shall I call Mother?'

Beth did not answer the first question; but in the dark one hand went involuntarily to her heart, as if the pain were there; with the other she held Jo fast, whispering eagerly, 'No, no, don't call her, don't tell her. I shall be better soon. Lie down here and "poor" my head. I'll be quiet, and go to sleep; indeed I will.'

Jo obeyed; but as her hand went softly to and fro across Beth's hot forehead and wet eyelids, her heart was very full, and she longed to speak. But young as she was, Jo had learned that hearts, like flowers, cannot be rudely handled, but must open naturally; so, though she believed she knew the cause of Beth's new pain, she only said, in her tenderest tone, 'Does anything trouble you, deary?'

'Yes, Jo,' after a long pause.

'Wouldn't it comfort you to tell me what it is?'

'Not now, not yet.'

'Then I won't ask; but remember, Bethy, that Mother and Jo are always glad to hear and help you, if they can.'

'I know it. I'll tell you by and by.'

'Is the pain better now?'

'Oh yes, much better; you are so comfortable, Jo!'

'Go to sleep, dear; I'll stay with you.'

So cheek to cheek they fell asleep, and on the morrow Beth seemed quite herself again; for at eighteen, neither heads nor hearts ache long, and a loving word can medicine most ills.

But Jo had made up her mind, and, after pondering over a project for some days, she confided it to her mother.

'You asked me the other day what my wishes were. I'll

tell you one of them, Marmee,' she began, as they sat alone together. 'I want to go away somewhere this winter for a change.'

'Why, Jo?' and her mother looked up quickly, as if the words suggested a double meaning.

With her eyes on her work, Jo answered soberly, 'I want something new; I feel restless, and anxious to be seeing, doing, and learning more than I am. I brood too much over my own small affairs, and need stirring up, so, as I can be spared this winter, I'd like to hop a little way, and try my wings.'

'Where will you hop?'

'To New York. I had a bright idea yesterday, and this is it. You know Mrs Kirke wrote to you for some respectable young person to teach her children and sew. It's rather hard to find just the thing, but I think I should suit if I tried.'

'My dear, go out to service in that great boarding-house!' and Mrs March looked surprised, but not displeased.

'It's not exactly going out to service; for Mrs Kirke is your friend – the kindest soul that ever lived – and would make things pleasant for me, I know. Her family is separate from the rest, and no one knows me there. Don't care if they do; it's honest work, and I'm not ashamed of it.'

'Nor I; but your writing?'

'All the better for the change. I shall see and hear new

things, get new ideas, and, even if I haven't much time there, I shall bring home quantities of material for my rubbish.'

'I have no doubt of it; but are these your only reasons for this sudden fancy?'

'No, Mother.'

'May I know the others?'

Jo looked up and Jo looked down, then said slowly, with sudden colour in her cheeks, 'It may be vain and wrong to say it, but – I'm afraid – Laurie is getting too fond of me.'

'Then you don't care for him in the way it is evident he begins to care for you?' and Mrs March looked anxious as she put the question.

'Mercy, no! I love the dear boy, as I always have, and am immensely proud of him; but as for anything more, it's out of the question.'

'I'm glad of that, Jo.'

'Why, please?'

'Because, dear, I don't think you are suited to one another. As friends you are very happy, and your frequent quarrels soon blow over but I fear you would both rebel if you were mated for life. You are too much alike and too fond of freedom, not to mention hot tempers and strong wills, to get on happily together, in a relation which needs infinite patience and forbearance, as well as love.'

'That's just the feeling I had, though I couldn't express

it. I'm glad you think he is only beginning to care for me. It would trouble me sadly to make him unhappy; for I couldn't fall in love with the dear old fellow merely out of gratitude, could I?'

'You are sure of his feeling for you?'

The colour deepened in Jo's cheeks, as she answered, with the look of mingled pleasure, pride, and pain which young girls wear when speaking of first lovers:

'I'm afraid it is so, Mother; he hasn't said anything, but he looks a great deal. I think I had better go away before it comes to anything.'

'I agree with you, and if it can be managed you shall go.'

Jo looked relieved, and, after a pause, said, smiling, 'How Mrs Moffat would wonder at your want of management, if she knew, and how she will rejoice that Annie still may hope.'

'Ah, Jo, mothers may differ in their management, but the hope is the same in all – the desire to see their children happy. Meg is so, and I am content with her success. You I leave to enjoy your liberty till you tire of it; for only then will you find that there is something sweeter. Amy is my chief care now, but her good sense will help her. For Beth, I indulge no hopes except that she may be well. By the way, she seems brighter this last day or two. Have you spoken to her?'

'Yes; she owned she had a trouble, and promised to tell

me by and by. I said no more, for I think I know it,' and Jo told her little story.

Mrs March shook her head, and did not take so romantic a view of the case, but looked grave, and repeated her opinion that, for Laurie's sake, Jo should go away for a time.

'Let us say nothing about it to him till the plan is settled; then I'll run away before he can collect his wits and be tragical. Beth must think I'm going to please myself, as I am, for I can't talk about Laurie to her; but she can pet and comfort him after I'm gone, and so cure him of this romantic notion. He's been through so many little trials of the sort, he's used to it, and will soon get over his love-lornity.'

Jo spoke hopefully, but could not rid herself of the foreboding fear that this 'little trial' would be harder than the others, and that Laurie would not get over his 'love-lornity' as easily as heretofore.

The plan was talked over in a family council, and agreed upon; for Mrs Kirke gladly accepted Jo, and promised to make a pleasant home for her. The teaching would render her independent; and such leisure as she got might be made profitable by writing, while the new scenes and society would be both useful and agreeable. Jo liked the prospect and was eager to be gone, for the home-nest was growing too narrow for her restless nature and adventurous spirit. When all was settled, with fear and trembling she told Laurie; but to her surprise he took it very quietly. He had been graver than usual of late, but very pleasant; and, when jokingly accused of turning over a new leaf, he answered soberly, 'So I am; and I mean this one shall stay turned.'

Jo was very much relieved that one of his virtuous fits should come on just then, and made her preparations with a lightened heart – for Beth seemed more cheerful – and hoped she was doing the best for all.

'One thing I leave to your especial care,' she said, the night before she left.

'You mean your papers?' asked Beth.

'No, my boy. Be very good to him, won't you?'

'Of course I will; but I can't fill your place, and he'll miss you sadly.'

'It won't hurt him; so remember, I leave him in your charge, to plague, pet, and keep in order.'

'I'll do my best for your sake,' promised Beth, wondering why Jo looked at her so queerly.

When Laurie said 'Goodbye,' he whispered significantly, 'It won't do a bit of good, Jo. My eye is on you; so mind what you do, or I'll come and bring you home.'

10

Jo's Journal

New York, November

Dear Marmee and Beth, – I'm going to write you a regular volume, for I've heaps to tell, though I'm not a fine young lady travelling on the continent. When I lost sight of Father's dear old face, I felt a trifle blue, and might have shed a briny drop or two, if an Irish lady with four small children, all crying more or less, hadn't diverted my mind; for I amused myself by dropping gingerbread nuts over the seat every time they opened their mouths to roar.

Soon the sun came out, and taking it as a good omen, I cleared up likewise, and enjoyed my journey with all my heart.

Mrs Kirke welcomed me so kindly I felt at home at once, even in that big house full of strangers. She gave me a funny little sky-parlour – all she had; but there is a stove in it, and a nice table in a sunny window, so I can sit here and write whenever I like.

A fine view and a church tower opposite atone for the many stairs, and I took a fancy to my den on the spot. The nursery, where I am to teach and sew, is a pleasant room next Mrs Kirke's private parlour, and the two little girls are pretty children – rather spoilt, I fancy, but they took to me after telling them *The Seven Bad Pigs*; and I've no doubt I shall make a model governess.

I am to have my meals with the children, if I prefer it to the great table, and for the present I do, for I *am* bashful, though no one will believe it.

'Now, my dear, make yourself at home,' said Mrs K. in her motherly way; 'I'm on the drive from morning to night, as you may suppose, with such a family; but a great anxiety will be off my mind if I know the children are safe with you. My rooms are always open to you, and your own shall be as comfortable as I can make it. There are some pleasant people in the house if you feel sociable, and your evenings are always free. Come to me if anything goes wrong, and be as happy as you can. There's the tea-bell; I must run and change my cap'; and off she bustled, leaving me to settle myself in my new nest.

As I went downstairs, soon after, I saw something I liked. The flights are very long in this tall house, and as I stood waiting at the head of the third one for a little servant-girl to lumber up, I saw a gentleman come along behind her, take the heavy hod of coal out of her hand, carry it all the way up, put it down at a door near by, and walk away, saying, with a kind nod and a foreign accent:

'It goes better so. The little back is too young to haf such heaviness.'

Wasn't it good of him? I like such things, for, as Father says, trifles show character. When I mentioned it to Mrs K., that evening, she laughed, and said:

'That must have been Professor Bhaer; he's always doing things of that sort.'

Mrs K. told me he was from Berlin; very learned and good, but poor as a church mouse, and gives lessons to support himself and two little orphan nephews whom he is educating here, according to the wishes of his sister, who married an American. Not a very romantic story, but it interested me; and I was glad to hear that Mrs K. lends him her parlour for some of his scholars. There is a glass door between it and the nursery, and I mean to peep at him, and then I'll tell you how he looks. He's almost forty, so it's no harm, Marmee.

After tea and a go-to-bed romp with the little girls, I attacked the big work-basket, and had a quiet evening chatting with my new friend. I shall keep a journal-letter, and send it once a week; so goodnight, and more tomorrow.

Had a lively time in my seminary this morning, for the children acted like Sancho; and at one time I really thought I should shake them all round. Some good angel inspired me to try gymnastics, and I kept it up till they were glad to sit down and keep still. After luncheon, the girl took them out for a walk, and I went to my needlework, like little Mabel, 'with a willing mind'. I was thanking my stars that I'd learned to make nice buttonholes, when the parlour door opened and shut, and someone began to hum:

'*Kennst du das land*'

like a big bumble-bee. It was dreadfully improper, I know, but I couldn't resist the temptation; and lifting one end of the curtain before the glass door, I peeped in. Professor Bhaer was there; and while he arranged his books, I took a good look at him. A regular German – rather stout, with brown hair tumbled all over his head, a bushy beard, good nose, the kindest eyes I ever saw, and a splendid big voice that does one's ears good, after our sharp or slipshod American gabble. His clothes were rusty, his hands were large, and he hadn't a really handsome feature in his face, except his beautiful teeth; yet I liked him, for he had a fine head; his linen was very nice, and he looked like a gentleman, though two buttons were off his coat, and there was a patch on one shoe. He looked sober in spite of his humming, till he went to the window to turn the hyacinth bulbs towards the sun, and stroke the cat, who received him like an old friend. Then he smiled; and when a tap came at the door, called out in a loud, brisk tone:

'Herein!'

I was just going to run, when I caught sight of a morsel of a child carrying a big book, and stopped to see what was going on.

'Me wants my Bhaer,' said the mite, slamming down her book, and running to meet him.

'Thou shalt haf thy Bhaer; come, then, and take a goot hug from him, my Tina,' said the professor, catching her up, with a laugh, and holding her so high over his head that she had to stoop her little face to kiss him.

'Now me mus tuddy my lessin,' went on the funny little thing; so he put her up at the table, opened the great dictionary she had brought, and gave her a paper and pencil, and she scribbled away, turning a leaf now and then, and passing her little fat finger down the page, as if finding a word, so soberly that I nearly betrayed myself by a laugh, while Mr Bhaer stood stroking her pretty hair, with a fatherly look, that made me think she must be his own, though she looked more French than German.

Another knock and the appearance of two young ladies sent me back to my work, and there I virtuously remained through all the noise and gabbling that went on next door. One of the girls kept laughing affectedly, and saying 'Now, Professor,' in a coquettish tone, and the other pronounced her German with an accent that must have made it hard for him to keep sober.

Both seemed to try his patience sorely; for more than once I heard him say emphatically, 'No, no, it is *not* so; you haf not attend to what I say'; and once there was a loud rap, as if he struck the table with his book, followed by the despairing exclamation, 'Prut! it all goes bad this day.'

Poor man, I pitied him; and when the girls were gone, took just one more peep, to see if he survived it. He seemed to have thrown himself back in his chair, tired out, and sat there with his eyes shut till the clock struck two, when he jumped up, put his books in his pocket, as if ready for another lesson, and, taking little Tina, who had fallen asleep on the sofa, in his arms, he carried her quietly away. I fancy he has a hard life of it.

Mrs Kirke asked me if I wouldn't go down to the five o'clock dinner; and, feeling a little bit homesick,

I thought I would, just to see what sort of people are under the same roof with me. So I made myself respectable, and tried to slip in behind Mrs Kirke but as she is short, and I'm tall, my efforts at concealment were rather a failure. She gave me a seat by her, and after my face cooled off, I plucked up courage, and looked about me. The long table was full, and everyone intent on getting their dinner – the gentlemen especially, who seemed to be eating on time, for they *bolted* in every sense of the word, vanishing as soon as they were done. There was the usual assortment of young men absorbed in themselves; young couples absorbed in each other; married ladies in their babies, and old gentlemen in politics. I don't think I shall care to have much to do with any of them, except one sweet-faced maiden lady, who looks as if she had something in her.

Cast away at the very bottom of the table was the professor, shouting answers to the questions of a very inquisitive, deaf old gentleman on one side, and talking philosophy with a Frenchman on the other. If Amy had been here, she'd have turned her back on him for ever, because, sad to relate, he had a great appetite, and shovelled in his dinner in a manner which would have horrified 'her ladyship'. I didn't mind, for I like 'to see folks eat with a relish', as

Hannah says, and the poor man must have needed a deal of food after teaching idiots all day.

As I went upstairs after dinner, two of the young men were settling their hats before the hall mirror, and I heard one say low to the other, 'Who's the new party?'

'Governess, or something of that sort.'

'What the deuce is she at our table for?'

'Friend of the old lady's.'

'Handsome head, but no style.'

'Not a bit of it. Give us a light and come on.'

I felt angry at first, and then I didn't care, for a governess is as good as a clerk, and I've got sense, if I haven't style, which is more than some people have, judging from the remarks of the elegant beings who clattered away, smoking like bad chimneys. I hate ordinary people!

Thursday

Yesterday was a quiet day, spent in teaching, sewing, and writing in my little room, which is very cosy, with a light and fire. I picked up a few bits of news, and was introduced to the professor. It seems that Tina is the child of the Frenchwoman who does the fine ironing in the laundry here. The little thing has lost her heart to Mr Bhaer, and follows him about the house like a dog whenever he is at home, which delights him, as he is very fond of children, though a 'bacheldore'. Kitty and Minnie Kirke likewise regard him with affection, and tell all sorts of stories about the plays he invents, the presents he brings, and the splendid tales he tells. The young men quiz him, it seems, call him Old Fritz, Lager Beer, Ursa Major, and make all manner of jokes on his name. But he enjoys it like a boy, Mrs K. says, and takes it so good-naturedly that they all like him, in spite of his foreign ways.

The maiden lady is a Miss Norton – rich, cultivated, and kind. She spoke to me at dinner today (for I went to table again, it's such fun to watch people), and asked me to come and see her at her room. She has fine books and pictures, knows interesting persons, and seems friendly; so I shall make myself agreeable, for I *do* want to get into good society, only it isn't the same sort that Amy likes.

I was in our parlour last evening, when Mr Bhaer came in with some newspapers for Mrs Kirke. She wasn't there, but Minnie, who is a little old woman, introduced me very prettily: 'This is Mamma's friend, Miss March.'

'Yes; and she's jolly and we like her lots,' added Kitty, who is an *enfant terrible*.

We both bowed, and then we laughed, for the

prim introduction and the blunt addition were rather a comical contrast.

'Ah, yes, I hear these naughty ones go to vex you, Mees Marsch. If so again, call at me and I come,' he said, with a threatening frown that delighted the little wretches.

I promised I would, and he departed; but it seems as if I was doomed to see a good deal of him, for today, as I passed his door on my way out, by accident I knocked against it with my umbrella. It flew open, and there he stood in his dressing-gown, with a big blue sock on one hand, and a darning-needle in the other; he didn't seem at all ashamed of it, for when I explained and hurried on, he waved his hand, sock and all, saying in his loud, cheerful way:

'You haf a fine day to make your walk. Bon voyage, mademoiselle.'

I laughed all the way downstairs; but it was a little pathetic, also, to think of the poor man having to mend his own clothes. The German gentlemen embroider, I know; but darning hose is another thing, and not so pretty.

Saturday

Nothing has happened to write about, except a call on Miss Norton, who has a room full of lovely things, and who was very charming, for she showed me all her treasures, and asked me if I would sometimes go with her to lectures and concerts, as her escort – if I enjoyed them. She put it as a favour, but I'm sure Mrs Kirke has told her about us, and she does it out of kindness to me. I'm as proud as Lucifer, but such favours from such people don't burden me, and I accepted gratefully.

When I got back to the nursery there was such an uproar in the parlour that I looked in; and there was Mr Bhaer down on his hands and knees, with Tina on his back, Kitty leading him with a jump-rope, and Minnie feeding two small boys with seed-cakes, as they roared and ramped in cages built of chairs.

'We are playing *nargarie*,' explained Kitty.

'Dis is mine effalunt!' added Tina, holding on by the professor's hair.

'Mamma always allows us to do what we like Saturday afternoon, when Franz and Emil come, doesn't she, Mr Bhaer?' said Minnie.

The 'effalunt' sat up, looking as much in earnest as any of them, and said soberly to me:

'I gif you my wort it is so. If we make too large a noise you shall say "Hush!" to us, and we go more softly.'

I promised to do so, but left the door open, and

enjoyed the fun as much as they did – for a more glorious frolic I never witnessed. They played tag and soldiers, danced and sung, and when it began to grow dark they all piled on to the sofa about the professor, while he told charming fairy stories of the storks on the chimney-tops, and the little 'kobolds', who ride the snowflakes as they fall. I wish Americans were as simple and natural as Germans, don't you?

I'm so fond of writing, I should go spinning on for ever if motives of economy didn't stop me; for though I've used thin paper and written fine, I tremble to think of the stamps this long letter will need. Pray forward Amy's as soon as you can spare them. My small news will sound very flat after her splendours, but you will like them, I know. Is Teddy studying so hard that he can't find time to write to his friends? Take good care of him for me, Beth, and tell me all about the babies, and give heaps of love to everyone.

From your faithful Jo

P.S. – On reading over my letter it strikes me as rather Bhaery; but I am always interested in odd people, and I really had nothing else to write about. Bless you!

My Precious Betsey, – As this is to be a scribble-scrabble letter, I direct it to you, for it may amuse you, and give you some idea of my goings on; for, though quiet, they are rather amusing, for which, oh, be joyful! After what Amy would call Herculaneum efforts, in the way of mental and moral agriculture, my young ideas begin to shoot and my little twigs to bend as I could wish. They are not so interesting to me as Tina and the boys, but I do my duty by them, and they are fond of me. Franz and Emil are jolly little lads, quite after my own heart; for the mixture of German and American spirit in them produces a constant state of effervescence. Saturday afternoons are riotous times, whether spent in the house or out; for on pleasant days they all go to walk, like a seminary, with the professor and myself to keep order; and then such fun!

We are very good friends now, and I've begun to take lessons. I really couldn't help it, and it all came about in such a droll way that I must tell you. To begin at the beginning, Mrs Kirke called to me, one day, as I passed Mr Bhaer's room, where she was rummaging.

'Did you ever see such a den, my dear? Just come and help me put these books to rights, for I've turned everything upside-down, trying to discover what he has done with the six new handkerchiefs I gave him not long ago.'

I went in, and while we worked I looked about me, for it was 'a den', to be sure. Books and papers everywhere; a broken meerschaum, and an old flute over the mantelpiece as if done with; a ragged bird, without any tail, chirped on one window seat, and a box of white mice adorned the other; half-finished boats and bits of string lay among the manuscripts; dirty little boots stood drying before the fire; and traces of the dearly beloved boys, for whom he makes a slave of himself, were to be seen all over the room. After a grand rummage three of the missing articles were found – one over the bird cage, one covered with ink, and a third burnt brown, having been used as a holder.

'Such a man!' laughed good-natured Mrs K., as she put the relics in the rag-bag. 'I suppose the others are torn up to rig ships, bandage cut fingers, or make kite tails. It's dreadful, but I can't scold him: he's so absent-minded and good-natured, he lets those boys ride over him roughshod. I agreed to do his washing and mending, but he forgets to give out his things and I forget to look them over, so he comes to a sad pass sometimes.'

'Let me mend them,' said I. 'I don't mind it, and

he needn't know. I'd like to – he's so kind to me about bringing my letters and lending books.'

So I have got his things in order, and knit heels into two pairs of the socks – for they were boggled out of shape with his queer darns. Nothing was said, and I hoped he wouldn't find it out, but one day last week he caught me at it. Hearing the lessons he gives to others has interested and amused me so much that I took a fancy to learn; for Tina runs in and out, leaving the door open, and I can hear. I had been sitting near this door, finishing off the last sock, and trying to understand what he said to a new scholar, who is as stupid as I am. The girl had gone, and I thought he had also, it was so still, and I was busily gabbling over a verb, and rocking to and fro in a most absurd way, when a little crow made me look up, and there was Mr Bhaer looking and laughing quietly, while he made signs to Tina not to betray him.

'So!' he said, as I stopped and stared like a goose, 'you peep at me, I peep at you, and that is not bad; but see, I am not pleasanting when I say, haf you a wish for German?'

'Yes; but you are too busy. I am too stupid to learn,' I blundered out, as red as a peony.

'Prut! we will make the time, and we fail not to find the sense. At evening I shall gif a little lesson with much gladness; for, like you, Mees Marsch, I haf this debt to pay,' and he pointed to my work. "'Yes," they say to one another, these so kind ladies, "he is a stupid old fellow; he will see not what we do; he will never observe that his sock-heels go not in holes any more, he will think his buttons grow out new when they fall, and believe that strings make theirselves." Ah! but I haf an eye, and I see much. I haf a heart, and I feel the thanks for this. Come, a little lesson then and now, or no more good fairy works for me and mine.'

Of course I couldn't say anything after that, and as it really is a splendid opportunity, I made the bargain, and we began. I took four lessons, and then I stuck fast in a grammatical bog. The professor was very patient with me, but it must have been torment to him, and now and then he'd look at me with such an expression of mild despair that it was a toss up with me whether to laugh or cry. I tried both ways; and when it came to a sniff of utter mortification and woe, he just threw the grammar on to the floor, and marched out of the room. I felt myself disgraced and deserted for ever, but didn't blame him a particle, and was scrambling my papers together, meaning to rush upstairs and shake myself hard, when in he came, as brisk and beaming as if I'd covered myself with glory.

'Now we shall try a new way. You and I will read these pleasant little Märchen together, and dig no more in that dry book, that goes in the corner for making us trouble.'

He spoke so kindly, and opened Hans Andersen's fairy tales so invitingly before me, that I was more ashamed than ever, and went at my lesson in a neck-or-nothing style that seemed to amuse him immensely. I forgot my bashfulness, and pegged away (no other word will express it) with all my might, tumbling over long words, pronouncing according to the inspiration of the minute, and doing my very best. When I finished reading my first page, and stopped for breath, he clapped his hands and cried out, in his hearty way, 'Das ist gut! Now we go well! My turn. I do him in German; gif me your ear.' And away he went, rumbling out the words with his strong voice, and a relish which was good to see as well as hear. Fortunately the story was 'The Constant Tin Soldier', which is droll, you know, so I could laugh – and I did – though I didn't understand half he read, for I couldn't help it, he was so earnest, I so excited, and the whole thing so comical.

After that we got on better, and now I read my lessons pretty well; for this way of studying suits me, and I can see that the grammar gets tucked into the tales and poetry as one gives pills in jelly. I like it very much, and he doesn't seem tired of it yet – which is very good of him, isn't it? I mean to give him something on Christmas, for I dare not offer money. Tell me something nice, Marmee.

I'm glad Laurie seems so happy and busy, that he has given up smoking, and lets his hair grow. You see Beth manages him better than I did. I'm not jealous, dear; do your best, only don't make a saint of him. I'm afraid I couldn't like him without a spice of human naughtiness. Read him bits of my letters. I haven't time to write much, and that will do just as well. Thank Heaven Beth continues so comfortable.

January

A Happy New Year to you all, my dearest family, which of course includes Mr L. and a young man by the name of Teddy. I can't tell you how much I enjoyed your Christmas bundle, for I didn't get it till night, and had given up hoping. Your letter came in the morning, but you said nothing about a parcel, meaning it for a surprise; so I was disappointed, for I'd had a 'kind of a feeling' that you wouldn't forget me. I felt a little low in my mind, as I sat up in my room, after tea; and when the big, muddy, battered-looking bundle was brought to me, I just hugged it, and pranced. It was so *homey* and refreshing, that I sat down on the floor and read and looked and ate and laughed and cried, in my usual absurd way. The things were just what I wanted, and all the better for being made instead of bought. Beth's new 'ink-bib' was capital; and Hannah's box of hard gingerbread will be a treasure. I'll be sure and wear the nice flannels you sent, Marmee, and read carefully the books Father has marked. Thank you all, heaps and heaps!

Speaking of books reminds me that I'm getting rich in that line, for, on New Year's Day, Mr Bhaer gave me a fine Shakespeare. It is one he values much, and I've often admired it, set up in the place of honour, with his German Bible, Plato, Homer, and Milton; so you may imagine how I felt when he brought it down, without its cover, and showed me my name in it, 'from my friend Friedrich Bhaer.'

'You say often you wish a library: here I gif you one; for between these lids (he meant covers) is many books in one. Read him well, and he will help you much; for the study of character in this book will help you to read it in the world and paint it with your pen.'

I thanked him as well as I could, and talk now about 'my library', as if I had a hundred books. I never knew how much there was in Shakespeare before; but then I never had a Bhaer to explain it to me. Now *don't* laugh at his horrid name; it isn't pronounced either Bear or Beer, as people *will* say it, but something between the two, as only Germans can give it. I'm glad you both like what I tell you about him, and hope you will know him some day. Mother would admire his warm heart, Father his wise head. I admire both, and feel rich in my new 'friend Friedrich Bhaer'.

Not having much money, or knowing what he'd like, I got several little things, and put them about the room, where he would find them unexpectedly. They were useful, pretty, or funny: a new standish on his table, a little vase for his flower – he always has one, or a bit of green in a glass, to keep him fresh, he says – and a holder for his blower, so that he needn't burn up what Amy calls 'mouchoirs'. I made it like those Beth invented – a big butterfly with a fat body, and black and yellow wings, worsted feelers, and bead eyes. It took his fancy immensely, and he put it on his mantelpiece as an article of virtu; so it was rather a failure after all. Poor as he is, he didn't forget a servant or a child in the house; and not a soul here, from the French laundry woman to Miss Norton, forgot him. I was so glad of that.

They got up a masquerade, and had a gay time

New Year's Eve. I didn't mean to go down, having no dress; but at the last minute, Mrs Kirke remembered some old brocades, and Miss Norton lent me lace and feathers; so I dressed up as Mrs Malaprop, and sailed in with a mask on. No one knew me, for I disguised my voice, and no one dreamed of the silent, haughty Miss March (for they think I am very stiff and cool, most of them; and so I am to whippersnappers) could dance and dress, and burst out into a 'nice derangement of epitaphs, like an allegory on the banks of the Nile'. I enjoyed it very much; and when we unmasked, it was fun to see them stare at me. I heard one of the young men tell another that he knew I'd been an actress; in fact, he thought he remembered seeing me at one of the minor theatres. Meg will relish that joke. Mr Bhaer was Nick Bottom, and Tina was Titania – a perfect little fairy in his arms. To see them dance was 'quite a landscape', to use a Teddyism.

I had a very happy New Year, after all; and when I thought it over in my room, I felt as if I was getting on a little in spite of my many failures; for I'm cheerful all the time now, work with a will, and take more interest in other people than I used to, which is satisfactory. Bless you all! Ever your loving

Jo

11

A Friend

Though very happy in the social atmosphere about her, and very busy with the daily work that earned her bread, and made it sweeter for the effort, Jo still found time for literary labours. The purpose which now took possession of her was a natural one to a poor and ambitious girl; but the means she took to gain her end were not the best. She saw that money conferred power: money and power, therefore, she resolved to have; not to be used for herself alone, but for those whom she loved more than self.

The dream of filling home with comforts, giving Beth everything she wanted, from strawberries in winter to an organ in her bedroom; going abroad herself, and always having *more* than enough, so that she might indulge in the luxury of charity, had been for years Jo's most cherished castle in the air.

The prize-story experience had seemed to open a way which might, after long travelling and much uphill work, lead to this delightful *château en Espagne*. But the novel disaster quenched her courage for a time, for public opinion is a giant which has frightened stouter-hearted Jacks on bigger beanstalks than hers. Like that immortal hero, she reposed awhile after the first attempt, which resulted in a tumble, and the least lovely of the giant's treasures, if I remember rightly. But the 'up again and take another' spirit was as strong in Jo as in Jack; so she scrambled up, on the shady side this time, and got more booty, but nearly left behind her what was far more precious than the money-bags.

She took to writing sensation stories; for in those dark ages, even all-perfect America read rubbish. She told no one, but concocted a 'thrilling tale', and boldly carried it herself to Mr Dashwood, editor of the *Weekly Volcano*. She had never read *Sartor Resartus*, but she had a womanly instinct that clothes possess an influence more powerful over many than the worth of character or the magic of manners. So she dressed herself in her best, and, trying to persuade herself that she was neither excited nor nervous, bravely climbed two pairs of dark and dirty stairs to find herself in a disorderly room, a cloud of cigar smoke, and the presence of three gentlemen, sitting with their heels rather higher than their hats, which articles of dress none of them took the trouble to remove on her appearance. Somewhat daunted by this reception, Jo hesitated on the threshold, murmuring in much embarrassment:

'Excuse me, I was looking for the *Weekly Volcano* office; I wished to see Mr Dashwood.'

Down went the highest pair of heels, up rose the smokiest gentleman, and, carefully cherishing his cigar between his fingers, he advanced, with a nod, and a countenance expressive of nothing but sleep. Feeling that she must get through the matter somehow, Jo produced her manuscript, and, blushing redder and redder with each sentence, blundered out fragments of the little speech carefully prepared for the occasion.

'A friend of mine desired me to offer – a story – just as an experiment – would like your opinion – be glad to write more if this suits.'

While she blushed and blundered, Mr Dashwood had taken the manuscript, and was turning over the leaves with a pair of rather dirty fingers, and casting critical glances up and down the neat pages.

'Not a first attempt, I take it?' observing that the pages were numbered, covered only on one side, and not tied up with a ribbon – sure sign of a novice.

'No, sir; she has had some experience, and got a prize for a tale in the *Blarneystone Banner*.'

'Oh, did she?' and Mr Dashwood gave Jo a quick look, which seemed to take note of everything she had on, from the bow in her bonnet to the buttons on her boots. 'Well, you can leave it, if you like. We've more of this sort of thing on hand than we know what to do with at present; but I'll run my eye over it, and give you an answer next week.'

Now, Jo did *not* like to leave it, for Mr Dashwood didn't suit her at all; but, under the circumstances, there was nothing for her to do but bow and walk away, looking particularly tall and dignified, as she was apt to do when nettled or abashed. Just then she was both; for it was perfectly evident, from the knowing glances exchanged among the gentlemen, that her little fiction of 'my friend' was considered a good joke; and a laugh, produced by some inaudible remark of the editor, as he closed the door, completed her discomfiture. Half resolving never to return, she went home, and worked off her irritation by stitching pinafores vigorously; and in an hour or two was cool enough to laugh over the scene, and long for next week.

When she went again, Mr Dashwood was alone, whereat she rejoiced; Mr Dashwood was much wider awake than before, which was agreeable; and Mr Dashwood was not too deeply absorbed in a cigar to remember his manners: so the second interview was much more comfortable than the first.

'We'll take this' – editors never say I – 'if you don't object to a few alterations. It's too long, but omitting the passages I've marked will make it just the right length,' he said, in a business-like tone.

Jo hardly knew her own manuscript again, so crumpled

and underscored were its pages and paragraphs; but, feeling as a tender parent might on being asked to cut off her baby's legs in order that it might fit into a new cradle, she looked at the marked passages, and was surprised to find that all the moral reflections – which she had carefully put in as ballast for much romance – had been stricken out.

'But, sir, I thought every story should have some sort of a moral, so I took care to have a few of my sinners repent.'

Mr Dashwood's editorial gravity relaxed into a smile, for Jo had forgotten her 'friend', and spoken as only an author could.

'People want to be amused, not preached at, you know. Morals don't sell nowadays'; which was not quite a correct statement, by the way.

'You think it would do with these alterations, then?'

'Yes, it's a new plot, and pretty well worked up – language good, and so on,' was Mr Dashwood's affable reply.

'What do you – that is, what compensation –' began Jo, not exactly knowing how to express herself.

'Oh, yes, well, we give from twenty-five to thirty for things of this sort. Pay when it comes out,' returned Mr Dashwood, as if that point had escaped him; such trifles often do escape the editorial mind, it is said.

'Very well; you can have it,' said Jo, handing back the

story, with a satisfied air; for, after the dollar-a-column work, even twenty-five seemed good pay.

'Shall I tell my friend you will take another if she has one better than this?' asked Jo, unconscious of her little slip of the tongue, and emboldened by her success.

'Well, we'll look at it; can't promise to take it. Tell her to make it short and spicy, and never mind the moral. What name would your friend like to put to it?' in a careless tone.

'None at all, if you please; she doesn't wish her name to appear, and has no *nom de plume*,' said Jo, blushing in spite of herself.

'Just as she likes, of course. The tale will be out next week; will you call for the money, or shall I send it?' asked Mr Dashwood, who felt a natural desire to know who his new contributor might be.

'I'll call. Good morning, sir.'

As she departed, Mr Dashwood put up his feet, with the graceful remark, 'Poor and proud, as usual, but she'll do.'

Following Mr Dashwood's directions, and making Mrs Northbury her model, Jo rashly took a plunge into the frothy sea of sensational literature; but, thanks to the life-preserver thrown her by a friend, she came up again, not much the worse for her ducking.

Like most young scribblers, she went abroad for her characters and scenery; and banditti, counts, gipsies, nuns, and duchesses appeared upon her stage, and played their parts with as much accuracy and spirit as could be expected. Her readers were not particular about such trifles as grammar, punctuation, and probability, and Mr Dashwood graciously permitted her to fill his columns at the lowest prices, not thinking it necessary to tell her that the real cause of his hospitality was the fact that one of his hacks, on being offered higher wages, had basely left him in the lurch.

She soon became interested in her work, for her emaciated purse grew stout, and the little hoard she was making to take Beth to the mountains next summer grew slowly but surely as the weeks passed. One thing disturbed her satisfaction, and that was that she did not tell them at home. She had a feeling that Father and Mother would not approve, and preferred to have her own way first, and beg pardon afterwards. It was easy to keep her secret, for no name appeared with her stories; Mr Dashwood had, of course, found it out very soon, but promised to be dumb; and, for a wonder, kept his word.

She thought it would do her no harm, for she sincerely meant to write nothing of which she should be ashamed, and quieted all pricks of conscience by anticipations of the happy minute when she should show her earnings and laugh over her well-kept secret.

But Mr Dashwood rejected any but thrilling tales; and, as thrills could not be produced except by harrowing up the souls of the readers, history and romance, land and sea, science and art, police records and lunatic asylums, had to be ransacked for the purpose. Jo soon found that her innocent experience had given her but few glimpses of the tragic world which underlies society; so, regarding it in a business light, she set about supplying her deficiencies with characteristic energy. Eager to find material for stories, and bent on making them original in plot, if not masterly in execution, she searched newspapers for accidents, incidents, and crimes; she excited the suspicions of public librarians for asking for works on poisons; she studied faces in the street, and characters, good, bad, and indifferent, all about her; she delved in the dust of ancient times for facts or fictions so old that they were as good as new, and introduced herself to folly, sin, and misery, as well as her limited opportunities allowed. She thought she was prospering finely; but, unconsciously, she was beginning to desecrate some of the womanliest attributes of a woman's character. She was living in bad society; and, imaginary though it was, its influence affected her, for she was feeding heart and fancy on dangerous and unsubstantial food, and was fast brushing the innocent bloom from her nature by a premature acquaintance with the darker side of life, which comes soon enough to all of us.

She was beginning to feel rather than see this, for much describing of other people's passions and feelings set her to studying and speculating about her own – a morbid amusement, in which healthy young minds do not voluntarily indulge. Wrong-doing always brings its own punishment; and, when Jo most needed hers, she got it.

I don't know whether the study of Shakespeare helped her to read character, or the natural instinct of a woman for what was honest, brave, and strong; but while endowing her imaginary heroes with every perfection under the sun, Jo was discovering a live hero, who interested her in spite of many human imperfections. Mr Bhaer, in one of their conversations, had advised her to study simple, true, and lovely characters, wherever she found them, as good training for a writer. Jo took him at his word, for she coolly turned round and studied him – a proceeding which would have much surprised him, had he known it, for the worthy professor was very humble in his own conceit.

Why everybody liked him was what puzzled Jo, at first. He was neither rich nor great, young nor handsome; in no respect what is called fascinating, imposing, or brilliant; and yet he was as attractive as a genial fire, and people seemed to gather about him as naturally as about a warm hearth. He was poor, yet always appeared to be giving something away; a stranger, yet everyone was his friend; no longer young, but as happy-hearted as a boy; plain and peculiar, yet his face looked beautiful to many, and his oddities were freely forgiven for his sake. Jo often watched him, trying to discover the charm, and, at last, decided that it was benevolence which worked the miracle. If he had any sorrow, 'it sat with its head under its wing', and he turned only his sunny side to the world. There were lines upon his forehead, but Time seemed to have touched him gently, remembering how kind he was to others. The pleasant curves about his mouth were the memorials of many friendly words and cheery laughs; his eyes were never cold or hard, and his big hand had a warm, strong grasp that was more expressive than words.

His very clothes seemed to partake of the hospitable nature of the wearer. They looked as if they were at ease, and liked to make him comfortable; his capacious waistcoat was suggestive of a large heart underneath; his rusty coat had a social air, and the baggy pockets plainly proved that little hands often went in empty and came out full; his very boots were benevolent, and his collars never stiff and raspy like other people's.

'That's it!' said Jo to herself, when she at length discovered that genuine goodwill towards one's fellow men could beautify and dignify even a stout German teacher, who shovelled in his dinner, darned his own socks, and was burdened with the name of Bhaer.

Jo valued goodness highly, but she also possessed a most feminine respect for intellect, and a little discovery which she made about the professor added much to her regard for him. He never spoke of himself, and no one ever knew that in his native city he had been a man much honoured and esteemed for learning and integrity, till a countryman came to see him, and, in a conversation with Miss Norton, divulged the pleasing fact. From her Jo learned it, and liked it all the better because Mr Bhaer had never told it. She felt proud to know that he was an honoured professor in Berlin, though only a poor language master in America; and his homely, hard-working life was much beautified by the spice of romance which this discovery gave it.

Another and a better gift than intellect was shown her in a most unexpected manner. Miss Norton had the entrée into literary society, which Jo would have had no chance of seeing but for her. The solitary woman felt an interest in the ambitious girl, and kindly conferred many favours of this sort both on Jo and the professor. She took them with her, one night, to a select symposium, held in honour of several celebrities.

Jo went prepared to bow down and adore the mighty ones whom she had worshipped with youthful enthusiasm afar off. But her reverence for genius received a severe shock that night, and it took her some time to recover from the discovery that the great creatures were only men and women after all. Imagine her dismay, on stealing a glance of timid admiration at the poet whose lines suggested an ethereal being fed on 'spirit, fire, and dew', to behold him devouring his supper with an ardour which flushed his intellectual countenance. Turning as from a fallen idol, she made other discoveries which rapidly dispelled her romantic illusions. The great novelist vibrated between two decanters with the regularity of a pendulum; the famous divine flirted openly with one of the Madame de Staëls of the age, who looked daggers at another Corinne, who was amiably satirizing her, after outmanoeuvring her in efforts to absorb the profound philosopher, who imbibed tea Johnsonianly and appeared to slumber, the loquacity of the lady rendering speech impossible. The scientific celebrities, forgetting their molluscs and glacial periods, gossiped about art, while devoting themselves to oysters and ices with characteristic energy; the young musician, who was charming the city like a second Orpheus, talked horses; and the specimen of the British nobility present happened to be the most ordinary man of the party.

Before the evening was half over, Jo felt so completely *désillusionée*, that she sat down in a corner to recover herself. Mr Bhaer soon joined her, looking rather out of his element, and presently several of the philosophers, each mounted on his hobby, came ambling up to hold an intellectual tournament in the recess. The conversation was miles beyond Jo's comprehension, but she enjoyed it, though Kant and Hegel were unknown gods, the Subjective and Objective unintelligible terms; and the only thing 'evolved from her inner consciousness', was a bad headache after it was all over. It dawned upon her gradually that the world was being picked to pieces, and put together on new, and, according to the talkers, on infinitely better principles than before; that religion was in a fair way to be reasoned into nothingness, and intellect was to be the only God. Jo knew nothing about philosophy or metaphysics of any sort, but a curious excitement, half pleasurable, half painful, came over her, as she listened with a sense of being turned adrift into time and space, like a young balloon out on a holiday.

She looked round to see how the professor liked it, and found him looking at her with the grimmest expression she had ever seen him wear. He shook his head, and beckoned her to come away; but she was fascinated, just then, by the freedom of Speculative Philosophy, and kept her seat, trying to find out what the wise gentlemen intended to rely upon after they had annihilated all the old beliefs.

Now, Mr Bhaer was a diffident man, and slow to offer his own opinions, not because they were unsettled, but too sincere and earnest to be lightly spoken. As he glanced from Jo to several other young people, attracted by the brilliancy of the philosophic pyrotechnics, he knit his brows, and longed to speak, fearing that some inflammable young soul would be led astray by the rockets, to find, when the display was over, that they had only an empty stick or a scorched hand.

He bore it as long as he could; but when he was appealed to for an opinion, he blazed up with honest indignation, and defended religion with all the eloquence of truth – an eloquence which made his broken English musical, and his plain face beautiful. He had a hard fight, for the wise men argued well; but he didn't know when he was beaten, and stood to his colours like a man. Somehow, as he talked, the world got right again to Jo; the old beliefs, that had lasted so long, seemed better than the new; God was not a blind force, and immortality was not a pretty fable, but a blessed fact. She felt as if she had solid ground under her feet again; and when Mr Bhaer paused, out-talked, but not one whit convinced, Jo wanted to clap her hands and thank him.

She did neither; but she remembered this scene, and gave the professor her heartiest respect, for she knew it cost him an effort to speak out then and there, because his conscience would not let him be silent. She began to see that character is a better possession than money, rank, intellect, or beauty; and to feel that if greatness is what a wise man has defined it to be, 'truth, reverence, and goodwill', then her friend Friedrich Bhaer was not only good, but great.

This belief strengthened daily. She valued his esteem, she coveted his respect, she wanted to be worthy of his friendship; and, just when the wish was sincerest, she came near losing everything. It all grew out of a cocked hat; for one evening the professor came in to give Jo her lesson, with a paper soldier cap on his head, which Tina had put there, and he had forgotten to take off.

'It's evident he doesn't look in his glass before coming down,' thought Jo, with a smile, as he said 'Good efening,' and sat soberly down, quite unconscious of the ludicrous contrast between his subject and his headgear, for he was going to read her the 'Death of Wallenstein'.

She said nothing at first, for she liked to hear him laugh out his big, hearty laugh, when anything funny happened, so she left him to discover it for himself, and presently forgot all about it; for to hear a German read Schiller is rather an absorbing occupation. After the reading came the lesson, which was a lively one, for Jo was in a gay mood that night, and the cocked hat kept her eyes dancing with merriment. The professor didn't know what to make of her, and stopped at last, to ask, with an air of mild surprise that was irresistible:

'Mees Marsch, for what do you laugh in your master's face? Haf you no respect for me, that you go on so bad?'

'How can I be respectful, sir, when you forget to take your hat off?' said Jo.

Lifting his hand to his head, the absent-minded professor gravely felt and removed the little cocked hat, looked at it a minute, and then threw back his head, and laughed like a merry bass-viol.

'Ah! I see him now; it is that imp Tina who makes me a fool with my cap. Well, it is nothing; but see you, if this lesson goes not well, you too shall wear him.'

But the lesson did not go at all for a few minutes,

because Mr Bhaer caught sight of a picture on the hat, and, unfolding it, said, with an air of great disgust:

'I wish these papers did not come in the house; they are not for children to see, nor young people to read. It is not well, and I haf no patience with those who make this harm.'

Jo glanced at the sheet, and saw a pleasing illustration composed of a lunatic, a corpse, a villain, and a viper. She did not like it; but the impulse that made her turn it over was not one of displeasure, but fear, because, for a minute, she fancied the paper was the *Volcano*. It was not, however, and her panic subsided as she remembered that, even if it had been, and one of her own tales in it, there would have been no name to betray her. She had betrayed herself, however, by a look and a blush; for, though an absent man, the professor saw a good deal more than people fancied. He knew that Jo wrote, and had met her down among the newspaper offices more than once; but as she never spoke of it, he asked no questions, in spite of a strong desire to see her work. Now it occurred to him that she was doing what she was ashamed to own, and it troubled him. He did not say to himself, 'It is none of my business; I've no right to say anything,' as many people would have done; he only remembered that she was young and poor, a girl far away from mother's love and father's care; and he was moved to help her with an impulse as quick and natural as that which would prompt him to put out his hand to save a baby from a puddle. All this flashed through his mind in a minute, but not a trace of it appeared in his face; and by the time the paper was turned, and Jo's needle threaded, he was ready to say quite naturally, but very gravely:

'Yes, you are right to put it from you. I do not like to think that good young girls should see such things. They are made pleasant to some, but I would more rather give my boys gunpowder to play with than this bad trash.'

'All may not be bad, only silly, you know; and if there is a demand for it, I don't see any harm in supplying it. Many very respectable people make an honest living out of what are called sensation stories,' said Jo, scratching gathers so energetically that a row of little slits followed her pin.

'There is a demand for whisky, but I think you and I do not care to sell it. If the respectable people knew what harm they did, they would not feel that the living *was* honest. They haf no right to put poison in the sugar-plum, and let the small ones eat it. No; they should think a little, and sweep mud in the street before they do this thing.'

Mr Bhaer spoke warmly, and walked to the fire, crumpling the paper in his hands. Jo sat still, looking as if the fire had come to her; for her cheeks burned long after the cocked hat had turned to smoke, and gone harmlessly up the chimney.

'I should like much to send all the rest after him,' muttered the professor, coming back with a relieved air.

Jo thought what a blaze her pile of papers upstairs would make, and her hard-earned money lay rather heavily on her conscience at that minute. Then she thought consolingly to herself, 'Mine are not like that; they are only silly, never bad, so I won't be worried'; and taking up her book, she said, with a studious face:

'Shall we go on, sir? I'll be very good and proper now.'

'I shall hope so,' was all he said, but he meant more than she imagined; and the grave, kind look he gave her made her feel as if the words *Weekly Volcano* were printed in large type on her forehead.

As soon as she went to her room, she got out her papers, and carefully re-read every one of her stories. Being a little short-sighted, Mr Bhaer sometimes used eye-glasses, and Jo had tried them once, smiling to see how they magnified the fine print of her book; now she seemed to have got on the professor's mental or moral spectacles also; for the faults of these poor stories glared at her dreadfully, and filled her with dismay.

'They *are* trash, and will soon be worse than trash if I go on for each is more sensational than the last. I've gone blindly on, hurting myself and other people, for the sake of money; I know it's so, for I can't read this stuff in sober earnest without being horribly ashamed of it; and what *should* I do if they were seen at home, or Mr Bhaer got hold of them?'

Jo turned hot at the bare idea, and stuffed the whole bundle into her stove, nearly setting the chimney afire with the blaze.

'Yes, that's the best place for such inflammable nonsense; I'd better burn the house down, I suppose, than let other people blow themselves up with my gunpowder,' she thought, as she watched the 'Demon of the Jura' whisk away, a little black cinder with fiery eyes.

But when nothing remained of all her three months' work except a heap of ashes, and the money in her lap, Jo looked sober, as she sat on the floor, wondering what she ought to do about her wages.

'I think I haven't done much harm *yet*, and may keep this to pay for my time,' she said, after a long meditation, adding impatiently, 'I almost wish I hadn't any conscience, it's so inconvenient. If I didn't care about doing right, and didn't feel uncomfortable when doing wrong, I should get on capitally. I can't help wishing sometimes, that Father and Mother hadn't been so particular about such things.'

Ah, Jo, instead of wishing that, thank God that 'Father and Mother *were* particular', and pity from your heart those who have no such guardians to hedge them round with principles which may seem like prison walls to impatient youth, but which will prove sure foundations to build character upon in womanhood.

Jo wrote no more sensational stories, deciding that the money did not pay for her share of the sensation; but, going to the other extreme, as is the way with people of her stamp, she took a course of Mrs Sherwood, Miss Edgeworth, and Hannah More; and then produced a tale which might have been more properly called an essay or a sermon, so intensely moral was it. She had her doubts about it from the beginning; for her lively fancy and girlish romance felt as ill at ease in the new style as she would have done masquerading in the stiff and cumbrous costume of the last century. She sent this didactic gem to several markets, but it found no purchaser; and she was inclined to agree with Mr Dashwood, that morals didn't sell.

Then she tried a child's story, which she could easily have disposed of if she had not been mercenary enough to demand filthy lucre for it. The only person who offered enough to make it worth her while to try juvenile literature was a worthy gentleman who felt it his mission to convert all the world to his particular belief. But much as she liked to write for children, Jo could not consent to depict all her naughty boys as being eaten by bears or tossed by mad bulls, because they did not go to a particular Sabbath-school, nor all the good infants, who did go, as rewarded by every kind of bliss, from gilded gingerbread to escorts of angels, when they departed this life with psalms or sermons on their lisping tongues. So nothing came of these trials; and Jo corked up her inkstand, and said, in a fit of very wholesome humility:

'I don't know anything; I'll wait till I do before I try again, and, meantime, "sweep mud in the street", if I can't do better; that's honest, at least'; which decision proved that her second tumble down the bean-stalk had done her some good.

While these internal revolutions were going on, her external life had been as busy and uneventful as usual; and if she sometimes looked serious or a little sad no one observed it but Professor Bhaer. He did it so quietly that Jo never knew he was watching to see if she would accept and profit by his reproof; but she stood the test, and he was satisfied; for, though no words passed between them, he knew that she had given up writing. Not only did he guess it by the fact that the second finger of her right hand was no longer inky, but she spent her evenings downstairs now, was met no more among newspaper offices, and studied with a dogged patience, which assured him that she was bent on occupying her mind with something useful, if not pleasant.

He helped her in many ways, proving himself a true friend, and Jo was happy; for, while her pen lay idle, she was learning other lessons beside German, and laying a foundation for the sensation story of her own life.

It was a pleasant winter and a long one, for she did not leave Mrs Kirke till June. Everyone seemed sorry when the time came; the children were inconsolable, and Mr Bhaer's hair stuck straight up all over his head, for he always rumpled it wildly when disturbed in mind.

'Going home? Ah, you are happy that you haf a home to go in,' he said, when she told him, and sat silently pulling his beard, in the corner, while she held a little levee on that last evening.

She was going early, so she bade them all goodbye over night; and when his turn came, she said warmly:

'Now, sir, you won't forget to come and see us, if you ever travel our way, will you? I'll never forgive you if you do, for I want them all to know my friend.'

'Do you? Shall I come?' he asked, looking down at her with an eager expression which she did not see.

'Yes, come next month; Laurie graduates then, and you'd enjoy Commencement as something new.'

'That is your best friend, of whom you speak?' he said, in an altered tone.

'Yes, my boy Teddy, I'm very proud of him, and should like you to see him.'

Jo looked up then, quite unconscious of anything but her own pleasure in the prospect of showing them to one another. Something in Mr Bhaer's face suddenly recalled the fact that she might find Laurie more than a 'best friend', and, simply because she particularly wished not to look as if anything was the matter, she involuntarily began to blush; and the more she tried not to, the redder she grew. If it had not been for Tina on her knee, she didn't know what would have become of her. Fortunately, the child was moved to hug her; so she managed to hide her face an instant, hoping the professor did not see it. But he did, and his own changed again from that momentary anxiety to its usual expression, as he said cordially:

'I fear I shall not make the time for that, but I wish the friend much success, and you all happiness. Gott bless you!' and with that, he shook hands warmly, shouldered Tina, and went away.

But after the boys were abed, he sat long before his fire, with the tired look on his face, and the *heimweh*, or homesickness, lying heavy at his heart. Once, when he remembered Jo, as she sat with the little child on her lap and that new softness in her face, he leaned his head on his hands a minute, and then roamed about the room, as if in search of something that he could not find.

'It is not for me; I must not hope it now,' he said to himself, with a sigh that was almost a groan; then, as if reproaching himself for the longing that he could not repress, he went and kissed the two tousled heads upon the pillow, took down his seldom used meerschaum, and opened his Plato.

He did his best, and did it manfully; but I don't think he found that a pair of rampant boys, a pipe, or even the divine Plato, were very satisfactory substitutes for wife and child and home.

Early as it was, he was at the station, next morning, to see Jo off; and, thanks to him, she began her solitary journey with the pleasant memory of a familiar face smiling its farewell, a bunch of violets to keep her company, and, best of all, the happy thought:

'Well, the winter's gone, and I've written no books, earned no fortune; but I've made a friend worth having, and I'll try to keep him all my life'.

12

Heartache

Whatever his motive might have been, Laurie studied to some purpose that year, for he graduated with honour, and gave the Latin oration with the grace of a Phillips and the eloquence of a Demosthenes, so his friends said. They were all there, his grandfather – oh, so proud! – Mr and Mrs March, John and Meg, Jo and Beth, and all exulted over him with the sincere admiration which boys make light of at the time, but fail to win from the world by any after-triumphs.

'I've got to stay for this confounded supper, but I shall be home early tomorrow; you'll come and meet me as usual, girls?' Laurie said, as he put the sisters into the carriage after the joys of the day were over. He said 'girls', but he meant Jo, for she was the only one who kept up the old custom; she had not the heart to refuse her splendid, successful boy anything, and answered warmly:

'I'll come, Teddy, rain or shine, and march before you, playing *Hail the conquering hero comes*, on a jew's-harp.'

Laurie thanked her with a look that made her think,

in a sudden panic, 'Oh, deary me! I know he'll say something, and then what shall I do?'

Evening meditation and morning work somewhat allayed her fears, and having decided that she wouldn't be vain enough to think people were going to propose when she had given them every reason to know what her answer would be, she set forth at the appointed time, hoping Teddy wouldn't do anything to make her hurt his poor little feelings. A call at Meg's, and a refreshing sniff and sip at the Daisy and Demijohn, still further fortified her for the *tête-à-tête* but when she saw a stalwart figure looming in the distance, she had a strong desire to turn about and run away.

'Where's the jew's harp, Jo?' cried Laurie, as soon as he was within speaking distance.

'I forgot it'; and Jo took heart again, for that salutation could not be called lover-like.

She always used to take his arm on these occasions; now she did not, and he made no complaint, which was a bad sign, but talked on rapidly about all sorts of far away subjects, till they turned from the road into the little path that led homeward through the grove. Then he walked more slowly, suddenly lost his fine flow of language, and, now and then, a dreadful pause occurred. To rescue the conversation from one of the wells of silence into which it kept falling, Jo said hastily:

'Now you must have a good long holiday!'

'I intend to.'

Something in his resolute tone made Jo look up quickly to find him looking down at her with an expression that assured her the dreaded moment had come, and made her put out her hand with an imploring:

'No, Teddy, please don't!'

'I will, and you *must* hear me. It's no use, Jo; we've got to have it out, and the sooner the better for both of us,' he answered, getting flushed and excited all at once.

'Say what you like, then; I'll listen,' said Jo, with a desperate sort of patience.

Laurie was a young lover, but he was in earnest, and meant to 'have it out', if he died in the attempt; so he plunged into the subject with characteristic impetuosity, saying in a voice that *would* get choky now and then, in spite of manful efforts to keep it steady:

'I've loved you ever since I've known you, Jo; couldn't help it, you've been so good to me. I've tried to show it, but you wouldn't let me; now I'm going to make you hear, and give me an answer, for I *can't* go on so any longer.'

'I wanted to save you this; I thought you'd understand –' began Jo, finding it a great deal harder than she expected.

'I know you did; but girls are so queer you never know what they mean. They say No when they mean Yes, and drive a man out of his wits just for the fun of it,' returned Laurie, entrenching himself behind an undeniable fact.

'*I* don't. I never wanted to make you care for me so, and I went away to keep you from it if I could.'

'I thought so; it was like you, but it was no use. I only loved you all the more, and I worked hard to please you, and I gave up billiards and everything you didn't like, and waited and never complained, for I hoped you'd love me, though I'm not half good enough –'. Here there was a choke that couldn't be controlled, so he decapitated buttercups while he cleared his 'confounded throat'.

'Yes, you are; you're a great deal too good for me, and I'm so grateful to you, and so proud and fond of you, I don't see why I can't love you as you want me to. I've tried, but I can't change the feeling, and it would be a lie to say I do when I don't.'

'Really, truly, Jo?'

He stopped short, and caught both her hands as he put his question with a look that she did not soon forget.

'Really, truly, dear.'

They were in the grove now, close by the stile; and when the last words fell reluctantly from Jo's lips, Laurie dropped her hands and turned as if to go on, but for once in his life that fence was too much for him; so he just laid his head down on the mossy post, and stood so still that Jo was frightened.

'O Teddy, I'm so sorry, so desperately sorry, I could kill myself if it would do any good! I wish you wouldn't take it so hard. I can't help it; you know it's impossible for people to make themselves love other people if they don't,' cried Jo inelegantly but remorsefully, as she softly patted his shoulder, remembering the time when he had comforted her so long ago.

'They do sometimes,' said a muffled voice from the post.

'I don't believe it's the right sort of love, and I'd rather not try it,' was the decided answer.

There was a long pause, while a blackbird sung blithely on the willow by the river, and the tall grass rustled in the wind. Presently Jo said very soberly, as she sat down on the step of the stile:

'Laurie, I want to tell you something.'

He started as if he had been shot, threw up his head, and cried out, in a fierce tone:

'*Don't* tell me that, Jo; I can't bear it now!'

'Tell what?' she asked, wondering at his violence.

'That you love that old man.'

'What old man?' demanded Jo, thinking he must mean his grandfather.

'That devilish professor you were always writing about. If you say you love him, I know I shall do something desperate'; and he looked as if he would keep his word as he clenched his hands, with a wrathful spark in his eyes.

Jo wanted to laugh, but restrained herself, and said warmly, for she, too, was getting excited with all this:

'Don't swear, Teddy! He isn't old, nor anything bad, but good and kind, and the best friend I've got, next to you.

Pray, don't fly into a passion; I want to be kind, but I know I shall get angry if you abuse my professor. I haven't the least idea of loving him or anybody else.'

'But you will after a while, and then what will become of me?'

'You'll love someone else too, like a sensible boy, and forget all this trouble.'

'I *can't* love anyone else; and I'll never forget you, Jo, never! never!' with a stamp to emphasize his passionate words.

'What *shall* I do with him?' sighed Jo, finding that emotions were more unmanageable than she expected. 'You haven't heard what I wanted to tell you. Sit down and listen; for indeed I want to do right and make you happy,' she said, hoping to soothe him with a little reason, which proved that she knew nothing about love.

Seeing a ray of hope in that last speech, Laurie threw himself down on the grass at her feet, leaned his arm on the lower step of the stile, and looked up at her with an expectant face. Now that arrangement was not conducive to calm speech or clear thought on Jo's part; for how *could* she say hard things to her boy while he watched her with eyes full of love and longing, and lashes still wet with the bitter drop or two her hardness of heart had wrung from him? She gently turned his head away, saying, as she stroked the wavy hair which had been allowed to grow for her sake – how touching that was, to be sure! –

'I agree with Mother that you and I are not suited to each other, because our quick tempers and strong wills would probably make us very miserable, if we were so foolish as to –' Jo paused a little over the last word, but Laurie uttered it with a rapturous expression:

'Marry – no, we shouldn't! If you loved me, Jo, I should be a perfect saint, for you could make me anything you like.'

'No, I can't, I've tried it and failed, and I won't risk our happiness by such a serious experiment. We don't agree and we never shall; so we'll be good friends all our lives, but we won't go and do anything rash.'

'Yes, we will if we get the chance,' muttered Laurie rebelliously.

'Now do be reasonable, and take a sensible view of the case,' implored Jo, almost at her wit's end.

'I won't be reasonable; I don't want to take what you call "a sensible view"; it won't help me, and it only makes you harder. I don't believe you've got any heart.'

'I wish I hadn't!'

There was a little quiver in Jo's voice, and, thinking it a good omen, Laurie turned round, bringing all his persuasive powers to bear as he said, in the wheedlesome tone that had never been so dangerously wheedlesome before:

'Don't disappoint us, dear! Everyone expects it. Grandpa has set his heart upon it, your people like it, and I can't get on without you. Say you will, and let's be happy. Do, do!'

Not until months afterwards did Jo understand how she had the strength of mind to hold fast to the resolution she had made when she decided that she did not love her boy, and never could. It was very hard to do, but she did it, knowing that delay was both useless and cruel.

'I can't say "Yes" truly, so I won't say it at all. You'll see that I'm right, by and by, and thank me for it –' she began solemnly.

'I'll be hanged if I do!' and Laurie bounded up off the grass, burning with indignation at the bare idea.

'Yes, you will!' persisted Jo; 'you'll get over this after a while, and find some lovely, accomplished girl, who will adore you, and make a fine mistress for your fine house. I shouldn't. I'm homely and awkward and odd and old, and you'd be ashamed of me, and we should quarrel – we can't help it even now, you see – and I shouldn't like elegant society and you would, and you'd hate my scribbling, and I couldn't get on without it, and we should be unhappy, and wish we hadn't done it, and everything would be horrid!'

'Anything more?' asked Laurie, finding it hard to listen patiently to this prophetic burst.

'Nothing more, except that I don't believe I shall ever marry. I'm happy as I am, and love my liberty too well to be in any hurry to give it up for any mortal man.'

'I know better!' broke in Laurie. 'You think so now; but there'll come a time when you *will* care for somebody, and you'll love him tremendously, and live and die for him. I know you will, it's your way, and I shall have to stand by and see it'; and the despairing lover cast his hat upon the ground with a gesture that would have seemed comical, if his face had not been so tragical.

'Yes, I *will* live and die for him, if he ever comes and makes me love him in spite of myself, and you must do the best you can!' cried Jo, losing patience with poor Teddy. 'I've done my best, but you *won't* be reasonable, and it's selfish of you to keep teasing for what I can't give. I shall always be fond of you, very fond indeed, as a friend, but I'll never marry you; and the sooner you believe it, the better for both of us – so now!'

That speech was like fire to gunpowder. Laurie looked at her a minute as if he did not quite know what to do with himself, then turned sharply away, saying, in a desperate sort of tone:

'You'll be sorry some day, Jo.'

'Oh, where are you going?' she cried, for his face frightened her.

'To the devil!' was the consoling answer.

For a minute Jo's heart stood still, as he swung himself down the bank, towards the river; but it takes much folly, sin, or misery to send a young man to a violent death, and Laurie was not one of the weak sort who are conquered by a single failure. He had no thought of a melodramatic plunge, but some blind instinct led him to fling hat and coat into his boat and row away with all his might, making better time up the river than he had done in many a race. Jo drew a long breath and unclasped her hands as she watched the poor fellow trying to outstrip the trouble which he carried in his heart.

'That will do him good, and he'll come home in such a tender, penitent state of mind, that I shan't dare to see him,' she said; adding, as she went slowly home, feeling as if she had murdered some innocent thing, and buried it under the leaves:

'Now I must go and prepare Mr Laurence to be very kind to my poor boy. I wish he'd love Beth; perhaps he may, in time, but I begin to think I was mistaken about her. Oh dear! how can girls like to have lovers and refuse them. I think it's dreadful.'

Being sure that no one could do it so well as herself, she went straight to Mr Laurence, told the hard story bravely through, and then broke down, crying so dismally over her own insensibility that the kind old gentleman, though sorely disappointed, did not utter a reproach. He found it difficult to understand how any girl could help loving Laurie, and hoped she would change her mind, but he knew even better than Jo that love cannot be forced, so he shook his head sadly, and resolved to carry his boy out of harm's way; for Young Impetuosity's parting words to Jo disturbed him more than he would confess.

When Laurie came home, dead tired, but quite composed, his grandfather met him as if he knew nothing, and kept up the delusion very successfully for an hour or two. But when they sat together in the twilight, the time they used to enjoy so much, it was hard work for the old man to ramble on as usual, and harder still for the young one to listen to praises of the last year's success, which to him now seemed love's labour lost. He bore it as long as he could, then went to his piano, and began to play. The windows were open; and Jo, walking in the garden with Beth, for once understood music better than her sister, for he played the *Sonata Pathétique*, and played it as he never did before.

'That's very fine, I dare say, but it's sad enough to make one cry; give us something gayer, lad,' said Mr Laurence, whose kind old heart was full of sympathy, which he longed to show, but knew not how.

Laurie dashed into a livelier strain, played stormily for several minutes, and would have got through bravely, if, in a momentary lull, Mrs March's voice had not been heard calling:

'Jo, dear, come in; I want you.'

Just what Laurie longed to say, with a different meaning! As he listened, he lost his place; the music ended with a broken chord, and the musician sat silent in the dark.

'I can't stand this,' muttered the old gentleman. Up he got, groped his way to the piano, laid a kind hand on either of the broad shoulders, and said, as gently as a woman:

'I know, my boy, I know.'

No answer for an instant; then Laurie asked sharply:

'Who told you?'

'Jo herself.'

'Then there's an end of it!' and he shook off his grandfather's hands with an impatient motion; for, though grateful for the sympathy, his man's pride could not bear a man's pity.

'Not quite; I want to say one thing, and then there shall be an end of it,' returned Mr Laurence, with unusual mildness. 'You won't care to stay at home just now, perhaps?'

'I don't intend to run away from a girl. Jo can't prevent my seeing her, and I shall stay and do it as long as I like,' interrupted Laurie, in a defiant tone.

'Not if you are the gentleman I think you. I'm disappointed, but the girl can't help it; and the only thing left for you to do is to go away for a time. Where will you go?'

'Anywhere. I don't care what becomes of me'; and Laurie got up, with a reckless laugh, that grated on his grandfather's ear.

'Take it like a man, and don't do anything rash, for

God's sake. Why not go abroad, as you planned, and forget it?'

'I can't.'

'But you've been wild to go, and I promised you should when you got through college.'

'Ah, but I didn't mean to go alone!' and Laurie walked fast through the room, with an expression which it was well his grandfather did not see.

'I don't ask you to go alone; there's someone ready and glad to go with you, anywhere in the world.'

'Who, sir?' stopping to listen.

'Myself.'

Laurie came back as quickly as he went, and put out his hand, saying huskily:

'I'm a selfish brute; but – you know – Grandfather –'

'Lord help me, yes, I do know, for I've been through it all before, once in my own young days, and then with your father. Now, my dear boy, just sit quietly down, and hear my plan. It's all settled, and can be carried out at once,' said Mr Laurence, keeping hold of the young man, as if fearful that he would break away, as his father had done before him.

'Well, sir, what is it?' and Laurie sat down, without a sign of interest in face or voice.

'There is business in London that needs looking after; I meant you should attend to it; but I can do it better myself, and things here will get on very well with Brooke to manage them. My partners do almost everything; I'm merely holding on till you take my place, and can be off at any time.'

'But you hate travelling, sir; I can't ask it of you at your age,' began Laurie, who was grateful for the sacrifice, but much preferred to go alone, if he went at all.

The old gentleman knew that perfectly well, and particularly desired to prevent it; for the mood in which he found his grandson assured him that it would not be wise to leave him to his own devices. So stifling a natural regret at the thought of the home comforts he would leave behind him, he said stoutly:

'Bless your soul, I'm not superannuated yet. I quite enjoy the idea; it will do me good, and my old bones won't suffer, for travelling nowadays is almost as easy as sitting in a chair.'

A restless movement from Laurie suggested that *his* chair was not easy, or that he did not like the plan, and made the old man add hastily:

'I don't mean to be a marplot or a burden; I go because I think you'd feel happier than if I was left behind. I don't intend to gad about with you, but leave you free to go where you like, while I amuse myself in my own way. I've friends in London and Paris, and should like to visit them; meantime you can go to Italy, Germany, Switzerland, where you will, and enjoy pictures, music, scenery, and adventures to your heart's content.'

Now, Laurie felt just then that his heart was entirely broken, and the world a howling wilderness; but at the sound of certain words which the old gentleman artfully introduced into his closing sentence, the broken heart gave an unexpected leap, and a green oasis or two suddenly appeared in the howling wilderness. He sighed, and then said, in a spiritless tone:

'Just as you like, sir; it doesn't matter where I go or what I do.'

'It does to me, remember that, my lad; I give you entire liberty, but I trust you to make an honest use of it. Promise me that, Laurie.'

'Anything you like, sir.'

'Good,' thought the old gentleman. 'You don't care now, but there'll come a time when that promise will keep you out of mischief, or I'm much mistaken.'

Being an energetic individual, Mr Laurence struck while the iron was hot; and before the blighted being recovered spirit enough to rebel, they were off. During the time necessary for preparation, Laurie bore himself as young gentlemen usually do in such cases. He was moody, irritable, and pensive by turns; lost his appetite, neglected his dress, and devoted much time to playing tempestuously on his piano; avoided Jo, but consoled himself by staring at her from his window, with a tragical face that haunted her dreams by night, and oppressed her with a heavy sense of guilt by day. Unlike some sufferers, he never spoke of his unrequited passion, and would allow no one, not even Mrs March, to attempt consolation or offer sympathy. On some accounts, this was a relief to his friends; but the weeks before his departure were very uncomfortable, and everyone rejoiced that the 'poor, dear fellow was going away to forget his trouble, and come home happy'. Of course, he smiled darkly at their delusion, but passed it by, with the sad superiority of one who knew that his fidelity, like his love, was unalterable.

When the parting came he affected high spirits, to conceal certain inconvenient emotions which seemed inclined to assert themselves. This gaiety did not impose upon anybody, but they tried to look as if it did, for his sake, and he got on very well till Mrs March kissed him, with a whisper full of motherly solicitude; then, feeling that he was going very fast, he hastily embraced them all round, not forgetting the afflicted Hannah, and ran downstairs as if for his life. Jo followed a minute after to wave her hand to him if he looked round. He did look round, came back, put his arms about her, as she stood on the step above him, and looked up at her with a face that made his short appeal both eloquent and pathetic.

'O Jo, can't you?'

'Teddy, dear, I wish I could!'

That was all, except a little pause; then Laurie straightened himself up, said 'It's all right, never mind,' and went away without another word. Ah, but it wasn't all right, and Jo *did* mind; for while the curly head lay on her arm a minute after her hard answer, she felt as if she had stabbed her dearest friend; and when he left her without a look behind him, she knew that the boy Laurie never would come again.

13

Beth's Secret

When Jo came home that spring, she had been struck with the change in Beth. No one spoke of it or seemed aware of it, for it had come too gradually to startle those who saw her daily; but to eyes sharpened by absence, it was very plain; and a heavy weight fell on Jo's heart as she saw her sister's face. It was no paler and but little thinner than in the autumn; yet there was a strange, transparent look about it, as if the mortal was being slowly refined away, and the immortal shining through the frail flesh with an indescribably pathetic beauty. Jo saw and felt it, but said nothing at the time, and soon the first impression lost much of its power; for Beth seemed happy, no one appeared to doubt that she was better; and, presently, in other cares, Jo for a time forgot her fear.

But when Laurie was gone, and peace prevailed again, the vague anxiety returned and haunted her. She had confessed her sins and been forgiven; but when she showed her savings and proposed the mountain trip, Beth had thanked her heartily, but begged not to go so far away from home. Another little visit to the seashore would suit her better, and, as Grandma could not be prevailed upon to leave the babies, Jo took Beth down to the quiet place, where she could live much in the open air, and let the fresh sea-breezes blow a little colour into her pale cheeks.

It was not a fashionable place, but, even among the pleasant people there, the girls made few friends, preferring to live for one another. Beth was too shy to enjoy society, and Jo too wrapped up in her to care for anyone else: so they were all in all to each other, and came and went, quite unconscious of the interest they excited in those about them, who watched with sympathetic eyes the strong sister and the feeble one, always together, as if they felt instinctively that a long separation was not far away.

They did feel it, yet neither spoke of it; for often between ourselves and those nearest and dearest to us there exists a reserve which it is very hard to overcome. Jo felt as if a veil had fallen between her heart and Beth's; but when she put out her hand to lift it up, there seemed something sacred in the silence, and she waited for Beth to speak. She wondered, and was thankful also, that her parents did not seem to see what she saw; and, during the quiet weeks, when the shadow grew so plain to her, she said nothing of it to those at home, believing that it would tell itself when Beth came back no better. She wondered still more if her sister really guessed the hard truth, and what thoughts were passing through her mind during the long hours when she lay on the warm rocks, with her head in Jo's lap, while the winds blew healthfully over her, and the sea made music at her feet.

One day Beth told her. Jo thought she was asleep, she lay so still; and, putting down her book, sat looking at her with wistful eyes, trying to see signs of hope in the faint colour on Beth's cheeks. But she could not find enough to satisfy her, for the cheeks were very thin, and the hands seemed too feeble to hold even the rosy little shells they had been gathering. It came to her then more bitterly than ever that Beth was slowly drifting away from her, and her arms instinctively tightened their hold upon the dearest treasure she possessed. For a minute her eyes were too dim for seeing, and, when they cleared, Beth was looking up at her so tenderly that there was hardly any need for her to say:

'Jo, dear, I'm glad you know it. I've tried to tell you, but I couldn't.'

There was no answer except her sister's cheek against her own, not even tears; for when most deeply moved, Jo did not cry. She was the weaker, then, and Beth tried to comfort and sustain her, with her arms about her, and the soothing words she whispered in her ear.

'I've known it for a good while, dear, and, now I'm used to it, it isn't hard to think of or to bear. Try to see it so, and don't be troubled about me, because it's best; indeed it is.'

'Is this what made you so unhappy in the autumn, Beth? You did not feel it then, and keep it to yourself so long, did you?' asked Jo, refusing to see or say that it *was* best, but glad to know that Laurie had no part in Beth's trouble.

'Yes, I gave up hoping then, but I didn't like to own it. I tried to think it was a sick fancy, and would not let it trouble anyone. But when I saw you all so well and strong, and full of happy plans, it was hard to feel that I could never be like you, and then I was miserable, Jo.'

'O Beth, and you didn't tell me, didn't let me comfort and help you! How could you shut me out, and bear it all alone?'

Jo's voice was full of tender reproach, and her heart ached to think of the solitary struggle that must have gone on while Beth learned to say goodbye to health, love, and life, and take up her cross so cheerfully.

'Perhaps it was wrong, but I tried to do right; I wasn't sure, no one said anything, and I hoped I was mistaken. It would have been selfish to frighten you all when Marmee was so anxious about Meg, and Amy away, and you so happy with Laurie – at least, I thought so then.'

'And I thought that you loved him, Beth, and I went away because I couldn't,' cried Jo, glad to say all the truth.

Beth looked so amazed at the idea that Jo smiled in spite of her pain, and added softly:

'Then you didn't, deary? I was afraid it was so, and

imagined your poor little heart full of love-lornity all that while.'

'Why, Jo, how could I, when he was so fond of you?' asked Beth, as innocently as a child. 'I do love him dearly; he is so good to me, how can I help it? But he never could be anything to me but my brother. I hope he truly will be, some time.'

'Not through me,' said Jo decidedly. 'Amy is left for him, and they would suit excellently; but I have no heart for such things, now. I don't care what becomes of anybody but you, Beth. You *must* get well.'

'I want to, oh, so much! I try, but every day I lose a little, and feel more sure that I shall never gain it back. It's like the tide, Jo, when it turns, it goes slowly, but it can't be stopped.'

'It *shall* be stopped, your tide must not turn so soon, nineteen is too young. Beth, I can't let you go. I'll work and pray and fight against it. I'll keep you in spite of everything; there must be ways, it can't be too late. God won't be so cruel as to take you from me,' cried poor Jo rebelliously, for her spirit was far less piously submissive than Beth's.

Simple, sincere people seldom speak much of their piety; it shows itself in acts, rather than in words, and has more influence than homilies or protestations. Beth could not reason upon or explain the faith that gave her courage and patience to give up life, and cheerfully wait for death. Like a confiding child, she asked no questions, but left everything to God and nature, Father and mother of us all, feeling sure they, and they only, could teach and strengthen heart and spirit for this life and the life to come. She did not rebuke Jo with saintly speeches, only loved her better for her passionate affection, and clung more closely to the dear human love, from which our Father never means us to be weaned, but through which He draws us closer to Himself. She could not say, 'I'm glad to go,' for life was very sweet to her; she could only sob out, 'I try to be willing,' while she held fast to Jo, as the first bitter wave of this great sorrow broke over them together.

By and by Beth said, with recovered serenity:

'You'll tell them this when we go home?'

'I think they will see it without words,' sighed Jo; for now it seemed to her that Beth changed every day.

'Perhaps not; I've heard that the people who love best are often blindest to such things. If they don't see it, you will tell them for me. I don't want any secrets, and it's kinder to prepare them. Meg has John and the babies to comfort her, but you must stand by Father and Mother, won't you, Jo?'

'If I can but, Beth, I don't give up yet; I'm going to believe that it *is* a sick fancy, and not let you think it's true,' said Jo, trying to speak cheerfully.

Beth lay a minute thinking, and then said in her quiet way:

'I don't know how to express myself, and shouldn't try to anyone but you, because I can't speak out, except to my Jo. I only mean to say that I have a feeling that it never was intended I should live long. I'm not like the rest of you; I never made any plans about what I'd do when I grew up; I never thought of being married, as you all did. I couldn't seem to imagine myself anything but stupid little Beth, trotting about at home, of no use anywhere but there. I never wanted to go away, and the hard part now is the leaving you all. I'm not afraid, but it seems as if I should be homesick for you even in heaven.'

Jo could not speak; and for several minutes there was no sound but the sigh of the wind and the lapping of the tide. A white-winged gull flew by, with the flash of sunshine on its silvery breast; Beth watched it till it vanished, and her eyes were full of sadness. A little grey-coated sand-bird came tripping over the beach, 'peeping' softly to itself, as if enjoying the sun and sea; it came quite close to Beth, looked at her with a friendly eye, and sat upon a warm stone, dressing its wet feathers, quite at home. Beth smiled, and felt comforted, for the tiny thing seemed to offer its small friendship, and remind her that a pleasant world was still to be enjoyed.

'Dear little bird! See, Jo, how tame it is. I like peeps better than the gulls: they are not so wild and handsome, but they seem happy, confiding little things. I used to call them my birds, last summer; and Mother said they reminded her of me – busy, quaker-coloured creatures, always near the shore, and always chirping that contented little song of theirs. You are the gull, Jo, strong and wild, fond of the storm and the wind, flying far out to sea, and happy all alone. Meg is the turtle dove, and Amy is like the lark she writes about, trying to get up among the clouds, but always dropping down into its nest again. Dear little girl! she's so ambitious, but her heart is good and tender; and no matter how high she flies, she never will forget home. I hope I shall see her again, but she seems *so* far away.'

'She is coming in the spring, and I mean that you shall be all ready to see and enjoy her. I'm going to have you well and rosy by that time,' began Jo, feeling that of all the changes in Beth, the talking change was the greatest, for it seemed to cost no effort now, and she thought aloud in a way quite unlike bashful Beth.

'Jo, dear, don't hope any more; it won't do any good, I'm sure of that. We won't be miserable, but enjoy being together while we wait. We'll have happy times, for I don't suffer much, and I think the tide will go out easily, if you help me.'

Jo leaned down to kiss the tranquil face; and with that silent kiss, she dedicated herself soul and body to Beth.

She was right: there was no need of any words when they got home, for Father and Mother saw plainly, now, what they had prayed to be saved from seeing. Tired with her short journey, Beth went at once to bed, saying how glad she was to be at home; and when Jo went down, she found that she would be spared the hard task of telling Beth's secret. Her father stood leaning his head on the mantelpiece, and did not turn as she came in; but her mother stretched out her arms as if for help, and Jo went to comfort her without a word.

14

New Impressions

At three o'clock in the afternoon, all the fashionable world at Nice may be seen on the Promenade des Anglais – a charming place; for the wide walk, bordered with palms, flowers, and tropical shrubs, is bounded on one side by the sea, on the other by the grand drive, lined with hotels and villas, while beyond lie orange orchards and the hills. Many nations are represented, many languages spoken, many costumes worn; and, on a sunny day, the spectacle is as gay and brilliant as a carnival. Haughty English, lively French, sober Germans, handsome Spaniards, ugly Russians, meek Jews, free-and-easy Americans, all drive, sit, or saunter here, chatting over the news, and criticizing the latest celebrity who has arrived – Ristori or Dickens, Victor Emmanuel or the Queen of the Sandwich Islands. The equipages are as varied as the company, and attract as much attention, especially the low basket barouches in which ladies drive themselves, with a pair of dashing ponies, gay nets to keep their voluminous flounces from overflowing the diminutive vehicles, and little grooms on the perch behind.

Along this walk, on Christmas Day, a tall young man walked slowly, with his hands behind him, and a somewhat absent expression of countenance. He looked like an Italian, was dressed like an Englishman, and had the independent air of an American – a combination which caused sundry pairs of feminine eyes to look approvingly after him, and sundry dandies in black velvet suits, with rose-coloured neckties, buff gloves, and orange flowers in their buttonholes, to shrug their shoulders, and then envy him his inches. There were plenty of pretty faces to admire, but the young man took little notice of them, except to glance, now and then, at some blonde girl, or lady in blue. Presently he strolled out of the promenade, and stood a moment at the crossing, as if undecided whether to go and listen to the band in the Jardin Publique, or to wander along the beach towards Castle Hill. The quick trot of ponies' feet made him look up, as one of the little carriages, containing a single lady, came rapidly down the street. The lady was young, blonde, and dressed in blue. He stared a minute, then his whole face woke up, and, waving his hat like a boy, he hurried forward to meet her.

'O Laurie, is it really you? I thought you'd never come!' cried Amy, dropping the reins, and holding out both hands, to the great scandalization of a French mamma, who hastened her daughter's steps, lest she should be demoralized by beholding the free manners of these 'mad English'.

'I was detained by the way, but I promised to spend Christmas with you, and here I am.'

'How is your grandfather? When did you come? Where are you staying?'

'Very well – last night – at the Chauvain. I called at your hotel, but you were all out.'

'I have so much to say, I don't know where to begin! Get in, and we can talk at our ease; I was going for a drive, and longing for company. Flo's saving up for tonight.'

'What happens then, a ball?'

'A Christmas party at our hotel. There are many Americans there, and they give it in honour of the day. You'll go with us, of course? Aunt will be charmed.'

'Thank you. Where now?' asked Laurie, leaning back and folding his arms, a proceeding which suited Amy, who preferred to drive; for her parasol-whip and blue reins over the white ponies' backs, afforded her infinite satisfaction.

'I'm going to the banker's first, for letters, and then to Castle Hill; the view is so lovely, and I like to feed the peacocks. Have you ever been there?'

'Often, years ago; but I don't mind having a look at it.'

'Now tell me all about yourself. The last I heard of you, your grandfather wrote that he expected you from Berlin.'

'Yes, I spent a month there, and then joined him in

Paris, where he has settled for the winter. He has friends there, and finds plenty to amuse him; so I go and come, and we get on capitally.'

'That's a sociable arrangement,' said Amy, missing something in Laurie's manner, though she couldn't tell what.

'Why, you see he hates to travel, and I hate to keep still; so we each suit ourselves, and there is no trouble. I am often with him, and he enjoys my adventures, while I like to feel that someone is glad to see me when I get back from my wanderings. Dirty old hole, isn't it?' he added, with a look of disgust, as they drove along the boulevard to the Place Napoleon, in the old city.

'The dirt is picturesque, so I don't mind. The river and the hills are delicious, and these glimpses of the narrow cross-streets are my delight. Now we shall have to wait for that procession to pass; it's going to the Church of St John.'

While Laurie listlessly watched the procession of priests under their canopies, white-veiled nuns bearing lighted tapers, and some brotherhood in blue, chanting as they walked, Amy watched him, and felt a new sort of shyness steal over her; for he was changed, and she could not find the merry-faced boy she left in the moody-looking man beside her. He was handsomer than ever, and greatly improved, she thought; but now that the flush of pleasure at meeting her was over, he looked tired and spiritless – not sick, or exactly unhappy, but older and graver than a year or two of prosperous life should have made him. She couldn't understand it, and did not venture to ask questions; so she shook her head, and touched up her ponies, as the procession wound away across the arches of the Paglioni bridge, and vanished in the church.

'Que pensez-vous?' she said, airing her French, which had improved in quantity, if not in quality, since she came abroad.

'That mademoiselle has made good use of her time, and the result is charming,' replied Laurie, bowing, with his hand on his heart, and an admiring look.

She blushed with pleasure, but somehow the compliment did not satisfy her like the blunt praises he used to give her at home, when he promenaded round her on festival occasions, and told her she was 'altogether jolly', with a hearty smile and an approving pat on the head. She didn't like the new tone; for, though not blasé, it sounded indifferent in spite of the look.

'If that's the way he's going to grow up, I wish he'd stay a boy,' she thought, with a curious sense of disappointment and discomfort, trying meantime to seem quite easy and gay.

At Avigdor's she found the precious home letters, and, giving the reins to Laurie, read them luxuriously as they wound up the shady road between green hedges, where tea-roses bloomed as freshly as in June.

'Beth is very poorly, Mother says. I often think I ought

to go home, but they all say "stay"; so I do, for I shall never have another chance like this,' said Amy, looking sober over one page.

'I think you are right, there; you could do nothing at home, and it is a great comfort to them to know that you are well and happy, and enjoying so much, my dear.'

He drew a little nearer, and looked more like his old self as he said that; and the fear that sometimes weighed on Amy's heart was lightened, for the look, the act, the brotherly 'my dear', seemed to assure her that if any trouble did come, she would not be alone in a strange land. Presently she laughed, and showed him a small sketch of Jo in her scribbling suit, with the bow rampantly erect upon her cap, and issuing from her mouth the words, 'Genius burns!'

Laurie smiled, took it, put it in his vest pocket, 'to keep it from blowing away', and listened with interest to the lively letter Amy read him.

'This will be a regularly merry Christmas to me, with presents in the morning, you and letters in the afternoon, and a party at night,' said Amy, as they alighted among the ruins of the old fort, and a flock of splendid peacocks came trooping about them, tamely waiting to be fed. While Amy stood laughing on the bank above him as she scattered crumbs to the brilliant birds, Laurie looked at her as she had looked at him, with a natural curiosity to see what changes time and absence had wrought. He found nothing to perplex or disappoint, much to admire and approve; for, overlooking a few little affectations of speech and manner, she was as sprightly and graceful as ever, with the addition of that indescribable something in dress and bearing which we call elegance. Always mature for her age, she had gained a certain aplomb in both carriage and conversation, which made her seem more of a woman of the world than she was; but her old petulance now and then showed itself, her strong will still held its own, and her native frankness was unspoiled by foreign polish.

Laurie did not read all this while he watched her feed the peacocks, but he saw enough to satisfy and interest him, and carried away a pretty little picture of a bright-faced girl standing in the sunshine, which brought out the soft hue of her dress, the fresh colour of her cheeks, the golden gloss of her hair, and made her a prominent figure in the pleasant scene.

As they came up on to the stone plateau that crowns the hill, Amy waved her hand as if welcoming him to her favourite haunt, and said, pointing here and there:

'Do you remember the cathedral and the Corso, the fishermen dragging their nets in the bay, and the lovely road to Villa Franca, Schubert's Tower, just below, and, best of all, that speck far out to sea which they say is Corsica?'

'I remember; it's not much changed,' he answered, without enthusiasm.

'What Jo would give for a sight of that famous speck!' said Amy, feeling in good spirits, and anxious to see him so also.

'Yes,' was all he said, but he turned and strained his eyes to see the island which a greater usurper than even Napoleon now made interesting in his sight.

'Take a good look at it for her sake, and then come and tell me what you have been doing with yourself all this while,' said Amy, seating herself, ready for a good talk.

But she did not get it; for, though he joined her, and answered all her questions freely, she could only learn that he had roved about the Continent and been to Greece. So, after idling away an hour, they drove home again; and, having paid his respects to Mrs Carrol, Laurie left them, promising to return in the evening.

It must be recorded of Amy that she deliberately 'prinked' that night. Time and absence had done its work on both the young people; she had seen her old friend in a new light; not as 'our boy', but as a handsome and agreeable man, and she was conscious of a very natural desire to find favour in his sight. Amy knew her good points, and made the most of them, with the taste and skill which is a fortune to a poor and pretty woman.

Tarlatan and tulle were cheap at Nice, so she enveloped herself in them on such occasions, and, following the sensible English fashion of simple dress for young girls, got up charming little toilettes with fresh flowers, a few trinkets, and all manner of dainty devices, which were both inexpensive and effective. It must be confessed that the artist sometimes got possession of the woman, and indulged in antique *coiffures*, statuesque attitudes, and classic draperies. But, dear heart, we all have our little weaknesses, and find it easy to pardon such in the young, who satisfy our eyes with their comeliness, and keep our hearts merry with their artless vanities.

'I do want him to think I look well, and tell them so at home,' said Amy to herself, as she put on Flo's old white silk ball-dress, and covered it with a cloud of fresh illusion, out of which her white shoulders and golden head emerged with a most artistic effect. Her hair she had the sense to let alone, after gathering up the thick waves and curls into a Hebe-like knot at the back of her head.

'It's not the fashion, but it's becoming, and I can't afford to make a fright of myself,' she used to say, when advised to frizzle, puff, or braid, as the latest style commanded.

Having no ornaments fine enough for this important occasion, Amy looped her fleecy skirts with rosy clusters of azalea, and framed the white shoulders in delicate green vines. Remembering the painted boots, she surveyed her white satin slippers with girlish satisfaction, and chasséd down the room, admiring her aristocratic feet all by herself.

'My new fan just matches my flowers, my gloves fit to a charm, and the real lace on Aunt's *mouchoir* gives an air to my whole dress. If I only had a classical nose and mouth I should be perfectly happy,' she said, surveying herself with a critical eye, and a candle in each hand.

In spite of this affliction, she looked unusually gay and graceful as she glided away; she seldom ran – it did not suit her style, she thought, for, being tall, the stately and Junoesque was more appropriate than the sportive or piquant. She walked up and down the long saloon while waiting for Laurie, and once arranged herself under the chandelier, which had a good effect upon her hair; then she thought better of it, and went away to the other end of the room, as if ashamed of the girlish desire to have the first view a propitious one. It so happened that she could not have done a better thing, for Laurie came in so quietly she did not hear him; and, as she stood at the distant window, with her head half turned, and one hand gathering up her dress, the slender, white figure against the red curtains was as effective as a well-placed statue.

'Good evening, Diana!' said Laurie, with the look of satisfaction she liked to see in his eyes when they rested on her.

'Good evening, Apollo!' she answered, smiling back at him, for he, too, looked unusually *débonnaire*, and the thought of entering the ballroom on the arm of such a personable man caused Amy to pity the four plain Misses Davis from the bottom of her heart.

'Here are your flowers; I arranged them myself, remembering that you didn't like what Hannah calls a "sotbookey",' said Laurie, handing her a delicate nosegay, in a holder that she had long coveted as she daily passed it in Cardiglia's window.

'How kind you are!' she exclaimed gratefully. 'If I'd known you were coming I'd have had something ready for you today, though not as pretty as this, I'm afraid.'

'Thank you; it isn't what it should be, but you have improved it,' he added, as she snapped the silver bracelet on her wrist.

'Please don't.'

'I thought you liked that sort of thing?'

'Not from you; it doesn't sound natural, and I like your old bluntness better.'

'I'm glad of it,' he answered, with a look of relief; then buttoned her gloves for her, and asked if his tie was straight, just as he used to do when they went to parties together, at home.

The company assembled in the long *salle-à-manger*, that evening, was such as one sees nowhere but on the Continent. The hospitable Americans had invited every acquaintance they had in Nice, and, having no prejudice against titles, secured a few to add lustre to their Christmas ball.

A Russian prince condescended to sit in a corner for an hour, and talk with a massive lady, dressed like Hamlet's mother, in black velvet, with a pearl bridle under her chin. A Polish count, aged eighteen, devoted himself to the ladies, who pronounced him 'a fascinating dear', and a German Serene Something, having come for the supper alone, roamed vaguely about, seeking what he might devour. Baron Rothschild's private secretary, a large-nosed Jew, in tight boots, affably beamed upon the world, as if his master's name crowned him with a golden halo; a stout Frenchman, who knew the emperor, came to indulge his mania for dancing, and Lady de Jones, a British matron, adorned the scene with her little family of eight. Of course, there were many light-footed, shrill-voiced American girls, handsome, lifeless-looking English ditto, and a few plain but piquant French demoiselles; likewise the usual set of travelling young gentlemen, who disported themselves gaily, while mammas of all nations lined the walls, and smiled upon them benignly when they danced with their daughters.

Any young girl can imagine Amy's state of mind when she 'took the stage' that night, leaning on Laurie's arm. She knew she looked well, she loved to dance, she felt that her foot was on her native heath in a ballroom, and enjoyed the delightful sense of power which comes when young girls first discover the new and lovely kingdom they are born to rule by virtue of beauty, youth, and womanhood. She did pity the Davis girls, who were awkward, plain, and destitute of escort, except a grim papa and three grimmer maiden aunts, and she bowed to them in her friendliest manner as she passed; which was good of her, as it permitted them to see her dress, and burn with curiosity to know who her distinguished-looking friend might be. With the first burst of the band Amy's colour rose, her eyes began to sparkle, and her feet to tap the floor impatiently; for she danced well, and wanted Laurie to know it: therefore the shock she received can better be imagined than described, when he said, in a perfectly tranquil tone:

'Do you care to dance?'

'One usually does at a ball.'

Her amazed look and quick answer caused Laurie to repair his error as fast as possible.

'I meant the first dance. May I have the honour?'

'I can give you one if I put off the count. He dances divinely; but he will excuse me, as you are an old friend,' said Amy, hoping that the name would have a good effect, and show Laurie that she was not to be trifled with.

'Nice little boy, but rather a short Pole to support

> *A daughter of the gods,*
> *Divinely tall, and most divinely fair,'*

was all the satisfaction she got, however.

The set in which they found themselves was composed of English, and Amy was compelled to walk decorously through a cotillon, feeling all the while as if she could dance the tarantella with a relish. Laurie resigned her to the 'nice little boy', and went to do his duty to Flo, without securing Amy for the joys to come, which reprehensible want of forethought was properly punished, for she immediately engaged herself till supper, meaning to relent if he then gave any signs of penitence. She showed him her ball-book with demure satisfaction when he strolled, instead of rushing, up to claim her for the next, a glorious polka *redowa*; but his polite regrets didn't impose upon her, and when she gallopaded away with the count, she saw Laurie sit down by her aunt with an actual expression of relief.

That was unpardonable; and Amy took no more notice of him for a long while, except a word now and then, when she came to her chaperon, between the dances, for a necessary pin or a moment's rest. Her anger had a good effect, however, for she hid it under a smiling face, and seemed unusually blithe and brilliant. Laurie's eyes followed her with pleasure, for she neither romped nor sauntered, but danced with spirit and grace, making the delightsome pastime what it should be. He very naturally fell to studying her from this new point of view; and, before the evening was half over, had decided that 'little Amy was going to make a very charming woman'.

It was a lively scene, for soon the spirit of the social season took possession of everyone, and Christmas merriment made all faces shine, hearts happy, and heels light. The musicians fiddled, tooted, and banged as if they enjoyed it; everybody danced who could, and those who couldn't admired their neighbours with uncommon warmth. The air was dark with Davises, and many Joneses gambolled like a flock of young giraffes. The golden secretary darted through the room like a meteor, with a dashing Frenchwoman, who carpeted the floor with her pink and satin train. The Serene Teuton found the supper table, and was happy, eating steadily through the bill of fare, and dismayed the *garçons* by the ravages he committed. But the emperor's friend covered himself with glory, for he danced everything, whether he knew it or not, and introduced impromptu pirouettes when the figures bewildered him. The boyish abandon of that stout man was charming to behold; for, though he 'carried weight', he danced like an india-rubber ball. He ran, he flew, he pranced; his face glowed, his bald head shone; his coat-tails waved wildly, his pumps actually twinkled in the air, and when the music stopped, he wiped the drops from his brow, and beamed upon his fellow men like a French Pickwick without glasses.

Amy and her Pole distinguished themselves by equal enthusiasm, but more graceful agility; and Laurie found himself involuntarily keeping time to the rhythmic rise and fall of the white slippers as they flew by as indefatigably as if winged. When little Vladimir finally relinquished her, with assurances that he was 'desolated to leave so early', she was ready to rest, and see how her recreant knight had borne his punishment.

It had been successful; for, at three-and-twenty, blighted affections find a balm in friendly society, and young nerves will thrill, young blood dance, and healthy young spirits rise, when subjected to the enchantment of beauty, light, music, and motion. Laurie had a waked-up look as he rose to give her his seat; and when he hurried away to bring her some supper, she said to herself, with a satisfied smile:

'Ah, I thought that would do him good!'

'You look like Balzac's "Femme peinte par elle-même"', he said, as he fanned her with one hand, and held her coffee cup in the other.

'My rouge won't come off'; and Amy rubbed her brilliant cheek, and showed him her white glove with a sober simplicity that made him laugh outright.

'What do you call this stuff?' he asked, touching a fold of her dress that had blown over his knee.

'Illusion.'

'Good name for it; it's very pretty – new thing, isn't it?'

'It's as old as the hills; you have seen it on dozens of girls, and you never found out that it was pretty till now – *stupide!*'

'I never saw it on you before, which accounts for the mistake, you see.'

'None of that, it is forbidden; I'd rather take coffee than

compliments just now. No, don't lounge, it makes me nervous.'

Laurie sat bolt upright, and meekly took her empty plate, feeling an odd sort of pleasure in having 'little Amy' order him about; for she had lost her shyness now, and felt an irresistible desire to trample on him, as girls have a delightful way of doing when lords of creation show any signs of subjection.

'Where did you learn all this sort of thing?' he asked, with a quizzical look.

'As "this sort of thing" is rather a vague expression, would you kindly explain?' returned Amy, knowing perfectly well what he meant, but wickedly leaving him to describe what is indescribable.

'Well – the general air, the style, the self-possession, the – the – illusion – you know,' laughed Laurie, breaking down, and helping himself out of his quandary with the new word.

Amy was gratified, but, of course, didn't show it, and demurely answered, 'Foreign life polishes one in spite of one's self; I study as well as play; and as for this' – with a little gesture towards her dress – 'why, tulle is cheap, posies to be had for nothing, and I am used to making the most of my poor little things.'

Amy rather regretted that last sentence, fearing it wasn't in good taste; but Laurie liked her the better for it, and found himself both admiring and respecting the brave patience that made the most of opportunity, and the cheerful spirit that covered poverty with flowers. Amy did not know why he looked at her so kindly, nor why he filled up her book with his own name, and devoted himself to her for the rest of the evening, in the most delightful manner; but the impulse that wrought this agreeable change was the result of one of the new impressions which both of them were unconsciously giving and receiving.

15

On the Shelf

In France the young girls have a dull time of it till they are married, when 'Vive la liberté' becomes their motto. In America, as everyone knows, girls early sign the declaration of independence, and enjoy their freedom with republican zest; but the young matrons usually abdicate with the first heir to the throne, and go into a seclusion almost as close as a French nunnery, though by no means as quiet. Whether they like it or not, they are virtually put upon the shelf as soon as the wedding excitement is over, and most of them might exclaim, as did a very pretty woman the other day, 'I'm as handsome as ever, but no one takes any notice of me because I'm married.'

Not being a belle or even a fashionable lady, Meg did not experience this affliction till her babies were a year old, for in her little world primitive customs prevailed, and she found herself more admired and beloved than ever.

As she was a womanly little woman, the maternal instinct was very strong, and she was entirely absorbed in her children, to the utter exclusion of everything and everybody else. Day and night she brooded over them with tireless devotion and anxiety, leaving John to the tender mercies of the help, for an Irish lady now presided over the kitchen department. Being a domestic man, John decidedly missed the wifely attentions he had been accustomed to receive; but, as he adored his babies, he cheerfully relinquished his comfort for a time, supposing, with masculine ignorance, that peace would soon be restored. But three months passed, and there was no return of repose; Meg looked worn and nervous, the babies absorbed every minute of her time, the house was neglected, and Kitty, the cook, who took life 'aisy', kept him on short commons. When he went out in the morning he was bewildered by small commissions for the captive mamma; if he came gaily in at night, eager to embrace his family, he was quenched by a 'Hush! they are just asleep after worrying all day.' If he proposed a little amusement at home, 'No, it would disturb the babies.' If he hinted at a lecture or concert, he was answered with a reproachful look, and a decided 'Leave my children for pleasure, never!' His sleep was broken by infant wails and visions of a phantom figure pacing noiselessly to and fro in the watches of the night; his meals were interrupted by the frequent flight of the presiding genius, who deserted him, half helped, if a muffled chirp sounded from the nest above; and when he read his paper of an evening, Demi's colic got into the shipping-list, and Daisy's fall affected the price of stocks, for Mrs Brooke was only interested in domestic news.

The poor man was very uncomfortable, for the children had bereft him of his wife; home was merely a nursery, and the perpetual 'hushing' made him feel like a brutal intruder whenever he entered the secret precincts of Babyland. He bore it very patiently for six months, and, when no signs of amendment appeared, he did what other paternal exiles do – tried to get a little comfort elsewhere. Scott had married and gone to housekeeping not far off, and John fell into the way of running over for an hour or two of an evening, when his own parlour was empty, and his own wife singing lullabies that seemed to have no end. Mrs Scott was a lively, pretty girl, with nothing to do but be agreeable, and she performed her mission most successfully. The parlour was always bright and attractive, the chess-board ready, the piano in tune, plenty of gay gossip, and a nice little supper set forth in tempting style.

John would have preferred his own fireside if it had not been so lonely; but as it was, he gratefully took the next best thing, and enjoyed his neighbour's society.

Meg rather approved of the new arrangement at first, and found it a relief to know that John was having a good time instead of dozing in the parlour, or tramping about the house and waking the children. But by and by, when the teething worry was over, and the idols went to sleep at proper hours, leaving Mamma time to rest, she began to miss John, and find her work-basket dull company, when he was not sitting opposite in his old dressing-gown, comfortably scorching his slippers on the fender. She would not ask him to stay at home, but felt injured because he did not know that she wanted him without being told, entirely forgetting the many evenings he had waited for her in vain. She was nervous and worn out with watching and worry, and in that unreasonable frame of mind which the best of mothers occasionally experience when domestic cares oppress them. Want of exercise robs them of cheerfulness, and too much devotion to that idol of American women, the teapot, makes them feel as if they were all nerve and no muscle.

'Yes,' she would say, looking in the glass, 'I'm getting old and ugly; John doesn't find me interesting any longer, so he leaves his faded wife and goes to see his pretty neighbour, who has no incumbrances. Well, the babies love me; they don't care if I am thin and pale, and haven't time to crimp my hair; they are my comfort, and some day John will see what I've gladly sacrificed for them, won't he, my precious?'

To which pathetic appeal Daisy would answer with a coo, or Demi with a crow, and Meg would put by her lamentations for a maternal revel, which soothed her solitude for the time being. But the pain increased as politics absorbed John, who was always running over to discuss interesting points with Scott, quite unconscious that Meg missed him. Not a word did she say, however, till her mother found her in tears one day, and insisted on knowing what the matter was, for Meg's drooping spirits had not escaped her observation.

'I wouldn't tell anyone except you, Mother; but I really do need advice, for, if John goes on so much longer I might as well be widowed,' replied Mrs Brooke, drying her tears on Daisy's bib, with an injured air.

'Goes on how, my dear?' asked her mother anxiously.

'He's away all day, and at night, when I want to see him, he is continually going over to the Scotts'. It isn't fair that I should have the hardest work, and never any amusement. Men are very selfish, even the best of them.'

'So are women; don't blame John till you see where you are wrong yourself.'

'But it can't be right for him to neglect me.'

'Don't you neglect him?'

'Why, Mother, I thought you'd take my part!'

'So I do, as far as sympathizing goes; but I think the fault is yours, Meg.'

'I don't see how.'

'Let me show you. Did John ever neglect you, as you call it, while you made it a point to give him your society of an evening, his only leisure time?'

'No; but I can't do it now, with two babies to tend.'

'I think you could, dear; and I think you ought. May I

speak quite freely, and will you remember that it's Mother who blames as well as Mother who sympathizes?'

'Indeed I will! Speak to me as if I were little Meg again. I often feel as if I need teaching more than ever since these babies look to me for everything.'

Meg drew her low chair beside her mother's, and, with a little interruption in either lap, the two women rocked and talked lovingly together, feeling that the tie of mother-hood made them more one than ever.

'You have only made the mistake that most young wives make – forgotten your duty to your husband in your love for your children. A very natural and forgivable mistake, Meg, but one that had better be remedied before you take to different ways; for children should draw you nearer than ever, not separate you, as if they were all yours, and John had nothing to do but support them. I've seen it for some weeks, but have not spoken, feeling sure it would come right in time.'

'I'm afraid it won't. If I ask him to stay, he'll think I'm jealous; and I wouldn't insult him by such an idea. He doesn't see that I want him, and I don't know how to tell him without words.'

'Make it so pleasant he won't want to go away. My dear, he's longing for his little home; but it isn't home without you, and you are always in the nursery.'

'Oughtn't I to be there?'

'Not all the time; too much confinement makes you

nervous, and then you are unfitted for everything. Besides, you owe something to John as well as to the babies; don't neglect husband for children, don't shut him out of the nursery, but teach him how to help in it. His place is there as well as yours, and the children need him; let him feel that he has his part to do, and he will do it gladly and faithfully, and it will be better for you all.'

'You really think so, Mother?'

'I know it, Meg, for I've tried it; and I seldom give advice unless I've proved its practicability. When you and Jo were little, I went on just as you are, feeling as if I didn't do my duty unless I devoted myself wholly to you. Poor Father took to his books, after I had refused all offers of help, and left me to try my experiment alone. I struggled along as well as I could, but Jo was too much for me. I nearly spoilt her by indulgence. You were poorly, and I worried about you till I fell sick myself. Then Father came to the rescue, quietly managed everything, and made himself so helpful that I saw my mistake, and never have been able to get on without him since. That is the secret of our home happiness: he does not let business wean him from the little cares and duties that affect us all, and I try not to let domestic worries destroy my interest in his pursuits. Each do our part alone in many things, but at home we work together, always.'

'It is so, Mother; and my great wish is to be to my

husband and children what you have been to yours. Show me how; I'll do anything you say.'

'You always were my docile daughter. Well, dear, if I were you, I'd let John have more to do with the management of Demi, for the boy needs training, and it's none too soon to begin. Then I'd do what I have often proposed, let Hannah come and help you; she is a capital nurse, and you may trust the precious babies to her while you do more housework. You need the exercise, Hannah would enjoy the rest, and John would find his wife again. Go out more; keep cheerful as well as busy, for you are the sunshine-maker of the family, and if you get dismal there is no fair weather. Then I'd try to take an interest in whatever John likes – talk with him, let him read to you, exchange ideas, and help each other in that way. Don't shut yourself up in a bandbox because you are a woman, but understand what is going on, and educate yourself to take your part in the world's work, for it all affects you and yours.'

'John is so sensible, I'm afraid he will think I'm stupid if I ask questions about politics and things.'

'I don't believe he would; love covers a multitude of sins, and of whom could you ask more freely than of him? Try it, and see if he doesn't find your society far more agreeable than Mrs Scott's suppers.'

'I will. Poor John! I'm afraid I *have* neglected him sadly, but I thought I was right, and he never said anything.'

'He tried not to be selfish, but he *has* felt rather forlorn, I fancy. This is just the time, Meg, when young married people are apt to grow apart, and the very time when they ought to be most together; for the first tenderness soon wears off, unless care is taken to preserve it; and no time is so beautiful and precious to parents as the first years of the little lives given them to train. Don't let John be a stranger to the babies, for they will do more to keep him safe and happy in this world of trial and temptation than anything else, and through them you will learn to know and love one another as you should. Now, dear, goodbye; think over Mother's preachment, act upon it if it seems good, and God bless you all!'

Meg did think it over, found it good, and acted upon it, though the first attempt was not made exactly as she planned to have it. Of course the children tyrannized over her, and ruled the house as soon as they found out that kicking and squalling brought them whatever they wanted. Mamma was an abject slave to their caprices, but Papa was not so easily subjugated, and occasionally afflicted his tender spouse by an attempt at paternal discipline with his obstreperous son. For Demi inherited a trifle of his sire's firmness of character – we won't call it obstinacy – and when he made up his little mind to have or to do anything, all the king's horses and all the king's men could not change that pertinacious little mind. Mamma thought the dear too young to be taught to conquer his prejudices, but Papa believed that it never was too soon to learn obedience; so Master Demi early discovered that when he undertook to 'wrastle' with 'Parpar', he always got the worst of it; yet, like the Englishman, Baby respected the man who conquered him, and loved the father whose grave 'No, no', was more impressive than all Mamma's love pats.

A few days after the talk with her mother, Meg resolved to try a social evening with John; so she ordered a nice supper, set the parlour in order, dressed herself prettily, and put the children to bed early, that nothing should interfere with her experiment. But, unfortunately, Demi's most unconquerable prejudice was against going to bed, and that night he decided to go on a rampage; so poor Meg sung and rocked, told stories, and tried every sleep-provoking wile she could devise, but all in vain, the big eyes wouldn't shut and long after Daisy had gone to byelow, like the chubby little bunch of good-nature she was, naughty Demi lay staring at the light, with the most discouragingly wide-awake expression of countenance.

'Will Demi lie still like a good boy, while Mamma runs down and gives poor Papa his tea?' asked Meg, as the hall door softly closed, and the well-known step went tiptoeing into the dining room.

'Me has tea!' said Demi, preparing to join in the revel.

'No; but I'll save you some little cakies for breakfast, if you'll go bye-bye like Daisy. Will you, lovey?'

'Iss!' and Demi shut his eyes tight, as if to catch sleep and hurry the desired day.

Taking advantage of the propitious moment, Meg slipped away, and ran down to greet her husband with a smiling face, and the little blue bow in her hair which was his especial admiration. He saw it at once, and said, with pleased surprise:

'Why, little mother, how gay we are tonight. Do you expect company?'

'Only you, dear.'

'Is it a birthday, anniversary, or anything?'

'No; I'm tired of being a dowdy, so I dressed up as a change. You always make yourself nice for table, no matter how tired you are; so why shouldn't I when I have the time?'

'I do it out of respect to you, my dear,' said old-fashioned John.

'Ditto, ditto, Mr Brooke,' laughed Meg, looking young and pretty again, as she nodded to him over the teapot.

'Well, it's altogether delightful, and like old times. This tastes right. I drink your health, dear.' And John sipped his tea with an air of reposeful rapture, which was of very short duration, however; for, as he put down his cup, the door handle rattled mysteriously, and a little voice was heard, saying impatiently:

'Opy doy; me's tummin!'

'It's that naughty boy. I told him to go to sleep alone,

and here he is, downstairs, getting his death a-cold pattering over that canvas,' said Meg, answering the call.

'Morning now,' announced Demi, in a joyful tone, as he entered, with his long night-gown gracefully festooned over his arm, and every curl bobbing gaily as he pranced about the table, eyeing the 'cakies' with loving glances.

'No, it isn't morning yet. You must go to bed, and not trouble poor Mamma; then you can have the little cake with sugar on it.'

'Me loves Parpar,' said the artful one, preparing to climb the paternal knee, and revel in forbidden joys. But John shook his head, and said to Meg:

'If you told him to stay up there, and go to sleep alone, make him do it, or he will never learn to mind you.'

'Yes, of course. Come, Demi'; and Meg led her son away, feeling a strong desire to spank the little marplot who hopped beside her, labouring under the delusion that the bribe was to be administered as soon as they reached the nursery.

Nor was he disappointed; for that short-sighted woman actually gave him a lump of sugar, tucked him into his bed, and forbade any more promenades till morning.

'Iss!' said Demi the perjured, blissfully sucking his sugar, and regarding his first attempt as eminently successful.

Meg returned to her place, and supper was progressing pleasantly, when the little ghost walked again, and exposed the maternal delinquencies by boldly demanding:

'More sudar, Marmar.'

'Now this won't do,' said John, hardening his heart against the engaging little sinner. 'We shall never know any peace till that child learns to go to bed properly. You have made a slave of yourself long enough; give him one lesson, and then there will be an end of it. Put him in his bed and leave him, Meg.'

'He won't stay there; he never does, unless I sit by him.'

'I'll manage him. Demi, go upstairs, and get into your bed, as Mamma bids you.'

'S'ant!' replied the young rebel, helping himself to the coveted 'cakie', and beginning to eat the same with calm audacity.

'You must never say that to Papa; I shall carry you if you don't go yourself.'

'Go 'way; me don't love Parpar'; and Demi retired to his mother's skirts for protection.

But even that refuge proved unavailing, for he was delivered over to the enemy, with a 'Be gentle with him, John,' which struck the culprit with dismay; for when Mamma deserted him, then the judgement day was at hand. Bereft of his cake, defrauded of his frolic, and borne away by a strong hand to that detested bed, poor Demi could not restrain his wrath, but openly defied Papa, and kicked and screamed lustily all the way upstairs. The minute he was put into bed on one side, he rolled out on the other, and made for the door, only to be ignominiously caught up by the tail of his little toga, and put back again, which lively performance was kept up till the young man's strength gave out, when he devoted himself to roaring at the top of his voice. This vocal exercise usually conquered Meg; but John sat as unmoved as the post which is popularly believed to be deaf. No coaxing, no sugar, no lullaby, no story; even the light was put out, and only the red glow of the fire enlivened the 'big dark' which Demi regarded with curiosity rather than fear. This new order of things disgusted him, and he howled dismally for 'Marmar', as his angry passions subsided, and recollections of his tender bondwoman returned to the captive autocrat. The plaintive wail which succeeded the passionate roar went to Meg's heart, and she ran up to say beseechingly:

'Let me stay with him; he'll be good, now, John.'

'No, my dear, I've told him he must go to sleep, as you bid him; and he must, if I stay here all night.'

'But he'll cry himself sick,' pleaded Meg, reproaching herself for deserting her boy.

'No, he won't, he's so tired he will soon drop off, and then the matter is settled; for he will understand that he has got to mind. Don't interfere; I'll manage him.'

'He's my child, and I can't have his spirit broken by harshness.'

'He's my child, and I won't have his temper spoilt by indulgence. Go down, my dear, and leave the boy to me.'

When John spoke in that masterful tone, Meg always obeyed, and never regretted her docility.

'Please let me kiss him once, John?'

'Certainly. Demi, say "goodnight" to Mamma, and let her go and rest, for she is very tired with taking care of you all day.'

Meg always insisted upon it that the kiss won the victory; for after it was given, Demi sobbed more quietly, and lay quite still at the bottom of the bed, whither he had wriggled in his anguish of mind.

'Poor little man, he's worn out with sleep and crying. I'll cover him up, and then go and set Meg's heart at rest,' thought John, creeping to the bedside, hoping to find his rebellious heir asleep.

But he wasn't; for the moment his father peeped at him, Demi's eyes opened, his little chin began to quiver, and he put up his arms, saying, with a penitent hiccough, 'Me's dood, now.'

Sitting on the stairs, outside, Meg wondered at the long silence which followed the uproar; and, after imagining all sorts of impossible accidents, she slipped into the room, to set her fears at rest. Demi lay fast asleep; not in his usual spread-eagle attitude, but in a subdued bunch, cuddled close in the circle of his father's arm and holding his father's finger as if he felt that justice was tempered with mercy, and had gone to sleep a sadder and a wiser baby. So held, John had waited with womanly patience till the little hand relaxed its hold; and, while waiting, had fallen asleep, more tired by that tussle with his son than with his whole day's work.

As Meg stood watching the two faces on the pillow, she smiled to herself, and then slipped away again, saying, in a satisfied tone:

'I never need fear that John will be too harsh with my babies: he *does* know how to manage them, and will be a great help, for Demi is getting too much for me.'

When John came down at last, expecting to find a pensive or reproachful wife, he was agreeably surprised to find Meg placidly trimming a bonnet, and to be greeted with the request to read something about the election, if he was not too tired. John saw in a minute that a revolution of some kind was going on, but wisely asked no questions, knowing that Meg was such a transparent little person, she couldn't keep a secret to save her life, and therefore the clue would soon appear. He read a long debate with the most amiable readiness, and then explained it in his most lucid manner, while Meg tried to look deeply interested, to ask intelligent questions, and keep her thoughts from wandering from the state of the nation to the state of her bonnet. In her secret soul, however, she decided that politics were as bad as mathematics, and that the mission of politicians seemed to be calling each other names; but she kept these feminine ideas to herself, and when John paused, shook her head, and said with what she thought diplomatic ambiguity:

'Well, I really don't see what we are coming to.'

John laughed, and watched her for a minute, as she poised a pretty little preparation of lace and flowers on her hand, and regarded it with the genuine interest which his harangue had failed to waken.

'She is trying to like politics for my sake, so I'll try and like millinery for hers, that's only fair,' thought John the Just, adding aloud:

'That's very pretty; is it what you call a breakfast cap?'

'My dear man, it's a bonnet! My very best go-to-concert-and-theatre bonnet.'

'I beg your pardon; it was so small, I naturally mistook it for one of the fly-away things you sometimes wear. How do you keep it on?'

'These bits of lace are fastened under the chin with a rosebud, so'; and Meg illustrated by putting on the bonnet, and regarding him with an air of calm satisfaction that was irresistible.

'It's a love of a bonnet, but I prefer the face inside, for it looks young and happy again,' and John kissed the smiling face, to the great detriment of the rosebud under the chin.

'I'm glad you like it, for I want you to take me to one of the new concerts some night; I really need some music to put me in tune. Will you, please?'

'Of course I will, with all my heart, or anywhere else you like. You have been shut up so long, it will do you no end of good, and I shall enjoy it, of all things. What put it into your head, little mother?'

'Well, I had a talk with Marmee the other day, and told her how nervous and cross and out of sorts I felt, and she said I needed change and less care; so Hannah is to help me with the children, and I'm to see to things about the house more, and now and then have a little fun, just to keep me from getting to be a fidgety, broken-down old woman before my time. It's only an experiment, John, and I want to try it for your sake as much as for mine, because I've neglected you shamefully lately, and I'm going to make home what it used to be, if I can. You don't object, I hope?'

Never mind what John said, or what a very narrow escape the little bonnet had from utter ruin; all that we have any business to know, is that John did *not* appear to object, judging from the changes which gradually took place in the house and its inmates. It was not all paradise by any means, but everyone was better for the division of labour system; the children throve under the paternal rule, for accurate, steadfast John brought order and obedience into Babydom, while Meg recovered her spirits and composed her nerves by plenty of wholesome exercise, a little pleasure, and much confidential conversation with her sensible husband. Home grew home-like again, and John had no wish to leave it, unless he took Meg with him. The Scotts came to the Brookes' now, and everyone found the little house a cheerful place, full of happiness, content, and family love. Even gay Sallie Moffat liked to go there. 'It is always so quiet and pleasant here; it does me good, Meg,' she used to say, looking about her with wistful eyes, as if trying to discover the charm, that she might use it in her great house, full of splendid loneliness; for there were no riotous, sunny-faced babies there, and Ned lived in a world of his own, where there was no place for her.

This household happiness did not come all at once, but John and Meg had found the key to it, and each year of married life taught them how to use it, unlocking the treasuries of real home-love and mutual helpfulness, which the poorest may possess, and the richest cannot buy. This is the sort of shelf on which young wives and mothers may consent to be laid, safe from the restless fret and fever of the world, finding loyal lovers in the little sons and daughters who cling to them, undaunted by sorrow, poverty, or age; walking side by side, through fair and stormy weather, with a faithful friend, who is, in the true sense of the good old Saxon word, the 'houseband', and learning, as Meg learned, that a woman's happiest kingdom is home, her highest honour the art of ruling it, not as a queen, but a wise wife and mother.

16

Lazy Laurence

Laurie went to Nice intending to stay a week, and remained a month. He was tired of wandering about alone, and Amy's familiar presence seemed to give a home-like charm to the foreign scenes in which she bore a part. He rather missed the 'petting' he used to receive, and enjoyed a taste of it again; for no attentions, however flattering, from strangers, were half so pleasant as the sisterly adoration of the girls at home. Amy never would pet him like the others, but she was very glad to see him now, and quite clung to him, feeling that he was the representative of the dear family for whom she longed more than she would confess. They naturally took comfort in each other's society, and were much together, riding, walking, dancing, or dawdling, for, at Nice, no one can be very industrious during the gay season. But, while apparently amusing themselves in the most careless fashion, they were half consciously making discoveries and forming opinions about each other. Amy rose daily in the estimation of her friend, but he sunk in hers, and each felt the truth before a word was spoken. Amy tried to please, and succeeded, for she was grateful for the many pleasures he gave her, and repaid him with the little services to which womanly women know how to lend an indescribable charm. Laurie made no effort of any kind, but just let himself drift along as comfortably as possible, trying to forget, and feeling that all women owed him a kind word because one had been cold to him. It cost him no effort to be generous, and he would have given Amy all the trinkets in Nice if she would have taken them; but, at the same time, he felt that he could not change the opinion she was forming of him, and he rather dreaded the keen blue eyes that seemed to watch him with such half-sorrowful, half-scornful surprise.

'All the rest have gone to Monaco for the day; I preferred to stay at home and write letters. They are done now, and I am going to Valrosa to sketch; will you come?' said Amy, as she joined Laurie one lovely day when he lounged in as usual, about noon.

'Well, yes; but isn't it rather warm for such a long walk?' he answered slowly, for the shaded *salon* looked inviting, after the glare without.

'I'm going to have the little carriage, and Baptiste can drive, so you'll have nothing to do but hold your umbrella and keep your gloves nice,' returned Amy, with a sarcastic glance at the immaculate kids, which were a weak point with Laurie.

'Then I'll go with pleasure'; and he put out his hand for her sketchbook. But she tucked it under her arm with a sharp –

'Don't trouble yourself; it's no exertion to me, but *you* don't look equal to it.'

Laurie lifted his eyebrows, and followed at a leisurely pace as she ran downstairs; but when they got into the carriage he took the reins himself, and left little Baptiste nothing to do but fold his arms and fall asleep on his perch.

The two never quarrelled – Amy was too well bred, and just now Laurie was too lazy; so, in a minute he peeped under her hat brim with an enquiring air; she answered with a smile, and they went on together in the most amicable manner.

It was a lovely drive, along winding roads rich in the picturesque scenes that delight beauty-loving eyes. Here an ancient monastery, whence the solemn chanting of the monks came down to them. There a bare-legged shepherd, in wooden shoes, pointed hat, and rough jacket over one shoulder, sat piping on a stone, while his goats skipped among the rocks or lay at his feet. Meek, mouse-coloured donkeys, laden with panniers of freshly cut grass, passed by, with a pretty girl in a *capaline* sitting between the green piles, or an old woman spinning with a distaff as she went. Brown, soft-eyed children ran out from the quaint stone hovels to offer nosegays, or bunches of oranges still on the bough. Gnarled olive trees covered the hills with their dusky foliage, fruit hung golden in the orchard, and great scarlet anemones fringed the roadside; while beyond green slopes and craggy heights, the Maritime Alps rose sharp and white against the blue Italian sky.

Valrosa well deserved its name, for, in that climate of perpetual summer, roses blossomed everywhere. They over-hung the archway, thrust themselves between the bars of the great gate with a sweet welcome to passers-by, and lined the avenue, winding through lemon-trees and feathery palms up to the villa on the hill. Every shadowy nook, where seats invited one to stop and rest, was a mass of bloom; every cool grotto had its marble nymph smiling from a veil of flowers, and every fountain reflected crimson, white, or pale pink roses, leaning down to smile at their own beauty. Roses covered the walls of the house, draped the cornices, climbed the pillars, and ran riot over the balustrade of the wide terrace, whence one looked down on the sunny Mediterranean, and the white-walled city on its shore.

'This is a regular honeymoon paradise, isn't it? Did you ever see such roses?' asked Amy, pausing on the terrace to enjoy the view and a luxurious whiff of perfume that came wandering by.

'No, nor felt such thorns,' returned Laurie, with his thumb in his mouth, after a vain attempt to capture a solitary scarlet flower that grew just beyond his reach.

'Try lower down, and pick those that have no thorns,' said Amy, gathering three of the tiny cream-coloured ones that starred the wall behind her. She put them in his buttonhole, as a peace offering, and he stood a minute looking down at them with a curious expression, for in the Italian part of his nature there was a touch of super-stition, and he was just then in that state of half-sweet, half-bitter melancholy, when imaginative young men find significance in trifles, and food for romance everywhere. He had thought of Jo in reaching after the thorny red rose, for vivid flowers became her, and she had often worn ones like that from the greenhouse at home. The pale roses Amy gave him were the sort that the Italians lay in dead hands, never in bridal wreaths, and, for a moment, he wondered if the omen was for Jo or for himself; but the next instant his American common sense got the better of sentimentality, and he laughed a heartier laugh than Amy had heard since he came.

'It's good advice; you'd better take it and save your fingers,' she said, thinking her speech amused him.

'Thank you, I will,' he answered in jest, and a few months later he did it in earnest.

'Laurie, when are you going to your grandfather?' she asked presently, as she settled herself on a rustic seat.

'Very soon.'

'You have said that a dozen times within the last three weeks.'

'I dare say; short answers save trouble.'

'He expects you, and you really ought to go.'

'Hospitable creature! I know it.'

'Then why don't you do it?'

'Natural depravity, I suppose.'

'Natural indolence, you mean. It's really dreadful!' and Amy looked severe.

'Not as bad as it seems, for I should only plague him if I went, so I might as well stay, and plague you a little longer, you can bear it better; in fact, I think it agrees with you excellently'; and Laurie composed himself for a lounge on the broad ledge of the balustrade.

Amy shook her head, and opened her sketch-book with an air of resignation; but she had made up her mind to lecture 'that boy', and in a minute she began again.

'What are you doing just now?'

'Watching lizards.'

'No, no; I mean what do you intend and wish to do?'

'Smoke a cigarette, if you'll allow me.'

'How provoking you are! I don't approve of cigars, and I will only allow it on condition that you let me put you into my sketch; I need a figure.'

'With all the pleasure in life. How will you have me – full-length or three-quarters, on my head or my heels? I should respectfully suggest a recumbent posture, then put yourself in also, and call it "Dolce far niente".'

'Stay as you are, and go to sleep if you like. *I* intend to work hard,' said Amy, in her most energetic tone.

'What delightful enthusiasm!' and he leaned against a tall urn with an air of entire satisfaction.

'What would Jo say if she saw you now?' asked Amy impatiently, hoping to stir him up by the mention of her still more energetic sister's name.

'As usual, "Go away, Teddy, I'm busy!"' He laughed as he spoke, but the laugh was not natural, and a shade passed over his face, for the utterance of the familiar name touched the wound that was not healed yet. Both tone and shadow struck Amy, for she had seen and heard them before, and now she looked up in time to catch a new expression on Laurie's face – a hard, bitter look, full of pain, dissatisfaction, and regret. It was gone before she could study it, and the listless expression back again. She watched him for a moment with artistic pleasure, thinking how like an Italian he looked, as he lay basking in the sun with uncovered head, and eyes full of southern dreaminess; for he seemed to have forgotten her, and fallen into a reverie.

'You look like the effigy of a young knight asleep on his tomb,' she said, carefully tracing the well-cut profile defined against the dark stone.

'Wish I was!'

'That's a foolish wish, unless you have spoilt your life. You are so changed, I sometimes think –' There Amy stopped, with a half-timid, half-wistful look, more significant than her unfinished speech.

Laurie saw and understood the affectionate anxiety which she hesitated to express, and looking straight into her eyes, said, just as he used to say it to her mother:

'It's all right, ma'am.'

That satisfied her and set at rest the doubts that had begun to worry her lately. It also touched her, and she showed that it did, by the cordial tone in which she said:

'I'm glad of that! I didn't think you'd been a very bad boy, but I fancied you might have wasted money at that wicked Baden-Baden, lost your heart to some charming Frenchwoman with a husband, or got into some of the scrapes that young men seem to consider a necessary part of a foreign tour. Don't stay out there in the sun; come and lie on the grass here, and "let us be friendly," as Jo used to say when we got in the sofa corner and told secrets.'

Laurie obediently threw himself down on the turf, and began to amuse himself by sticking daisies into the ribbons of Amy's hat, that lay there.

'I'm all ready for the secrets'; and he glanced up with a decided expression of interest in his eyes.

'I've none to tell; you may begin.'

'Haven't one to bless myself with. I thought perhaps you'd had some news from home.'

'You have heard all that has come lately. Don't you hear often? I fancied Jo would send you volumes.'

'She's very busy; I'm roving about so, it's impossible to be regular, you know. When do you begin your great work of art, Raphaella?' he asked, changing the subject abruptly after another pause, in which he had been wondering if Amy knew his secret, and wanted to talk about it.

'Never,' she answered, with a despondent but decided air. 'Rome took all the vanity out of me; for after seeing the wonders there, I felt too insignificant to live, and gave up all my foolish hopes in despair.'

'Why should you, with so much energy and talent?'

'That's just why – because talent isn't genius, and no amount of energy can make it so. I want to be great, or nothing. I won't be a commonplace dauber, so I don't intend to try any more.'

'And what are you going to do with yourself now, if I may ask?'

'Polish up my other talents, and be an ornament to society, if I get the chance.'

It was a characteristic speech, and sounded daring; but audacity becomes young people, and Amy's ambition had a good foundation. Laurie smiled, but he liked the spirit with which she took up a new purpose when a long-cherished one died, and spent no time lamenting.

'Good! and here is where Fred Vaughn comes in, I fancy.'

Amy preserved a discreet silence, but there was a

conscious look in her downcast face, and made Laurie sit up and say gravely:

'Now I'm going to play brother, and ask questions. May I?'

'I don't promise to answer.'

'Your face will, if your tongue won't. You aren't woman of the world enough yet to hide your feelings, my dear. I heard rumours about Fred and you last year, and it's my private opinion that, if he had not been called home so suddenly and detained so long, something would have come of it – hey?'

'That's not for me to say,' was Amy's prim reply; but her lips would smile, and there was a traitorous sparkle of the eye, which betrayed that she knew her power and enjoyed the knowledge.

'You are not engaged, I hope?' and Laurie looked very elder brotherly and grave all of a sudden.

'No.'

'But you will be, if he comes back and goes properly down upon his knees, won't you?'

'Very likely.'

'Then you are fond of old Fred?'

'I could be, if I tried.'

'But you don't intend to try till the proper moment? Bless my soul, what unearthly prudence! He's a good fellow, Amy, but not the man I fancied you'd like.'

'He is rich, a gentleman, and has delightful manners,'

began Amy, trying to be quite cool and dignified, but feeling a little ashamed of herself, in spite of the sincerity of her intentions.

'I understand; queens of society can't get on without money, so you mean to make a good match, and start in that way? Quite right and proper, as the world goes, but it sounds odd from the lips of one of your mother's girls.'

'True, nevertheless.'

A short speech, but the quiet decision with which it was uttered contrasted curiously with the young speaker. Laurie felt this instinctively, and laid himself down again, with a sense of disappointment which he could not explain. His look and silence, as well as a certain inward self-disapproval, ruffled Amy, and made her resolve to deliver her lecture without delay.

'I wish you'd do me the favour to rouse yourself a little,' she said sharply.

'Do it for me, there's a dear girl.'

'I could, if I tried'; and she looked as if she would like doing it in the most summary style.

'Try, then; I give you leave,' returned Laurie, who enjoyed having someone to tease, after his long abstinence from his favourite pastime.

'You'd be angry in five minutes.'

'I'm never angry with you. It takes two flints to make a fire: you are as cool and soft as snow.'

'You don't know what I can do; snow produces a glow

and a tingle, if applied rightly. Your indifference is half affectation, and a good stirring up would prove it.'

'Stir away; it won't hurt me and it may amuse you, as the big man said when his little wife beat him. Regard me in the light of a husband or a carpet, and beat till you are tired, if that sort of exercise agrees with you.'

Being decidedly nettled herself, and longing to see him shake off the apathy that so altered him, Amy sharpened both tongue and pencil, and began:

'Flo and I have got a new name for you; it's "Lazy Laurence". How do you like it?'

She thought it would annoy him; but he only folded his arms under his head, with an imperturbable 'That's not bad. Thank you, ladies.'

'Do you want to know what I honestly think of you?'

'Pining to be told.'

'Well, I despise you.'

If she had even said 'I hate you,' in a petulant or coquettish tone, he would have laughed, and rather liked it; but the grave, almost sad, accent of her voice made him open his eyes, and ask quickly:

'Why, if you please?'

'Because, with every chance for being good, useful, and happy, you are faulty, lazy, and miserable.'

'Strong language, mademoiselle.'

'If you like it, I'll go on.'

'Pray, do; it's quite interesting.'

'I thought you'd find it so; selfish people always like to talk about themselves.'

'Am *I* selfish?' The question slipped out involuntarily and in a tone of surprise, for the one virtue on which he prided himself was generosity.

'Yes, very selfish,' continued Amy, in a calm, cool voice, twice as effective, just then, as an angry one. 'I'll show you how, for I've studied you while we have been frolicking, and I'm not at all satisfied with you. Here you have been abroad nearly six months, and done nothing but waste time and money and disappoint your friends.'

'Isn't a fellow to have any pleasure after a four years' grind?'

'You don't look as if you'd had much; at any rate, you are none the better for it, as far as I can see. I said, when we first met, that you had improved. Now I take it all back, for I don't think you half so nice as when I left you at home. You have grown abominably lazy; you like gossip, and waste time on frivolous things; you are contented to be petted and admired by silly people, instead of being loved and respected by wise ones. With money, talent, position, health, and beauty – ah, you like that, Old Vanity! but it's the truth, so I can't help saying it – with all these splendid things to use and enjoy, you can find nothing to do but dawdle; and, instead of being the man you might and ought to be, you are only –' There she stopped, with a look that had both pain and pity in it.

'Saint Laurence on a gridiron,' added Laurie, blandly finishing the sentence. But the lecture began to take effect, for there was a wide-awake sparkle in his eyes now, and a half-angry, half-injured expression replaced the former indifference.

'I supposed you'd take it so. You men tell us we are angels, and say we can make you what we will; but the instant we honestly try to do you good, you laugh at us, and won't listen, which proves how much your flattery is worth.' Amy spoke bitterly, and turned her back on the exasperating martyr at her feet.

In a minute a hand came down over the page, so that she could not draw, and Laurie's voice said, with a droll imitation of a penitent child:

'I will be good, oh, I will be good!'

But Amy did not laugh, for she was in earnest; and, tapping on the outspread hand with her pencil, said soberly:

'Aren't you ashamed of a hand like that? It's as soft and white as a woman's, and looks as if it never did anything but wear Jouvin's best gloves, and pick flowers for ladies. You are not a dandy, thank Heavens! so I'm glad to see there are no diamonds or big seal rings on it, only the little old one Jo gave you so long ago. Dear soul, I wish she was here to help me!'

'So do I!'

The hand vanished as suddenly as it came, and there

was energy enough in the echo of her wish to suit even Amy. She glanced down at him with a new thought in her mind; but he was lying with his hat half over his face, as if for shade, and his moustache hid his mouth. She only saw his chest rise and fall, with a long breath that might have been a sigh, and the hand that wore the ring nestled down into the grass, as if to hide something too precious or too tender to be spoken of. All in a minute various hints and trifles assumed shape and significance in Amy's mind, and told her what her sister never had confided to her. She remembered that Laurie never spoke voluntarily of Jo; she recalled the shadow on his face just now, the change in his character, and the wearing of the little old ring, which was no ornament to a handsome hand. Girls are quick to read such signs and feel their eloquence. Amy had fancied that perhaps a love trouble was at the bottom of the alteration, and now she was sure of it. Her keen eyes filled, and, when she spoke again, it was in a voice that could be beautifully soft and kind when she chose to make it so.

'I know I have no right to talk so to you, Laurie; and if you weren't the sweetest-tempered fellow in the world, you'd be very angry with me. But we are all so fond and proud of you, I couldn't bear to think they should be disappointed in you at home as I have been, though, perhaps, they would understand the change better than I do.'

'I think they would,' came from under the hat, in a grim tone, quite as touching as a broken one.

'They ought to have told me, and not let me go blundering and scolding, when I should have been more kind and patient than ever. I never did like that Miss Randal, and now I hate her!' said artful Amy, wishing to be sure of her facts this time.

'Hang Miss Randal!' and Laurie knocked the hat off his face with a look that left no doubt of his sentiments towards that young lady.

'I beg pardon; I thought –' And there she paused diplomatically.

'No, you didn't; you knew perfectly well I never cared for anyone but Jo.' Laurie said that in his old, impetuous tone, and turned his face away as he spoke.

'I did think so; but as they never said anything about it, and you came away, I supposed I was mistaken. And Jo wouldn't be kind to you? Why, I was sure she loved you dearly.'

'She *was* kind, but not in the right way; and it's lucky for her she didn't love me, if I'm the good-for-nothing fellow you think me. It's her fault, though, and you may tell her so.'

The hard, bitter look came back again as he said that, and it troubled Amy, for she did not know what balm to apply.

'I was wrong, I didn't know, I'm very sorry I was so

cross, but I can't help wishing you'd bear it better, Teddy, dear.'

'Don't, that's her name for me!' and Laurie put up his hand with a quick gesture to stop the words spoken in Jo's half-kind, half-reproachful tone. 'Wait till you've tried it yourself,' he added, in a low voice, as he pulled up the grass by the handful.

'I'd take it manfully, and be respected if I couldn't be loved,' said Amy, with the decision of one who knew nothing about it.

Now, Laurie flattered himself that he *had* borne it remarkably well, making no moan, asking no sympathy, and taking his trouble away to live it down alone. Amy's lecture put the matter in a new light, and for the first time it did look weak and selfish to lose heart at the first failure, and shut himself up in moody indifference. He felt as if suddenly shaken out of a pensive dream, and found it impossible to go to sleep again. Presently he sat up, and asked slowly:

'Do you think Jo would despise me as you do?'

'Yes, if she saw you now. She hates lazy people. Why don't you do something splendid, and *make* her love you?'

'I did my best, but it was no use.'

'Graduating well, you mean? That was no more than you ought to have done, for your grandfather's sake. It would have been shameful to fail after spending so much time and money, when everyone knew you *could* do well.'

'I did fail, say what you will, for Jo wouldn't love me,' began Laurie, leaning his head on his hand in a despondent attitude.

'No, you didn't, and you'll say so in the end, for it did you good, and proved that you could do something if you tried. If you'd only set about another task of some sort, you'd soon be your hearty, happy self again, and forget your trouble.'

'That's impossible.'

'Try it and see. You needn't shrug your shoulders, and think, "Much she knows about such things". I don't pretend to be wise, but I *am* observing, and I see a great deal more than you'd imagine. I'm interested in other people's experiences and inconsistencies; and, though I can't explain, I remember and use them for my own benefit. Love Jo all your days, if you choose, but don't let it spoil you, for it's wicked to throw away so many good gifts because you can't have the one you want. There, I won't lecture any more, for I know you'll wake up and be a man in spite of that hard-hearted girl.'

Neither spoke for several minutes. Laurie sat turning the little ring on his finger, and Amy put the last touches to the hasty sketch she had been working at while she talked. Presently she put it on his knee, merely saying:

'How do you like that?'

He looked and then he smiled, as he could not well help doing, for it was capitally done – the long, lazy figure on the grass, with listless face, half-shut eyes, and one hand holding a cigar, from which came the little wreath of smoke that encircled the dreamer's head.

'How well you draw!' he said, with genuine surprise and pleasure at her skill, adding, with a half-laugh:

'Yes, that's me.'

'As you are: this is as you were'; and Amy laid another sketch beside the one he held.

It was not nearly so well done, but there was a life and spirit in it which atoned for many faults, and it recalled the past so vividly that a sudden change swept over the young man's face as he looked. Only a rough sketch of Laurie taming a horse; hat and coat were off, and every line of the active figure, resolute face, and commanding attitude, was full of energy and meaning. The handsome brute, just subdued, stood arching his neck under the tightly drawn rein, with one foot impatiently pawing the ground, and ears pricked up as if listening for the voice that had mastered him. In the ruffled mane, the rider's breezy hair and erect attitude, there was a suggestion of suddenly arrested motion, of strength, courage, and youthful buoyancy, that contrasted sharply with the supine grace of the 'Dolce far niente' sketch. Laurie said nothing but, as his eye went from one to the other, Amy saw him flush up and fold his lips together as if he read and accepted the little lesson she had given him.

That satisfied her; and, without waiting for him to speak, she said, in her sprightly way:

'Don't you remember the day you played Rarey with Puck, and we all looked on? Meg and Beth were frightened, but Jo clapped and pranced, and I sat on the fence and drew you. I found that sketch in my portfolio the other day, touched it up, and kept it to show you.'

'Much obliged. You've improved immensely since then, and I congratulate you. May I venture to suggest in "a honeymoon paradise" that five o'clock is the dinner-hour at your hotel?'

Laurie rose as he spoke, returned the pictures with a smile and a bow, and looked at his watch, as if to remind her that even moral lectures should have an end. He tried to resume his former easy, indifferent air, but it *was* an affectation now, for the rousing had been more efficacious than he would confess. Amy felt the shade of coldness in his manner, and said to herself:

'Now I've offended him. Well, if it does him good, I'm glad; if it makes him hate me, I'm sorry; but it's true, and I can't take back a word of it.'

They laughed and chatted all the way home; and little Baptiste, up behind, thought that monsieur and mademoiselle were in charming spirits. But both felt ill at ease; the friendly frankness was disturbed, the sunshine had a shadow over it, and, despite their apparent gaiety, there was a secret discontent in the heart of each.

'Shall we see you this evening, *mon frère*?' asked Amy as they parted at her aunt's door.

'Unfortunately I have an engagement. Au revoir, mademoiselle,' and Laurie bent as if to kiss her hand, in the foreign fashion, which became him better than many men. Something in his face made Amy say quickly and warmly:

'No; be yourself with me, Laurie, and part in the good old way. I'd rather have a hearty English handshake than all the sentimental salutations in France.'

'Goodbye, dear,' and with these words, uttered in the tone she liked, Laurie left her, after a handshake almost painful in its heartiness.

Next morning, instead of the usual call, Amy received a note which made her smile at the beginning and sigh at the end:

My Dear Mentor, – Please make my adieux to your aunt, and exult within yourself, for 'Lazy Laurence' has gone to his grandpa, like the best of boys. A pleasant winter to you, and may the gods grant you a blissful honeymoon at Valrosa! I think Fred would be benefited by a rouser. Tell him so, with my congratulations.

Yours gratefully,
Telemachus.

'Good boy! I'm glad he's gone,' said Amy, with an approving smile; the next minute her face fell as she glanced about the empty room, adding, with an involuntary sigh:

'Yes, I *am* glad, but how I shall miss him!'

17

The Valley of the Shadow

When the first bitterness was over, the family accepted the inevitable, and tried to bear it cheerfully, helping one another by the increased affection which comes to bind households tenderly together in times of trouble. They put away their grief, and each did his or her part towards making that last year a happy one.

The pleasantest room in the house was set apart for Beth, and in it was gathered everything that she most loved – flowers, pictures, her piano, the little worktable, and the beloved pussies. Father's best books found their way there, Mother's easy chair, Jo's desk, Amy's finest sketches; and every day Meg brought her babies on a loving pilgrimage, to make sunshine for Aunty Beth. John quietly set apart a little sum, that he might enjoy the pleasure of keeping the invalid supplied with the fruit she loved and longed for; old Hannah never wearied of concocting dainty dishes to tempt a capricious appetite, dropping tears as she worked; and from across the sea came little gifts and cheerful letters, seeming to bring breaths of warmth and fragrance from lands that know no winter.

Here, cherished like a household saint in its shrine, sat Beth, tranquil and busy as ever; for nothing could change the sweet, unselfish nature, and even while preparing to leave life, she tried to make it happier for those who should remain behind. The feeble fingers were never idle, and one of her pleasures was to make little things for the school-children daily passing to and fro – to drop a pair of mittens from her window for a pair of purple hands, a needlebook for some small mother of many dolls, pen-wipers for young penmen toiling through forests of pot-hooks, scrapbooks for picture-loving eyes, and all manner of pleasant devices, till the reluctant climbers up the ladder of learning found their way strewn with flowers, as it were, and came to regard the gentle giver as a sort of fairy godmother, who sat above there, and showered down gifts miraculously suited to their tastes and needs. If Beth had wanted any reward, she found it in the bright little faces always turned up to her window, with nods and smiles, and the droll little letters which came to her, full of blots and gratitude.

The first few months were very happy ones, and Beth often used to look round, and say, 'How beautiful this is!' as they all sat together in her sunny room, the babies kicking and crowing on the floor, mother and sisters working near, and Father reading, in his pleasant voice, from the wise old books which seemed rich in good and comfortable words, as applicable now as when written centuries ago; a little chapel, where a paternal priest taught his flock the hard lessons all must learn, trying to show them that hope can comfort love, and faith make resignation possible. Simple sermons, that went straight to the souls of those who listened; for the father's heart was in the minister's religion, and the frequent falter in the voice gave a double eloquence to the words he spoke or read.

It was well for all that this peaceful time was given them as preparation for the sad hours to come; for, by and by, Beth said the needle was 'so heavy', and put it down for ever; talking wearied her, faces troubled her, pain claimed her for its own, and her tranquil spirit was sorrowfully perturbed by the ills that vexed her feeble flesh. Ah me! such heavy days, such long, long nights, such aching hearts and imploring prayers, when those who loved her best were forced to see the thin hands stretched out to them beseechingly, to hear the bitter cry, 'Help me, help me!' and to feel that there was no help. A sad eclipse of the serene soul, a sharp struggle of the young life with death; but both were mercifully brief, and then, the natural rebellion over, the old peace returned more beautiful than ever. With the wreck of her frail body, Beth's soul grew strong; and, though she said little, those about her felt that she was ready, saw that the first pilgrim called was likewise the fittest, and waited with her on the shore, trying to see the Shining Ones coming to receive her when she crossed the river.

Jo never left her for an hour since Beth had said, 'I feel stronger when you are here'. She slept on a couch in the room, waking often to renew the fire, to feed, lift, or wait upon the patient creature who seldom asked for anything, and 'tried not to be a trouble'. All day she haunted the room, jealous of any other nurse, and prouder of being chosen then than of any honour her life ever brought her. Precious and helpful hours for Jo, for now her heart received the teaching that it needed; lessons in patience were so sweetly taught her that she could not fail to learn them; charity for all, the lovely spirit that can forgive and truly forget unkindness, the loyalty to duty that makes the hardest easy, and the sincere faith that fears nothing, but trusts undoubtingly.

Often, when she woke, Jo found Beth reading in her well-worn little book, heard her singing softly, to beguile the sleepless night, or saw her lean her face upon her hands, while slow tears dropped through the transparent fingers; and Jo would lie watching her, with thoughts too deep for tears, feeling that Beth, in her simple, unselfish way, was trying to wean herself from the dear old life, and fit herself for the life to come, by sacred words of comfort, quiet prayers, and the music she loved so well.

Seeing this did more for Jo than the wisest sermons, the saintliest hymns, the most fervent prayers that any voice could utter; for, with eyes made clear by many tears, and a heart softened by the tenderest sorrow, she recognized the beauty of her sister's life – uneventful, unambitious, yet full of the genuine virtues which 'smell sweet, and blossom in the dust', the self-forgetfulness that makes the humblest on earth remembered soonest in heaven, the true success which is possible to all.

One night, when Beth looked among the books upon her table, to find something to make her forget the mortal weariness that was almost as hard to bear as pain, as she turned the leaves of her old favourite *Pilgrim's Progress*, she found a little paper, scribbled over in Jo's hand. The name caught her eye, and the blurred look of the lines made her sure that tears had fallen on it.

'Poor Jo! she's fast asleep, so I won't wake her to ask leave; she shows me all her things, and I don't think she'll mind if I look at this,' thought Beth, with a glance at her sister, who lay on the rug, with the tongs beside her, ready to wake up the minute the log fell apart.

MY BETH

> *Sitting patient in the shadow*
> *Till the blessed light shall come,*
> *A serene and saintly presence*
> *Sanctifies our troubled home.*
> *Earthly joys and hopes and sorrows*
> *Break like ripples on the strand*

Of the deep and solemn river
  Where her willing feet now stand.

O my sister, passing from me,
  Out of human care and strife,
Leave me, as a gift, those virtues
  Which have beautified your life.
Dear, bequeath me that great patience
  Which has power to sustain
A cheerful, uncomplaining spirit
  In its prison-house of pain.

Give me, for I need it sorely,
  Of that courage, wise and sweet,
Which has made the path of duty
  Green beneath your willing feet.
Give me that unselfish nature,
  That with charity divine
Can pardon wrong for love's dear sake –
  Meek heart, forgive me mine!

Thus our parting daily loseth
  Something of its bitter pain,
And while learning this hard lesson,
  My great loss becomes my gain.
For the touch of grief will render
  My wild nature more serene,

Give to life new aspirations,
    A new trust in the unseen.

Henceforth, safe across the river,
    I shall see for ever more
A beloved, household spirit
    Waiting for me on the shore.
Hope and faith, born of my sorrow,
    Guardian angels shall become,
And the sister gone before me
    By their hands shall lead me home.

Blurred and blotted, faulty and feeble, as the lines were, they brought a look of inexpressible comfort to Beth's face, for her one regret had been that she had done so little; and this seemed to assure her that her life had not been useless, that her death would not bring the despair she feared. As she sat with the paper folded between her hands, the charred log fell asunder. Jo started up, revived the blaze, and crept to the bedside, hoping Beth slept.

'Not asleep, but so happy, dear. See, I found this and read it; I knew you wouldn't care. Have I been all that to you, Jo?' she asked, with wistful, humble earnestness.

'O Beth, so much, so much!' and Jo's head went down upon the pillow, beside her sister's.

'Then I don't feel as if I'd wasted my life. I'm not so good as you make me, but I *have* tried to do right; and now, when it's too late to begin even to do better, it's such a comfort to know that someone loves me so much, and feels as if I'd helped them.'

'More than anyone in the world, Beth. I used to think I couldn't let you go; but I'm learning to feel that I don't lose you; that you'll be more to me than ever, and death can't part us, though it seems to.'

'I know it cannot, and I don't fear it any longer, for I'm sure I shall be your Beth still, to love and help you more than ever. You must take my place, Jo, and be everything to Father and Mother when I'm gone. They will turn to you, don't fail them; and if it's hard work alone, remember that I don't forget you, and that you'll be happier in doing that than writing splendid books or seeing all the world; for love is the only thing that we can carry with us when we go, and it makes the end so easy.'

'I'll try, Beth'; and then and there Jo renounced her old ambition, pledged herself to a new and better one, acknowledging the poverty of other desires, and feeling the blessed solace of a belief in the immortality of love.

So the spring days came and went, the sky grew clearer, the earth greener, the flowers were up fair and early, and the birds came back in time to say goodbye to Beth, who, like a tired but trustful child, clung to the hands that had led her all her life, as Father and Mother guided her tenderly through the Valley of the Shadow, and gave her up to God.

Seldom, except in books, do the dying utter memorable words, see visions, or depart with beatified countenances; and those who have sped many parting souls know that to most the end comes as naturally and simply as sleep. As Beth had hoped, the 'tide went out easily'; and in the dark hour before the dawn, on the bosom where she had drawn her first breath, she quietly drew her last, with no farewell but one loving look, one little sigh.

With tears and prayers and tender hands, mother and sisters made her ready for the long sleep that pain would never mar again, seeing with grateful eyes the beautiful serenity that soon replaced the pathetic patience that had wrung their hearts so long, and feeling, with reverent joy, that to their darling death was a benignant angel, not a phantom full of dread.

When morning came, for the first time in many months the fire was out, Jo's place was empty, and the room was very still. But a bird sang blithely on a budding bough, close by, the snowdrops blossomed freshly at the window, and the spring sunshine streamed in like a benediction over the placid face upon the pillow – a face so full of painless peace that those who loved it best smiled through their tears, and thanked God that Beth was well at last.

18

Learning to Forget

Amy's lecture did Laurie good, though, of course, he did not own it till long afterward; men seldom do, for when women are the advisers, the lords of creation don't take the advice till they have persuaded themselves that it is just what they intended to do; then they act upon it, and, if it succeeds, they give the weaker vessel half the credit of it; if it fails, they generously give her the whole. Laurie went back to his grandfather, and was so dutifully devoted for several weeks that the old gentleman declared the climate of Nice had improved him wonderfully, and he had better try it again. There was nothing the young gentleman would have liked better, but elephants could not have dragged him back after the scolding he had received; pride forbid, and whenever the longing grew very strong, he fortified his resolution by repeating the words that had made the deepest impression, 'I despise you'; 'Go and do something splendid that will *make* her love you'.

Laurie turned the matter over in his mind so often that

he soon brought himself to confess that he *had* been selfish and lazy; but then when a man has a great sorrow, he should be indulged in all sorts of vagaries till he has lived it down. He felt that his blighted affections were quite dead now; and, though he should never cease to be a faithful mourner, there was no occasion to wear his weeds ostentatiously. Jo *wouldn't* love him, but he might *make* her respect and admire him by doing something which should prove that a girl's 'No' had not spoilt his life. He had always meant to do something, and Amy's advice was quite unnecessary. He had only been waiting till the aforesaid blighted affections were decently interred; that being done, he felt that he was ready to 'hide his stricken heart, and still toil on'.

As Goethe, when he had a joy or a grief, put it into a song, so Laurie resolved to embalm his love-sorrow in music, and compose a requiem which should harrow up Jo's soul and melt the heart of every hearer. Therefore the next time the old gentleman found him getting restless and moody, and ordered him off, he went to Vienna, where he had musical friends, and fell to work with the firm determination to distinguish himself. But, whether the sorrow was too vast to be embodied in music, or music too ethereal to uplift a mortal woe, he soon discovered that the requiem was beyond him, just at present. It was evident that his mind was not in working order yet, and his ideas needed clarifying; for often in the middle of a plaintive strain, he would find himself humming a dancing tune that vividly recalled the Christmas ball at Nice, especially the stout Frenchman, and put an effectual stop to tragic composition for the time being.

Then he tried an opera, for nothing seemed impossible in the beginning; but here, again, unforeseen difficulties beset him. He wanted Jo for his heroine, and called upon his memory to supply him with tender recollections and romantic vision of his love. But memory turned traitor; and, as if possessed by the perverse spirit of the girl, would only recall Jo's oddities, faults, and freaks, would only show her in the most unsentimental aspects – beating mats with her head tied up in a bandanna, barricading herself with the sofa pillow, or throwing cold water over his passion *à la* Gummidge – and an irresistible laugh spoilt the pensive picture he was endeavouring to paint. Jo wouldn't be put into the opera at any price, and he had to give her up with a 'Bless that girl, what a torment she is!' and a clutch at his hair, as became a distracted composer.

When he looked about him for another and less intractable damsel to immortalize in melody, memory produced one with the most obliging readiness. This phantom wore many faces, but it always had golden hair, was enveloped in a diaphanous cloud, and floated airily before his mind's eye in a pleasing chaos of roses, peacocks, white ponies, and blue ribbons. He did not give the complacent wraith any name, but he took her for his heroine, and grew quite fond of her, as well he might; for he gifted her with every gift and grace under the sun, and escorted her, unscathed, through trials which would have annihilated any mortal woman.

Thanks to this inspiration, he got on swimmingly for a time, but gradually the work lost its charm, and he forgot to compose, while he sat musing, pen in hand, or roamed about the gay city to get new ideas and refresh his mind, which seemed to be in a somewhat unsettled state that winter. He did not do much, but he thought a great deal and was conscious of a change of some sort going on in spite of himself. 'It's genius simmering, perhaps. I'll let it simmer, and see what comes of it,' he said, with a secret suspicion, all the while, that it wasn't genius, but something far more common. Whatever it was, it simmered to some purpose, for he grew more and more discontented with his desultory life, began to long for some real and earnest work to go at, soul and body, and finally came to the wise conclusion that everyone who loved music was not a composer. Returning from one of Mozart's grand operas, splendidly performed at the Royal Theatre, he looked over his own, played a few of the best parts, sat staring up at the busts of Mendelssohn, Beethoven, and Bach, who stared benignly back again; then suddenly he tore up his music-sheets, one by one, and, as the last fluttered out of his hand, he said soberly to himself:

'She is right! Talent isn't genius, and you can't make it so. That music has taken the vanity out of me as Rome took it out of her, and I won't be a humbug any longer. Now what shall I do?'

That seemed a hard question to answer, and Laurie began to wish he had to work for his daily bread. Now, if ever, occurred an eligible opportunity for 'going to the devil', as he once forcibly expressed it, for he had plenty of money and nothing to do, and Satan is proverbially fond of providing employment for full and idle hands. The poor fellow had temptations enough from without and from within, but he withstood them pretty well; for, much as he valued liberty, he valued good faith and confidence more, so his promise to his grandfather, and his desire to be able to look honestly into the eyes of the women who loved him, and say, 'All's well', kept him safe and steady.

Very likely some Mrs Grundy will observe, 'I don't believe it; boys will be boys, young men must sow their wild oats, and women must not expect miracles'. I dare say *you* don't, Mrs Grundy, but it's true nevertheless. Women work a good many miracles, and I have a persuasion that they may perform even that of raising the standard of manhood by refusing to echo such sayings. Let the boys be boys, the longer the better, and let the young men sow their wild oats if they must; but mothers, sisters, and friends may help to make the crop a small one, and keep many tares from spoiling the harvest, by believing, and showing that they believe, in the possibility of loyalty to the virtues which make men manliest in good women's eyes. If it *is* a feminine delusion, leave us to enjoy it while we may, for without it half the beauty and the romance of life is lost, and sorrowful forebodings would embitter all our hopes of the brave, tender-hearted little lads, who still love their mothers better than themselves, and are not ashamed to own it.

Laurie thought that the task of forgetting his love for Jo would absorb all his powers for years; but, to his great surprise, he discovered it grew easier every day. He refused to believe it at first, got angry with himself, and couldn't understand it; but these hearts of ours are curious and contrary things, and time and nature work their will in spite of us. Laurie's heart *wouldn't* ache; the wound persisted in healing with a rapidity that astonished him, and, instead of trying to forget, he found himself trying to remember. He had not foreseen this turn of affairs, and was not prepared for it. He was disgusted with himself, surprised at his own fickleness, and full of a queer mixture of disappointment and relief that he could recover from such a tremendous blow so soon. He carefully stirred up the embers of his lost love, but they refused to burst into a blaze: there was only a comfortable glow that warmed and did him good without putting him into a fever, and he was reluctantly obliged to confess that the boyish

passion was slowly subsiding into a more tranquil sentiment, very tender, a little sad and resentful still, but that
was sure to pass away in time, leaving a brotherly affection
which would last unbroken to the end.

As the word 'brotherly' passed through his mind in
one of these reveries, he smiled, and glanced up at the
picture of Mozart that was before him:

'Well, he was a great man; and when he couldn't have
one sister he took the other, and was happy.'

Laurie did not utter the words, but he thought them;
and the next instant kissed the little old ring, saying to
himself:

'No, I won't! I haven't forgotten, I never can. I'll try
again, and if that fails, why, then –'

Leaving his sentence unfinished, he seized pen and
paper and wrote to Jo, telling her that he could not settle
to anything while there was the least hope of her changing
her mind. Couldn't she, wouldn't she, and let him come
home and be happy? While waiting for an answer he did
nothing, but he did it energetically, for he was in a fever
of impatience. It came at last, and settled his mind effec-
tually on one point, for Jo decidedly couldn't and wouldn't.
She was wrapped up in Beth, and never wished to hear
the word 'love' again. Then she begged him to be happy
with somebody else, but always to keep a little corner of
his heart for his loving sister Jo. In a postscript she desired
him not to tell Amy that Beth was worse; she was coming

home in the spring, and there was no need of saddening the remainder of her stay. That would be time enough, please God, but Laurie must write to her often, and not let her feel lonely, homesick, or anxious.

'So I will, at once. Poor little girl; it will be a sad going home for her, I'm afraid'; and Laurie opened his desk, as if writing to Amy had been the proper conclusion of the sentence left unfinished some weeks before.

But he did not write the letter that day; for, as he rummaged out his best paper, he came across something which changed his purpose. Tumbling about in one part of the desk, among bills, passports, and business documents of various kinds, were several of Jo's letters, and in another compartment were three notes from Amy, carefully tied up with one of her blue ribbons, and sweetly suggestive of the little dead roses put away inside. With a half-repentant, half-amused expression, Laurie gathered up all Jo's letters, smoothed, folded, and put them neatly into a small drawer of the desk, stood a minute turning the ring thoughtfully on his finger, then slowly drew it off, laid it with the letters, locked the drawer, and went out to hear High Mass at Saint Stefan's, feeling as if there had been a funeral; and, though not overwhelmed with affliction, this seemed a more proper way to spend the rest of the day than in writing letters to charming young ladies.

The letter went very soon, however, and was promptly

answered, for Amy *was* homesick, and confessed it in the most delightfully confiding manner. The correspondence flourished famously, and letters flew to and fro, with unfailing regularity, all through the early spring. Laurie sold his busts, made *allumettes* of his opera, and went back to Paris, hoping somebody would arrive before long. He wanted desperately to go to Nice, but would not till he was asked; and Amy would not ask him, for just then she was having little experiences of her own, which made her rather wish to avoid the quizzical eyes of 'our boy'.

Fred Vaughn had returned, and put the question to which she had once decided to answer 'Yes, thank you'; but now she said, 'No, thank you,' kindly but steadily; for, when the time came, her courage failed her, and she found that something more than money and position was needed to satisfy the new longing that filled her heart so full of tender hopes and fears. The words, 'Fred is a good fellow, but not at all the man I fancied you would ever like', and Laurie's face when he uttered them, kept returning to her as pertinaciously as her own did when she said in look, if not in words, 'I shall marry for money'. It troubled her to remember that now, she wished she could take it back, it sounded so unwomanly. She didn't want Laurie to think her a heartless, worldly creature; she didn't care to be a queen of society now half so much as she did to be a lovable woman; she was so glad he didn't hate her for the dreadful things she said, but took them so beautifully, and was kinder than ever. His letters were such a comfort, for the home letters were very irregular, and were not half so satisfactory as his when they did come. It was not only a pleasure, but a duty to answer them, for the poor fellow was forlorn, and needed petting, since Jo persisted in being stony-hearted. She ought to have made an effort, and tried to love him; it couldn't be very hard, many people would be proud and glad to have such a dear boy care for them; but Jo never would act like other girls, so there was nothing to do but be very kind, and treat him like a brother.

If all brothers were treated as well as Laurie was at this period, they would be a much happier race of beings than they are. Amy never lectured now; she asked his opinion on all subjects; she was interested in everything he did, made charming little presents for him, and sent him two letters a week, full of lively gossip, sisterly confidences, and captivating sketches of the lovely scenes about her. As few brothers are complimented by having their letters carried about in their sisters' pockets, read and re-read diligently, cried over when short, kissed when long, and treasured carefully, we will not hint that Amy did any of these fond and foolish things. But she certainly did grow a little pale and pensive that spring, lost much of her relish for society, and went out sketching alone a good deal. She never had much to show when she came home, but was studying nature, I dare say, while she sat for hours, with her hands folded, on the terrace at Valrosa, or absently sketched any fancy that occurred to her – a stalwart knight carved on a tomb, a young man asleep in the grass, with his hat over his eyes, or a curly-haired girl in gorgeous array, promenading down a ballroom on the arm of a tall gentleman, both faces being left a blur according to the last fashion in art, which was safe but not altogether satisfactory.

Her aunt thought that she regretted her answer to Fred; and, finding denials useless and explanations impossible, Amy left her to think what she liked, taking care that Laurie should know that Fred had gone to Egypt. That was all, but he understood it, and looked relieved, as he said to himself, with a venerable air:

'I was sure she would think better of it. Poor old fellow! I've been through it all, and I can sympathize.'

With that he heaved a great sigh, and then, as if he had discharged his duty to the past, put his feet up on the sofa, and enjoyed Amy's letter luxuriously.

While these changes were going on abroad, trouble had come at home; but the letter telling that Beth was failing never reached Amy, and when the next found her, the grass was green above her sister. The sad news met her at Vevay, for the heat had driven them from Nice in May, and they had travelled slowly to Switzerland, by way of Genoa and the Italian lakes. She bore it very well, and quietly submitted to the family decree that she should not shorten her visit, for, since it was too late to say goodbye to Beth, she had better stay, and let absence soften her sorrow. But her heart was very heavy; she longed to be at home, and every day looked wistfully across the lake, waiting for Laurie to come and comfort her.

He did come very soon; for the same mail brought letters to them both, but he was in Germany, and it took some days to reach him. The moment he read it, he packed his knapsack, bade adieu to his fellow pedestrians, and was off to keep his promise, with a heart full of joy and sorrow, hope and suspense.

He knew Vevay well; and as soon as the boat touched the little quay, he hurried along the shore to La Tour, where the Carrols were living *en pension*. The *garçon* was in despair that the whole family had gone to take a promenade on the lake; but no, the blonde mademoiselle might be in the château garden. If monsieur would give himself the pain of sitting down, a flash of time should present her. But monsieur could not wait even 'a flash of time', and, in the middle of the speech, departed to find mademoiselle himself.

A pleasant old garden on the borders of the lovely lake, with chestnuts rustling overhead, ivy climbing everywhere, and the black shadow of the tower falling far across the sunny water. At one corner of the wide, low wall was a seat, and here Amy often came to read or work, or console herself with the beauty all about her. She was sitting here that day, leaning her head on her hand, with a homesick heart and heavy eyes, thinking of Beth, and wondering why Laurie did not come. She did not hear him cross the courtyard beyond, nor see him pause in the archway that led from the subterranean path into the garden. He stood a minute, looking at her with new eyes, seeing what no one had ever seen before – the tender side of Amy's character. Everything about her mutely suggested love and sorrow – the blotted letters in her lap, the black ribbon that tied up her hair, the womanly pain and patience in her face; even the little ebony cross at her throat seemed pathetic to Laurie, for he had given it to her, and she wore it as her only ornament. If he had any doubts about the reception she would give him, they were set at rest the minute she looked up and saw him; for, dropping everything, she ran to him, exclaiming, in a tone of unmistakable love and longing:

'O Laurie, Laurie, I knew you'd come to me!'

I think everything was said and settled then; for, as they stood together quite silent for a moment, with the dark head bent down protectingly over the light one, Amy felt that no one could comfort and sustain her so well as Laurie, and Laurie decided that Amy was the only woman in the world who could fill Jo's place, and make him happy. He did not tell her so; but she was not disappointed, for both felt the truth, were satisfied, and gladly left the rest to silence.

In a minute Amy went back to her place; and, while

she dried her tears, Laurie gathered up the scattered papers, finding in the sight of sundry well-worn letters and suggestive sketches good omens for the future. As he sat down beside her, Amy felt shy again, and turned rosy red at the recollection of her impulsive greeting.

'I couldn't help it; I felt so lonely and sad, and was so very glad to see you. It was such a surprise to look up and find you, just as I was beginning to fear you wouldn't come,' she said, trying in vain to speak quite naturally.

'I came the minute I heard. I wish I could say something to comfort you for the loss of dear little Beth; but I can only feel, and –' He could not get any further, for he, too, turned bashful all of a sudden, and did not quite know what to say. He longed to lay Amy's head down on his shoulder, and tell her to have a good cry, but he did not dare; so took her hand instead, and gave it a sympathetic squeeze that was better than words.

'You needn't say anything; this comforts me,' she said softly. 'Beth is well and happy, and I mustn't wish her back; but I dread the going home, much as I long to see them all. We won't talk about it now, for it makes me cry, and I want to enjoy you while you stay. You needn't go right back, need you?'

'Not if you want me, dear.'

'I do, so much. Aunt and Flo are very kind; but you seem like one of the family, and it would be so comfortable to have you for a little while.'

Amy spoke and looked so like a homesick child, whose heart was full, that Laurie forgot his bashfulness all at once, and gave her just what she wanted – the petting she was used to and the cheerful conversation she needed.

'Poor little soul, you look as if you'd grieved yourself half sick! I'm going to take care of you, so don't cry any more, but come and walk about with me; the wind is too chilly for you to sit still,' he said, in the half-caressing, half-commanding way that Amy liked, as he tied on her hat, drew her arm through his, and began to pace up and down the sunny walk, under the new-leaved chestnuts. He felt more at ease upon his legs; and Amy found it very pleasant to have a strong arm to lean upon, a familiar face to smile at her, and a kind voice to talk delightfully for her alone.

The quaint old garden had sheltered many pairs of lovers, and seemed expressly made for them, so sunny and secluded was it, with nothing but the tower to over-look them, and the wide lake to carry away the echo of their words, as it rippled by below. For an hour this new pair walked and talked, or rested on the wall, enjoying the sweet influences which gave such a charm to time and place; and when an unromantic dinner-bell warned them away, Amy felt as if she left her burden of loneliness and sorrow behind her in the château garden.

The moment Mrs Carrol saw the girl's altered face, she was illuminated with a new idea, and exclaimed to herself,

'Now I understand it all – the child has been pining for young Laurence. Bless my heart, I never thought of such a thing!'

With praiseworthy discretion, the good lady said nothing, and betrayed no sign of enlightenment; but cordially urged Laurie to stay, and begged Amy to enjoy his society, for it would do her more good than so much solitude. Amy was a model of docility; and, as her aunt was a good deal occupied with Flo, she was left to entertain her friend, and did it with more than her usual success.

At Nice, Laurie had lounged and Amy had scolded; at Vevay, Laurie was never idle, but always walking, riding, boating, or studying, in the most energetic manner, while Amy admired everything he did, and followed his example as far and as fast as she could. He said the change was owing to the climate, and she did not contradict him, being glad of a like excuse for her own recovered health and spirits.

The invigorating air did them both good, and much exercise worked wholesome changes in minds as well as bodies. They seemed to get clearer views of life and duty up there among the everlasting hills; the fresh winds blew away desponding doubts, delusive fancies, and moody mists; the warm spring sunshine brought out all sorts of aspiring ideas, tender hopes, and happy thoughts; the lake seemed to wash away the troubles of the past, and the grand old mountains to look benignly down upon them, saying 'Little children, love one another'.

In spite of the new sorrow, it was a very happy time, so happy that Laurie could not bear to disturb it by a word. It took him a little while to recover from his surprise at the rapid cure of his first, and, as he had firmly believed, his last and only love. He consoled himself for the seeming disloyalty by the thought that Jo's sister was almost the same as Jo's self, and the conviction that it would have been impossible to love any other woman but Amy so soon and so well. His first wooing had been of the tempestuous order, and he looked back upon it as if through a long vista of years, with a feeling of compassion blended with regret. He was not ashamed of it, but put it away as one of the bitter-sweet experiences of his life, for which he could be grateful when the pain was over. His second wooing he resolved should be as calm and simple as possible; there was no need of having a scene, hardly any need of telling Amy that he loved her; she knew it without words, and had given him his answer long ago. It all came about so naturally that no one could complain, and he knew that everybody would be pleased, even Jo. But when our first little passion has been crushed, we are apt to be wary and slow in making a second trial; so Laurie let the days pass, enjoying every hour, and leaving to chance the utterance of the word that would put an end to the first and sweetest part of his new romance.

He had rather imagined that the denouement would take place in the château garden by moonlight, and in the most graceful and decorous manner; but it turned out exactly the reverse, for the matter was settled on the lake, at noonday, in a few blunt words. They had been floating about all the morning, from gloomy St Gingolf to sunny Montreux, with the Alps of Savoy on one side, Mont St Bernard and the Dent du Midi on the other, pretty Vevay in the valley, and Lausanne upon the hill beyond, a cloudless blue sky overhead, and the bluer lake below, dotted with the picturesque boats that look like white-winged gulls.

They had been talking of Bonnivard, as they glided past Chillon, and of Rousseau, as they looked up at Clarens, where he wrote his *Héloise*. Neither had read it, but they knew it was a love-story, and each privately wondered if it was half as interesting as their own. Amy had been dabbling her hand in the water during the little pause that fell between them, and, when she looked up, Laurie was leaning on his oars, with an expression in his eyes that made her say hastily, merely for the sake of saying something:

'You must be tired; rest a little, and let me row; it will do me good; for, since you came, I have been altogether lazy and luxurious.'

'I'm not tired; but you may take an oar, if you like. There's room enough, though I have to sit nearly in the middle, else the boat won't trim,' returned Laurie, as if he rather liked the arrangement.

Feeling that she had not mended matters much, Amy took the offered third of a seat, shook her hair over her face, and accepted an oar. She rowed as well as she did many other things; and, though she used both hands, and Laurie but one, the oars kept time, and the boat went smoothly through the water.

'How well we pull together, don't we?' said Amy, who objected to silence just then.

'So well that I wish we might always pull in the same boat. Will you, Amy?' very tenderly.

'Yes, Laurie,' very low.

Then they both stopped rowing, and unconsciously added a pretty little tableau of human love and happiness to the dissolving views reflected in the lake.

19

All Alone

It was easy to promise self-abnegation when self was wrapped up in another, and heart and soul were purified by a sweet example; but when the helpful voice was silent, the daily lesson over, the beloved presence gone, and nothing remained but loneliness and grief, then Jo found her promise very hard to keep. How could she 'comfort Father and Mother', when her own heart ached with a ceaseless longing for her sister; how could she 'make the house cheerful', when all its light and warmth and beauty seemed to have deserted it when Beth left the old home for the new; and where in all the world could she 'find some useful, happy work to do', that would take the place of the loving service which had been its own reward? She tried in a blind, hopeless way to do her duty, secretly rebelling against it all the while, for it seemed unjust that her few joys should be lessened, her burdens made heavier, and life get harder and harder as she toiled along. Some people seemed to get all sunshine, and some all shadow; it was not fair, for she tried more than Amy to be good, but never got any reward, only disappointment, trouble, and hard work.

Poor Jo, these were dark days to her, for something like despair came over her when she thought of spending all her life in that quiet house, devoted to humdrum cares, a few small pleasures, and the duty that never seemed to grow any easier. 'I can't do it. I wasn't meant for a life like this, and I know I shall break away and do something desperate if somebody don't come and help me,' she said to herself, when her first efforts failed, and she fell into the moody, miserable state of mind which often comes when strong wills have to yield to the inevitable.

But someone did come and help her, though Jo did not recognize her good angels at once, because they wore familiar shapes, and used the simple spells best fitted to poor humanity. Often she started up at night, thinking Beth called her; and when the sight of the little empty bed made her cry with the bitter cry of an unsubmissive sorrow, 'O Beth, come back! come back!' she did not stretch out her yearning arms in vain; for, as quick to hear her sobbing as she had been to hear her sister's faintest whisper, her mother came to comfort her, not with words only, but the patient tenderness that soothes by a touch, tears that were mute reminders of a greater grief than Jo's, and broken whispers, more eloquent than prayers, because hopeful resignation went hand-in-hand with natural sorrow. Sacred moments, when heart talked to heart in the silence of the night, turning affliction to a blessing, which chastened grief and strengthened love. Feeling this, Jo's burden seemed easier to bear, duty grew sweeter, and life looked more endurable, seen from the safe shelter of her mother's arms.

When aching heart was a little comforted, troubled mind likewise found help; for one day she went to the study, and, leaning over the good grey head lifted to welcome her with a tranquil smile, she said, very humbly:

'Father, talk to me as you did to Beth. I need it more than she did, for I'm all wrong.'

'My dear, nothing can comfort me like this,' he answered, with a falter in his voice, and both arms round her, as if he, too, needed help, and did not fear to ask it.

Then, sitting in Beth's chair close beside him, Jo told her troubles – the resentful sorrow for her loss, the fruit-less efforts that discouraged her, the want of faith that made life look so dark, and all the sad bewilderment which we call despair. She gave him entire confidence, he gave her the help she needed, and both found consolation in the act; for the time had come when they could talk together not only as father and daughter, but as man and woman, able and glad to serve each other with mutual sympathy as well as mutual love. Happy, thoughtful times there in the old study which Jo called 'the church of one member', and from which she came with fresh courage, recovered cheerfulness, and a more submissive spirit; for the parents who had taught one child to meet death without fear, were trying now to teach another to accept life without despondency or distrust, and to use its beautiful opportunities with gratitude and power.

Other helps had Jo – humble, wholesome duties and delights that would not be denied their part in serving her, and which she slowly learned to see and value. Brooms and dishcloths never could be as distasteful as they once had been, for Beth had presided over both; and something of her housewifely spirit seemed to linger round the little mop and the old brush, that was never thrown away. As she used them, Jo found herself humming the songs Beth used to hum, imitating Beth's orderly ways, and giving the little touches here and there that kept everything fresh and cosy, which was the first step towards making home happy, though she didn't know it, till Hannah said with an approving squeeze of the hand:

'You thoughtful creter, you're determined we shan't miss that dear lamb ef you can help it. We don't say much, but we see it, and the Lord will bless you for't, see ef He don't.'

As they sat sewing together, Jo discovered how much improved her sister Meg was; how well she could talk, how much she knew about good, womanly impulses, thoughts, and feelings, how happy she was in husband and children, and how much they were all doing for each other.

'Marriage is an excellent thing, after all. I wonder if I

should blossom out half as well as you have, if I tried it?' said Jo, as she constructed a kite for Demi, in the topsy-turvy nursery.

'It's just what you need to bring out the tender, womanly half of your nature, Jo. You are like a chestnut burr, prickly outside, but silky soft within, and a sweet kernel, if one can only get at it. Love will make you show your heart some day, and then the rough burr will fall off.'

'Frost opens chestnut burrs, ma'am, and it takes a good shake to bring them down. Boys go nutting, and I don't care to be bagged by them,' returned Jo, pasting away at the kite which no wind that blows would ever carry up, for Daisy had tied herself on as a bob.

Meg laughed, for she was glad to see a glimmer of Jo's old spirit, but she felt it her duty to enforce her opinion by every argument in her power; and the sisterly chats were not wasted, especially as two of Meg's most effective arguments were the babies, whom Jo loved tenderly. Grief is the best opener for some hearts, and Jo's was nearly ready for the bag: a little more sunshine to ripen the nut, then, not a boy's impatient shake, but a man's hand reached up to pick it gently from the burr, and find the kernel sound and sweet. If she had suspected this, she would have shut up tight, and been more prickly than ever; fortunately she wasn't thinking about herself, so, when the time came, down she dropped.

Now, if she had been the heroine of a moral storybook,

she ought at this period of her life to have become quite saintly, renounced the world, and gone about doing good in a mortified bonnet, with tracts in her pocket. But, you see, Jo wasn't a heroine; she was only a struggling human girl, like hundreds of others, and she just acted out her nature, being sad, cross, listless, or energetic, as the mood suggested. It's highly virtuous to say we'll be good, but we can't do it all at once, and it takes a long pull, a strong pull, and a pull all together, before some of us even get our feet set in the right way. Jo had got so far, she was learning to do her duty, and to feel unhappy if she did not; but to do it cheerfully – ah, that was another thing! She had often said she wanted to do something splendid, no matter how hard; and now she had her wish, for what could be more beautiful than to devote her life to Father and Mother, trying to make home as happy to them as they had to her? And, if difficulties were necessary to increase the splendour of the effort, what could be harder for a restless, ambitious girl than to give up her own hopes, plans, and desires, and cheerfully live for others?

Providence had taken her at her word; here was the task, not what she had expected, but better, because self had no part in it: now, could she do it? She decided that she would try; and, in her first attempt, she found the helps I have suggested. Still another was given her, and she took it, not as a reward, but as a comfort, as Christian took the refreshment afforded by the little arbour where he rested, as he climbed the hill called Difficulty.

'Why don't you write? That always used to make you happy,' said her mother, once, when the desponding fit over-shadowed Jo.

'I've no heart to write, and if I had, nobody cares for my things.'

'We do; write something for us, and never mind the rest of the world. Try it, dear; I'm sure it would do you good, and please us very much.'

'Don't believe I can'; but Jo got out her desk, and began to overhaul her half-finished manuscripts.

An hour afterwards her mother peeped in, and there she was, scratching away, with her black pinafore on, and an absorbed expression, which caused Mrs March to smile, and slip away, well pleased with the success of her suggestion. Jo never knew how it happened, but something got into that story that went straight to the hearts of those who read it; for, when her family had laughed and cried over it, her father sent it, much against her will, to one of the popular magazines, and, to her utter surprise, it was not only paid for, but others requested. Letters from several persons, whose praise was honour, followed the appearance of the little story, newspapers copied it, and strangers as well as friends admired it. For a small thing it was a great success; and Jo was more astonished than when her novel was commended and condemned all at once.

'I don't understand it. What *can* there be in a simple little story like that, to make people praise it so?' she said, quite bewildered.

'There is truth in it, Jo, that's the secret; humour and pathos make it alive, and you have found your style at last. You wrote with no thought of fame or money, and put your heart into it, my daughter; you have had the bitter, now comes the sweet. Do your best, and grow as happy as we are in your success.'

'If there *is* anything good or true in what I write, it isn't mine; I owe it all to you and Mother and to Beth,' said Jo, more touched by her father's words than by any amount of praise from the world.

So, taught by love and sorrow, Jo wrote her little stories, and sent them away to make friends for themselves and her, finding it a very charitable world to such humble wanderers; for they were kindly welcomed, and sent home comfortable tokens to their mother, like dutiful children whom good fortune overtakes.

When Amy and Laurie wrote of their engagement, Mrs March feared that Jo would find it difficult to rejoice over it, but her fears were soon set at rest; for, though Jo looked grave at first, she took it very quietly, and was full of hopes and plans for 'the children' before she read the letter twice. It was a sort of written duet, wherein each glorified the other in lover-like fashion, very pleasant to read and satisfactory to think of, for no one had any objection to make.

'You like it, Mother?' said Jo, as they laid down the closely written sheets, and looked at one another.

'Yes, I hoped it would be so, ever since Amy wrote that she had refused Fred. I felt sure then that something better than what you call the "mercenary spirit" had come over her, and a hint here and there in her letters made me suspect that love and Laurie would win the day.'

'How sharp you are, Marmee, and how silent! You never said a word to me.'

'Mothers have need of sharp eyes and discreet tongues when they have girls to manage. I was half afraid to put the idea into your head, lest you should write and congratulate them before the thing was settled.'

'I'm not the scatter-brain I was; you may trust me, I'm sober and sensible enough for anyone's confidante now.'

'So you are, dear, and I should have made you mine, only I fancied it might pain you to learn that your Teddy loved anyone else.'

'Now, Mother, did you really think I could be so silly and selfish, after I'd refused his love, when it was freshest, if not best?'

'I knew you were sincere then, Jo, but lately I have thought that if he came back, and asked again, you might, perhaps, feel like giving another answer. Forgive me, dear, I can't help seeing that you are very lonely, and sometimes there is a hungry look in your eyes that goes to my heart;

so I fancied that your boy might fill the empty place if he tried now.'

'No, Mother, it is better as it is, and I'm glad Amy has learned to love him. But you are right in one thing: I *am* lonely, and perhaps if Teddy had tried again, I might have said "Yes," not because I love him any more, but because I care more to be loved than when he went away.'

'I'm glad of that, Jo, for it shows that you are getting on. There are plenty to love you, so try to be satisfied with Father and Mother, sisters and brothers, friends and babies, till the best lover of all comes to give you your reward.'

'Mothers are the *best* lovers in the world; but I don't mind whispering to Marmee that I'd like to try all kinds. It's very curious, but the more I try to satisfy myself with all sorts of natural affections, the more I seem to want. I'd no idea hearts could take in so many; mine is so elastic, it never seems full now, and I used to be quite contented with my family. I don't understand it.'

'I do'; and Mrs March smiled her wise smile, as Jo turned back the leaves to read what Amy said of Laurie.

'It is so beautiful to be loved as Laurie loves me; he isn't sentimental, doesn't say much about it, but I see and feel it in all he says and does, and it makes me so happy and so humble that I don't seem to be the same girl I was. I never knew how good and generous and tender he was till now, for he lets me read his heart, and I find it full of noble impulses and hopes and purposes, and am so proud to know it's mine. He says he feels as if he "could make a prosperous voyage now with me aboard as mate, and lots of love for ballast". I pray he may, and try to be all he believes me, for I love my gallant captain with all my heart and soul and might, and never will desert him, while God lets us be together. O Mother, I never knew how much like heaven this world could be, when two people love and live for one another!'

'And that's our cool, reserved, and worldly Amy! Truly, love does work miracles. How very, very happy they must be!' And Jo laid the rustling sheets together with a careful hand, as one might shut the covers of a lovely romance, which holds the reader fast till the end comes, and he finds himself alone in the workaday world again.

By and by Jo roamed away upstairs, for it was rainy, and she could not walk. A restless spirit possessed her, and the old feeling came again, not bitter as it once was, but a sorrowfully patient wonder why one sister should have all she asked, the other nothing. It was not true; she knew that, and tried to put it away, but the natural craving for affection was strong, and Amy's happiness woke the hungry longing for someone to 'love with heart and soul, and cling to while God let them be together'.

Up in the garret, where Jo's unquiet wanderings ended, stood four little wooden chests in a row, each marked with its owner's name, and each filled with relics of the childhood and girlhood ended now for all. Jo glanced into them, and when she came to her own, leaned her chin on the edge, and stared absently at the chaotic collection, till a bundle of old exercise books caught her eyes. She drew them out, turned them over, and relived that pleasant winter at kind Mrs Kirke's. She had smiled at first, then she looked thoughtful, next sad, and when she came to a little message written in the professor's hand, her lips began to tremble, the books slid out of her lap, and she sat looking at the friendly words, as if they took a new meaning, and touched a tender spot in her heart.

'Wait for me, my friend. I may be a little late, but I shall surely come.'

'Oh, if he only would! So kind, so good, so patient with me always; my dear old Fritz, I didn't value him half enough when I had him, but now how I should love to see him, for everyone seems going away from me, and I'm all alone.'

And holding the little paper fast, as if it were a promise yet to be fulfilled, Jo laid her head down on a comfortable rag-bag, and cried, as if in opposition to the rain pattering on the roof.

Was it all self-pity, loneliness, or low spirits? or was it the waking up of a sentiment which had bided its time as patiently as its inspirer? Who shall say?

20

Surprises

Jo was alone in the twilight, lying on the old sofa, looking at the fire, and thinking. It was her favourite way of spending the hour of dusk; no one disturbed her, and she used to lie there on Beth's little red pillow, planning stories, dreaming dreams, or thinking tender thoughts of the sister who never seemed far away. Her face looked tired, grave and rather sad; for tomorrow was her birthday, and she was thinking how fast the years went by, how old she was getting, and how little she seemed to have accomplished. Almost twenty-five, and nothing to show for it. Jo was mistaken in that; there was a good deal to show, and by and by she saw, and was grateful for it.

'An old maid, that's what I'm to be. A literary spinster, with a pen for a spouse, a family of stories for children, and twenty years hence a morsel of fame, perhaps; when, like poor Johnson, I'm old, and can't enjoy it, solitary, and can't share it, independent, and don't need it. Well, I needn't be a sour saint nor a selfish sinner; and, I dare say, old maids are very comfortable when they get used to it; but –' And there Jo sighed, as if the prospect was not inviting.

It seldom is, at first, and thirty seems the end of all things to five-and-twenty; but it's not so bad as it looks, and one can get on quite happily if one has something in one's self to fall back upon. At twenty-five, girls begin to talk about being old maids, but secretly resolve that they never will be; at thirty they say nothing about it, but quietly accept the fact, and, if sensible, console themselves by remembering that they have twenty more useful, happy years, in which they may be learning to grow old gracefully. Don't laugh at the spinsters, dear girls, for often very tender, tragical romances are hidden away in the hearts that beat so quietly under the sober gowns, and many silent sacrifices of youth, health, ambition, love itself, make the faded faces beautiful in God's sight. Even the sad, sour sisters should be kindly dealt with, because they have missed the sweetest part of life, if for no other reason; and, looking at them with compassion, not contempt, girls in their gloom should remember that they too may miss the blossom time; that rosy cheeks don't last for ever, that silver threads will come in the bonnie brown hair, and that, by and by, kindness and respect will be as sweet as love and admiration now.

Gentlemen, which means boys, be courteous to the old

maids, no matter how poor and plain and prim, for the only chivalry worth having is that which is the readiest to pay deference to the old, protect the feeble, and serve woman-kind, regardless of rank, age, or colour. Just recollect the good aunts who have not only lectured and fussed, but nursed and petted, too often without thanks; the scrapes they have helped you out of; the 'tips' they have given you from their small store, the stitches the patient old fingers have set for you, the steps the willing old feet have taken, and gratefully pay the dear old ladies the little attentions that women love to receive as long as they live. The bright-eyed girls are quick to see such traits, and will like you all the better for them; and if death, almost the only power that can part mother and son, should rob you of yours, you will be sure to find a tender welcome and maternal cherishing from some Aunt Priscilla, who has kept the warmest corner of her lonely old heart for 'the best nevvy in the world'.

Jo must have fallen asleep (as I dare say my reader has during this little homily), for suddenly Laurie's ghost seemed to stand before her – a substantial, lifelike ghost – leaning over her, with the very look he used to wear when he felt a good deal and didn't like to show it. But, like Jenny in the ballad:

She could not think it he,

and lay staring up at him in startled silence, till he stooped and kissed her. Then she knew him, and flew up, crying joyfully:

'O my Teddy! O my Teddy!'

'Dear Jo, you are glad to see me, then?'

'Glad! My blessed boy, words can't express my gladness. Where's Amy?'

'Your mother has got her down at Meg's. We stopped there by the way, and there was no getting my wife out of their clutches.'

'Your what?' cried Jo, for Laurie uttered those two words with an unconscious pride and satisfaction which betrayed him.

'Oh, the dickens! now I've done it'; and he looked so guilty that Jo was down upon him like a flash.

'You've gone and got married!'

'Yes, please, but I never will again'; and he went down upon his knees, with a penitent clasping of hands, and a face full of mischief, mirth, and triumph.

'Actually married?'

'Very much so, thank you.'

'Mercy on us! What dreadful thing will you do next?' and Jo fell into her seat, with a gasp.

'A characteristic, but not exactly complimentary, congratulation,' returned Laurie, still in an abject attitude, but beaming with satisfaction.

'What can you expect, when you take one's breath away,

creeping in like a burglar, and letting cats out of bags like that? Get up, you ridiculous boy, and tell me all about it.'

'Not a word, unless you let me come in my old place, and promise not to barricade.'

Jo laughed at that as she had not done for many a long day, and patted the sofa invitingly, as she said, in a cordial tone:

'The old pillow is up in the garret, and we don't need it now; so, come and 'fess, Teddy.'

'How good it sounds to hear you say "Teddy"! No one ever calls me that but you'; and Laurie sat down, with an air of great content.

'What does Amy call you?'

'My lord.'

'That's like her. Well, you look it'; and Jo's eyes plainly betrayed that she found her boy comelier than ever.

The pillow was gone, but there *was* a barricade, nevertheless – a natural one, raised by time, absence, and change of heart. Both felt it, and for a minute looked at one another as if that invisible barrier cast a shadow over them. It was gone directly, however, for Laurie said, with a vain attempt at dignity:

'Don't I look like a married man and the head of a family?'

'Not a bit, and you never will. You've grown bigger and bonnier, but you are the same scapegrace as ever.'

'Now, really, Jo, you ought to treat me with more respect,' began Laurie, who enjoyed it all immensely.

'How can I, when the mere idea of you, married and settled, is so irresistibly funny that I can't keep sober!' answered Jo, smiling all over her face, so infectiously that they had another laugh, and then settled down for a good talk, quite in the pleasant old fashion.

'It's no use your going out in the cold to get Amy, for they are all coming up presently. I couldn't wait; I wanted to be the one to tell you the grand surprise, and have "first skim", as we used to say when we squabbled about the cream.'

'Of course you did, and spoilt your story by beginning at the wrong end. Now, start right, and tell me how it all happened; I'm pining to know.'

'Well, I did it to please Amy,' began Laurie, with a twinkle that made Jo exclaim:

'Fib number one; Amy did it to please you. Go on, and tell the truth, if you can, sir.'

'Now she's beginning to marm it; isn't it jolly to hear her?' said Laurie to the fire, and the fire glowed and sparkled as if it quite agreed. 'It's all the same, you know, she and I being one. We planned to come home with the Carrols, a month or more ago, but they suddenly changed their minds, and decided to pass another winter in Paris. But Grandpa wanted to come home; he went to please me, and I couldn't let him go alone, neither could I leave Amy; and Mrs Carrol had got English notions about chaperons and such nonsense, and wouldn't let Amy come with us. So I just settled the difficulty by saying "Let's be married, and then we can do as we like".'

'Of course you did; you always have things to suit you.'

'Not always'; and something in Laurie's voice made Jo say hastily:

'How did you ever get Aunt to agree?'

'It was hard work; but, between us, we talked her over, for we had heaps of good reasons on our side. There wasn't time to write and ask leave, but you all liked it, had consented to it by and by, and it was only "taking Time by the fetlock," as my wife says.'

'Aren't we proud of those two words, and don't we like to say them?' interrupted Jo, addressing the fire in her turn, and watching with delight the happy light it seemed to kindle in the eyes that had been so tragically gloomy when she saw them last.

'A trifle, perhaps; she's such a captivating little woman I can't help being proud of her. Well, then, Uncle and Aunt were there to play propriety; we were so absorbed in one another we were of no mortal use apart, and that charming arrangement would make everything easy all round; so we did it.'

'When, where, how?' asked Jo, in a fever of feminine interest and curiosity, for she could not realize it a particle.

'Six weeks ago, at the American consul's, in Paris; a very quiet wedding, of course, for even in our happiness we didn't forget dear little Beth.'

Jo put her hand in his as he said that, and Laurie gently smoothed the little red pillow, which he remembered well.

'Why didn't you let us know afterwards?' asked Jo, in a quieter tone, when they had sat quite still a minute.

'We wanted to surprise you; we thought we were coming directly home, at first; but the dear old gentleman, as soon as we were married, found he couldn't be ready under a month, at least, and sent us off to spend our honeymoon wherever we liked. Amy had once called Valrosa a regular honeymoon home, so we went there, and were as happy as people are but once in their lives. My faith! wasn't it love among the roses!'

Laurie seemed to forget Jo for a minute, and Jo was glad of it; for the fact that he told her these things so freely and naturally assured her that he had quite forgiven and forgotten. She tried to draw away her hand; but, as if he guessed the thought that prompted the half-involuntary impulse, Laurie held it fast, and said, with a manly gravity she had never seen in him before:

'Jo, dear, I want to say one thing, and then we'll put it by for ever. As I told you in my letter, when I wrote that Amy had been so kind to me, I never shall stop loving you; but the love is altered, and I have learned to see that it is better as it is. Amy and you change places in my heart, that's all. I think it was meant to be so, and would have come about naturally, if I had waited, as you tried to make me; but I never could be patient, and so I got a heartache. I was a boy then, headstrong and violent; and it took a hard lesson to show me my mistake. For it *was* one, Jo, as you said, and I found it out, after making a fool of myself. Upon my word, I was so tumbled up in my mind, at one time, that I didn't know which I loved best, you or Amy, and tried to love both alike; and I couldn't, and when I saw her in Switzerland, everything seemed to clear up all at once. You both got into your right places, and I felt sure that it was well off with the old love before it was on with the new; that I could honestly share my heart between sister Jo and wife Amy, and love them both dearly. Will you believe it, and go back to the happy old times when we first knew one another?'

'I'll believe it, with all my heart; but, Teddy, we never can be boy and girl again: the happy old times can't come back, and we mustn't expect it. We are man and woman now, with sober work to do, for playtime is over, and we must give up frolicking. I'm sure you feel this; I see the change in you, and you'll find it in me. I shall miss my boy, but I shall love the man as much, and admire him more, because he means to be what I hoped he would. We can't be little playmates any longer, but we will be brother and sister, to love and help one another all our lives, won't we, Laurie?'

He did not say a word, but took the hand she offered him, and laid his face down on it for a minute, feeling that out of the grave of a boyish passion, there had risen a beautiful, strong friendship to bless them both. Presently Jo said cheerfully, for she didn't want the coming home to be a sad one:

'I can't make it true that you children are really married, and going to set up housekeeping. Why, it seems only yesterday that I was buttoning Amy's pinafore, and pulling your hair when you teased. Mercy me, how time does fly!'

'As one of the children is older than yourself, you needn't talk so like a grandma. I flatter myself I'm a "gentleman growed," as Peggotty said of David; and when you see Amy, you'll find her rather a precocious infant,' said Laurie, looking amused at her maternal air.

'You may be a little older in years, but I'm ever so much older in feeling, Teddy. Women always are; and this last year has been such a hard one that I feel forty.'

'Poor Jo! we left you to bear it alone, while we went pleasuring. You *are* older; here's a line, and there's another; unless you smile, your eyes look sad, and when I touched the cushion, just now, I found a tear on it. You've had a great deal to bear, and had to bear it all alone. What a selfish beast I've been!' and Laurie pulled his own hair, with a remorseful look.

But Jo only turned over the traitorous pillow, and answered, in a tone which she tried to make quite cheerful:

'No, I had Father and Mother to help me, the dear babies to comfort me, and the thought that you and Amy were safe and happy, to make the troubles here easier to bear. I *am* lonely, sometimes, but I dare say it's good for me, and –'

'You never shall be again,' broke in Laurie, putting his arm about her, as if to fence out every human ill. 'Amy and I can't get on without you, so you must come and teach "the children" to keep house, and go halves in everything, just as we used to do, and let us pet you, and all be blissfully happy and friendly together.'

'If I shouldn't be in the way, it would be very pleasant. I begin to feel quite young already; for, somehow, all my troubles seemed to fly away when you came. You always were a comfort, Teddy'; and Jo leaned her head on his shoulder, just as she did years ago, when Beth lay ill, and Laurie told her to hold on to him.

He looked down at her, wondering if she remembered the time, but Jo was smiling to herself, as if, in truth, her troubles *had* all vanished at his coming.

'You are the same Jo still, dropping tears about one minute, and laughing the next. You look a little wicked now; what is it, Grandma?'

'I was wondering how you and Amy get on together.'

'Like angels!'

'Yes, of course, at first; but which rules?'

'I don't mind telling you that she does, now; at least I let her think so – it pleases her, you know. By and by we shall take turns, for marriage, they say, halves one's rights and doubles one's duties.'

'You'll go on as you begin, and Amy will rule you all the days of your life.'

'Well, she does it so imperceptibly that I don't think I shall mind much. She is the sort of woman who knows how to rule well; in fact, I rather like it, for she winds one round her finger as softly and prettily as a skein of silk, and makes you feel as if she was doing you a favour all the while.'

'That ever I should live to see you a henpecked husband and enjoying it!' cried Jo, with uplifted hands.

It was good to see Laurie square his shoulders, and smile with masculine scorn at that insinuation, as he replied, with his 'high and mighty' air:

'Amy is too well bred for that, and I am not the sort of man to submit to it. My wife and I respect ourselves and one another too much ever to tyrannize or quarrel.'

Jo liked that, and thought the new dignity very becoming, but the boy seemed changing very fast into the man, and regret mingled with her pleasure.

'I am sure of that; Amy and you never did quarrel as we used to. She is the sun and I the wind, in the fable, and the sun managed the man best, you remember.'

'She can blow him up as well as shine on him,' laughed Laurie. 'Such a lecture as I got at Nice! I give you my word it was a deal worse than any of your scoldings – a regular rouser. I'll tell you all about it some time – *she* never will, because, after telling me that she despised and was ashamed of me, she lost her heart to the despicable party and married the good-for-nothing.'

'What baseness! Well, if she abuses you, come to me, and I'll defend you.'

'I look as if I needed it, don't I?' said Laurie, getting up and striking an attitude which suddenly changed from the imposing to the rapturous, as Amy's voice was heard calling:

'Where is she? Where's my dear old Jo?'

In trooped the whole family, and everyone was hugged and kissed all over again, and, after several vain attempts, the three wanderers were set down to be looked at and exulted over. Mr Laurence, hale and hearty as ever, was quite as much improved as the others by his foreign tour, for the crustiness seemed to be nearly gone, and the old-fashioned courtliness had received a polish which made it kindlier than ever. It was good to see him beam at 'my children', as he called the young pair; it was better still to see Amy pay him the daughterly duty and affection which completely won his old heart; and best of all, to watch Laurie revolve about the two, as if never tired of enjoying the pretty picture they made.

The minute she put her eyes upon Amy, Meg became conscious that her own dress hadn't a Parisian air, that young Mrs Moffat would be entirely eclipsed by young Mrs Laurence, and that 'her ladyship' was altogether a most elegant and graceful woman. Jo thought, as she watched the pair, 'How well they look together! I was right, and Laurie has found the beautiful, accomplished girl who will become his home better than clumsy old Jo, and be a pride, not a torment to him'. Mrs March and her husband smiled and nodded at each other with happy faces, for they saw that their youngest had done well, not only in worldly things, but the better wealth of love, confidence, and happiness.

For Amy's face was full of the soft brightness which betokens a peaceful heart, her voice had a new tenderness in it, and the cool, prim carriage was changed to a gentle dignity, both womanly and winning. No little affectations marred it, and the cordial sweetness of her manner was more charming than the new beauty or the old grace, for it stamped her at once with the unmistakable sign of the true gentlewoman she had hoped to become.

'Love has done much for our little girl,' said her mother softly.

'She has had a good example before her all her life, my dear,' Mr March whispered back, with a loving look at the worn face and grey head beside him.

Daisy found it impossible to keep her eyes off her 'pitty aunty', but attached herself like a lapdog to the wonderful chatelaine full of delightful charms. Demi paused to consider the new relationship before he compromised himself by the rash acceptance of a bribe, which took the tempting form of a family of wooden bears from Berne.

A flank movement produced an unconditional surrender, however, for Laurie knew where to have him.

'Young man, when I first had the honour of making your acquaintance you hit me in the face: now I demand the satisfaction of a gentleman'; and with that the tall uncle proceeded to toss and tousle the small nephew in a way that damaged his philosophical dignity as much as it delighted his boyish soul.

'Blest if she ain't in silk from head to foot! Ain't it a relishin' sight to see her settin' there as fine as a fiddle, and hear folks calling little Amy, Mrs Laurence?' muttered old Hannah, who could not resist frequent 'peeks' through the slide as she set the table in a most decidedly promiscuous manner.

Mercy on us, how they did talk! first one, then the other, then all burst out together, trying to tell the history of three years in half an hour. It was fortunate that tea was at hand, to produce a lull and provide refreshment, for they would have been hoarse and faint if they had gone on much longer. Such a happy procession as filed away into the little dining room! Mr March proudly escorted 'Mrs Laurence'; Mrs March as proudly leaned on the arm of 'my son'; the old gentleman took Jo, with a whispered 'You must be my girl now,' and a glance at the empty corner by the fire, that made Jo whisper back, with trembling lips, 'I'll try to fill her place, sir.'

The twins pranced behind, feeling that the millennium

was at hand, for everyone was so busy with the newcomers that they were left to revel at their own sweet will, and you may be sure they made the most of the opportunity. Didn't they steal sips of tea, stuff gingerbread *ad libitum*, get a hot biscuit apiece, and, as a crowning trespass, didn't they each whisk a captivating little tart into their tiny pockets, there to stick and crumble treacherously, teaching them that both human nature and pastry are frail? Burdened with the guilty consciousness of the sequestered tarts, and fearing that Dodo's sharp eyes would pierce the thin disguise of cambric and merino which hid their booty, the little sinners attached themselves to 'Dranpa', who hadn't his spectacles on. Amy, who was handed about like refreshments, returned to the parlour on Father Laurence's arm; the others paired off as before, and this arrangement left Jo companionless. She did not mind it at the minute, for she lingered to answer Hannah's eager enquiry:

'Will Miss Amy ride in her coop (coupé), and use all them lovely silver dishes that's stored away over yander?'

'Shouldn't wonder if she drove six white horses, ate off gold plate, and wore diamonds and point lace every day. Teddy thinks nothing too good for her,' returned Jo with infinite satisfaction.

'No more there is! Will you have hash or fish balls for breakfast?' asked Hannah, who wisely mingled poetry and prose.

'I don't care'; and Jo shut the door, feeling that food

was an uncongenial topic just then. She stood a minute looking at the party vanishing above, and, as Demi's short plaid legs toiled up the last stair, a sudden sense of loneliness came over her so strongly that she looked about her with dim eyes, as if to find something to lean upon, for even Teddy had deserted her. If she had known what birthday gift was coming every minute nearer and nearer, she would not have said to herself, 'I'll weep a little weep when I go to bed; it won't do to be dismal now.' Then she drew her hand over her eyes – for one of her boyish habits was never to know where her handkerchief was – and had just managed to call up a smile when there came a knock at the porch door.

She opened it with hospitable haste, and started as if another ghost had come to surprise her; for there stood a tall, bearded gentleman, beaming on her from the darkness like a midnight sun.

'O Mr Bhaer, I *am* so glad to see you!' cried Jo, with a clutch, as if she feared the night would swallow him up before she could get him in.

'And I to see Miss Marsch – but no, you haf a party –' And the professor paused as the sound of voices and the tap of dancing feet came down to them.

'No, we haven't, only the family. My sister and friends have just come home, and we are all very happy. Come in, and make one of us.'

Though a very social man, I think Mr Bhaer would

have gone decorously away, and come again another day; but how could he, when Jo shut the door behind him, and bereft him of his hat? Perhaps her face had something to do with it, for she forgot to hide her joy at seeing him, and showed it with a frankness that proved irresistible to the solitary man, whose welcome far exceeded his boldest hopes.

'If I shall not be Monsieur de Trop, I will so gladly see them all. You haf been ill, my friend?'

He put the question abruptly, for, as Jo hung up his coat, the light fell on her face, and he saw a change in it.

'Not ill, but tired and sorrowful. We have had trouble since I saw you last.'

'Ah, yes, I know. My heart was sore for you when I heard that'; and he shook hands again, with such a sympathetic face that Jo felt as if no comfort could equal the look of the kind eyes, the grasp of the big, warm hand.

'Father, Mother, this is my friend, Professor Bhaer,' she said, with a face and tone of such irrepressible pride and pleasure that she might as well have blown a trumpet and opened the door with a flourish.

If the stranger had any doubts about his reception, they were set at rest in a minute by the cordial welcome he received. Everyone greeted him kindly, for Jo's sake at first, but very soon they liked him for his own. They could not help it, for he carried the talisman that opens all hearts, and these simple people warmed to him at once, feeling even the more friendly because he was poor; for poverty enriches those who live above it, and is a sure passport to truly hospitable spirits. Mr Bhaer sat looking about him with the air of a traveller who knocks at a strange door, and, when it opens, finds himself at home. The children went to him like bees to a honey-pot; and, establishing themselves on each knee, proceeded to captivate him by rifling his pockets, pulling his beard, and investigating his watch, with juvenile audacity. The women telegraphed their approval to one another, and Mr March, feeling that he had got a kindred spirit, opened his choicest stores for his guest's benefit, while silent John listened and enjoyed the talk, but said not a word, and Mr Laurence found it impossible to go to sleep.

If Jo had not been otherwise engaged, Laurie's behaviour would have amused her; for a faint twinge, not of jealousy, but something like suspicion, caused that gentleman to stand aloof at first, and observe the newcomer with brotherly circumspection. But it did not last long. He got interested in spite of himself, and, before he knew it, was drawn into the circle; for Mr Bhaer talked well in this genial atmosphere, and did himself justice. He seldom spoke to Laurie, but he looked at him often, and a shadow would pass across his face, as if regretting his own lost youth, as he watched the young man in his prime. Then his eye would turn to Jo so wistfully that she would have surely answered the mute enquiry if she

340

had seen it; but Jo had her own eyes to take care of, and, feeling that they could not be trusted, she prudently kept them on the little sock she was knitting, like a model maiden aunt.

A stealthy glance now and then refreshed her like sips of fresh water after a dusty walk, for the sidelong peeps showed her several propitious omens. Mr Bhaer's face had lost the absent-minded expression, and looked all alive with interest in the present moment, actually young and handsome, she thought, forgetting to compare him with Laurie, as she usually did strange men, to their great detriment. Then he seemed quite inspired, though the burial customs of the ancients, to which the conversation had strayed, might not be considered an exhilarating topic. Jo quite glowed with triumph when Teddy got quenched in an argument, and thought to herself, as she watched her father's absorbed face, 'how he would enjoy having such a man as my professor to talk with every day!' Lastly, Mr Bhaer was dressed in a new suit of black, which made him look more like a gentleman than ever. His bushy hair had been cut and smoothly brushed, but didn't stay in order long, for, in exciting moments, he rumpled it up in the droll way he used to do; and Jo liked it rampantly erect better than flat, because she thought it gave his fine forehead a Jove-like aspect. Poor Jo, how she did glorify that plain man, as she sat knitting away so quietly, yet letting nothing escape her, not even the fact that Mr Bhaer actually had gold sleeve-buttons in his immaculate wristbands!

'Dear old fellow! He couldn't have got himself up with more care if he'd been going a-wooing,' said Jo to herself; and then a sudden thought, born of the words, made her blush so dreadfully that she had to drop her ball, and go down after it to hide her face.

The manoeuvre did not succeed as well as she expected, however; for, though just in the act of setting fire to a funeral pile, the professor dropped his torch, metaphorically speaking, and made a dive after the little ball. Of course they bumped their heads smartly together, saw stars, and both came up flushed and laughing, without the ball, to resume their seats, wishing they had not left them.

Nobody knew where the evening went to; for Hannah skilfully abstracted the babies at an early hour, nodding like two rosy poppies, and Mr Laurence went home to rest. The others sat round the fire, talking away, utterly regardless of the lapse of time, till Meg, whose maternal mind was impressed with a firm conviction that Daisy had tumbled out of bed, and Demi set his night-gown afire studying the structure of matches, made a move to go.

'We must have our sing, in the good old way, for we are all together again once more,' said Jo, feeling that a good shout would be a safe and pleasant vent for the jubilant emotions of her soul.

They were not *all* there. But no one found the words thoughtless or untrue; for Beth still seemed among them, a peaceful presence, invisible, but dearer than ever, since death could not break the household league that love made indissoluble. The little chair stood in its old place; the tidy basket, with the bit of work she left unfinished when the needle grew 'so heavy', was still on its accustomed shelf; the beloved instrument, seldom touched now, had not been moved; and above it Beth's face, serene and smiling, as in the early days, looked down upon them, seeming to say, 'Be happy. I am here.'

'Play something, Amy. Let them hear how much you have improved,' said Laurie, with pardonable pride in his promising pupil.

But Amy whispered, with full eyes, as she twirled the faded stool:

'Not tonight, dear. I can't show off tonight.'

But she did show something better than brilliancy or skill; for she sung Beth's songs with a tender music in her voice which the best master could not have taught, and touched the listeners' hearts with a sweeter power than any other inspiration could have given her. The room was very still, when the clear voice failed suddenly at the last line of Beth's favourite hymn. It was hard to say:

'*Earth hath no sorrow that heaven cannot heal*';

and Amy leaned against her husband, who stood behind her, feeling that her welcome home was not quite perfect without Beth's kiss.

'Now, we must finish with Mignon's song; for Mr Bhaer sings that,' said Jo, before the pause grew painful. And Mr Bhaer cleared his throat with a gratified 'Hem!' as he stepped into the corner where Jo stood, saying:

'You will sing with me? We go excellently well together.'

A pleasing fiction, by the way; for Jo had no more idea of music than a grasshopper. But she would have consented if he had proposed to sing a whole opera, and warbled away, blissfully regardless of time and tune. It didn't much matter; for Mr Bhaer sang like a true German, heartily and well; and Jo soon subsided into a subdued hum, that she might listen to the mellow voice that seemed to sing for her alone.

'*Know'st thou the land where the citron blooms*',

used to be the professor's favourite line, for 'das land' meant Germany to him; but now he seemed to dwell, with peculiar warmth and melody, upon the words:

> '*There, oh there, might I with thee,*
>   *O my beloved, go!*'

and one listener was so thrilled by the tender invitation that she longed to say she did know the land, and would joyfully depart thither whenever he liked.

The song was considered a great success, and the singer retired covered with laurels. But a few minutes afterwards, he forgot his manners entirely, and stared at Amy putting on her bonnet; for she had been introduced simply as 'my sister', and no one had called her by her new name since he came. He forgot himself still further when Laurie said, in his most gracious manner, at parting:

'My wife and I are very glad to meet you, sir. Please remember that there is always a welcome waiting for you over the way.'

Then the professor thanked him so heartily, and looked so suddenly illuminated with satisfaction, that Laurie thought him the most delightfully demonstrative old fellow he ever met.

'I too shall go; but I shall gladly come again, if you will gif me leave, dear madame, for a little business in the city will keep me here some days.'

He spoke to Mrs March, but he looked at Jo; and the mother's voice gave as cordial an assent as did the daughter's eyes; for Mrs March was not so blind to her children's interest as Mrs Moffat supposed.

'I suspect that is a wise man,' remarked Mr March, with placid satisfaction, from the hearth-rug, after the last guest had gone.

'I know he is a good one,' added Mrs March, with decided approval, as she wound up the clock.

'I thought you'd like him,' was all Jo said, as she slipped away to her bed.

She wondered what the business was that brought Mr Bhaer to the city, and finally decided that he had been appointed to some great honour, somewhere, but had been too modest to mention the fact. If she had seen his face when, safe in his own room, he looked at the picture of a severe and rigid young lady, with a good deal of hair, who appeared to be gazing darkly into futurity, it might have thrown some light upon the subject, especially when he turned off the gas, and kissed the picture in the dark.

21

My Lord and Lady

'Please, Madam Mother, could you lend me my wife for half an hour. The luggage has come, and I've been making hay of Amy's Paris finery, trying to find some things I want,' said Laurie, coming in the next day to find Mrs Laurence sitting in her mother's lap, as if being made 'the baby' again.

'Certainly. Go, dear; I forget that you have any home but this,' and Mrs March pressed the white hand that wore the wedding-ring, as if asking pardon for her maternal covetousness.

'I shouldn't have come over if I could have helped it; but I can't get on without my little woman any more than a –'

'Weathercock can without wind,' suggested Jo, as he paused for a simile; Jo had grown quite her own saucy self again since Teddy came home.

'Exactly; for Amy keeps me pointing due west most of the time, with only an occasional whiffle round to the south, and I haven't had an easterly spell since I was married; don't know anything about the north, but am altogether salubrious and balmy, hey, my lady?'

'Lovely weather so far; I don't know how long it will last, but I'm not afraid of storms, for I'm learning how to sail my ship. Come home, dear, and I'll find your bootjack; I suppose that's what you are rummaging after among my things. Men are *so* helpless, Mother,' said Amy, with a matronly air, which delighted her husband.

'What are you going to do with yourselves after you get settled?' asked Jo, buttoning Amy's cloak as she used to button her pinafores.

'We have our plans; we don't mean to say much about them yet, because we are such very new brooms, but we don't intend to be idle. I'm going into business with a devotion that shall delight Grandfather, and prove to him that I'm not spoilt. I need something of the sort to keep me steady. I'm tired of dawdling, and mean to work like a man.'

'And Amy, what is she going to do?' asked Mrs March, well pleased at Laurie's decision, and the energy with which he spoke.

'After doing the civil all round, and airing our best bonnet, we shall astonish you by the elegant hospitalities of our mansion, the brilliant society we shall draw about us, and the beneficial influence we shall exert over the world at large. That's about it, isn't it, Madame Récamier?' asked Laurie, with a quizzical look at Amy.

'Time will show. Come away, Impertinence, and don't shock my family by calling me names before their faces,' answered Amy, resolving that there should be a home with a good wife in it before she set up a *salon* as a queen of society.

'How happy those children seem together!' observed Mr March, finding it difficult to become absorbed in his Aristotle after the young couple had gone.

'Yes, and I think it will last,' added Mrs March, with the restful expression of a pilot who has brought a ship safely into port.

'I know it will. Happy Amy!' and Jo sighed, then smiled brightly as Professor Bhaer opened the gate with an impatient push.

Later in the evening, when his mind had been set at rest about the bootjack, Laurie said suddenly to his wife, who was flitting about, arranging her new art treasures:

'Mrs Laurence.'

'My lord!'

'That man intends to marry our Jo!'

'I hope so; don't you, dear?'

'Well, my love, I consider him a trump, in the fullest sense of that expressive word, but I do wish he was a little younger and a good deal richer.'

'Now, Laurie, don't be too fastidious and worldly-minded. If they love one another it doesn't matter a particle how old they are nor how poor. Women *never* should marry for money –' Amy caught herself up short as the words escaped her, and looked at her husband, who replied, with malicious gravity:

'Certainly not, though you do hear charming girls say that they intend to do it sometimes. If my memory serves me, you once thought it your duty to make a rich match; that accounts, perhaps, for your marrying a good-for-nothing like me.'

'O my dearest boy, don't, don't say that! I forgot you were rich when I said "Yes." I'd have married you if you hadn't a penny, and I sometimes wish you *were* poor that I might show how much I love you'; and Amy, who was very dignified in public and very fond in private, gave convincing proofs of the truth of her words.

'You don't really think I am such a mercenary creature as I tried to be once, do you? It would break my heart if you didn't believe that I'd gladly pull in the same boat with you, even if you had to get your living by rowing on the lake.'

'Am I an idiot and a brute? How could I think so, when you refused a richer man for me, and won't let me give you half I want to now, when I have the right? Girls do it every day, poor things, and are taught to think it is their only salvation; but you had better lessons, and, though I trembled for you at one time, I was not disappointed, for the daughter was true to the mother's teaching. I told Mamma so yesterday, and she looked as glad and grateful as if I'd given her a cheque for a million, to be spent in charity. You are not listening to my moral remarks, Mrs Laurence'; and Laurie paused, for Amy's eyes had an absent look, though fixed upon his face.

'Yes, I am, and admiring the dimple in your chin at the same time. I don't wish to make you vain, but I must confess that I'm prouder of my handsome husband than of all his money. Don't laugh, but your nose is *such* a comfort to me'; and Amy softly caressed the well-cut feature with artistic satisfaction.

Laurie had received many compliments in his life, but never one that suited him better, as he plainly showed, though he did laugh at his wife's peculiar taste, while she said slowly:

'May I ask you a question, dear?'

'Of course you may.'

'Shall you care if Jo does marry Mr Bhaer?'

'Oh, that's the trouble, is it? I thought there was something in the dimple that didn't suit you. Not being a dog in the manger, but the happiest fellow alive, I assure you I can dance at Jo's wedding with a heart as light as my heels. Do you doubt it, my darling?'

Amy looked up at him, and was satisfied; her last little jealous fear vanished for ever, and she thanked him, with a face full of love and confidence.

'I wish we could do something for that capital old professor. Couldn't we invent a rich relation, who shall obligingly die out there in Germany, and leave him a tidy little fortune?' said Laurie, when they began to pace up and down the long drawing room, arm-in-arm, as they were fond of doing, in memory of the château garden.

'Jo would find us out, and spoil it all; she is very proud of him, just as he is, and said yesterday that she thought poverty was a beautiful thing.'

'Bless her dear heart! she won't think so when she has a literary husband, and a dozen little professors and professorins to support. We won't interfere now, but watch our chance, and do them a good turn in spite of themselves. I owe Jo for a part of my education, and she believes in people's paying their honest debts, so I'll get round her in that way.'

'How delightful it is to be able to help others, isn't it? That was always one of my dreams, to have the power of giving freely; and, thanks to you, the dream has come true.'

'Ah! we'll do quantities of good, won't we? There's one sort of poverty that I particularly like to help. Out-and-out beggars get taken care of; but poor gentle-folks fare badly, because they won't ask, and people don't dare to offer charity; yet there are a thousand ways of helping them, if one only knows how to do it so delicately that it does not offend. I must say, I like to serve a decayed gentleman better than a blarneying beggar; I suppose it's wrong, but I do, though it is harder.'

'Because it takes a gentleman to do it,' added the other member of the domestic admiration society.

'Thank you, I'm afraid I don't deserve that pretty compliment. But I was going to say that while I was dawdling about abroad, I saw a good many talented young fellows making all sorts of sacrifices, and enduring real hardships, that they might realize their dreams. Splendid fellows, some of them, working like heroes, poor and friendless, but so full of courage, patience, and ambition, that I was ashamed of myself, and longed to give them a right good lift. Those are people whom it's a satisfaction to help, for if they've got genius, it's an honour to be allowed to serve them, and not let it be lost or delayed for want of fuel to keep the pot boiling; if they haven't, it's a pleasure to comfort the poor souls, and keep them from despair when they find it out.'

'Yes, indeed; and there's another class who can't ask, and who suffer in silence. I know something of it, for I belonged to it before you made a princess of me, as the king does the beggar-maid in the old story. Ambitious girls have a hard time, Laurie, and often have to see youth, health and precious opportunities go by, just for want of a little help at the right minute. People have been very kind to me and whenever I see girls struggling along, as we used to do, I want to put out my hand and help them, as I was helped.'

'And so you shall, like an angel as you are!' cried Laurie

resolving, with a glow of philanthropic zeal, to found and endow an institution for the express benefit of young women with artistic tendencies. 'Rich people have no right to sit down and enjoy themselves, or let their money accumulate for others to waste. It's not half so sensible to leave legacies when one dies as it is to use the money wisely while alive, and enjoy making one's fellow creatures happy with it. We'll have a good time ourselves, and add an extra relish to our own pleasure by giving other people a generous taste. Will you be a little Dorcas, going about emptying a big basket of comforts, and filling it up with good deeds?'

'With all my heart, if you will be a brave St Martin, stopping, as you ride gallantly through the world, to share your cloak with the beggar.'

'It's a bargain, and we shall get the best of it!'

So the young pair shook hands upon it, and then paced happily on again, feeling that their pleasant home was more home-like because they hoped to brighten other homes, believing that their own feet would walk more uprightly along the flowery path before them, if they smoothed rough ways for other feet, and feeling that their hearts were more closely knit together by a love which could tenderly remember those less blest than they.

22

Daisy and Demi

I cannot feel that I have done my duty as humble histor-
ian of the March family, without devoting at least one
chapter to the two most precious and important members
of it. Daisy and Demi had now arrived at years of discretion; for in this fast age babies of three or four assert their
rights, and get them, too, which is more than many of
their elders do. If there ever were a pair of twins in danger
of being utterly spoilt by adoration, it was these prattling
Brookes. Of course they were the most remarkable children ever born, as will be shown when I mention that
they walked at eight months, talked fluently at twelve
months, and at two years they took their places at table,
and behaved with a propriety which charmed all beholders.
At three, Daisy demanded a 'needler', and actually made
a bag with four stitches in it; she likewise set up housekeeping in the sideboard, and managed a microscopic
cooking-stove with a skill that brought tears of pride to
Hannah's eyes, while Demi learned his letters with his
grandfather, who invented a new mode of teaching the

alphabet by forming the letters with his arms and legs, thus uniting gymnastics for head and heels. The boy early developed a mechanical genius which delighted his father and distracted his mother, for he tried to imitate every machine he saw, and kept the nursery in a chaotic condition, with his 'sewin sheen' – a mysterious structure of string, chairs, clothes-pins, and spools, for wheels to go 'wound and wound'; also a basket hung over the back of a big chair, in which he vainly tried to hoist his too confiding sister, who, with feminine devotion, allowed her little head to be bumped till rescued, when the young inventor indignantly remarked, 'Why, Marmar, dat's my lellywaiter, and me's trying to pull her up.'

Though utterly unlike in character, the twins got on remarkably well together, and seldom quarrelled more than thrice a day. Of course, Demi tyrannized over Daisy, and gallantly defended her from every other aggressor; while Daisy made a galley slave of herself, and adored her brother as the one perfect being in the world. A rosy, chubby, sunshiny little soul was Daisy, who found her way to everybody's heart, and nestled there. One of the captivating children, who seem made to be kissed and cuddled, adorned and adored like little goddesses, and produced for general approval on all festive occasions. Her small virtues were so sweet that she would have been quite angelic if a few small naughtinesses had not kept her delightfully human. It was all fair weather in her world, and every morning she scrambled up to the window in her little nightgown to look out, and say, no matter whether it rained or shone, 'Oh, pitty day, oh, pitty day!' Everyone was a friend, and she offered kisses to a stranger so confidingly that the most inveterate bachelor relented, and baby-lovers became faithful worshippers.

'Me loves evvybody,' she once said, opening her arms, with her spoon in one hand, and her mug in the other, as if eager to embrace and nourish the whole world.

As she grew, her mother began to feel that the Dovecote would be blest by the presence of an inmate as serene and loving as that which had helped to make the old house home, and to pray that she might be spared a loss like that which had lately taught them how long they had entertained an angel unawares. Her grandfather often called her 'Beth', and her grandmother watched over her with untiring devotion, as if trying to atone for some past mistake, which no eye but her own could see.

Demi, like a true Yankee, was of an enquiring turn, wanting to know everything, and often getting much disturbed because he could not get satisfactory answers to his perpetual 'What for?'

He also possessed a philosophic bent, to the great delight of his grandfather, who used to hold Socratic conversations with him, in which the precocious pupil occasionally posed his teacher, to the undisguised satisfaction of the women folk.

'What makes my legs go, dranpa?' asked the young philosopher, surveying those active portions of his frame with a meditative air, while resting after a go-to-bed frolic one night.

'It's your little mind, Demi,' replied the sage, stroking the yellow head respectfully.

'What is a little mine?'

'It is something which makes your body move, as the spring made the wheels go in my watch when I showed it to you.'

'Open me; I want to see it go wound.'

'I can't do that any more than you could open the watch. God winds you up, and you go till he stops you.'

'Does I?' and Demi's brown eyes grew big and bright as he took in the new thought. 'Is I wounded up like the watch?'

'Yes; but I can't show you how; for it is done when we don't see.'

Demi felt of his back, as if expecting to find it like that of the watch, and then gravely remarked:

'I dess Dod does it when I's asleep.'

A careful explanation followed, to which he listened so attentively that his anxious grandmother said:

'My dear, do you think it wise to talk about such things to that baby? He's getting great bumps over his eyes, and learning to ask the most unanswerable questions.'

'If he is old enough to ask the questions he is old enough

to receive true answers. I am not putting the thoughts into his head, but helping him unfold those already there. These children are wiser than we are, and I have no doubt the boy understands every word I have said to him. Now, Demi, tell me where you keep your mind?'

If the boy had replied like Alcibiades, 'By the gods, Socrates, I cannot tell', his grandfather would not have been surprised; but when, after standing a moment on one leg, like a meditative young stork, he answered, in a tone of calm conviction, 'In my little belly,' the old gentleman could only join in Grandma's laugh, and dismiss the class in metaphysics.

There might have been cause for maternal anxiety, if Demi had not given convincing proofs that he was a true boy, as well as a budding philosopher; for, often, after a discussion which caused Hannah to prophesy, with ominous nods, 'That child ain't long for this world', he would turn about and set her fears at rest by some of the pranks with which dear, dirty, naughty little rascals distract and delight their parents' souls.

Meg made many moral rules, and tried to keep them; but what mother was ever proof against the winning wiles, the ingenious evasions, or the tranquil audacity of the miniature men and women who so early show themselves accomplished Artful Dodgers?

'No more raisins, Demi, they'll make you sick,' says Mamma to the young person who offers his services in the kitchen with unfailing regularity on plum-pudding day.

'Me likes to be sick.'

'I don't want to have you, so run away and help Daisy make patty cakes.'

He reluctantly departs, but his wrongs weigh upon his spirit; and, by and by, when an opportunity comes to redress them, he outwits Mamma by a shrewd bargain.

'Now you have been good children, and I'll play anything you like,' says Meg, as she leads her assistant cook upstairs, when the pudding is safely bouncing in the pot.

'Truly, Marmar?' asks Demi, with a brilliant idea in his well-powdered head.

'Yes, truly; anything you say,' replies the shortsighted parent, preparing herself to sing 'The Three Little Kittens' half a dozen times over, or to take her family to 'Buy a penny bun', regardless of wind or limb. But Demi corners her by the cool reply:

'Then we'll go and eat up all the raisins.'

Aunt Dodo was chief playmate and confidante of both children, and the trio turned the little house topsy-turvy. Aunt Amy was as yet only a name to them, Aunt Beth soon faded into a pleasantly vague memory, but Aunt Dodo was a living reality, and they made the most of her, for which compliment she was deeply grateful. But when Mr Bhaer came, Jo neglected her playfellows, and dismay and desolation fell upon their little souls. Daisy, who was fond of going about peddling kisses, lost her best customer and became bankrupt; Demi, with infantile penetration, soon discovered that Dodo liked to play with 'the bear man' better than she did with him; but, though hurt, he concealed his anguish, for he hadn't the heart to insult a rival who kept a mine of chocolate drops in his waistcoat pocket, and a watch that could be taken out of its case and freely shaken by ardent admirers.

Some persons might have considered these pleasing liberties as bribes; but Demi didn't see it in that light, and continued to patronize the 'bear man' with pensive affability, while Daisy bestowed her small affections upon him at the third call, and considered his shoulder her throne, his arm her refuge, his gifts treasures of surpassing wealth.

Gentlemen are sometimes seized with sudden fits of admiration for the young relatives of ladies whom they honour with their regard; but this counterfeit philoprogenitiveness sits uneasily upon them, and does not deceive anybody a particle. Mr Bhaer's devotion was sincere, however likewise effective – for honesty is the best policy in love as in law; he was one of the men who are at home with children, and looked particularly well when little faces made a pleasant contrast with his manly one. His business, whatever it was, detained him from day to day, but evening seldom failed to bring him out to see – well, he always asked for Mr March, so I suppose *he* was the attraction. The excellent Papa laboured under the delusion that he was, and revelled in long discussions with the kindred spirit, till a chance remark of his more observing grandson suddenly enlightened him.

Mr Bhaer came in one evening to pause on the threshold of the study, astonished by the spectacle that met his eye. Prone upon the floor lay Mr March, with his respectable legs in the air, and beside him, likewise prone, was Demi, trying to imitate the attitude with his own short, scarlet-stockinged legs, both grovellers so seriously absorbed that they were unconscious of spectators, till Mr Bhaer laughed his sonorous laugh, and Jo cried out, with a scandalized face:

'Father, Father, here's the professor!'

Down went the black legs and up came the grey head, as the preceptor said, with undisturbed dignity:

'Good evening, Mr Bhaer. Excuse me for a moment; we are just finishing our lesson. Now, Demi, make the letter and tell its name.'

'I knows him!' and, after a few convulsive efforts, the red legs took the shape of a pair of compasses, and the intelligent pupil triumphantly shouted, 'It's a We, Danpa, it's a We!'

'He's a born Weller,' laughed Jo, as her parent gathered himself up, and her nephew tried to stand on his head, as the only mode of expressing his satisfaction that school was over.

'What have you been at today, *bübchen*?' asked Mr Bhaer, picking up the gymnast.

'Me went to see little Mary.'

'And what did you there?'

'I kissed her,' began Demi, with artless frankness.

'Prut! thou beginnest early. What did the little Mary say to that?' asked Mr Bhaer, continuing to confess the young sinner, who stood upon his knee, exploring the waistcoat-pocket.

'Oh, she liked it, and she kissed me, and I liked it. *Don't* little boys like little girls?' added Demi, with his mouth full, and an air of bland satisfaction.

'You precocious chick! Who put that into your head?' said Jo, enjoying the innocent revelations as much as the professor.

'"Tisn't in mine head; it's in mine mouf,' answered literal Demi, putting out his tongue, with a chocolate-drop on it, thinking she alluded to confectionery, not ideas.

'Thou shouldst save some for the little friend: sweets to the sweet, mannling'; and Mr Bhaer offered Jo some, with a look that made her wonder if chocolate was not the nectar drunk by the gods. Demi also saw the smile, was impressed by it, and artlessly enquired:

'Do great boys like great girls, too, 'Fessor?'

Like young Washington, Mr Bhaer 'couldn't tell a lie'; so he gave the somewhat vague reply that he believed they did sometimes, in a tone that made Mr March put down his clothes brush, glance at Jo's retiring face, and then sink into his chair, looking as if the 'precocious chick' had put an idea into *his* head that was both sweet and sour.

Why Dodo, when she caught him in the china-closet half an hour afterwards, nearly squeezed the breath out of his little body with a tender embrace, instead of shaking him for being there, and why she followed up this novel performance by the unexpected gift of a big slice of bread and jelly, remained one of the problems over which Demi puzzled his small wits, and was forced to leave unsolved for ever.

23

Under the Umbrella

While Laurie and Amy were taking conjugal strolls over velvet carpets, as they set their house in order, and planned a blissful future, Mr Bhaer and Jo were enjoying promenades of a different sort, along muddy roads and sodden fields.

'I always do take a walk towards evening, and I don't know why I should give it up, just because I often happen to meet the professor on his way out,' said Jo to herself, after two or three encounters; for, though there were two paths to Meg's, whichever one she took she was sure to meet him, either going or returning. He was always walking rapidly, and never seemed to see her till quite close, when he would look as if his short-sighted eyes had failed to recognize the approaching lady till that moment. Then, if she was going to Meg's, he always had something for the babies; if her face was turned homeward, he had merely strolled down to see the river, and was just about returning, unless they were tired of his frequent calls.

Under the circumstances, what could Jo do but greet

him civilly, and invite him in? If she *was* tired of his visits, she concealed her weariness with perfect skill, and took care that there should be coffee for supper, 'as Friedrich – I mean Mr Bhaer – doesn't like tea'.

By the second week, everyone knew perfectly well what was going on, yet everyone tried to look as if they were stone-blind to the changes in Jo's face. They never asked why she sang about her work, did up her hair three times a day, and got so blooming with her evening exercise; and no one seemed to have the slightest suspicion that Professor Bhaer, while talking philosophy with the father, was giving the daughter lessons in love.

Jo couldn't even lose her heart in a decorous manner, but sternly tried to quench her feelings; and, failing to do so, led a somewhat agitated life. She was mortally afraid of being laughed at for surrendering, after her many and vehement declarations of independence. Laurie was her especial dread; but, thanks to the new manager, he behaved with praiseworthy propriety, never called Mr Bhaer 'a capital old fellow' in public, never alluded, in the remotest manner, to Jo's improved appearance, or expressed the least surprise at seeing the professor's hat on the Marches' hall table nearly every evening. But he exulted in private and longed for the time to come when he could give Jo a piece of plate, with a bear and a ragged staff on it as an appropriate coat of arms.

For a fortnight, the professor came and went with

lover-like regularity; then he stayed away for three whole days, and made no sign – a proceeding which caused everybody to look sober, and Jo to become pensive, at first, and then – alas for romance! – very cross.

'Disgusted, I dare say, and gone home as suddenly as he came. It's nothing to me, of course; but I *should* think he would have come and bid us goodbye, like a gentleman,' she said to herself, with a despairing look at the gate, as she put on her things for the customary walk, one dull afternoon.

'You'd better take the little umbrella, dear; it looks like rain,' said her mother, observing that she had on her new bonnet, but not alluding to the fact.

'Yes, Marmee; do you want anything in town? I've got to run in and get some paper,' returned Jo, pulling out the bow under her chin before the glass as an excuse for not looking at her mother.

'Yes; I want some twilled silesia, a paper of number nine needles, and two yards of narrow lavender ribbon. Have you got your thick boots on, and something warm under your cloak?'

'I believe so,' answered Jo absently.

'If you happen to meet Mr Bhaer, bring him home to tea. I quite long to see the dear man,' added Mrs March.

Jo heard *that*, but made no answer, except to kiss her mother, and walk rapidly away, thinking with a glow of gratitude, in spite of her heartache:

'How good she is to me! What *do* girls do who haven't any mothers to help them through their troubles?'

The dry goods stores were not down among the counting-houses, banks, and wholesale warerooms, where gentlemen most do congregate; but Jo found herself in that part of the city before she did a single errand, loitering along as if waiting for someone, examining engineering instruments in one window and samples of wool in another with most unfeminine interest; tumbling over barrels, being half smothered by descending bales, and hustled unceremoniously by busy men who looked as if they wondered 'how the deuce she got there'. A drop of rain on her cheek recalled her thoughts from baffled hopes to ruined ribbons; for the drops continued to fall, and, being a woman as well as a lover, she felt that, though it was too late to save her heart, she might her bonnet. Now she remembered the little umbrella, which she had forgotten to take in her hurry to be off; but regret was unavailing, and nothing could be done but borrow one or submit to a drenching. She looked up at the lowering sky, down at the crimson bow already flecked with black, forward along the muddy street, then one long, lingering look behind, at a certain grimy warehouse, with 'Hoffmann, Swartz, & Co.' over the door, and said to herself, with a sternly reproachful air:

'It serves me right! What business had I to put on all my best things and come philandering down here, hoping to see the professor? Jo, I'm ashamed of you! No, you shall *not* go there to borrow an umbrella, or find out where he is, from his friends. You shall trudge away, and do your errands in the rain; and if you catch your death and ruin your bonnet, it's no more than you deserve. Now then!'

With that she rushed across the street so impetuously that she narrowly escaped annihilation from a passing truck, and precipitated herself into the arms of a stately old gentleman, who said, 'I beg pardon, ma'am,' and looked mortally offended. Somewhat daunted, Jo righted herself, spread her handkerchief over the devoted ribbons, and, putting temptation behind her, hurried on, with increasing dampness about the ankles, and much clashing of umbrellas overhead. The fact that a somewhat dilapidated blue one remained stationary above the unprotected bonnet, attracted her attention; and, looking up, she saw Mr Bhaer looking down.

'I feel to know the strong-minded lady who goes so bravely under many horse-noses, and so fast through much mud. What do you down here, my friend?'

'I'm shopping.'

Mr Bhaer smiled, as he glanced from the pickle factory on one side, to the wholesale hide and leather concern on the other; but he only said politely:

'You haf no umbrella. May I go also, and take for you the bundles?'

'Yes, thank you.'

Jo's cheeks were as red as her ribbon, and she wondered what he thought of her; but she didn't care, for in a minute she found herself walking away arm-in-arm with her professor, feeling as if the sun had suddenly burst out with uncommon brilliancy, that the world was all right again, and that one thoroughly happy woman was paddling through the wet that day.

'We thought you had gone,' said Jo hastily, for she knew he was looking at her. Her bonnet wasn't big enough to hide her face, and she feared he might think the joy it betrayed unmaidenly.

'Did you believe that I should go with no farewell to those who haf been so heavenly kind to me?' he asked so reproachfully that she felt as if she had insulted him by the suggestion, and answered heartily:

'No, *I* didn't; I knew you were busy about your own affairs, but we rather missed you – Father and Mother especially.'

'And you?'

'I'm always glad to see you, sir.'

In her anxiety to keep her voice quite calm, Jo made it rather cool, and the frosty little monosyllable at the end seemed to chill the professor, for his smile vanished, as he said gravely:

'I thank you, and come one time more before I go.'

'You *are* going then?'

'I haf no longer any business here; it is done.'

'Successfully, I hope?' said Jo, for the bitterness of disappointment was in that short reply of his.

'I ought to think so, for I haf a way opened to me by which I can make my bread and gif my *Jünglings* much help.'

'Tell me, please! I like to know all about the – the boys,' said Jo eagerly.

'That is so kind, I gladly tell you. My friends find for me a place in a college, where I teach as at home, and earn enough to make the way smooth for Franz and Emil. For this I should be grateful, should I not?'

'Indeed you should. How splendid it will be to have you doing what you like, and be able to see you often, and the boys!' cried Jo, clinging to the lads as an excuse for the satisfaction she could not help betraying.

'Ah! but we shall not meet often, I fear; this place is at the West.'

'So far away!' and Jo left her skirts to their fate, as if it didn't matter now what became of her clothes or herself.

Mr Bhaer could read several languages, but he had not learned to read women yet. He flattered himself that he knew Jo pretty well, and was, therefore, much amazed by the contradictions of voice, face, and manner, which she showed him in rapid succession that day, for she was in half a dozen different moods in the course of half an hour. When she met him she looked surprised, though it was impossible to help suspecting that she had come for that express purpose. When he offered her his arm, she took it with a look that filled him with delight; but when he asked if she missed him, she gave such a chilly, formal reply that despair fell upon him. On learning his good fortune she almost clapped her hands: was the joy all for the boys? Then, on hearing his destination, she said, 'So far away!' in a tone of despair that lifted him on to a pinnacle of hope; but the next minute she tumbled him down again by observing, like one entirely absorbed in the matter –

'Here's the place for my errands; will you come in? It won't take long.'

Jo rather prided herself upon her shopping capabilities, and particularly wished to impress her escort with the neatness and dispatch with which she would accomplish the business. But, owing to the flutter she was in, everything went amiss; she upset the tray of needles, forgot the silesia was to be 'twilled' till it was cut off, gave the wrong change, and covered herself with confusion by asking for lavender ribbon at the calico counter. Mr Bhaer stood by, watching her blush and blunder; and, as he watched, his own bewilderment seemed to subside, for he was beginning to see that on some occasions women, like dreams, go by contraries.

When they came out, he put the parcel under his arm with a more cheerful aspect, and splashed through the puddles as if he rather enjoyed it, on the whole.

'Should we not do a little what you call shopping for the babies, and haf a farewell feast tonight if I go for my last call at your so pleasant home?' he asked, stopping before a window full of fruit and flowers.

'What will we buy?' said Jo, ignoring the latter part of his speech, and sniffing the mingled odours with an affectation of delight as they went in.

'May they haf oranges and figs?' asked Mr Bhaer, with a paternal air.

'They eat them when they can get them.'

'Do you care for nuts?'

'Like a squirrel.'

'Hamburg grapes; yes, we shall surely drink to the Fatherland in those?'

Jo frowned upon that piece of extravagance, and asked why he didn't buy a frail of dates, a cask of raisins, and a bag of almonds, and done with it? Whereat Mr Bhaer confiscated her purse, produced his own, and finished the marketing by buying several pounds of grapes, a pot of rosy daisies, and a pretty jar of honey, to be regarded in the light of a demijohn. Then, distorting his pockets with the knobby bundles, and giving her the flowers to hold, he put up the old umbrella, and they travelled on again.

'Miss Marsch, I haf a great favour to ask of you,' began the professor, after a moist promenade of half a block.

'Yes, sir'; and Jo's heart began to beat so hard she was afraid he would hear it.

'I am bold to say it in spite of the rain, because so short a time remains to me.'

'Yes, sir'; and Jo nearly crushed the small flowerpot with the sudden squeeze she gave it.

'I wish to get a little dress for my Tina, and I am too stupid to go alone. Will you kindly gif me a word of taste and help?'

'Yes, sir'; and Jo felt as calm and cool, all of a sudden, as if she had stepped into a refrigerator.

'Perhaps also a shawl for Tina's mother, she is so poor and sick, and the husband is such a care. Yes, yes, a thick, warm shawl would be a friendly thing to take the little mother.'

'I'll do it with pleasure, Mr Bhaer.'

'I'm going very fast and he's getting dearer every minute,' added Jo to herself; then, with a mental shake, she entered into the business with an energy which was pleasant to behold.

Mr Bhaer left it all to her, so she chose a pretty gown for Tina, and then ordered out the shawls. The clerk, being a married man, condescended to take an interest in the couple, who appeared to be shopping for their family.

'Your lady may prefer this; it's a superior article, a most desirable colour, quite chaste and genteel,' he said, shaking out a comfortable grey shawl, and throwing it over Jo's shoulders.

'Does this suit you, Mr Bhaer?' she asked, turning her

back to him, and feeling deeply grateful for the chance of hiding her face.

'Excellently well; we will haf it,' answered the professor, smiling to himself as he paid for it, while Jo continued to rummage the counters like a confirmed bargain-hunter.

'Now, shall we go home?' he asked, as if the words were very pleasant to him.

'Yes, it's late, and I'm *so* tired.' Jo's voice was more pathetic than she knew; for now the sun seemed to have gone in as suddenly as it came out, the world grew muddy and miserable again, and for the first time she discovered that her feet were cold, her head ached, and that her heart was colder than the former, fuller of pain than the latter. Mr Bhaer was going away; he only cared for her as a friend; it was all a mistake, and the sooner it was over the better. With this idea in her head, she hailed an approaching omnibus with such a hasty gesture that the daisies flew out of the pot and were badly damaged.

'This is not our omniboos,' said the professor, waving the loaded vehicle away, and stopping to pick up the poor little flowers.

'I beg your pardon, I didn't see the name distinctly. Never mind, I can walk. I'm used to plodding in the mud,' returned Jo, winking hard, because she would have died rather than openly wipe her eyes.

Mr Bhaer saw the drops on her cheeks, though she turned her head away; the sight seemed to touch him very much, for, suddenly stooping down, he asked in a tone that meant a great deal:

'Heart's dearest, why do you cry?'

Now, if Jo had not been new to this sort of thing she would have said she wasn't crying, had a cold in her head, or told any other feminine fib proper to the occasion; instead of which that undignified creature answered, with an irrepressible sob:

'Because you are going away.'

'Ach, mein Gott, that is *so* good!' cried Mr Bhaer, managing to clasp his hands in spite of the umbrella and the bundles. 'Jo, I haf nothing but much love to gif you; I came to see if you could care for it, and I waited to be sure that I was something more than a friend. Am I? Can you make a little place in your heart for old Fritz?' he added, all in one breath.

'Oh, yes!' said Jo; and he was quite satisfied, for she folded both hands over his arm, and looked up at him with an expression that plainly showed how happy she would be to walk through life beside him, even though she had no better shelter than the old umbrella, if he carried it.

It was certainly proposing under difficulties, for, even if he had desired to do so, Mr Bhaer could not go down upon his knees, on account of the mud; neither could he offer Jo his hand, except figuratively, for both were full; much less could he indulge in tender demonstrations in the open street, though he was near it: so the only way in which he could express his rapture was to look at her, with an expression which glorified his face to such a degree that there actually seemed to be little rainbows in the drops that sparkled on his beard. If he had not loved Jo very much, I don't think he could have done it *then*, for she looked far from lovely, with her skirts in a deplorable state, her rubber boots splashed to the ankle, and her bonnet a ruin. Fortunately, Mr Bhaer considered her the most beautiful woman living, and she found him more 'Jove-like' than ever, though his hat brim was quite limp with the little rills trickling thence upon his shoulders (for he held the umbrella all over Jo), and every finger of his gloves needed mending.

Passers-by probably thought them a pair of harmless lunatics, for they entirely forgot to hail a bus, and strolled leisurely along, oblivious of deepening dusk and fog. Little they cared what anybody thought, for they were enjoying the happy hour that seldom comes but once in any life, the magical moment which bestows youth on the old, beauty on the plain, wealth on the poor, and gives human hearts a foretaste of heaven. The professor looked as if he had conquered a kingdom, and the world had nothing more to offer him in the way of bliss; while Jo trudged beside him, feeling as if her place had always been there, and wondering how she ever could have chosen any other lot. Of course, she was the first to speak – intelligibly, I mean, for the emotional remarks which followed her impetuous 'Oh, yes!' were not of a coherent or reportable character.

'Friedrich, why didn't you –'

'Ah, heaven, she gifs me the name that no one speaks since Minna died!' cried the professor, pausing in a puddle to regard her with grateful delight.

'I always call you so to myself – I forgot; but I won't, unless you like it.'

'Like it? It is more sweet to me than I can tell. Say "thou," also, and I shall say your language is almost as beautiful as mine.'

'Isn't "thou" a little sentimental?' asked Jo, privately thinking it a lovely monosyllable.

'Sentimental? Yes. Thank Gott, we Germans believe in sentiment, and keep ourselves young mit it. Your English "you" is so cold, say "thou," heart's dearest, it means so much to me,' pleaded Mr Bhaer, more like a romantic student than a grave professor.

'Well, then, why didn't thou tell me all this sooner?' asked Jo bashfully.

'Now I shall haf to show thee all my heart, and I so gladly will, because thou must take care of it hereafter. See, then, my Jo – ah, the dear, funny little name! – I had a wish to tell something the day I said goodbye, in New York; but I thought the handsome friend was betrothed to thee, and so I spoke not. Wouldst thou have said "Yes," then, if I *had* spoken?'

'I don't know; I'm afraid not, for I didn't have any heart just then.'

'Prut! that I do not believe. It was asleep till the fairy prince came through the wood, and waked it up. Ah, well, "Die erste Liebe ist die beste"; but that I should not expect.'

'Yes, the first love *is* the best; so be contented, for I never had another. Teddy was only a boy, and soon got over his little fancy,' said Jo, anxious to correct the professor's mistake.

'Good! then I shall rest happy, and be sure that thou givest me all. I haf waited so long, I am grown selfish, as thou wilt find, Professorin.'

'I like that,' cried Jo, delighted with her new name. 'Now tell me what brought you, at last, just when I most wanted you?'

'This'; and Mr Bhaer took a little worn paper out of his waistcoat pocket.

Jo unfolded it, and looked much abashed, for it was one of her own contributions to a paper that paid for poetry, which accounted for her sending it an occasional attempt.

'How could that bring you?' she asked, wondering what he meant.

'I found it by chance; I knew it by the names and the initials, and in it there was one little verse that seemed to call me. Read and find him; I will see that you go not in the wet.'

Jo obeyed, and hastily skimmed through the lines which she had christened:

Four little chests all in a row,
  Dim with dust, and worn by time,
All fashioned and filled, long ago,
  By children now in their prime.
Four little keys hung side by side,
  With faded ribbons, brave and gay
When fastened there, with childish pride,
  Long ago, on a rainy day.
Four little names, one on each lid,
  Carved out by a boyish hand,
And underneath there lieth hid
  Histories of the happy band
Once playing here, and pausing oft
  To hear the sweet refrain,
That came and went on the roof aloft,
  In the falling summer rain.

'Meg' on the first lid, smooth and fair.
  I look in with loving eyes,
For folded here, with well-known care,
  A goodly gathering lies,
The record of a peaceful life –
  Gifts to gentle child and girl,
A bridal gown, lines to a wife,

A tiny shoe, a baby curl.
No toys in this first chest remain.
  For all are carried away,
In their old age, to join again
  In another small Meg's play.
Ah, happy mother! well I know
  You hear, like a sweet refrain,
Lullabies ever soft and low
  In the falling summer rain.

'Jo' on the next lid, scratched and worn,
  And within a motley store
Of headless dolls, of school-books torn,
  Birds and beasts that speak no more;
Spoils brought home from the fairy ground
  Only trod by youthful feet,
Dreams of a future never found,
  Memories of a past still sweet;
Half-writ poems, stories wild,
  April letters, warm and cold,
Diaries of a wilful child,
  Hints of a woman early old;
A woman in a lonely home,
  Hearing, like a sad refrain –
'Be worthy love, and love will come,
  In the falling summer rain'.

My Beth! the dust is always swept
  From the lid that bears your name,
As if by loving eyes that wept,
  By careful hands that often came.
Death canonized for us one saint,
  Ever less human than divine,
And still we lay, with tender plaint,
  Relics in this household shrine –
The silver bell, so seldom rung,
  The little cap which last she wore,
The fair, dead Catherine that hung
  By angels borne above her door;
The songs she sang, without lament,
  In her prison-house of pain,
For ever are they sweetly blent
  With the falling summer rain.

Upon the last lid's polished field –
  Legend now both fair and true –
A gallant knight bears on his shield
  'Amy', in letters gold and blue.
Within lie snoods that bound her hair.
  Slippers that have danced their last,
Faded flowers laid by with care,
  Fans whose airy toils are past;
Gay valentines, all ardent flames,

Trifles that have borne their part
In girlish hopes and fears and shames –
  The record of a maiden heart
Now learning fairer, truer spells,
  Hearing, like a blithe refrain,
The silver sound of bridal bells
  In the falling summer rain.

Four little chests all in a row,
  Dim with dust, and worn by time,
Four women, taught by weal and woe
  To love and labour in their prime.
Four sisters, parted for an hour,
  None lost, one only gone before,
Made by love's immortal power,
  Nearest and dearest evermore.
Oh, when these hidden stores of ours
  Lie open to the Father's sight,
May they be rich in golden hours,
  Deeds that show fairer for the light,
Lives whose brave music long shall ring,
  Like a spirit-stirring strain,
Souls that shall gladly soar and sing
  In the long sunshine after rain.

J.M.

'It's very bad poetry, but I felt it when I wrote it, one day when I was very lonely, and had a good cry on a rag-bag. I never thought it would go where it could tell tales,' said Jo, tearing up the verses the professor had treasured so long.

'Let it go, it has done its duty, and I will haf a fresh one when I read all the brown book in which she keeps her little secrets,' said Mr Bhaer, with a smile, as he watched the fragments fly away on the wind. 'Yes,' he added earnestly, 'I read that, and I think to myself, "She has a sorrow, she is lonely, she would find comfort in true love. I haf a heart full, full for her; shall I not go and say, 'If this is not too poor a thing to gif for what I shall hope to receive, take it in Gott's name'?"'

'And so you came to find that it was not too poor, but the one precious thing I needed,' whispered Jo.

'I had no courage to think that at first, heavenly kind as was your welcome to me. But soon I began to hope, and then I said, "I will haf her if I die for it," and so I will!' cried Mr Bhaer, with a defiant nod, as if the walls of mist closing round them were barriers which he was to surmount or valiantly knock down.

Jo thought that was splendid, and resolved to be worthy of her knight, though he did not come prancing on a charger in gorgeous array.

'What made you stay away so long?' she asked presently, finding it so pleasant to ask confidential questions and get delightful answers that she could not keep silent.

'It was not easy, but I could not find the heart to take you from that so happy home until I could haf a prospect of one to give you, after much time, perhaps, and hard work. How could I ask you to gif up so much for a poor old fellow, who has no fortune but a little learning?'

'I'm glad you *are* poor; I couldn't bear a rich husband,' said Jo decidedly, adding, in a softer tone, 'Don't fear poverty; I've known it long enough to lose my dread, and be happy working for those I love; and don't call yourself old – forty is the prime of life. I couldn't help loving you if you were seventy!'

The professor found that so touching that he would have been glad of his handkerchief, if he could have got at it; as he couldn't, Jo wiped his eyes for him, and said, laughing, as she took away a bundle or two:

'I may be strong-minded, but no one can say I'm out of my sphere now, for woman's special mission is supposed to be drying tears and bearing burdens. I'm to carry my share, Friedrich, and help to earn the home. Make up your mind to that, or I'll never go,' she added resolutely, as he tried to reclaim his load.

'We shall see. Haf you patience to wait a long time, Jo? I must go away and do my work alone. I must help my boys first, because, even for you, I may not break my word to Minna. Can you forgif that, and be happy while we hope and wait?'

'Yes, I know I can; for we love one another, and that

makes all the rest easy to bear. I have my duty, also, and my work. I couldn't enjoy myself if I neglected them even for you, so there's no need of hurry or impatience. You can do your part out West, I can do mine here, and both be happy hoping for the best, and leaving the future to be as God wills.'

'Ah! thou gifest me such hope and courage, and I haf nothing to gif back but a full heart and these empty hands,' cried the professor, quite overcome.

Jo never, never would learn to be proper; for when he said that as they stood upon the steps, she just put both hands into his, whispering tenderly, 'Not empty now'; and, stooping down, kissed her Friedrich under the umbrella. It was dreadful, but she would have done it if the flock of draggle-tailed sparrows on the hedge had been human beings, for she was very far gone indeed, and quite regardless of everything but her own happiness. Though it came in such a very simple guise, that was the crowning moment of both their lives, when, turning from the night and storm and loneliness to the household light and warmth and peace waiting to receive them, with a glad 'Welcome home!' Jo led her lover in, and shut the door.

24

Harvest Time

For a year Jo and her professor worked and waited, hoped and loved, met occasionally, and wrote such voluminous letters that the rise in the price of paper was accounted for, Laurie said. The second year began rather soberly, for their prospects did not brighten, and Aunt March died suddenly. But when their first sorrow was over – for they loved the old lady in spite of her sharp tongue – they found they had cause for rejoicing, for she had left Plumfield to Jo, which made all sorts of joyful things possible.

'It's a fine old place, and will bring a handsome sum; for of course you intend to sell it,' said Laurie, as they were all talking the matter over, some weeks later.

'No, I don't,' was Jo's decided answer, as she petted the fat poodle, whom she had adopted, out of respect to his former mistress.

'You don't mean to live there?'

'Yes, I do.'

'But, my dear girl, it's an immense house, and will take

a power of money to keep it in order. The garden and orchard alone need two or three men, and farming isn't in Bhaer's line, I take it.'

'He'll try his hand at it there, if I propose it.'

'And you expect to live on the produce of the place? Well, that sounds paradisaical, but you'll find it desperate hard work.'

'The crop we are going to raise is a profitable one'; and Jo laughed.

'Of what is this fine crop to consist, ma'am?'

'Boys. I want to open a school for little lads – a good, happy, home-like school, with me to take care of them, and Fritz to teach them.'

'There's a truly Joian plan for you! Isn't that just like her?' cried Laurie, appealing to the family, who looked as much surprised as he.

'I like it,' said Mrs March decidedly.

'So do I,' added her husband, who welcomed the thought of a chance for trying the Socratic method of education on modern youth.

'It will be an immense care for Jo,' said Meg, stroking the head of her one all-absorbing son.

'Jo can do it, and be happy in it. It's a splendid idea. Tell us all about it,' cried Mr Laurence, who had been longing to lend the lovers a hand, but knew that they would refuse his help.

'I knew you'd stand by me, sir. Amy does too – I see it

in her eyes, though she prudently waits to turn it over in her mind before she speaks. Now, my dear people,' continued Jo earnestly, 'just understand that this isn't a new idea of mine, but a long-cherished plan. Before my Fritz came, I used to think how, when I'd made my fortune, and no one needed me at home, I'd hire a big house, and pick up some poor, forlorn little lads, who hadn't any mothers, and take care of them, and make life jolly for them before it was too late. I see so many going to ruin, for want of help at the right minute; I love so to do anything for them; I seem to feel their wants, and sympathize with their troubles, and, oh, I should *so* like to be a mother to them!'

Mrs March held out her hand to Jo, who took it, smiling, with tears in her eyes, and went on in the old enthusiastic way, which they had not seen for a long while.

'I told my plan to Fritz once, and he said it was just what he would like, and agreed to try it when we got rich. Bless his dear heart, he's been doing it all his life – helping poor boys, I mean, not getting rich; and he'll never be; money doesn't stay in his pocket long enough to lay up any. But now, thanks to my good old aunt, who loved me better than I ever deserved, *I'm* rich, at least I feel so, and we can live at Plumfield perfectly well, if we have a flourishing school. It's just the place for boys, the house is big, and the furniture strong and plain. There's plenty of room for dozens inside, and splendid grounds outside. They could help in the garden and orchard: such work is healthy, isn't it, sir? Then Fritz can train and teach in his own way, and Father will help him. I can feed and nurse and pet and scold them; and Mother will be my stand-by. I've always longed for lots of boys, and never had enough; now I can fill the house full, and revel in the little dears to my heart's content. Think what luxury – Plumfield my own, and a wilderness of boys to enjoy it with me!'

As Jo waved her hands, and gave a sigh of rapture, the family went off into a gale of merriment, and Mr Laurence laughed till they thought he'd have an apoplectic fit.

'I don't see anything funny,' she said gravely, when she could be heard. 'Nothing could be more natural or proper than for my professor to open a school, and for me to prefer to reside on my own estate.'

'She is putting on airs already,' said Laurie, who regarded the idea in the light of a capital joke. 'But may I enquire how you intend to support the establishment? If all the pupils are little ragamuffins, I'm afraid your crop won't be profitable in a worldly sense, Mrs Bhaer.'

'Now don't be a wet blanket, Teddy. Of course I shall have rich pupils, also – perhaps begin with such altogether; then, when I've got a start, I can take a ragamuffin or two, just for a relish. Rich people's children often need care and comfort, as well as poor. I've seen unfortunate little creatures left to servants, or backward ones pushed forward, when it's real cruelty. Some are naughty through mismanagement or neglect, and some lose their mothers. Besides, the best have to get through the hobbledehoy age, and that's the very time they need most patience and kindness. People laugh at them, and hustle them about, try to keep them out of sight, and expect them to turn, all at once, from pretty children into fine young men. They don't complain much – plucky little souls – but they feel it. I've been through something of it, and I know all about it. I've a special interest in such young bears, and like to show them that I see the warm, honest, well-meaning boys' hearts, in spite of the clumsy arms and legs and the topsy-turvy heads. I've had experience, too, for haven't I brought up one boy to be a pride and honour to his family?'

'I'll testify that you tried to do it,' said Laurie, with a grateful look.

'And I've succeeded beyond my hopes; for here you are, a steady, sensible business man, doing heaps of good with your money, and laying up the blessings of the poor, instead of dollars. But you are not merely a business man: you love good and beautiful things, enjoy them yourself, and let others go halves, as you always did in the old times. I *am* proud of you, Teddy, for you get better every year, and everyone feels it, though you won't let them say so. Yes, and when I have my flock, I'll just point to you, and say, "There's your model, my lads".'

Poor Laurie didn't know where to look; for, man though

he was, something of the old bashfulness came over him as this burst of praise made all faces turn approvingly upon him.

'I say, Jo, that's rather too much,' he began, just in his old boyish way. 'You have all done more for me than I can ever thank you for, except by doing my best not to disappoint you. You have rather cast me off lately, Jo, but I've had the best of help, nevertheless; so, if I've got on at all, you may thank these two for it'; and he laid one hand gently on his grandfather's white head, the other on Amy's golden one, for the three were never far apart.

'I do think that families are the most beautiful things in all the world!' burst out Jo, who was in an unusually uplifted frame of mind just then. 'When I have one of my own, I hope it will be as happy as the three I know and love the best. If John and my Fritz were only here, it would be quite a little heaven on earth,' she added more quietly. And that night, when she went to her room, after a blissful evening of family counsels, hopes, and plans, her heart was so full of happiness that she could only calm it by kneeling beside the empty bed always near her own, and thinking tender thoughts of Beth.

It was a very astonishing year altogether, for things seemed to happen in an unusually rapid and delightful manner. Almost before she knew where she was, Jo found herself married and settled at Plumfield. Then a family of six or seven boys sprung up like mushrooms, and flourished surprisingly, poor boys as well as rich; for Mr Laurence was continually finding some touching case of destitution, and begging the Bhaers to take pity on the child, and he would gladly pay a trifle for its support. In this way the sly old gentleman got round proud Jo, and furnished her with the style of boy in which she most delighted.

Of course it was uphill work at first, and Jo made queer mistakes; but the wise professor steered her safely into calmer waters, and the most rampant ragamuffin was conquered in the end. How Jo did enjoy her 'wilderness of boys', and how poor, dear Aunt March would have lamented had she been there to see the sacred precincts of prim, well-ordered Plumfield overrun with Toms, Dicks, and Harrys! There was a sort of poetic justice about it, after all, for the old lady had been the terror of the boys for miles round; and now the exiles feasted freely on forbidden plums, kicked up the gravel with profane boots unreproved, and played cricket in the big field where the irritable 'cow with a crumpled horn' used to invite rash youths to come and be tossed. It became a sort of boy's paradise, and Laurie suggested that it should be called the 'Bhaer garten', as a compliment to its master and appropriate to its inhabitants.

It never was a fashionable school, and the professor did not lay up a fortune; but it *was* just what Jo intended it to be – 'a happy, home-like place for boys, who needed teaching, care, and kindness'. Every room in the big house was soon full; every little plot in the garden soon had its owner; a regular menagerie appeared in barn and shed, for pet animals were allowed; and, three times a day, Jo smiled at her Fritz from the head of a long table lined on either side with rows of happy young faces, which all turned to her with affectionate eyes, confiding words, and grateful hearts, full of love for 'Mother Bhaer'. She had boys enough now, and did not tire of them, though they were not angels, by any means, and some of them caused both professor and professorin much trouble and anxiety. But her faith in the good spot which exists in the heart of the naughtiest, sauciest, most tantalizing little raga-muffin gave her patience, skill, and, in time, success; for no mortal boy could hold out long with Father Bhaer shining on him as benevolently as the sun, and Mother Bhaer forgiving him seventy times seven. Very precious to Jo was the friendship of the lads; their penitent sniffs and whispers after wrong-doing; their droll or touching little confidences; their pleasant enthusiasms, hopes, and plans; even their misfortunes, for they only endeared them to her all the more. There were slow boys and bashful boys; feeble boys and riotous boys; boys that lisped and boys that stuttered; one or two lame ones; and a merry little quadroon, who could not be taken in elsewhere, but who was welcome to the 'Bhaer garten', though some people predicted that his admission would ruin the school.

Yes; Jo was a very happy woman there, in spite of hard work, much anxiety, and a perpetual racket. She enjoyed it heartily, and found the applause of her boys more satisfying than any praise of the world; for now she told no stories except to her flock of enthusiastic believers and admirers. As the years went on, two little lads of her own came to increase her happiness – Rob, named for Grandpa, and Teddy, a happy-go-lucky baby, who seemed to have inherited his papa's sunshiny temper as well as his mother's lively spirit. How they ever grew up alive in that whirlpool of boys was a mystery to their grandma and aunts; but they flourished like dandelions in spring, and their rough nurses loved and served them well.

There were a great many holidays at Plumfield, and one of the most delightful was the yearly apple-picking; for then the Marches, Laurences, Brookes, and Bhaers turned out in full force, and made a day of it. Five years after Jo's wedding, one of these fruitful festivals occurred – a mellow October day, when the air was full of an exhilarating freshness which made the spirits rise, and the blood dance healthily in the veins. The old orchard wore its holiday attire; golden-rod and asters fringed the mossy walls; grasshoppers skipped briskly in the sere grass, and crickets chirped like fairy pipes at a feast; squirrels were busy with their small harvesting; birds twittered their adieux from the alders in the lane; and every tree stood ready to send down its shower of red or yellow apples at the first shake.

Everybody was there; everybody laughed and sang, climbed up and tumbled down; everybody declared that there never had been such a perfect day or such a jolly set to enjoy it; and everyone gave themselves up to the simple pleasures of the hour as freely as if there were no such things as care or sorrow in the world.

Mr March strolled placidly about, quoting Tusser, Cowley, and Columella to Mr Laurence, while enjoying

'The gentle apple's winey juice.'

The professor charged up and down the green aisles like a stout Teutonic knight, with a pole for a lance, leading on the boys, who made a hook and ladder company of themselves, and performed wonders in the way of ground and lofty tumbling. Laurie devoted himself to the little ones, rode his small daughter in a bushel-basket, took Daisy up among the birds' nests, and kept adventurous Rob from breaking his neck. Mrs March and Meg sat among the apple piles like a pair of Pomonas, sorting the contributions that kept pouring in; while Amy, with a beautiful motherly expression in her face, sketched the various groups, and watched over one pale lad, who sat adoring her with his little crutch beside him.

Jo was in her element that day, and rushed about, with her gown pinned up, her hat anywhere but on her head, and her baby tucked under her arm, ready for any lively adventure which might turn up. Little Teddy bore a charmed life, for nothing ever happened to him, and Jo never felt any anxiety when he was whisked up into a tree by one lad, galloped off on the back of another, or supplied with sour russets by his indulgent papa, who laboured under the Germanic delusion that babies could digest anything, from pickled cabbage to buttons, nails, and their own small shoes. She knew that little Ted would turn up again in time, safe and rosy, dirty and serene, and she always received him back with a hearty welcome, for Jo loved her babies tenderly.

At four o'clock a lull took place, and baskets remained empty, while the apple-pickers rested, and compared rents and bruises. Then Jo and Meg, with a detachment of the bigger boys, set forth the supper on the grass, for an out-of-door tea was always the crowning joy of the day. The land literally flowed with milk and honey on such occasions, for the lads were not required to sit at table, but allowed to partake of refreshments as they liked – freedom being the sauce best beloved by the boyish soul. They availed themselves of the rare privilege to the fullest extent, for some tried the pleasing experiment of drinking milk while standing on their heads, others lent a charm to leap-frog by eating pie in the pauses of the game, cookies were sown broadcast over the field, and apple-turnovers roosted in the trees like a new style of bird. The little girls had a private tea party, and Ted roved among the edibles at his own sweet will.

When no one could eat any more, the professor proposed the first regular toast, which was always drunk at such times – 'Aunt March, God bless her!' A toast heartily given by the good man, who never forgot how much he owed her, and quietly drunk by the boys, who had been taught to keep her memory green.

'Now, Grandma's sixtieth birthday! Long life to her, with three times three!'

That was given with a will, as you may well believe; and the cheering once begun, it was hard to stop it. Everybody's health was proposed, from Mr Laurence, who was considered their special patron, to the astonished guinea-pig, who had strayed from its proper sphere in search of its young master. Demi, as the oldest grandchild, then presented the queen of the day with various gifts, so numerous that they were transported to the festive scene in a wheelbarrow. Funny presents some of them but what would have been defects to other eyes were ornaments to Grandma's – for the children's gifts were all their own. Every stitch Daisy's patient little fingers had put into the handkerchiefs she hemmed was better than embroidery to Mrs March; Demi's shoe-box was a miracle of mechanical skill, though the cover wouldn't shut; Rob's footstool had a wiggle in its uneven legs, that she declared was very soothing; and no page of the costly book Amy's child gave her was so fair as that on which appeared, in tipsy capitals, the words – 'To dear Grandma, from her little Beth'.

During this ceremony the boys had mysteriously disappeared; and, when Mrs March had tried to thank her children, and broken down, while Teddy wiped her eyes on his pinafore, the professor suddenly began to sing. Then, from above him, voice after voice took up the words, and from tree to tree echoed the music of the unseen choir, as the boys sung, with all their hearts, the little song Jo had written, Laurie set to music, and the professor trained his lads to give with the best effect. This was something altogether new, and it proved a grand success; for Mrs March couldn't get over her surprise, and insisted on shaking hands with every one of the featherless birds, from tall Franz and Emil to the little quadroon, who had the sweetest voice of all.

After this, the boys dispersed for a final lark, leaving Mrs March and her daughters under the festival tree.

'I don't think I ever ought to call myself "Unlucky Jo" again, when my greatest wish has been so beautifully gratified,' said Mrs Bhaer, taking Teddy's little fist out of the milk pitcher, in which he was rapturously churning.

'And yet your life is very different from the one you pictured so long ago. Do you remember our castles in the air?' asked Amy, smiling as she watched Laurie and John playing cricket with the boys.

'Dear fellows! It does my heart good to see them forget business, and frolic for a day,' answered Jo, who now spoke in a maternal way of all mankind. 'Yes, I remember; but the life I wanted then seems selfish, lonely, and cold to me now. I haven't given up the hope that I may write a good book yet, but I can wait, and I'm sure it will be all the better for such experiences and illustrations as these'; and Jo pointed from the lively lads in the distance to her father, leaning on the professor's arm, as they walked to and fro in the sunshine, deep in one of the conversations which both enjoyed so much, and then to her mother, sitting enthroned among her daughters, with their children in her lap and at her feet, as if all found help and happiness in the face which never could grow old to them.

'My castle was the most nearly realized of all. I asked for splendid things, to be sure, but in my heart I knew I should be satisfied, if I had a little home, and John, and some dear children like these. I've got them all, thank God, and am the happiest woman in the world'; and Meg laid her hand on her tall boy's head, with a face full of tender and devout content.

'My castle is very different from what I planned, but I would not alter it, though, like Jo, I don't relinquish all my artistic hopes, or confine myself to helping others fulfil their dreams of beauty. I've begun to model a figure of baby, and Laurie says it is the best thing I've ever done. I think so myself, and mean to do it in marble, so that, whatever happens, I may at least keep the image of my little angel.'

As Amy spoke, a great tear dropped on the golden hair of the sleeping child in her arms; for her one well-beloved daughter was a frail little creature and the dread of losing her was the shadow over Amy's sunshine. This cross was doing much for both father and mother, for one love and sorrow bound them closely together. Amy's nature was growing sweeter, deeper, and more tender; Laurie was growing more serious, strong, and firm; and both were learning that beauty, youth, good fortune, even love itself, cannot keep care and pain, loss and sorrow, from the most blest; for

> *Into each life some rain must fall,*
> *Some days must be dark and sad and dreary.*

'She is growing better, I am sure of it, my dear. Don't despond, but hope and keep happy,' said Mrs March, as tender-hearted Daisy stooped from her knee, to lay her rosy cheek against her little cousin's pale one.

'I never ought to, while I have you to cheer me up, Marmee, and Laurie to take more than half of every burden,' replied Amy warmly. 'He never lets me see his anxiety, but is so sweet and patient with me, so devoted to Beth, and such a stay and comfort to me always, that

I can't love him enough. So, in spite of my one cross, I can say with Meg, "Thank God, I'm a happy woman".

'There's no need for me to say it, for everyone can see that I'm far happier than I deserve,' added Jo, glancing from her good husband to her happy children, tumbling on the grass beside her. 'Fritz is getting grey and stout; I'm growing as thin as a shadow, and am thirty; we never shall be rich, and Plumfield may burn up any night, for that incorrigible Tommy Bangs *will* smoke sweet-fern cigars under the bedclothes, though he's set himself afire three times already. But in spite of these unromantic facts, I have nothing to complain of, and never was so jolly in my life. Excuse the remark, but living among boys, I can't help using their expressions now and then.'

'Yes, Jo, I think your harvest will be a good one,' began Mrs March, frightening away a big black cricket that was staring Teddy out of countenance.

'Not half so good as yours, Mother. Here it is, and we never can thank you enough for the patient sowing and reaping you have done,' cried Jo, with the loving impetuosity which she never could outgrow.

'I hope there will be more wheat and fewer tares every year,' said Amy softly.

'A large sheaf, but I know there's room in your heart for it, Marmee dear,' added Meg's tender voice.

Touched to the heart, Mrs March could only stretch out her arms, as if to gather children and grandchildren to herself, and say, with face and voice full of motherly love, gratitude, and humility:

'O my girls, however long you may live, I never can wish you a greater happiness than this!'

Good Wives

With Puffin Classics, the adventure isn't
over when you reach the final page.
Want to discover more about your favourite
characters, their creators and their worlds?
Read on . . .

CONTENTS

NAME: Louisa May Alcott
BORN: 29 November 1832 in Germantown, Pennsylvania
DIED: 6 March 1888 in Boston, Massachusetts
NATIONALITY: American
LIVED: Grew up in Concord, Massachusetts. The family moved countless times, but the family plot (where Alcott is buried) is in Concord.

What was she like?

Even as a child Alcott was an avid reader and writer. She was surrounded by philosophers and writers as her father was part of a group of transcendentalists (who, above all, believe in the influence of nature and reason) and this had a lasting effect on her. Yet she was not entirely a quiet, bookish girl. Like the fictional character Jo March, Alcott was a tomboy who struggled against society's genteel expectations of young ladies. Also like her protagonist, she spent her life struggling to control her quick temper.

Alcott was a feminist and never married – unwilling to make the sacrifices to her career that becoming a wife would entail. Yet she was devoted to her family, and when her younger sister Abba died, she adopted her two-year-old daughter (also named Louisa May, but nicknamed 'Lulu').

During her time working as a nurse, Alcott contracted typhoid fever and pneumonia. She was treated with mercury which, in turn, gave her mercury poisoning, and the remainder of her life was riddled with pain and ill-health. But, a determined soul, Alcott never let it defeat her and she continued to work hard at her writing.

Where did she grow up?
Alcott grew up in Concord, Massachusetts, where she loved roaming through the fields and running wild. But the family were compelled by poverty to move from place to place in search of work.

What did she do apart from writing books?
Because of the family's financial difficulties (her father's radical ideology resulted in failed schemes at a severe cost to the Alcotts), Louisa May had to earn money from an early age and as a teenager began writing sensational short stories for newspapers and magazines. She also worked as a governess, teacher, seamstress and domestic help. Driven by her disappointment at not being able to fight in the Civil War, in 1862 she spent six weeks in Georgetown, Washington DC, working as a nurse. This career was cut short by the appalling conditions that resulted in her contracting typhoid and pneumonia.

Alcott was a staunch feminist and, as a fervent supporter of women's suffrage, was the first woman to register to vote in Concord.

What did people think of Little Women when it was first published in the 1860s?
The book was originally serialized in a magazine and was an immediate hit with both adults and children, who eagerly awaited the next instalment of the family drama. The book

itself, which appeared in 1868, was the first American book to become a children's classic. *Good Wives*, first published in 1869, is often published together with *Little Women* as if it were a single work. *Good Wives* picks up three years after the events in the last chapter of *Little Women* ('Aunt March Settles the Question'), and includes characters and events often felt by fans to be essential to the *Little Women* story.

Where did Louisa May Alcott get the idea for the series?

Despite acclaim for her adult novel *Moods* and her series of *Hospital Sketches* based on her time as a nurse (both published in 1864), Alcott was not gaining widespread success as a writer. Then an astute publisher suggested that she tried her hand at writing a children's book. Alcott was not enthusiastic at first, until she realized that her own family (she came from a family of four sisters, one of whom, Lizzie, died in her early twenties) was the ideal model for an interesting family saga. Louisa wrote *Little Women* in Orchard House, the Alcott family home, and set the lives of the March girls within it. Thus, although not entirely factual, *Little Women* is semi-autobiographical.

What other books did she write?

Louisa May Alcott was a prolific writer. Under the pseudonym of A. M. Barnard, she wrote numerous 'potboilers' (melodramatic stories with selfish, wilful protagonists), and under her own name the aforementioned *Moods* (based on her love for Henry David Thoreau – one of the philosophers she grew up around) and *Hospital Sketches*. Yet on receiving resounding acclaim for *Little Women*, she returned to writing books for adults only twice (one of which was an anonymous work). As well as the renowned sequels that followed *Little Women* – *Good Wives*; *Little Men*, which tells of Jo's life at Plumfield, where she runs a school for boys; and *Jo's Boys*, which continues the adventures of the boys from Jo's school – Alcott had over a dozen more children's books published, writing industriously right up until her death.

Meg March – the eldest of the March sisters, Meg is kind and sweet-natured, and always tries to please other people. She marries John Brooke, with whom she is very much in love, and tries to forego her longing for luxury and nice things, which John is too poor to provide. Meg can also be influenced by others and tempted into making wrong decisions.

Jo March – Jo, once the tomboy of the family, with a fiery temper, is still sensitive and high-spirited but she eventually learns to calm her behaviour when she decides to marry Professor Bhaer and live at Plumfield – the house left to her by Aunt March in her will.

Beth March – the third March sister, Beth is quiet and homely, and is especially close to Jo. But, unlike her sisters, Beth has never made plans for her future, as if she has always known that she would not live a long life.

Amy March – the youngest of the March sisters, Amy is now a stylish and independent young lady, and a gifted artist, but still a little spoiled and used to getting her own way. But her natural sweet nature and kind-heartedness grow deeper when she marries Laurie.

John Brooke – John is married to Meg. He is a good, honest, hard-working man who is poor and not able to give Meg any of the finery for which she yearns. But he is loyal and patient, and he and Meg are very much in love.

Marmee (Mrs March) – the mother and guiding light of the March girls. Considerate, passionate and honest, Marmee continues to lead her daughters on the correct moral path with a sense of humour and not a hint of sanctimony.

Mr March – the March girls' father who is home from service in the Civil War. Although he doesn't appear very often in the story, his gentle, philosophical character is evident throughout.

Daisy and Demi – Meg and John's twins. Although completely different in personality, the twins get along very well together.

Laurie (Teddy Laurence) – grandson to the Marches' rich neighbour. Laurie is as charming and impetuous as ever, and feels closest to Jo. His affection for her grows but Jo can only see him as a brother. Laurie realizes that it is Amy with whom he is in love and eventually they get married.

Aunt March – spinster and aunt to the March girls, Aunt March is, on the surface, a disagreeable and stern old lady, but although critical she clearly adores all her nieces.

Aunt Carrol – the March girls' aunt. Aunt Carrol chooses to take Amy with her to Paris instead of Jo because she thinks that Amy is more ladylike. She has a daughter named Florence who also goes to Paris with them.

Professor Friedrich Bhaer – the German language teacher who meets Jo in New York. He is a kind man who suggests to Jo that she adopts a simpler writing style in order to become successful. Friedrich and Jo fall in love, and when she returns home he follows her and they marry a year later.

Mrs Kirke – manages the boarding house in New York where Jo lives for a short time.

Florence – Aunt Carrol's daughter and a cousin of the March sisters who accompanies her mother and Amy to Paris.

The Hummels – a very poor family who are the beneficiaries of much charity from the March family.

Sallie Moffat – Meg's well-off friend who has enough money to buy all the nice things Meg so longs to have.

Good Wives, which was published in 1869 after the publication of its predecessor, *Little Women,* in 1868, has been read by children and adults alike for over a century and is still being enjoyed today. What do you think it is that attracts readers to Louisa May Alcott's story of growing up and learning about oneself?

Do you agree with the way in which Louisa May Alcott ends *Good Wives*? If you were the author of the book, is there anything that you would change about the ending?

What do you think about the title '*Good Wives*'? Can you think of any alternatives?

Here are some quotes from *Good Wives.* Can you work out who said them?

1. '*I'm not afraid, but it seems as if I should be homesick for you even in heaven.*'

2. '*It may be vain and wrong to say it, but – I'm afraid – Laurie is getting too fond of me.*'

3. '*I often feel as if I need teaching more than ever since these babies look to me for everything.*'

4. 'O my girls, however long you may live, I never can wish you a greater happiness than this!'

5. 'Then I must *have* a lobster, for tongue alone won't do.'

* How would you portray a modern adaptation of *Good Wives*? Why not include your friends in this task and put on a performance of the book, setting it in modern times?

* Are you happy with the pairings of couples at the end of the book? If so, write a paragraph explaining why you think that a particular couple are well suited. If not, write a paragraph explaining whom you think would be better suited as a couple and why you think this.

* Who is your favourite character and why? Put together a character profile, including interesting facts about them and why you like them. If you're feeling really creative, why not include an illustration of how you imagine them to look and dress?

* Choose your favourite character in the novel and write a letter to them, telling them all about your home, your family and your friends. What do you think they would have thought about your modern-day life?

* The March family home is based on Louisa May Alcott's family home where she lived with her father, Amos Bronson, her mother, Abigail May, and her sisters, Anna, Louisa and May.

* Due to the great success of *Little Women* and *Good Wives*, Alcott wrote *Little Men,* which focuses on Jo and the lives of the students at Plumfield Estate School.

* Beth March is modelled on Alcott's sister, Elizabeth ('Lizzie'), who died of scarlet fever when she was only twenty-three.

* *Little Women* is semi-autobiographical as Alcott bases the book on some of her childhood experiences with her sisters. However, *Good Wives* is fictional as it concentrates on the relationships and marriages of the March sisters. Alcott wrote *Good Wives* in response to readers' letters asking for more about the love lives of the March sisters.

* *Little Women* and *Good Wives* portray ambitious women in a positive light such as the protagonist, Jo. In doing so, Alcott challenged traditional gender stereotypes at the time and many women reading the novels would have found Jo an innovative and inspiring character.

* Louisa May Alcott and Jo are similar – they are both passionate about writing, are one of four sisters and they are religious. However, unlike Jo, Alcott never married. In the nineteenth century when the book was written and set,

the concept of the female heroine not finding happiness through marriage at the end of the novel was unconventional. Therefore, Alcott includes Jo's relationship and marriage to Professor Bhaer in order to conform to the normalities of the time.

* Orchard House is the Alcott family home in Concord, Massachusetts, USA, where Alcott grew up and then returned to from Boston, to write *Little Women*. Readers are able to go on a tour of Orchard House where they can see the writing desk where Alcott wrote her marvellous story.

GLOSSARY

afflatus   a divine inspiration

bower   a pleasant, shady outdoor place

conflagration   a huge fire

dyspeptic   having indigestion, and feeling bad-tempered

freedman   a person freed from slavery

furbelows   fancy frills on a woman's dress

mantua   a loose-fitting gown worn in the seventeenth and eighteenth centuries

moire   a silk fabric dress with a rippled appearance

Newfoundland   a type of dog: large, highly intelligent with a thick dark coat

nil desperandum   Latin for 'never despair'

Niobe   in Greek mythology, Niobe is a bereaved mother

omnibus   a horse-drawn bus

philanthropic   seeking to promote the welfare of others, being generous and kind

senna   a tropical plant with a fruit that is often used to make a medicine

| **tatting** | a kind of knotted lace, made by hand using a special tool |
| **truckle** | to submit or behave in a servile manner |

If you have enjoyed
Good Wives, you may like to read
Little Men – the next book in the lives of
the March sisters.

1

Nat

'Please, sir, is this Plumfield?' asked a ragged boy of the man who opened the great gate at which the omnibus left him.

'Yes; who sent you?'

'Mr Laurence. I have got a letter for the lady.'

'All right; go up to the house, and give it to her; she'll see to you, little chap.'

The man spoke pleasantly, and the boy went on, feeling much cheered by the words. Through the soft spring rain that fell on sprouting grass and budding trees, Nat saw a large square house before him – a hospitable-looking house, with an old-fashioned porch, wide steps, and lights shining in many windows. Neither curtains nor shutters hid the cheerful glimmer; and, pausing a moment before he rang, Nat saw many little shadows dancing on the walls, heard the pleasant hum of young voices, and felt that it was hardly possible that the light and warmth and comfort within could be for a homeless 'little chap' like him.

'I hope the lady *will* see to me,' he thought; and gave a

timid rap with the great bronze knocker, which was a jovial griffin's head.

A rosy-faced servant-maid opened the door, and smiled as she took the letter which he silently offered. She seemed used to receiving strange boys, for she pointed to a seat in the hall, and said, with a nod,

'Sit there and drip on the mat a bit, while I take this in to missis.'

Nat found plenty to amuse him while he waited, and stared about him curiously, enjoying the view, yet glad to do so unobserved in the dusky recess by the door.

The house seemed swarming with boys, who were beguiling the rainy twilight with all sorts of amusements. There were boys everywhere, 'upstairs and downstairs and in the lady's chamber', apparently, for various open doors showed pleasant groups of big boys, little boys, and middle-sized boys in all stages of evening relaxation, not to say effervescence. Two large rooms on the right were evidently schoolrooms, for desks, maps, blackboards, and books were scattered about. An open fire burned on the hearth, and several indolent lads lay on their backs before it, discussing a new cricket-ground, with such animation that their boots waved in the air. A tall youth was practising on the flute in one corner, quite undisturbed by the racket all about him. Two or three others were jumping over the desks, pausing, now and then, to get their breath, and laugh at the droll sketches of a little wag who was caricaturing the whole household on a blackboard.

In the room on the left a long supper table was seen, set forth with great pitchers of new milk, piles of brown and white bread, and perfect stacks of the shiny ginger-bread so dear to boyish souls. A flavour of toast was in the air, also suggestions of baked apples, very tantalizing to one hungry little nose and stomach.

The hall, however, presented the most inviting prospect of all, for a brisk game of tag was going on in the upper entry. One landing was devoted to marbles, the other to checkers, while the stairs were occupied by a boy reading, a girl singing lullaby to her doll, two puppies, a kitten, and a constant succession of small boys sliding down the banisters, to the great detriment of their clothes, and danger to their limbs.

So absorbed did Nat become in this exciting race, that he ventured farther and farther out of his corner; and when one very lively boy came down so swiftly that he could not stop himself, but fell off the banisters, with a crash that would have broken any head but one rendered nearly as hard as a cannon-ball by eleven years of constant bumping, Nat forgot himself, and ran up to the fallen rider, expecting to find him half dead. The boy, however, only winked rapidly for a second, then lay calmly looking up at the new face with a surprised 'Hullo!'

'Hallo!' returned Nat, not knowing what else to say, and thinking that form of reply both brief and easy.

'Are you a new boy?' asked the recumbent youth, without stirring.

'Don't know yet.'

'What's your name?'

'Nat Blake.'

'Mine's Tommy Bangs; come up and have a go, will you?' and Tommy got upon his legs like one suddenly remembering the duties of hospitality.

'Guess I won't, till I see whether I'm going to stay or not,' returned Nat, feeling the desire to stay increase every moment.

'I say, Demi, here's a new one. Come and see to him'; and the lively Thomas returned to his sport with unabated relish.

At his call, the boy reading on the stairs looked up with a pair of big brown eyes, and after an instant's pause, as if a little shy, he put the book under his arm, and came soberly down to greet the newcomer, who found something very attractive in the pleasant face of this slender, mild-eyed boy.

'Have you seen Aunt Jo?' he asked, as if that was some sort of important ceremony.

'I haven't seen anybody yet but you boys; I'm waiting,' answered Nat.

Little Men is available in Puffin Classics.